PRAISE FOR *PERFECTLY IMPOSSIBLE*

"Reading *Perfectly Impossible* was like eating imported macarons while getting a massage and having someone else figure out your tax prep— all at the same time. With deft precision and humor, Topp chronicles every delicious detail of what it takes to run the lives of the 1 percent. I loved it."

—Nicola Kraus, coauthor of *The Nanny Diaries*

Perfectly Impossible

Perfectly Impossible

a novel

Elizabeth Topp

Little
a

Text copyright © 2020 Elizabeth Topp
All rights reserved.

Published by Little A, New York

www.apub.com

Amazon, the Amazon logo, and Little A are trademarks of Amazon.com, Inc., or its affiliates.

ISBN-13: 9781542018678 (hardcover)
ISBN-10: 1542018676 (hardcover)

ISBN-13: 9781542018685 (paperback)
ISBN-10: 1542018684 (paperback)

Cover design by Rex Bonomelli

Cover illustration by Micaela Alcaino

Printed in the United States of America

First edition

This one's for all the assistants out there.

ONE

December 27

Park Avenue cooperatives announced their inverse relationship to reality first with the lobby's temperature. The colder it was outside, the hotter the climate in the marble entrance hall. In the steamy heat of August, gusts of icy air escaped through the iron doors each time a white glove held them open. When the building's residents crossed the pavement from their town cars, they unavoidably experienced several seconds of weather, like everyone, but once inside they could rest instantly reassured of exclusive and constant comfort. The doors stayed wide open to the street on only a few ideal days each year, the climate inside and out equivalent.

This day—a tooth-clacking seventeen degrees—a hot blast hit Anna in the face as Brian held the door for her. "You made it! All this way in this snow," he remarked.

"Gotta keep the wheels rollin', Bri." She unzipped her coat and fanned her face to avoid perspiring. "What is it, ninety degrees in here?"

"Eighty-seven today. Hey, what are you even doing here? Aren't they away?"

"Indeed they are, Bri!" she said cheerily, stepping onto the elevator. Brian pushed the button for her from the podium, and the Von Bizmark lower floor button, "8," illuminated itself with a tidy ding.

Anna felt good. Optimistic even. She loved this dead week in the office after Christmas and before the New Year when she was left to her own devices. She could come in late—a glance at her watch told her it was already 10:37 a.m.—but there was no one upstairs to complain. The gargantuan duplex remained quiet, and Anna would dispatch with the previous year's business, carefully documenting what money went where for what and then sending it all filed, labeled, and boxed to Marco, the Von Bizmark forever accountant. It was easy and cathartic work that never ran late, and Anna was always out the door and headed for her studio before six.

Both Von Bizmarks were in Aspen with the kids, their kids' friends, and a few hangers-on in a house so large no one knew exactly who or how many people were under its roof at the end of all the skiing, après skiing, après après, dinners, clubs, and clandestine rendezvous. Anna had had to book three separate jets to carry the whole entourage back East: one to Boston, one to Exeter, and one to New York. But that was still several glorious and calm days hence, after New Year's at Aspen's Caribou Club.

Without the family in residence and with the employees on vacation, there could be no surprises, which made Anna's life much, much easier, since her main purpose at the Von Bizmark residence was to make sure nothing unexpected happened to them. Every task flowed from that rule: staffing, researching, cleaning, maintaining, scheduling, confirming, reconfirming, and then maybe just one more confirmation. She could never know what, exactly, was going to be important to her employer on a moment-to-moment basis, which required her to keep tabs on an infinite number of details. Phone calls, emails, letters, cards, flowers with cards, gifts with notes. Requests, events, parties. *Where is the car? Where is the Magritte sketch? Where is the scuba gear? Where does so-and-so live? In January? What do you think of this dress? Email? Person? Bracelet? Behind-the-scenes drama at the opera? What is the name of the person I am thinking of?* The answers had to be not simply correct but perfect.

No one understood. After two decades, Anna gave up trying to explain, mostly unbothered by what her friends, family, and the people she met at gallery openings and cocktail parties thought a "private assistant" actually did. Those three days each week supported her creative work. PAing had always been her sustenance, a vocation that lived in its own tidy box in her mind labeled "day job." Anna knew it was precisely this—that she thought of herself primarily as an artist—that made Anna so good in a role that could easily eclipse a lesser identity.

Another few dings as the elevator doors opened into the Von Bizmark anteroom, a tiny holding area whose walls crawled with hand-painted vines that extended into the carved double doors, which remained open when the family was in residence but locked otherwise. In the absence of staff, who usually made Anna her coffee and midday meal, she contemplated the delicious lunch she would order on Mrs. Von Bizmark's credit card—a little treat for working through the holiday. Maybe a rack of ribs, chicken parmesan, one of those custom chopped salads with all the premium toppings and her favorite: double avocado.

But before Anna could turn her key in the lock, the doors fell open. She stepped inside the vast foyer, where the ivy pattern from the anteroom retreated into cabinet marquetry and the foresty color scheme was muted into creamy monotone. If the foyer door was open, that meant someone was inside the apartment: Anna had locked this door herself the evening before. She said uncertainly, "Hello?" No response.

The squeaking of her rubber boots on the walnut floors filled the long hallway, quiet kitchen, and then the office, a large airy space, all clean, white, and ordered. This was a room of systems and processes, lots of hard copies and matching staplers in a midcentury modern lime green. Mrs. Von Bizmark's broad desk of reclaimed wood occupied nearly a quarter of the space on its own platform. Anna's desk spanned the other side of the room, partially reserved for Julie, the other assistant, on the one day in the week when they overlapped. In between their two workspaces, the enormous, ledger-like leather-bound calendar splayed open in the sun like a cat. All the machines remained dark and quiet—as they should when the Von Bizmarks were away.

Yet arrayed there, on Anna's keyboard, a stack of handwritten notes: black Sharpie scrawled over personalized bloodred-on-chambray Kissy V. Bizmark stationery. In the office, this was Mrs. Von Bizmark's primary method of communicating all her most important thoughts, which inevitably occurred outside of the workday. These notes were piled in reverse order over the previous twelve hours, during which time the Von Bizmarks had not been in Aspen but home in New York after all. Was someone injured? Sick? Dead? The doorman would have known, said something. They kept track of the tenants on a little pegboard at their podium, yet Brian had also seemed ignorant of the Von Bizmarks' early return.

How had they even gotten home anyway? People like the Von Bizmarks frequently enjoyed a handful of everyman activities—grocery shopping, driving, mowing the lawn—that the rest of us would gladly avoid. For them, menial tasks provided a sense of misplaced nostalgia, not for a period of their lives but for the normalcy that would always elude them. More complicated everyman tasks like altering travel plans or navigating technical difficulties of any kind were essentially out of reach for them. Mr. and Mrs. had called Anna from a Parisian restaurant for the correct spelling of a particular wine, from Santa Fe to get the *Financial Times* delivered, from Boston to arrange the gift wrapping of a brand-new Jeep. They preferred to make requests of their personal staff, even if someone else with the answers stood directly in front of them. Anna's eyes narrowed. Florence, Mr. Von Bizmark's assistant of thirty years, had had a hand in this for sure.

Anna dialed Florence as she sifted through the notes on her desk. Piled in reverse order, the frantic scrawl quieted into more recognizable script:

Seriously, where are you

Buzz me AS SOON AS YOU GET IN.

Where are you? It's 10:14 AM.

EST

A—it's 10:05. Buzz me when you get in. KVB

VERY IMPORTANT—BUZZ ME WHEN YOU ARE HERE.

WE ARE BEING HONORED AT THE NEW YORK OPERA BALL!!!!!!!

So much to plan!

You won't believe what happened!

"Mr. Von Bizmark's office, this is—"

"Florence! What is going on?" Anna said. "Are they here?"

"She specifically told me not to call you. 'There's no reason to bother her,' she said," Florence reported primly.

"But . . . but . . . ," Anna sputtered. "Not even a text?"

"Anna!" Mrs. Von Bizmark stood at the door to the office, her tone 60 percent concerned, 40 percent "you're fired." Anna hung up on Florence. The notes fanned out in Anna's right hand; her beat-up nylon purse hung open from the left. Her goofy woolen hat with the braided earflaps sat slightly crooked on her head. Mrs. Von Bizmark wore head-to-toe chocolate cashmere. Her impeccably highlighted hair curved robustly just under her shoulders. If she could still move her eyebrows, they would have creased in agitation, but her face remained seamless, pliant. Lasered, injected, and tweaked, she looked about two decades younger than reality, which would make her and Anna about the same age.

Bambi Von Bizmark was known to staff as "Mrs. Von Bizmark." Only her husband called her "Bambi." To friends and press, on her social stationery, and at the opera, she was always "Kissy V. Bizmark." Although few others knew this, the V. for "Von" stood also for her maiden name, Verhuvenvel, a mass of v's that defied penmanship. Though Anna called her "Mrs. Von Bizmark" to her face, with employees, colleagues, and vendors she was "the Mrs." and in writing simply "KVB." The building staff referred to her as "KGB" only behind her back for her exactingness and seemingly random visitations to various storage facilities in the basement. Peter Von Bizmark, her husband, was "Mr. Von Bizmark," or "PVB," to all except cable news networks, who tended to use his name in its momentous entirety. Only Mrs. Von Bizmark and Avi, their personal lawyer, thought of him as a "Peter."

"Hello, Mrs. Von Bizmark. I must admit I'm rather surprised to see you," Anna said.

"In my own home?" Mrs. Von Bizmark replied, instantly indignant.

Cristina, the severe Polish housekeeper in a gray maid's uniform, poked her head around the pocket doors of the office. "Morning, Anna!" She hurried by, exhorting the two Salvadorean maids to follow her upstairs to the residential wing. These three were known to everyone in the building as "the ladies," and how they had come to be here on a day Anna knew they had off was confounding. Florence must have called everyone but her. Anna burned with annoyance—so much for double avocado.

"Is everything all right?" she asked.

"Fabulous, why would you ask?" Mrs. Von Bizmark and her circle were always, *always* fabulous, and to imply otherwise was ever-so-slightly offensive.

"Well, you're home five days early."

Mrs. Von Bizmark turned to the two-foot-high stack of new glossy magazines on the central island and absentmindedly dropped them one by one into the pewter trash can as she talked, gazing at each one for a few seconds before letting it fall. "Oh, yes, well . . . the snow was mediocre . . ." She held up a *New York* magazine—a close-up of the extremely liberal mayor of New York with the headline, "The City's Socialist Revolution." "Yuckapoo," she said, letting it fall. "Anyway, the kids and Peter were just so bored. They were *all* complaining, so I said why don't we just go home, then? The kids thought *that* was a great idea, of course." She paused, forced a chuckle, but her hands stopped. "And so did Peter . . . ," she added. Her shoulders slumped as she let out a sigh.

Uh-oh. The Von Bizmarks were not getting along. Which happened every so often—the Mrs. puffing up with dissatisfaction, the Mr. disappearing into work. And while it had always righted itself, the Von Bizmark marriage functioned as the cornerstone of an enormous enterprise that included staff, property, vendors—practically a whole economy unto itself. If the house divided, that economy would radically shrink. In other words, they could all be out of work.

"But wait . . . ," Anna said. "Why were the foyer doors closed if you are here?"

"I need to talk to you about that," Mrs. Von Bizmark said. "Mr. Von Bizmark has some security . . ." She waved her hand in the air, as if she might find the word there. Although she was perfectly coiffed and styled after a vacation of not just skiing but spa services and shopping, Anna could tell Mrs. Von Bizmark was out of sorts. "*Issues,*" she finally said.

Anna's employers frequently spoke in code. Valued most highly were those employees who could intuit meaning from the fewest, vaguest words, those who knew when to ask questions and those who knew when to let it lie. Furthermore, to have "security issues" in the Von Bizmarks' hyperexclusive Park Avenue co-op fell somewhere on the spectrum between extremely unlikely and completely impossible.

"And what about the ball?" Anna always tried to turn things toward the positive for her employers.

"Exactly!" Mrs. Von Bizmark said, moving to her desk in its elevated nook surrounded by built-in shelves lined with extraordinarily expensive bulbs Anna had had to order weeks in advance from Germany. All the while she nattered on, happy to have a flattering subject. "So we were at the Smythesons'—you know, Guy and Libba—they have this outrageous place out there, looks like somewhere Dracula might live or something. Anyway, they always have this big party where we get to see everyone, and it just so happened that it was Richard's last night in town. Anyway, when he sees me, he beelines over, snubbing Prince Valdobianno, who you know is a tremendous opera buff, and he finally takes both my hands in his and says, 'Just who I've been looking for, the belle of my ball.'"

Internally, Anna rolled her eyes. A very public budget shortfall had turned Richard Gross, the opera's executive director, into a rabidly obsequious fundraising machine. Meanwhile, a scathing *New York Times* article had pondered whether opera had run its course as an art form. Richard knew the answer to this lay in a blockbuster season, starting with the opening-night gala: he had been saying this in emails, phone calls, and letters to the entire board of trustees for at least three months.

"Richard got the board to vote"—Mrs. Von Bizmark bubbled over with delight—"on Christmas Eve morning and"—practically panting with eagerness—"they're going to honor Mr. Von Bizmark and *me*!" Effectively, this meant the Von Bizmarks were now on the hook to give or raise from their friends millions of additional dollars for the opera, a huge coup for Richard. In return, he would elevate the Von Bizmarks before their cohort of the richest, most well-connected people in North America; it was like the Von Bizmarks got to be king and queen of the prom, only this was not high school but New York City.

The Mrs. burst with such girlish glee at the prospect it was hard not to be a little happy for her. If philanthropy were Mrs. Von Bizmark's "career," then this would be the highlight of her curriculum vitae. Various institutions honored the Von Bizmarks all the time, but despite its financial woes, the New York City Opera was the most prestigious by a league. For the Mrs., it was the ultimate social credential, the jewel in her crown for which she had fought long and hard in the Park Avenue trenches. "That's the *real* reason we came back from Aspen early."

As exciting as this all was, Anna could see through this ruse. Since all the logistics for the ball could have been handled by phone, this meant the Von Bizmarks were definitely at odds. Next would be a trip to the couples counselor followed by a renegotiation of their wills. While this had all happened before, Anna had never known them to end a vacation early. Except the time Mrs. Von Bizmark had feigned a stomach illness to disembark prematurely from a friend's yacht in Portofino ("It was like escaping a prison!" Mrs. Von Bizmark later gushed).

"Well, congratulations!" Anna said; in her seat, she always had to play along.

"I know we've done plenty of balls and galas and parties . . ." Mrs. Von Bizmark began a pep talk but instantly lost her train of thought, traveling back through the annals of her social calendar. "Dinners . . . concerts . . ."

"Yes, I was—" Anna started.

"But this one, Anna," Mrs. Von Bizmark interrupted. "This one is . . ."

"A really big deal," Anna said.

"First there's the luncheon. The opera will handle the production and almost all of the gala, other than seating. But the luncheon! It's up to us."

All major happenings in New York society called for at least one significant "preparty" in order to build momentum, raise more money, and capture any potential attendees with conflicts for the main do. It was like you couldn't throw a successful party without actually having at least two. Typically, the first was less formal and held at someone's home to limit expenditures, maximize profits, and dangle a rare opportunity to see the inner sanctum of another multimillionaire's life.

"Should we have it—" Anna started.

"At home, exactly!" Mrs. Von Bizmark interrupted again. Cristina brought her an espresso, setting it down on top of a small tangerine cotton bar square.

"And you were thinking of doing it when?" Anna asked.

"I don't know . . . a few weeks from now? Less than two months. Richard says ASAP." Of course Richard would want the cash to start flowing. With the help of her colleague, Julie, Anna would have to put on a perfect ladies' luncheon for one hundred—maximum capacity in the Von Bizmark living and dining rooms—in about six weeks' time.

"That's going to be tough with New Year's at the end of the week," Anna said, hoping to buy a month.

"It's just a lunch," Mrs. Von Bizmark said with a flick of her wrist. "Get Richard, please."

Anna quickly did so, and Mrs. Von Bizmark picked up breathlessly, as if she'd run to the phone. "Richard!" She laughed. "You know, Peter and I are just so excited about this, and I wanted to get with you right away on choosing a luncheon date . . . uh-huh. Right. I'm sorry? . . . uh-huh. Uh-huh. Oh! My goodness. What's the budget?" She wrote down a number many digits long and poked her fountain pen at the end of it, creating a big black dot. "And this *includes* Opal's participation as creative director?" Her eyes narrowed. "Yes, do double-check, will you, Richard?"

Mrs. Von Bizmark placed the phone down and sighed. "They want us to pay for the whole production . . . the performers, the costumes, set"—she looked at her notes—"the webcast, this Austrian conductor . . ." Her eyes narrowed on the incredibly long figure she had just jotted down. "I'll have to discuss it with Peter." Even for the Von Bizmarks, there were such things as "significant purchases."

As if snapping out of a trance, Mrs. Von Bizmark said, "What time is my facial?"

"Two p.m.," Anna said, although of course there was technically no such appointment since Mrs. Von Bizmark was supposed to be in Aspen. These particulars were of no interest to Kissy V. Bizmark. "The car will be downstairs at one fifteen. In ten minutes." Anna quickly texted the Von Bizmark chauffeur: SOS, their code for *Be here now*.

"So, Anna, just get the ball rolling, all right?" Mrs. Von Bizmark said. As she pulled on a random fur from the office armoire, she asked, "Are you free to come in tomorrow?"

"Of course," Anna said. In fact, it was good timing for Anna to work more at the Von Bizmarks', as she was in between projects in the studio. There was always a natural lull in between creative bursts, followed by a few weeks of stalling and procrastination.

But this was different. Anna was waiting to get the call from the gallery where she had submitted her work. Surely once she signed with them, they would want to influence her future pieces, depending on the reaction to the series Anna had recently completed. It was her strongest work to date, and Anna just had a feeling it was going to sell and sell well. She smiled to herself, imagining a feature in *BOMB* magazine, her picture on the cover of the Arts section in the *Times* . . .

The ding-ding-ding of the front door announcing Mrs. Von Bizmark's departure snapped Anna back to the task at hand. She dialed the salon downtown. Every Tuesday when the temperature fell below freezing, Mrs. Von Bizmark went for a facial with Ping. It had to be with Ping or else. Dozens of Park Avenue ladies fought for a spot in Ping's chair, with her various needles and potions and her skilled hands. Anna silently prayed to the aesthetician gods as she dialed.

"I'm just calling to confirm today's appointment."

"We don't have anything today for Mrs. Von Bizmark, and Ping is totally booked."

"We'll pay double," Anna said.

"Aaahhhh . . ." The receptionist wavered.

"Triple."

"Hold, please." Anna imagined the vivid conversation in Mandarin happening in the back corridors of the salon before the receptionist popped back on and agreed to the deal. Anna breathed a sigh of relief.

Before she could even start thinking about the luncheon, the day and all its complexities had to be unfolded. Anna went upstairs to find Cristina to make a grocery list now that the Von Bizmarks were unexpectedly in residence. If the Mrs. didn't have her staples—cold-pressed juice, cold-brewed coffee, farm-fresh organic half-and-half, and pistachio gelato (imported from Milan)—then everyone was in trouble. The Mr. required only an evening cognac, and they had enough in his cabinet to last a nuclear winter.

The Von Bizmark bedroom, a fifteen-hundred-square-foot former living room, retained the paneling and the fireplace, of course, but a huge bed sprawled where another family might have put their couch. On every surface—the white suede chaise, the coffee table, the easy chairs—sumptuous clothes lay strewn in the hopes that not every single item would need to be pressed. But of course, they all would. Open suitcases and steamer trunks crammed the floor space.

Cristina, in her gray maid's uniform, stood steaming a white silk Brunello Cucinelli gown. Alicia, perpetually cheerful, spry, and ageless for her sixty-two years, and in pink, wrestled with a fox cape, while plumper, younger Josefina, wearing powder blue, folded a silk caftan with her twelve-year-old daughter, Ilana. When Ilana had been accepted at a gifted school for the visual arts in Harlem the year before, Josefina had proudly informed Anna that her daughter was going to be an artist—just like Anna. Since they lived over an hour away in the Bronx, Anna had negotiated with the Mrs. to allow Josefina to bring Ilana to work on occasional half days at school, but this had grown to include whenever school was not in session. Ilana was supposed to sit in the maids' room and do homework, but Anna frequently found her in the apartment helping her mom, which was lovely but, according to Avi, a violation of child labor laws.

"Ilana! Don't you have homework?" Anna asked.

"It's winter break, Anna." Ilana grinned at her.

"Still, isn't there a reading list? Shouldn't you be sketching or something?"

"There's so much work here—I thought I'd help out."

"Go, go," Josefina said, smiling proudly and waving Ilana away.

"OK, OK," Ilana said on her way out the door.

"What do you want?" Cristina asked Anna sharply.

"Grocery list, please."

"Come on! The usual stuff," Cristina said.

"Give me a break, Cristina."

"All right, I'm coming. You two, back working. Do the sweaters in tissue. Hear me? *Tissue.*"

The back doorbell rang. "I'll get it," Anna said to Cristina. "You make the list."

Brian, the doorman, nearly finished with his break, stood with his hat in his hand. He was a short portly fellow, a third-generation doorman. "Anna, I'm sorry I didn't know they were home," he said. "Barclay didn't tell me. He was so surprised to see them last night, and it was just him, so he had to unload all the bags and everything himself. He forgot to mark the board."

"Thanks, Brian," Anna said. "I appreciate your coming up here."

They shook hands. The Italian guys, Joe and Alfie, might have kissed her check. Brian stepped back, skirting the large trash cans where all the household waste went, and stepped onto the service elevator.

"Hey, Bri, happy New Year!" Anna said.

For things to work seamlessly in the lives of the co-op's residents—called "shareholders"—all the cogs needed to whir together, flushing the back channels behind the landmarked facades of Park Avenue. Plus, Brian and the boys knew that Anna was ultimately responsible for ensuring the heft and accuracy of their recent Christmas tips, the massive windfall when the best white-glove building staff made half their salary. Generally, the month before Christmas the service level went from premium to optimal as everyone toiled in thirsty anticipation.

While Cristina bustled around the kitchen checking supplies in the freezers, wine fridges, pantry, and both fridges, Anna turned her attention to party planning. First she solicited menus and bids from the Von Bizmarks' favorite three caterers and put them all on hold. She specced out an invitation and ordered proofs from two stationers.

"You want lunch?" Cristina asked from the office doorway. "We have chicken from the plane." She brought Anna a plate to eat at her desk while she continued to make phone calls and cross things off her list: flowers, check; music, check; photographer, check. At some point, Mrs. Von Bizmark came home with a list of various people she wanted to see and things she needed to buy, which she handed off to Anna before going to take a nap. After dealing with that, Anna made a list of all the things she'd have to take care of the following day because it was already after five: rentals, publicity, an apartment walk-through . . .

Anna's mobile phone rang—an unknown 212 number. Probably her sister, Lindsay, calling from some conference room at her job to heckle her about coming over for New Year's Eve. Anna reluctantly answered, preparing to reject her invitation. Again.

"Hi, this is Chad calling from the Miranda Chung Gallery. Is this Anna?"

"Yes, this is Anna," she heard herself say, suddenly very much outside her own body. It felt like receiving biopsy results. She held her breath, anticipating good news.

"Hi, Anna!" He sounded friendly! Definitely positive. "Thanks so much for sending in your portfolio"—he flipped through some papers—"'Taken From.' So much good stuff here!" This was it! Her moment! "But we are just all *full up* at the moment. Thanks for thinking of us. And please do come and collect your work by the end of the week, okaaaay?" She must have agreed and hung up.

The bottom fell out of her stomach.

Anna had not known until then how much she had expected to win this time, how much she felt entitled to it. A gallery, Miranda Chung. In the darkest corner of her mind, she unfolded a note that read *Your last chance* before it ignited and turned to dust in her hands.

Dazed, Anna departed Park Avenue for the subway, the city like the cold dark bottom of the ocean, streetlights bobbing above, taxis swimming by. Anna felt like a smudge of herself, oozing down the sidewalk. On the subway, an old lady in a knit beret munched noisily on some unidentifiable food she'd plucked from a brown paper bag. The crunching felt like a balled-up piece of aluminum foil rolling around the inside of Anna's skull. The city could become like this when it turned on you: saturated, intense, and overwhelming.

Carroll Gardens' narrow streets and short redbrick buildings cozied up to you, while Park Avenue stood back. Anna and Adrian's little walkup sat modestly on a residential block with an uneven sidewalk and variously maintained converted brownstones. Usually their neighborhood felt homey, welcoming, but tonight this short walk meant that there were only a few precious moments left before she would have to speak aloud and thereby make real her rejection.

Anna dreaded Adrian's reaction, which she knew would be something kind like, "Just keep painting." Which, like, yeah, but this wasn't a simple hobby for her. After an overpriced MFA at Yale and a few reasonably successful exhibitions as a student, she was thirsty for some outside affirmation that her efforts, her vision, her creativity were actually worthwhile. Adrian—with his meaningful work helping less-fortunate city dwellers receive free, high-quality prepared food that would otherwise be discarded—never seemed to fully get that Anna was not just creating her large vivid paintings for only her friends and family to see.

Anna climbed to the third floor, feeling heavy with disappointment, when a sudden unexpected sound from inside the apartment jarred her. A woman's high laugh. Without deciding to, Anna stopped breathing. Just froze, a foot and a half away, the thin door of the cheaply renovated townhome doing little to stop the speakers on Adrian's computer from broadcasting the contents of his conversation.

"Would love . . . of course . . . ," the woman's voice said.

Anna felt . . . puzzled. Adrian was FaceTiming with another woman? She didn't recognize the voice. She quietly clicked open the door behind him and slipped inside. On his screen, a woman with a crisp dark bob in a suit at her desk. Adrian held one index finger up off camera at Anna: *One sec.*

"I really appreciate your time," he said.

Adrian turned to Anna in his swivel chair. From the waist down he wore sweatpants and gym socks, but his top half was interview ready. Crisp white button-down shirt, hair carefully tousled. His cheeks were just the right amount of dewy over his carefully cropped beard. He was too scruffy, round in the gut, and disinterested in fashion, generally, to qualify as metrosexual; Adrian's facial hair, hearty appetite, and interest in nonprofit work further distinguished him in the New York design scene.

Anna stared at him until he finally blurted, "I'm applying for a job." She prodded him with her raised eyebrows. "At LVMH."

A set of emotional waves cycled in and began crashing over Anna's head. First, the sense that somehow he was moving forward and she was stuck in a rut. Nonsensically, Adrian's interview made Anna feel Miranda's pass even more keenly. Then, the surprise. Had he purposely kept this from her? Did he suspect Anna would not be completely supportive about the sudden deletion of the word *nonprofit* from his résumé? Was that in fact the case?

"What about Food Blast?" she said.

"You said"—he drew air quotes to emphasize—"'The writing's on the wall.' Remember?"

This was true. When Adrian had first built the app, it was to help real people. Food Blast connected food stamp recipients with elaborate, upscale food marketplaces in New York that threw away leftovers. The only problem was that twentysomethings were also enjoying free delectables, and for months Adrian had been complaining about his inability to stop those kids from taking advantage. It was only a matter of time before their funders found out and shut them down. But Anna had always presumed he would go on to found another ethically motivated nonprofit technology company.

"But LVMH?" Anna said, confused.

"Yes! The world's preeminent high-quality product conglomerate," he added, as if reading off their website.

"I'm sorry. I just"—*received the most crushing professional rejection*—"was surprised. That's all. Why didn't you tell me?"

"I didn't want to say anything until after the interview. I think it went well! They want me to come in tomorrow. You know how those corporate types are." Yes, Anna did know. Boring. And old. At least Adrian would have more to say to Lindsay's finance friends at the next event Anna couldn't wriggle out of.

"That's really . . ." She chided herself: this wasn't about her! Internally, she tried to shake off her shame for a moment. She rushed to Adrian and threw her arms around him, in part to hide the lack of a smile on her face. "Great!" she said into his starchy collar. This, the sort of stiff, tidy shirt he would be wearing every day now.

Adrian ran a disruptive hand through his hair and sighed. No doubt, this decision was hard for him too. "It's a great place to work, you know," he said, puzzled at her lack of enthusiasm. She knew that most people would be happy if their partner was trying to find a more lucrative job to advance their life together.

But Anna had been dragging her feet about next steps with Adrian—any next steps that would take them off the free, creative path she thought they walked hand in hand. Saving for an apartment, considering children, marriage?! All of that still loomed far off in Anna's distant future, when they were real adults: she an accomplished artist, he a tech entrepreneur churning out socially responsible app after app. Not now, with Adrian toiling away at a luxury-goods conglomerate and Anna having nowhere to display or sell her work.

Still, she dimly realized that she was acting like a jerk. "Oh, babe!" She forced herself to reach for Adrian's hand and say with all the sincerity she could muster, "I'm so proud of you." No way she could tell him about Miranda Chung now. "Let's celebrate!" she said instead.

TWO

M orning!" Julie said, breezing into the office in a vintage sable swing coat and a matching hat so wide she had to shove it under her desk along with her black leather handbag shaped like an enormous crow—surely one of her own designs.

The two had met while they were both failing the same fashion class. Anna focused on high-concept geometric garments that proved structurally impossible. Julie's work was high quality but too weird for anyone else to wear: pants entirely made of zippers, T-shirts with enormous feathered tails. Julie still enjoyed expressing herself through her own daily fashion choices, but artistically they had both moved on to other things: Anna to oil and collage, Julie to handbags, which she sold on Etsy.

Underneath her fur, Julie revealed a red vintage power suit from the eighties with matching pumps that she slid into after putting her moon boots away. She fastened big gold swirls to her earlobes and patted her perfect blonde updo: a wig over her natural long black hair.

"She's out. I haven't checked the voice mail or the email, and here's what she left us." Anna handed over the stack of Mrs. Von Bizmark's notes.

Did we hear from Opal yet?

Ralph Lauren, Carolina Herrera, Tom Ford

I'll be back around 11.

PRESS RELEASE!

Where is the foundation checkbook?

Can't sleep. We have to pick a date for the lunch.

I know! Let's salute Opal! At the lunch?

Go over apartment with Miguel. ☹ ASAP!

Gown? Possible designers?

"I'm calling Miguel now," Anna said. It felt good to pour herself into work and obliterate all thoughts of Miranda Chung. Anna never mentioned it to Adrian—had tried, in fact, to force herself into a state of amnesia about it. When the thought so much as crossed her mind, it dragged along endless negative implications Anna was not ready to face.

"Ugh," Julie said, leafing through Mrs. Von Bizmark's notes while Anna asked Barclay the doorman to send Miguel, the building's much-disliked superintendent, up. Julie dangled the note with the designers—*Ralph Lauren, Carolina Herrera, Tom Ford*. "So. Dull," she said, sighing heavily. She came to the missive about Opal and said, "Now this one, this one I have a really bad feeling about. The opera never honors anyone."

"Sure they do. They . . ." Anna suddenly realized what Julie was getting at.

"*Always* honor Opal." Julie finished Anna's sentence.

Opal had been the creative director at the opera for a million years; it would be impossible to overstate her aesthetic gravity. Ageless. Timeless. Classic. Of the moment. Stylistically unimpeachable. It was rumored she had masterminded transformations for both Madonna and Beyoncé, as a side gig. One could only imagine how Opal, a behind-the-scenes diva of world renown, would receive the news that this year's ball would have a new belle. Even though the Von Bizmarks' participation guaranteed money the opera so desperately needed, the question remained: How much would this negatively impact the production itself, which would surely suffer without Opal's wholehearted participation? The last thing Mrs. Von Bizmark wanted was for the opera to stink, which meant people would leave before the gala. The momentary picture of Mrs. Von Bizmark dressed to kill sitting at an empty table made Anna shudder.

"How much do you think this is going to cost?" she asked.

"Five million," Julie said.

"I'll say ten."

"Can they really use foundation money?" These were not idle posers but rather a significant part of Anna's job. She had to ask the right questions to the appropriate people at the correct time. "Will Opal really participate, do you think?" Julie continued her slew of questions.

There was only one way to find out.

"What can I do for you, Anna?" Richard said when Anna called.

"So I understand the Von Bizmarks are being honored at this year's gala?"

"Yes," he said.

"And part of that honor includes underwriting the entire production?"

"That's correct."

"And what is the budget?"

"Twelve point four million."

"I see," Anna said, imagining how creative their finance officer had been in coming up with this figure. "And will they have any input into the opera, or will Opal handle all art direction?"

"That remains to be seen."

Hardly an encouraging response.

"I'll have to consult our accountant," Anna said, dreading the call. This was the guy who made sure that the Von Bizmarks did not give a single additional dollar to the government after taking advantage of every possible loophole and workaround. The Von Bizmark tax bill was an item of gossip among the staff, as it had been rumored that one year Marco had brought it down to zero. He was methodical. In love with tax law. Mr. Von Bizmark had hired him to manage his finances when they were both in college—Von Bizmark at Princeton and Marco at Rutgers. All those years of quiet math meant when Marco did get the chance to talk to a live human being, he ran with it.

"Whoa, whoa, whoa, first of all, let's go back to square one," Marco said on the phone, which was how he responded to any question, ever. "So the Von Bizmarks are being honored by the New York City Opera." She could hear him scratching at a legal pad. "And for this their name will be mentioned on all preevent materials, which could be viewed as publicity. Do they get to pick the opera? The cast?"

"That remains to be seen."

"And they want them to pay twelve point four million dollars. What do they get in return? Do they get to invite their friends? Eat dinner? Yes, of course! It's a *gala!*" Marco laughed at his own question. "There's a lot here, Anna. I mean, could we find one or two things that they could pay for with foundation money? Sure. Probably. But, Anna, have I told you about—"

"Myron Moneybags?" Anna interjected. Marco had two parables he loved to employ, this one and the bagel story. Once he started, there was no point trying to stop him.

"Yes, exactly! Myron Moneybags gave a museum ten million, and they named it after him. Moneybags Museum! Anyway, the IRS takes a look at this: the big party they threw for Myron, the way he got to smash the champagne against the new sign with his name on it. And Myron didn't have a good PA like you who made sure he had a letter from the museum that explicitly said, and I quote"—as he spoke these words, Anna mouthed along—"'No goods or services were received in exchange for this contribution.' Are you with me so far?"

"Yup," Anna said.

"But what about the opera? If the Von Bizmarks pay for the costume tailoring, for example, it's not like they actually received a good or service. Are you following me?"

"*So* closely!"

"Playbills, plastic cups at the bar . . . maybe they pay for the cleaning of the hall afterward. You see, we're in a really murky area here. For example, did you know that if you buy a bagel, uncut, there's no tax, but if they cut it, they add tax? It's like that. We're dealing here in the very, very gray area full of land mines, so it's just not a great idea to push the envelope." The only thing Marco loved more than a long tax discussion was a mixed metaphor.

"OK, so you're saying maybe?" Anna said, egging him on.

"I'm saying no! No, no, no. No. It's not worth the risk!" Anna felt Marco's blood pressure rising through the phone.

"So you're going to send me that list of things we can pay for with foundation money?"

"Not. Worth. It . . . don't make me say that word . . ."

"Meatballs?"

"Audit!" Marco shouted. "Audit!" Anna imagined Marco bolting awake in the middle of the night screaming *Audit!*

"Look, I can't stop her."

"Hide the checkbook if you have to," Marco suggested. Anna's jaw fell open. This betrayal hung in the air between them. "Just joking!

Ha ha," Marco finally added nervously. When the back doorbell rang, Anna begged off the phone with Marco and went to find Cristina in the laundry room delicately ironing Mr. Von Bizmark's boxers. Ilana sat at the washing machine sketching her hand in pencil.

"Hey, Anna, did you have to do this stupid assignment?" she asked without looking up.

"Every semester."

As Cristina and Anna walked to the back door to let Miguel in, Cristina mumbled under her breath, "This guy's no good."

Miguel wore a khaki suit and paisley tie, which no one could explain since he was a superintendent meant to do things like fix leaky sinks, recalibrate expensive chef's ovens, and quiet military-grade alarm systems.

"What's up, girl?" he said with his characteristic sneer, and Anna grimaced. Cristina handed him blue booties to put over his shoes, although they were wing tips, not work boots.

"We're having a lunch here, and everything needs to be shipshape, top to bottom."

Miguel loudly rubbed his hands together. Cristina guided them through every detail and function of the ten-thousand-square-foot apartment. They started in the grand living room, half a city block long. Against the far wall, two identical slate couches abutted the marble mantel, creating mirror-image seating areas. A cream chenille ottoman invited you to warm yourself by the fire, which could be lit at any time with the toss of a single match. On the other side of the room, a massive custom sectional couch so large it had had to be constructed in the room sat before a wall that doubled as an enormous screen.

They traveled down the row of built-in climate-control units, turning them all on, feeling the heat and then flipping them over to air-conditioning until a crisp breeze flooded the room. Anna tested the cognac cabinet door, held closed by museum putty. Cristina produced a magnifying glass to inspect the detailed work of the hand-painted floors and walls while Miguel examined the seams in every corner, the function of every lighting fixture. Each faucet was made to run hot, cold, and the all-important full stop: no dripping sinks here. Cristina pointed out all the chips in the cabinetry, tiny stains nearly invisible to the naked eye on couches and pillows. Anna took notes. They skipped the Von Bizmark bedroom and finally arrived at the ninth and final bathroom, in the upstairs hall.

"The toilet doesn't work so good," Cristina explained. Depressing the silver handle resulted only in a stirring of the water. "You have to jiggle," she said, wiggling the fixture and coaxing the water to swirl and drain away. "You could make a sign?" she suggested.

"That says what? 'Please jiggle the handle a bit'?" Anna said. "Let's just keep the door closed, and the chances are no one will even be up here."

"I can fix it," Miguel volunteered. "No problem." Most people in fact would have loved their building superintendent to address broken fixtures so promptly, but in the Von Bizmark apartment, systems were so precise and rarefied (and generally made in Europe or Japan) it was risky to rely on house staff for anything beyond the smallest tweak.

Furthermore, each room was crowded with valuables, and Miguel was neither a talented handyman nor a graceful human being. The last time Miguel tried to deal with a minor plumbing problem in the Von Bizmark home, he had put his foot through a $50,000 piece of art deco etched glass, a momentary physical error that had taken many phone calls, drawn-out conversations, lengthy and repetitive emails, moments of doubt and anxiety, and months upon months just to get back to where they had started. Even though this bathroom had probably never been used in the two decades the Von Bizmarks had lived there, no expense had been spared in the mosaic floor and custom glass faucets . . . was that a real Magritte sketch on the wall? Anna was eager to avoid any sort of project with Miguel.

"How long will it take?"

"An hour. Tops."

"Let me ask Mrs. Von Bizmark if it's really necessary," she said, stopping Miguel from removing his jacket to get right to work. "I'll call you."

"Up to you," he said, reshouldering his blazer. "I wouldn't wait on that, though. It could clean break in the middle of the party, start a flood. Disaster," he said, heading down the hallway with his head down, like a general leaving the battlefield. Cristina rolled her eyes.

"Please!" she whispered to Anna. Cristina held up her hand, rubbing her fingers together to indicate that Miguel was only interested in money.

"And," he said, standing with his hand on the back doorknob, "you don't really have to worry about upsetting seven."

An ancient woman, Mrs. Forstbacher, inhabited the seventh floor like a painted hermit, interacting mostly with building staff, who claimed that she held a stethoscope to the walls of the apartment when she sensed the slightest disturbance in order to call downstairs and complain. This was, after all, her way of socializing. In any case, the dysfunctional Von Bizmark toilet seemed a safe distance away, a whole floor between them.

"I'll let you know," Anna said curtly. "Thank you." She closed the door.

Back in the office, Julie scribbled on an antiquated carbon copy pad that ensured no phone message was ever completely lost. The teensy-tiny slips forced you to whittle each voluminous, nuanced message down to about eleven words. Julie, sweating underneath her wig, ripped off another draft and crumpled it.

"Everything OK?" Anna asked.

"Vera tried to get the jet for the weekend. To Jamaica, of all places!" Vera was the Von Bizmarks' second child and a senior at Phillips Exeter. "When I told her no, she asked to speak to my manager."

"I'll call her back," Anna said, winking. "As your manager."

"And Avi called three times!" Julie said. "First he said he was returning his phone call, then hers, and this last time he wouldn't even tell me who he wanted to speak to; he just asked exactly who was in the apartment. Do we have to write that one down even?"

Avi the lawyer's hallmark was the cluster call. He would try the home office, then Mrs. Von Bizmark's cell phone, then email, then text her, then Mr. Von Bizmark's cell phone, then office, then back to the beginning until he got a Von Bizmark on the phone. Unlike Marco, he never, ever wanted to speak to anyone but a Von Bizmark about anything. Rumor had it he was former Israeli intelligence.

"He'll just keep calling until he reaches one of them. No need for a message," Anna said.

"He's a weird one," Julie said. "How'd it go with Miguel?"

Although by nearly anyone else's lights, the apartment and all its contents were pristine—practically unlived in!—by Von Bizmark entertaining standards, the place needed a lot of work.

"Eh," Anna said vaguely.

Julie opened the snack drawer between them. They munched anxiously on truffle popcorn, Indonesian raw cashews, grain-free coconut granola.

"Miranda Chung passed," Anna blurted.

"Oh, shit," Julie said. She squeezed Anna's hand over the snack drawer. "Shit, shit, shit!"

Tears unexpectedly filled Anna's eyes. She blinked, and there they were on her cheeks.

"Oh, no!" Julie exclaimed, handing her a tissue.

"I just don't know what to do now."

"Well, I mean, just keep painting. Obviously."

Anna suppressed a small sob.

"I mean, it's not like Miranda Chung is the only game in town, Anna," Julie said.

"And Adrian is leaving Food Blast to go work for Louis Vuitton! Louis fucking Vuitton!" Anna added, quaking a little. Again, it seemed somehow that he was moving up in the world, and that meant she was going down.

Julie looked confused. "Well, that sounds like good news?"

Anna quickly swiped her face and blew her nose when they heard the elevator door ding and then four hard heels on the marble. Both Von Bizmarks? Mr. Von Bizmark went straight upstairs while the Mrs. paused in the kitchen to gather herself before charging into the office. She wore her hair back with sunglasses and a trim down vest: no need for a full coat in a car.

"Good morning," Mrs. Von Bizmark said, rushing to the relatively dim lighting around her desk, keeping her owlish sunglasses on. Her skin looked puffy and pink. If she had come home alone, there would be some office speculation about where she had been: The dermatologist for a quick peel or laser? The shrink for a new Xanax prescription? Out for an unusual jog on this brisk day? But the two of them together like this on a workday, even if it was the quiet before New Year's Eve, plus Avi's frantic calls, could only mean one thing: they had, in fact, redone their wills.

Lately it seemed they treated will revision as if it were bad couples therapy; neither of them could now force the other to sign a postnuptial agreement, so instead they focused on bludgeoning one another with postmortem scenarios. Other husbands and wives fought bitterly and threatened to leave their spouses in their most inner sanctums. The Von Bizmarks did battle in the cool corporate setting of a lawyer's office, where they would demonstrate through subtext and math laid out by their legal representatives how far the other had fallen in their esteem.

"Anyway," Mrs. Von Bizmark said as if they were in the middle of a conversation, "I had an idea!" She took a seat at her desk and announced to Anna and Julie, both at attention, sitting straight up in their Aeron chairs: "Let's send the opera a foundation check."

This made sense in that if the marriage was in trouble, Mrs. Von Bizmark would wish to avoid dipping into her own personal trust. Anna presumed Mrs. Von Bizmark had just cooked up this idea in the car because there was no way Marco would have given her disinformation. Either way, it suddenly felt very much up to Anna to prevent this from happening. Personal assistants often found themselves in positions of maximum responsibility with minimal power. Florence always said, *Never do more or less than you are asked.* Somehow, it had never been easy for Anna to keep herself within those limits.

"Well . . . ," Anna said.

"We *absolutely* can," Mrs. Von Bizmark said sternly. Anna would have to prevent her from committing tax fraud either at a later date or surreptitiously. "And furthermore, we decided to go out East for New Year's Eve," Mrs. Von Bizmark said without ceremony.

"You're going to Coolwater?" Anna said, taken aback. The Von Bizmark country home had been most memorably described by *Architectural Digest* as "the most relevant take on a sixteenth-century chateau ever seen in the Hamptons." Mrs. Von Bizmark rarely referred to it by name, preferring the more subtle phrasing of *out East* or *the beach.* Behind their backs, the staff called it the Castle. The Von Bizmarks spent weekends there Memorial to Labor Day plus two weeks in August, then Thanksgiving with the family, and that was it.

Phil, the house manager, was probably at that moment snuggled up by the fire with a new off-season friend, someone like a buff contractor, several decades his junior. Or he could be gallivanting in the Caribbean with the same. The winter was his downtime, and in the ten years Anna had worked for the Von Bizmarks, it had never been interrupted.

"Yes, Anna, today. Julie, please tell them to get the cars ready," Mrs. Von Bizmark said pointedly. At least that was better than taking a helicopter, their usual mode of Hamptons transfer, which would get them to the Castle too soon for even the heat to be on.

The Von Bizmarks had no idea how difficult it could be to actualize their last-minute whims. They didn't care how the sausage was made, as long as it was delicious, fast, and ready when wanted. Speaking of sausage, what would they eat? The chef was at home in her native Colombia. Who would snatch all the sheets from the furniture, tuck the linens into the beds, set out towels in the bathrooms? Who would prep the grounds, distribute flowers, replace light bulbs? These tasks would require immediate sustained attention from the skeleton crew of year-round staff who lived in the Hamptons. If he started now, Phil would still be unprepared, and Anna was sure to hear about all this from him directly, as soon as he had five minutes to himself again.

"Does Phil know you're coming?" Anna asked, hoping maybe she had given him a heads-up.

"I trust you'll take care of that for me," Mrs. Von Bizmark said.

"OK, I'll just give him a . . ." Anna reached for the phone.

"Later. I have to go over everything, and I can't keep Mr. Von Bizmark waiting." Mrs. Von Bizmark always referred to the Mr. formally when she wanted to underline his authority. "I have a list here," she said, opening a white leather dossier within which lay a personalized Kissy V. Bizmark notepad, and pointed her fountain pen at each item in turn.

"I want to invite the Petzers right away."

There weren't that many rungs above the Von Bizmarks on the New York City social ladder, but the Petzers stood—smugly—on one of them. *Pippy and Charles Petzer* adorned the opera hall itself, and Mrs. Petzer chaired the committee raising money to endow a position in Opal's name and secure her a sizable pension. Mrs. Petzer claimed *Mayflower* heritage, a Roosevelt cousin, a library at Harvard: an untouchable elitist skeptical of all friendly overtures. So instead, Mrs. Von Bizmark had started with Charlie Petzer, artfully stalking him around town over the course of many years, slowly cultivating his acquaintance, until he'd introduced her to his wife enough times that Mrs. Petzer could no longer ignore Mrs. Von Bizmark.

"Dear Charlie, hope you and Pippy will join Peter and I in our box for the Opera Ball."

Anna jotted this down, wordlessly correcting the *I* to *me*. "Email, letter, orchid?"

"Just an email. Keep it light. And we're going to need to get that wine we had that one time . . . what was it? Maybe it was two years ago." Anna recalled the conversation. Mrs. Von Bizmark had said it was the perfect "lunch" wine, which meant it had been a summer event. One large enough that they would have had to order wine rather than rely on the thousand-bottle cellar, which meant at least fifty guests. There had been three such lunches in the past eighteen months. Anna opened each file on her computer in turn, scanning catering contracts and follow-up emails.

"You know, the wine, it had that really uninspired label . . ."

Anna closed in on the answer: the wine for the third lunch was a French chardonnay.

"*Vivre!*" Anna said, triumphant.

"That's it!" agreed Mrs. Von Bizmark.

"What?" Julie said.

"V-I-V-R-E," said Mrs. Von Bizmark while Julie wrote it down. "*Vivre.* It means 'live' in French."

Julie giggled. "In college, we used to drink this terrible wine called Vida. I'm not even sure it was really wine, more like grain alcohol . . ." Mrs. Von Bizmark's lips pressed together, and she sighed deeply through slightly flared nostrils. Julie trailed off. "Anyway . . ."

"Julie," Mrs. Von Bizmark said a little sternly, "order the wine, please, and call the boutiques on my list and have them send some gowns. Nothing too avant-garde, OK? Has Opal called about the lunch?"

"Not yet!" Anna said, knowing that Opal had not even been invited.

"We need to call Max about a press release!"

"Won't the opera handle press?"

"We can't trust them to do that. I want Max to work on the narrative of why they picked us, if you know what I mean," Mrs. Von Bizmark said. Anna read the subtext: Max, Mrs. Von Bizmark's longtime publicist, would have to figure out how to rewrite history so that it would not appear that the Von Bizmarks had smacked Opal from the marquee with their fat checkbooks. Max's talent lay in making moneyed folk look beneficent, effortlessly terrific, and otherwise totally normal.

"I'll call him, but what about invitations? Entertainment? Food?"

"Yes, of course . . ." Mrs. Von Bizmark stood and leaned over her desk to peer down the hallway. She inched her shades down her nose. Anna and Julie exchanged a puzzled glance. "I hired Sydney Bloom," Mrs. Von Bizmark stage-whispered.

Sydney Bloom was one of the best-known party planners in New York City and therefore the world, and working with her was both a relief and a terror. On the one hand, everything about the party instantly became Bloom's responsibility, which was great because she was exceedingly good at her job. Anna had no doubt the whole event itself would go swimmingly.

However, this shifted Anna's role from party planning to managing the party planner, who had, the last two times she'd worked with the Von Bizmarks, padded the bill so baroquely that they had ended up spending more than double the estimate.

"Oh, OK, so—" Anna started.

"She'll be here Monday," Mrs. Von Bizmark interrupted as heels struck the floor at the end of the hallway.

"What about a budget? Two fifty?"

"OK! *Sssshhh* . . . ," Mrs. Von Bizmark said, paddling the air for Anna to start talking about something else before Mr. Von Bizmark appeared at the office door.

"Bambi, let's go." Mr. Von Bizmark loomed at the open double doors of the office, scowling. A physically imposing man, made more so by a posture slightly bent forward from the waist, his barrel chest tilted aggressively, large hands frequently grasping and twitching at his sides. The very top button of his button-down shirt was undone, no tie: his casual look. "Anna," he said, inclining his head in her direction. "Gemma," he said to Julie.

"Julie," Mrs. Von Bizmark corrected.

"I know!" he snapped.

Mr. Von Bizmark was hardly ever around. The Von Bizmark Organization, or VBO, took up all his time and attention, or at least so he claimed. Given the boatloads of money the company generated through its vast international holdings, which spanned a dozen sectors, it was plausible that the man just worked all the time. Still, something was definitely wrong. The Von Bizmarks looked uncertainly at one another in a way that suggested there was more to this weekend than just "getting away."

"Your phone!" Cristina barked, suddenly popping into view and thrusting Mr. Von Bizmark's phone at him. He slipped it into his pocket, but before he could thank her, Cristina had yapped, "So forgetful!" She waved her hand in Mr. Von Bizmark's face and was gone.

"Bambi, let's go!" he said sternly, and Mrs. Von Bizmark stood.

"Quick question," Anna said, stopping them at the office door. "The upstairs hall bathroom toilet is a little wonky." Both Von Bizmarks stared at Anna as if she were suddenly speaking in Mandarin. Wonkiness was not a feature of their lives. "You have to, you know, jiggle the handle to get it to work." To illustrate, Anna wiggled an imaginary handle in midair.

"And?" Mr. Von Bizmark said, his eyes widening behind his tortoiseshell glasses.

"Should we have it fixed or leave it—"

"Fix it," he said. "Can't Miguel do it?"

"He's not a plumber, but I guess he can," Anna replied, wishing she had just called Ariadne Plumbing.

Anna was about to broach the topic of not using the foundation funds to underwrite the opera production when Mrs. Von Bizmark shrieked.

"Mommy?" said Peony Von Bizmark, the youngest and frequently forgotten third child, her hand on the back of her mother's thigh. The nastiest gossip on the Mrs. Von Bizmark side concerned Peony and how the Mrs.'s chief interest in her had been to appear younger, as if just having a baby at home with a nanny took five years off your face. Mrs. Von Bizmark liked to tell people Peony was a surprise baby, and if that were true, that she had spontaneously—ooops!—gotten pregnant at forty-nine, it surely would have been. But the machinations involved in securing the best egg, the right surrogate, and the desired third child had drained almost all the unexpectedness out of this reproduction.

"You surprised me, sweetheart," Mrs. Von Bizmark said, peering down at Peony, a quiet nine-year-old with a knack for invisibility. Mr. Von Bizmark's glowering softened only slightly at the sight of his youngest daughter. Peony's nanny—who had introduced herself to Anna as "Nanny" but whose born Indonesian name was surely something else—stood silently at the entryway of the office, waiting for her charge. Nanny had raised all the Von Bizmark children and was a fixture of the household. Mrs. Von Bizmark had made clear that Nanny was the only residential employee who existed outside of Anna's purview; in fact, she lived outside of almost everyone's consciousness. Except of course Peony, who loved Nanny but understood she could never wholly replace her mother.

"May I please go in the car with you?" Peony asked Mrs. Von Bizmark.

"No, darling, there's not enough room in Daddy's car." The Von Bizmarks avoided the everyman tedium of a long car ride with potential traffic jams and a child by sending the nanny up separately with the driver.

"We'll play when you get there," Mr. Von Bizmark said. Mrs. Von Bizmark snorted quietly—surely this was a rare occurrence. Mr. Von Bizmark glared at her.

"Come, come," Nanny said, Peony's audience with her parents at an end. They all shuffled down the hallway and out the door.

Anna slowly, finally, unwrapped her breakfast sandwich, the egg firmed up at room temperature, and bit into it, famished. Delicious. She imagined the Mrs. heading down in the elevator, she and Mr. Von Bizmark facing forward in silence; settling in the car, draping some sort of cashmere wrap over her legs; bound for the Long Island Expressway. Then she would reach for her phone, in her handbag, to call Anna and ask her to FedEx something completely unimportant and replaceable: lip balm, a certain sweater, a book.

Meanwhile, Anna dialed Vera, who was probably on her way to volleyball practice.

"Vera, it's Anna. What can I do for you?"

"Oh hi, Anna!" Vera knew she'd get further with a little sugar, a trick she'd learned from Mommy. "How *are* you?"

"Fine, thanks, and you?"

"You know. Studying."

"Yes, I know. I'm sure you're working very hard," Anna said blandly.

"So, what I was thinking was that I, like, deserved a little something after finals. You know, a little reward."

"I wonder what you had in mind."

"Well! I was *thinking* . . . it's the perfect time of year to hit Jamaica. Or Saint Barts. And my friends are also really stressed out . . . so. Can you send the jet next Friday?"

"Let's see here. You would like me to send the G-7 up to Exeter next week to pick up you and your other seventeen-year-old friends—"

"Clementine is eighteen!" Vera interjected.

"Right, of course. Clementine." Anna unfurled the name. "Anyway, you, Clementine, and company climb on the jet, with its fully stocked bar, of course. Let's say Friday. Three p.m. or fourish?"

"Four's good," Vera said.

"You zip on down to Jamaica to stay at a Round Hill villa all by yourselves for two nights? Or would three be better?"

"Two is fine."

"And I'll just call the resort and get you a chef and twice-daily housekeeping. How about water sports? Want to take the yacht out or anything?"

"Uh, sure?" Vera said, sensing a trap.

"OK, great! I've got this all written down, and all we have to do now is . . . run it by your mom!" Anna let this hang there for a moment before delivering the death blow. "And dad!"

"Never mind." Vera hung up.

"I see what you're saying about the sleeves, Greta," Julie said into her phone, studying the image of a jade velvet Ralph Lauren gown on her computer screen.

"No velvet," Anna said. "It's the spring."

"I'm hearing no velvet, Greta," Julie said, and she switched to another image of something satiny, sleek.

When the phone rang again, Anna expected Mrs. Von Bizmark but instead got gruff Richard Gross. "I'm returning her call," Richard said. Anna put down her sandwich.

"She called you?"

"She called Opal."

"She's in the car, but I know Mrs. Von Bizmark wants to honor Opal at the pregala luncheon."

"Unfortunately, because the lunch is right around the corner, we already extended that offer to Felix Mercurion."

One of the world's most famous art collectors and gallerists, Felix Mercurion came from a family who built their business on pieces stolen from the Jews during World War II. He was the sort frequently photographed on Mediterranean yachts, chomping a cigar, gut hanging out, yelling at someone on the phone, a bored model smoking in the background. Famous philanderer. It was hard to know if this would be received as good or bad news. Anna sighed and hung up.

"Oh shit, I never called Phil," Anna suddenly realized.

It was 2:00 p.m. The Von Bizmarks had left at noon. They would likely stop for lunch. Unless they were fighting. In which case, they would arrive in thirty minutes. Phil's phone rang and rang. The second before it was going to go to voice mail, in midlaugh, chew, or something, Phil answered. "Yeah, hello."

"Phil, they're coming!"

"Who is this?" he said, quieting a man's voice in the background.

"Phil, it's Anna. The Von Bizmarks are going to arrive at the Castle in as soon as thirty minutes."

"What the fuck, Anna!" Phil said, dropping the phone. It clattered to the floor, and she heard a man laugh in the background, only to have Phil hiss him silent. "Are you shitting me?" he said. "Seriously."

"This is not a drill. Repeat: this is not a drill."

"I gotta go," Phil said and then hung up on her. Diva.

"Was he pissed?" Julie said, hanging up with the wine vendor.

"He's totally freaked," Anna said, already dialing Miguel. "So about this toilet . . ." Oh, this seemed like such a bad idea. "Can you fix it next week?"

"No problem," he said smoothly. Anna's guts twisted.

Anna had agreed to meet Adrian for dinner at a Pakistani hole-in-the-wall spot, right by Food Blast and a favorite with taxi drivers. They claimed two out of five stools at the short counter to eat their samosas and goat curry. As they sipped hot sweet tea, Adrian told her about his second-round interview. "I think this could work out," he said, knocking his knuckles on the particleboard counter. "Have you heard anything?" he asked.

As much as she wanted to continue pretending, Anna could not bring herself to lie to him. "Miranda Chung passed," Anna said, the tears right there already. Adrian hugged her, and she nuzzled into the scratchy wool of his coat.

"Oh, babe," he whispered into her hair. Even though they sat on stools, squashed into a tiny corner reeking of curry, snot pooling on Adrian's collar, Anna felt the teensiest bit better for a second. "What did she say?" he asked, breaking away to look at her.

"No, I didn't . . . I spoke to . . ." Anna realized she wasn't even sure whom she'd spoken to.

"So you don't even know if she saw your work!"

"Yeah, but . . ." Anna didn't know how to finish the sentence.

"Come with me."

Adrian pulled Anna outside and around the corner. A long line of people in their twenties, faces lit up by iPhone screens, waited outside the Food Blast pop-up store. Peppered among them, a few homeless people looked uncomfortable in the spotlight all the extra space around them created. "Food Blast is not helping the right people," Adrian said.

"But . . ." Anna instinctively resisted the LVMH job, and not just because it made her feel like a failure. With his app, Adrian had carried the ethical weight for both of them. Anna could feel OK at her frivolous job because her partner was actually doing something good for the city's poorest residents. Even more deeply, Anna dimly realized that she had been clinging to the belief that neither of them ever really had to compromise on their dreams and ideals. "You're still fighting food waste."

Adrian scrunched up his face. "I don't know if that's enough for me. Or for us. Don't you want to have a normal, rodent-free life?"

"We have a normal life!" Anna insisted; the word *normal* rankled. "Rodents are normal."

"But, Anna, what about, you know, adult things?"

There it was. That word: *adult.*

"Buying an apartment, having a baby . . ."

A tiny part of her jumped to hear the word *baby* coming from Adrian's mouth. But she couldn't help worrying about what it would mean to have a child. The way things were shaping up, she would inevitably end up giving up on art to change diapers and wipe boogers. And Adrian—what about his meaningful work?

"Look, Anna, this new job means you can use this space to do your own show!" He gestured at the Food Blast storefront, a twenty-by-twenty-foot box with a broad plate-glass window. Just enough space to display all thirteen pieces in her "Taken From" series. Adrian watched her eyes travel over the three blank walls where her work could hang. He was as eager and excited as if it were his art that would show there.

But . . . this was just not a part of Anna's plans. Showing your work in a gallery meant the endorsement of the gallerist; putting on your own exhibition was like publicly admitting you had failed to interest such an entity. Plus, Anna would have to do all the work. Adrian sensed her hesitation. "If I get the LVMH job, I'm closing Food Blast, effective immediately. You just have to get the show together before January fifteenth, when the lease here runs out." Only two weeks to plan the whole thing, but she had accomplished more in far less time. "Screw Miranda Chung!" he said, and Anna winced. "Or get Miranda Chung or whoever to come and really see your work, hung and lit and the way it's meant to be."

She hadn't thought of it like that—like another bite at the apple. "But can I really pull it off? By myself?" she asked.

Adrian draped his arm over Anna's shoulders, and she leaned into him. "Who said you had to do it by yourself?"

THREE

When they arrived at the Castle, Bambi felt none the happier. Peter had driven grim faced and distracted the whole while: a forced march. They never went out East off season, but after having her vacation so unceremoniously snatched away, then an unpleasant round of legal rejiggering with that stickler Avi, Bambi felt entitled to some sort of reparation. And how could Peter deny her a trip to their very own country home? An unusually simple request, for Bambi.

But as they approached the gatehouse, she could not help but notice that no one had put on the dramatic lights that illuminated each two-hundred-year-old tree trunk along the drive, which made approaching Coolwater feel quite grand. Rather than looking festive and inviting, the darkened tree-lined road snaked ominously up to the stone residence. The bare branches in silhouette against the gray sky conjured in Bambi a series of wailing women, arms outstretched. Coolwater itself blended into the monotone clouds overhead and the gravel underneath. The flower beds were covered in burlap, the fountain shut off . . .

"Looks like no one's home," Peter said grimly, parking the car directly in front of the front door for someone else to move later. "Phil does know we're coming, right?"

"I'm sure Anna called him," Bambi responded. But had she? The place seemed abandoned. Peter and Bambi climbed the stairs to the never-locked front entrance and found it would not budge. Neither she nor Peter had a key; why would they need such a thing? Bambi felt her sadness sharpen into annoyance. She tugged fruitlessly on the iron handle, then began jabbing at the doorbell, the stentorian gong reverberating through the metal entry. Bambi leaned in to peer through the glass and was momentarily distracted by a sheen of dirt. And inside: Was that a sheet? On a couch? They stepped back out into the spacious grand drive. Bambi saw the silhouette of a blanket sailing through the air like a giant manta ray upstairs, where all the lights were on. Yet no one was answering the door. Annoyance blossomed into frustration.

Bambi and Peter stood there for a moment, stymied. Peter glared at Bambi, blaming her of course for this shocking delay. How ludicrous, to be shut out of their own home. Then Bambi remembered there were other points of ingress (in fact, there were six additional doors into the building). Bambi and Peter traveled around the side of the house to the kitchen, an entry they had not been through since Coolwater was under construction. The surprises kept coming as they found Phil himself unloading Bambi's fresh green juices into the fridge.

"Mr. and Mrs. Von Bizmark, hello!" Phil said, tossing the last juice in a little roughly, in Bambi's opinion, while upstairs there was this tremendous pounding noise. A light bulb needed replacing over the sink. The room was hardly any warmer than the temperature outside. No flowers? It looked so . . . stark in the grand kitchen. Only the overhead lights glared at full power. The light pained her eyes. Inattention to detail depressed her. And what was that racket upstairs? "Happy New Year!" Phil continued, coming toward them with an outstretched hand to shake Peter's. Bambi eyed their house manager, tufts of white hair sticking out at odd angles underneath his watchman's cap. She kissed him on both cheeks—he smelled like alcohol.

"Phil, don't you have people for that?" she said, gesturing at the sad empty Juice Press bag deflating on the counter. Upstairs, another series of thumps. But before he could answer, she added with more urgency, "And what is that noise?"

"What noise?" Phil said, blinking. There it was again, pound-*pound-pound*.

"*That* noise!" Bambi insisted. Did he think she could not hear? They were in a large house with only one distinct sound in it, and she wanted to know what was causing it.

"That's the new maid."

"Is she an elephant? What the devil is she doing up there?"

"Mrs. Von Bizmark, she's running. From the linen closet in the south corridor to your bedroom in the east wing. It's about an eighth of a mile round trip . . ."

Bambi cocked her head at him and sighed. "Phil, dear, it does seem like things are a smidge out of order," Bambi observed, her eyes ticking off the expired bulb, the empty vases. She shivered a little to underline her point.

"Well, we are making all good haste to have everything ready for you."

"What does that mean, Phil? Is the house somehow *not* ready?" It was a building made out of rocks full of inanimate objects. What on earth did anyone have to do to "get it ready"? And it was their home! Sometimes it seemed like people forgot that Bambi and Peter were two human beings with those sorts of basic needs: warmth, light, sustenance.

"Of course, Coolwater is always ready for you, Mrs. Von Bizmark!" he enthused, even as observable facts suggested otherwise. Sometimes staff could be so . . . *evasive*!

Bambi's eyes narrowed. "Why is it so cold in here, then?"

"The system takes a good forty-eight hours to get up to speed . . ."

"Peony can't come here, then! Forty-eight hours! The little dear will freeze to death. Call Nanny and tell them to turn around, please." Phil pulled out his mobile phone and dialed, but before it could start ringing, it occurred to Bambi that she herself was still cold and destined to be so for at least two full days. "Wait!" she said. "What about us?"

"I lit a fire in your bedroom, the east library, the upstairs and downstairs sitting rooms . . . ," Phil began as Nanny's phone rang.

"Not the corner room?"

"I'll light that right now." Phil hustled off, barking into the phone at Nanny to "Turn around! Right away!"

Peter looked longingly after him and said, "I have to make some calls," trying also to escape. Everyone always scattered when Bambi was even the slightest bit cross. Did no one wish to soothe her?

Before Peter had made it out of the kitchen, Bambi asked, "What would you like to eat tonight, dear?"

"Whatever you like, dear."

"Phil! Phil!" Mrs. Von Bizmark called, and Phil came running back, down two flights of stairs, through the great room and dining room, and into the kitchen. He caught his breath as subtly as possible.

"Who do we have to cook for us?" Bambi lobbed this, knowing it would stump him, but she was tired of Phil yessing her all the time. Plus she longed for Chef's slimming delights. Only in her hands could Bambi truly relax and just enjoy her food in still-tiny but calorically safe quantities.

"Ahhhhh . . ." Phil stalled, pained by his own lack of an answer. "How about the new steak place in Southampton?"

"Steak, dear?" Bambi called.

"Yes, dear," Peter responded. "You know I like steak." Yes, of course Bambi knew this, just as Peter knew she never ate red meat. But no one cared. *Sigh*. Not the way she did, always sacrificing for her kids, her husband, and the demands of their lives together. Would Bambi herself never get exactly what she wanted? There was still the opera to discuss, and after all the sacrifices she had made recently, all the indignities, she had it coming to her.

The steak restaurant was far too loud and public for such a conversation. Their meal was interrupted every half hour by people, some reasonably well known to them, others just wanting to kiss the Von Bizmark ring. It was tedious; it prolonged the meal and called attention to Bambi's sad, vaguely gray and pasty-looking steamed vegetable plate. Peter had outrageously ordered the rib eye for two and had somehow managed to saw through two-thirds of it before she stayed him with a hand on the wrist.

"Think of your heart," she murmured, which she knew did not endear her to him, but enough already. She'd hoped to ask him over his customary bottomless cognac back at the house, but instead of going to the bar, which was about as warm and welcoming as a meat locker, they'd gone up to the bedroom, where two fires had burned all day. Peter disappeared into the bathroom to come out a moment later with his disgusting mouth guard, a customized plastic item that he required in order not to grind his teeth to dust in his sleep. He showed it to Bambi—yellowing and crusty. She shivered in disgust.

"This thing is too old," he said. "Where is there another one?"

"You're asking me?" Bambi responded.

"Who else?" Peter asked.

"Phil?" Bambi suggested.

"Darling, it's nearly eleven p.m. Do you mean to tell me this is the only one of these we have here, when we literally have at least two of everything else?"

"I suppose it is," Bambi said primly.

"Literally, dear, this is the one thing I require. I will have a tremendous headache tomorrow if I do not wear one, and this thing is unusable."

"I can have another one sent up tomorrow."

"Yes, do that, will you," he said, throwing it in a wastepaper basket and storming down the hallway to "make some calls."

True, he conducted business all over the world, but surely he didn't need to do so at every possible moment, she pouted to herself in their bedroom.

The next morning, Bambi woke up agitated, and it took no time at all to determine why. The house was still freezing. Freezing! Bambi slipped into her terry cloth slippers and thin cotton robe—garments utterly inappropriate for the refrigerator her house had become. She crossed the room to squint at the digital thermostat: sixty-seven degrees! Freezing!

"Phil, why is the house so cold? It's practically uninhabitable," she said without a hello into the phone.

"Well, it takes a few days for the system to—"

"A few days? *A few days?*" She was so tired lately. "Phil, love, I am freezing *right* now at this very moment. Do you see our problem? Here's a thought . . . how about you upgrade the system to something that actually *works*. I may just like coming out here in the winter." Which couldn't be further from the truth. The house, the Hamptons, the beach, all so dreary out of season, with nothing to do and only one or two excessively large parties to decline. She didn't have her hormone patch or any of her favorite yoga pants. She could hardly even remember how they had agreed to go out East in the first place.

Bambi tied up her robe and went to find her husband, who no doubt was still working. But no, not in his office. Not in the TV room. Not in the gym, obviously. Finally she found him in the sunroom, a blanket over his shoulders, drinking coffee. Someone had gotten pastries and a *Wall Street Journal*, which he did not look up from. There was her plate of sliced papaya, her mineral water and vitamins. It was a few degrees warmer in here, which explained why both she and Peter were in the sunroom together for the first time ever. The window seat, encased in glass and lined with pillows, did look rather inviting, situated as it was facing the ocean.

"Has this room always had a window seat?" she asked Peter, joining him at the table.

"I have no idea," he said without looking up.

Bambi knew she should be canny about approaching the opera topic when Peter was so distracted. But priorities mattered too. It was always about his job or some obligation or the kids, never about Bambi. So she dived right in. "You said we would talk about it when we got here, Peter."

"Talk about what, Bambi?" He folded his paper finally and tucked it under his plate.

"The budget. For the opera," she said, sulking a little because he did not even remember something so important to her.

"Well?" he said.

Bambi paused, suddenly reticent. Was she the tiniest bit embarrassed, maybe, to want to spend so much money on one evening? But then, Richard had had no shame in asking for it, and the Petzers would never balk.

"What is it?" he asked.

Bambi mumbled something that sounded like *twaffle*.

"Speak up, darling!" Peter snipped like he was addressing a poorly behaved child.

"A bit over twelve," she said more clearly.

Peter flushed with outrage. In earlier days, Bambi used to tease him, saying that you could tell Peter's mood by the amount of red in his face. He rapidly approached ripe tomato. "Absolutely not, no," he said through clenched teeth. "Do you not remember coming home from Aspen for the security issues? Remember? And the business problems?"

Peter had always been so insecure! Bambi could never understand it. She kept thinking that as his company and their bank account grew exponentially each year, eventually the numbers would get big enough that he could sit back, relax. But instead, the mass of his achievements had made him focus like a laser on every deal that might lose money, reflect badly on him, be the beginning of the end.

"Yes, dear, I remember why my vacation, which I look forward to all year, was cut short. Because you may be having some . . ." Bambi tried to find the exact belittling word for it. "Snafus." That was why they had come to the Castle, she remembered. She had complained about being stuck in the city for the holiday, and somehow the beach had seemed better, but only because she had never been to Coolwater in winter before. She looked out the window at the shrubs, which seemed at least still mostly leafy, until she realized they were wearing little plastic jackets decorated with faux greenery to protect them from the harsh winter. The sky was that unpromising gray that just added pressure rather than snow.

"Snafus!" Peter exploded. "Snafus?! Bambi, use your brain, love! We are way overextended in real estate. If the city backs out of this deal, we are totally screwed. I could be out."

On the inside, Bambi trembled momentarily before getting a grip on herself.

Peter Von Bizmark ousted as the head of the Von Bizmark Organization? It fell somewhere on the spectrum between highly unlikely and legally impossible. "Sweetheart," Bambi countered icily, "aren't you being just a touch dramatic?" How could they, the Von Bizmarks, be facing any real financial problems?

"This fucking communist mayor could really, really screw us on this," he said loudly. "It's just not the time to take on another nine-digit expense, and the way things are shaping up, we won't even need the deduction this year."

"But, Peter, I've already agreed."

"You want to support the opera, you pay for it," Peter said. "You have the money, remember?" Which was true, of course: she did have the money. In a trust that Bambi strongly preferred never to touch. It was her emergency fund, not a party budget. And anyway, the principle was important, and the principle was that she was entitled to spend her husband's money. Everyone knew that. Peter stormed out and headed down the hallway to the left but quickly realized this was not the way to his office and stormed back, passing the open doorway at full tilt.

It's too cold to eat papaya, Bambi thought dolefully. Instead, she figured she might as well take a pill to quell the unusual fluttering in her stomach. What was bothering her exactly—arguing with her husband? That nonsense about "security issues"? Certainly not money!

The house phone rang. Bambi thought about ignoring it, but the little screen said it was Phil. "Please send over that new person to make me some oatmeal," she said without a hello.

"Will do! And great news! The heating will be replaced with a new White House–grade heating system. You will never be cold again. And I got Chef!"

"Oh goody! Will she be here for lunch today?"

"Well, she's coming from Colombia, so probably not until tomorrow."

"Oh, OK." Another disappointment. Chef could have been on the jet yesterday if Phil or Anna or anyone on their personal staff had thought it through more carefully. "I suppose that will have to do."

FOUR

December 31

Anna had been ignoring her sister for days. Sometimes it just felt too much like acting to pick up the phone and pretend like she was still killing it, still the cool one, still so brave and creative. Lately it seemed like she could only tap out texts that sounded defensive and unconvincing; she'd had to erase most of them. But now that Anna had a plan, however skimpy, for her art, she felt finally ready to take Lindsay's call during the contained space of time walking from her apartment to the subway.

"We have champagne!" Lindsay announced straightaway. "Two cases!"

"Linds, sorry, I'm—"

"Don't say it. Don't tell me you're not coming."

"We just like to spend the holiday—"

"Alone! I get it. Just come for drinks then . . ."

A small voice in Anna's head said, *This is* nice. *Lindsay's being nice to me.* But a much larger part of her felt like her sister just wanted to rub Anna's nose in her champagne flutes—sixteen pristine crystal vessels from Tiffany—and her friends, lawyers and bankers in nondescript couplets of suits and little black dresses. Anna, in her snug hand-me-down couture, would have to answer the same two questions all night, always with air quotes: "But what does it *mean* to 'be an artist'?" "But what does it *mean* to 'be a private assistant'?"

"The thing is, Linds, I'm doing a show of my work, like, tomorrow," Anna said. "The space just came through, and I have so much to take care of."

"No way!" Lindsay said, instantly excited. "A, that's *great!* *What* can I do to help?" Was Lindsay patronizing her? Just the fleeting thought of this left Anna rankled. She was the older sister, after all.

"I'll let you know, thanks." Anna was about to hang up—she had arrived at the station—when she heard Lindsay say, "Happy New Year, A!" Guilt stabbed her in the kidney.

"Happy New Year, Linds."

At work, the day of New Year's Eve kicked up a whirlwind of sending things to the Castle that had been forgotten due to the unusual circumstances of the weekend. They had, for example, only a few cold-weather clothes there, stashed in the safe room. The Mrs. needed her hormone patch, the Mr. his mouth guard, as the one there was "too old for him to put in his mouth." Of course he had at least a half dozen brand-new ones stashed away at Coolwater, somewhere, but the new maid had no idea where and sounded too terrified to poke around. This told Anna that Phil could not find or compel the housekeeper or three longtime maids to come. Phil himself was probably running all over the Hamptons sourcing the food and beverages they would need for New Year's Eve.

Anna spoke to Mrs. Von Bizmark herself only once, in the late morning. She launched into a rambling preamble about their favorite Montauk diner, "Which had the *best* doughnuts, which of course I couldn't eat more than a *few* bites of . . ." While she talked, Josefina placed the latest request, a prescription dandruff shampoo for Mr. Von Bizmark that the Mrs. had dubbed "his special hair wash," in a ziplock bag, which went into a shopping bag along with the Mrs.'s satin pillow and a box of Kleenex that she swore just were not the same when purchased at the local IGA. "In any case we drove all the way out there, and it's freezing, by the way, very cold in a different way than Aspen, where, you know, you *expect* it to be cold . . ."

"Please put this all in a shopping bag," Anna mouthed to Josefina, who went to the large closet reserved for their shopping-bag collection. She pulled out an enormous Prada bag and placed everything inside it. Anna wrote out a label (*TO BE PICKED UP BY CAR—VON BIZMARK*), stuck this on the bag, and mouthed, "Please send this downstairs."

"All the way . . . all the way out there, and can you believe there were *no* doughnuts?" Mrs. Von Bizmark loved to talk and talk when she was sad. Perhaps this doughnut disappointment had also occasioned just a half a pill too many.

Before she could launch into another lengthy aimless narrative, Anna interjected, "How about invitations for the lunch? I was thinking we should hop on that if you want to do the lunch in just six weeks."

"Yes. Something spring, hopeful . . . green." Anna wrote these three words down.

"Remember the font we used for the Frick cocktails? It was, like, blocky but also rounded." Anna added these words to her list, while the Mrs. rambled on about invitations prior. "Don't do anything like the botanical garden. I hate those garish flowers all over them. Or the Ecology Now people—their stuff is so serious." Anna jotted these notes down. "Just . . . do it perfectly, Anna, OK?" Anna heard Mr. Von Bizmark's annoyed voice in the background, and the Mrs. abruptly hung up.

Anna said, "Happy New Year," into the dead phone.

A few minutes later, the Castle called back. But it was only the frightened maid. "Mrs. Von Bizmark wanted me to call you to say Happy New Year!" Which wasn't quite the same as an actual personal call but was better than nothing. When the phone rang again from the Castle, Anna started to wonder if she'd ever get out of the office.

"Forget something?" Anna said by way of hello.

"Did you know things were this bad?" Phil complained. "She's all over my ass." In general, the Mrs. became impossible to please when the Von Bizmarks were not getting along.

"Well, it's been this tense before, right?"

"Anna, I'm replacing the entire heating system. In a summer home! Summer!"

Anna felt that her job extended to fielding calls like these from overstressed employees; no one could perform under duress. "It's OK, Phil, so you'll replace the heating—"

"Pain in my ass, Anna!" he interrupted. "Do you know how many times I'm gonna have to talk to Marco about this?" Indeed, that would be excruciating.

"I understand—"

"And that's not even why I'm calling!" he interrupted again. "I need you to wire Chef ten thousand dollars." Phil said it like he was asking for a few singles to tip the valet.

"I'm sorry?"

"Florence sent the jet for her in Colombia, but you know how fishy that looks? Last-minute private jet out of Bogotá on New Year's Eve? So she had to, you know, grease a few palms, and now we owe her."

The Von Bizmark chef was a compact lesbian with sleeve tattoos who had some sort of magical hold on Mrs. Von Bizmark's taste buds. Mr. Von Bizmark would eat whatever medium-rare, dry-aged, on-the-bone steak you put in front of him, but she had to have ten thousand calories of taste packed into a package of one hundred.

"Uh-huh. So now we're reimbursing the chef for bribes to Colombian immigration officials? Something just seems a little off about this to me."

"Listen, Anna, we do what we have to do to get the job done. You know it. I know it. And I'm not cooking, you hear? She kept eyeballing me like she expected me to put on an apron, and it was not happening!" Anna sighed. Phil could be so dramatic. "What difference does it make anyway? She got here, threw lunch together, and they loved it. It was the first time they laughed. Well, she laughed. Tomorrow morning, Chef's making those flavorless cardboard vegan raw whatever muffin balls that the Mrs. loves. Right now, it's the only thing that's making her happy, and no one's asking what it costs."

When Anna called Marco to transfer the money, it was after five on New Year's Eve. Not only did he answer his phone, but of course he was ready with his customary response: "Let's go back to square one," he said.

"I promise—you don't want to know, Marco."

"Now I definitely want to know."

"Chef needed to bribe Colombian—"

"Never mind," Marco said.

In this way, Mrs. Von Bizmark was guaranteed her favorite breakfast pastry. That critical task dispatched, Anna dismissed the ladies and raced through the rest of her work, leaving voice mails at the dry cleaners, the contractor, the artist to touch up all those hand-painted leaves and vines. Just as she'd turned out the light, the phone rang one last time. Boston area code.

"Hi, Chester." Anna greeted the eldest and perhaps least bright Von Bizmark child, a sophomore at Harvard.

"Anna! Happy New Year!" he gushed, possibly already drunk. "Listen, me and some of my friends from the club realized we failed to make a reservation for the private dining room at the Charles. Would you pretty please call? Everyone always does what you say when you call from Mummy's office."

"Here's a tip, Chester. How about you ask one of your friends to call and say that they are in Bambi Von Bizmark's office? How would the hostess ever know they weren't?"

"What a fantastic idea!" Chester said, truly impressed. "Thanks, Anna! Have a rager tonight."

Anna raced through the apartment making sure all the lights were out, windows closed, air-conditioning and heating units off, and appropriate cabinets and doors locked. She wished both doormen and two porters happy New Year as she flagged a cab—a New Year's treat to herself—to get home sooner, where Adrian would surely be preparing his delicious bolognese, their New Year's Eve tradition.

But at the front door of their apartment, Anna paused. The rich sounds of Bill Withers drifted out along with the unusual scent of . . . eucalyptus? Lavender? Inside, the sheer cleanliness disoriented her. All her clothes, picked up and put away. Everything vacuumed and shiny. There on the kitchen counter, a bottle of prosecco tilted in ice and two brand-new flutes, of all things. Adrian, in a flattering thin black wool sweater and what appeared to be . . . tailored slacks, stood at the ready.

"Hi," Anna murmured, gawking at their suddenly immaculate apartment. Adrian gave her a warm kiss. He took her coat, and instead of draping it over his desk chair, he put it on a hanger and into the closet.

As Adrian poured the bubbly, he said, "I got the LVMH job."

Anna rushed to embrace him and kissed his face, carried away with good feelings. Was she imaging that he felt extra smooth and, weirdly, that he smelled a little different? A little cleaner. A new cologne? An LVMH brand, perhaps? "I'm proud of you, babe!" she said.

He reached behind her to flip open his laptop. "Take a look." It was her website, a work in progress that had not progressed much recently. "I had to finish it before I start work on Monday," he added. The home page had become an exhibition announcement. *SEE ART NOW*, it read in bold, the text shimmering and superimposed over one of her favorite canvases—a dark skyline behind a serene country pond where a frilly Victorian lady floated in her simple canoe. The piece's autobiographical secret hid in the parasol, where she had layered marigold impasto paint with bits of thread snipped from the monogram on Lindsay's guest room towels. Anna recalled how she'd felt beholding those golden initials on those linens in that apartment: outpaced by a sibling years younger who had lagged behind for most of their lives, only to emerge at twenty-six as if fully formed—with a mortgage, an MBA, and a rock-solid career, married to the same. Anna imagined that she was the lady in the canoe, her sister the specter of capitalism looming in the background.

"It's all there—all the work, your bio, everything."

"Oh my God, Adrian! That's wonderful." She flooded with appreciation. Any lingering doubts that Adrian was selling out were, if not eliminated, momentarily forgotten. They were, in fact, adults, and it was time to act like it, she told herself sternly. "*And* you cleaned the apartment?!" Anna asked.

"Well, I don't think I'm going to be at home a lot once I start my new job. Figured I'd go out with a bang." This sounded vaguely ominous to Anna. She gulped her prosecco while eyeballing the pristine kitchen: No bolognese?

Following her gaze, Adrian said, "I made reservations at that French place you've been wanting to try . . ."

She couldn't stop herself from pining for Adrian's home cooking, the messy kitchen, the late dinners. God, what was wrong with her? Anna wondered.

"We need a week to empty out the Food Blast pop-up," he said. "But the space is ours until the fifteenth, so that gives you a weekend to set up, a night for an opening, and a few days after for sales."

That's right, a show. Her show. Anna momentarily indulged in her favorite pastime—fantasizing about future success. Here, the glowing article in *ARTnews* about the bold new artist who didn't wait for a gallery. Anna imagined her smuggest MFA classmates' oohs and aahs, their envious faces as journalists snapped her picture. Adrian by her side, Lindsay looking on in renewed awe.

As they stepped out onto their uneven Brooklyn street, arm in arm, professional lives about to blossom, Anna was stirred by a sense of optimism and security that she had not felt since she was an overconfident undergraduate, or maybe even before that—a pompous teen.

"You going to invite all your new fancy colleagues to the exhibition?"

"Definitely," he said. In her fantasy, she added a few black-clad fashion types with statement glasses and hairstyles that required product. It all made sense. Perhaps everything would work out after all.

Over the holiday, Anna devoted herself to the exhibition. The most important thing was who would attend: publications, gallerists, buyers. She made lists of people she knew in those categories and people she knew who knew those people. She wrote a pitch email and tweaked it for each recipient. There would be publicity efforts; should she write her own press release? Adrian seemed to think so, and he forwarded a few samples from work, where he spent the holiday. This was just one aspect of the show that Anna was not prepared to take care of.

"Don't worry," Adrian said, just before passing out on the couch when he got home.

Anna bounced out of bed Monday morning secure in identity and purpose. Everything on her *NOW* list had been crossed off. This would be her year, she told herself, leaving her apartment with a travel mug of fresh coffee and a full half hour to spare. By the time Julie arrived around ten a.m., Anna jittered with caffeine. Her boot heel smacked the floor unevenly as her leg shook.

"You OK?" Julie asked. She wore a velour tracksuit that read *IRONY* across the ass. Her hair twisted up in two cone-shaped buns on top of her head, like little horns. Bright-purple eyeliner and lacquer lip balm. All she needed was a lollipop and she could go straight to a rave.

"Nope!" Anna said cheerily. "I decided to do my own show. Next week."

"Cool!" Julie said encouragingly, her eyes on Anna's knee bouncing up and down. "And?"

"There's just, like, so much to do."

"And?"

"Well, I mean . . ."

"Anna, if anyone can pull off simultaneous extraordinary logistical challenges, it's you, right?"

"I guess?" Anna said, unconvinced but happy to be able to subvert her anxiety with the day's Von Bizmark business: the luncheon of the century. The phone lit up with vendors returning Anna's calls; emails poured in with quotes and appointment times. The back doorbell rang, and no one answered it. It rang again two times.

"Where's Cristina?" Anna asked no one in particular. She let in a woman in her sixties in a smock, with her steel hair in a regal bun, and her assistant, who carried a small piece of scaffolding and several klieg lights. Anna went to find the ladies, presumably finishing up in the Von Bizmark bedroom.

The two maids sat together on an ottoman, Alicia comforting Josefina, who was in tears. Cristina stood over them, arms crossed, clearly counting the seconds until she could interrupt their tableau.

"What's happening now?" Anna asked Josefina.

"Ilana's school is full of lead," Alicia explained, speaking very quietly. "They gave this to Josefina this morning at drop-off." Josefina handed over the letter to Anna, who scanned it briefly. At the top it read, *NOTICE OF SCHOOL CLOSURE*.

"Oh no," Anna said.

"If Ilana can't go to that school, Josefina cannot come to work," Cristina said.

"The other school is too far away," Alicia added. "The school bus won't go from the Bronx to Queens, and Josefina could never take her all the way there and get here on time."

"Maybe you can help?" Josefina said to Anna, wiping away her tears.

Cristina snapped, "Come on! What can Anna do?"

Although she was probably right—what *could* Anna do?—hearing Cristina say so irked Anna. Sure, her professional life consisted of the most frivolous pursuits taken to the furthest extreme, but here was something real. Something important. "Let me look into it," Anna finally said, reaching for the letter.

Cristina lightly clapped her hands together. "Come on, back to work. Be grateful you have your family with you. Me, I'm all alone." This was a frequent refrain of Cristina's, usually followed by, "But *I* don't complain!"

Cristina hurried after Anna to answer the back door. The contractor, a gorgeous paragon of capability Julie and Anna called "the Silver Fox," assessed the cabinetry requirements while his three guys waited with two enormous toolboxes. Anna showed him the most pressing problem. The world's largest couch set before the world's largest television. The TV would have to stay: it was literally the wall of the room. But the couch? The Silver Fox ran his hands over the piece like he was feeling the withers of a horse, looking for a weakness. He lay down on the floor and studied its underside with his pinky-size flashlight.

"Welp," he said, "they built this couch in this room, right?" Anna recalled the six summer weeks when a team of Italian furniture makers had set up shop there, somehow producing bowls of pasta and a few bottles of chianti each day from their bags for a leisurely two-hour lunch. "We can take it apart with a chainsaw, basically, but it'll never be quite right again."

"'Not quite right' is definitely wrong. Let me think about it."

Miguel showed up to do the toilet and traveled upstairs with an impossibly small tool bag and a nervous Josefina, charged with safeguarding the fixtures, while Anna ran to answer the ringing phone; Julie was on two other lines.

"Don't talk, Anna, just listen," Phil stage-whispered. "I don't know what this even means, but the Mrs. told me to call you and say, 'Bloom is coming at noon to see the space.'" Anna's eyes flew to the office clock: 11:53 a.m. "Does that make any sense to you? Oh God, here she comes."

"Bloom's coming in five minutes," Anna said to Julie, off the phone.

"What now?" Julie asked.

"I forgot," Anna admitted. The Mrs. had said something about Bloom coming, and it had uncharacteristically slipped her mind.

"How are you going to keep Bloom under budget?" Julie asked. "She just stopped telling us about new expenses last time, remember?"

Yes, Anna remembered Bloom arguing with the fire of a thousand suns, as if she were talking about her very own child and not a soufflé station: "Which element would you have me cut? You tell me! You take out one piece, and the whole thing becomes tacky. Half-done. That's not me! That's not what I do! We agreed if we were going to do an Ali Baba theme, it had to be Dubai, not Vegas. Am I right or am I right, here?"

Not everyone loved a Sydney Bloom event, most particularly Mr. Von Bizmark after the last budget blowout.

"I'm open to suggestions!" Anna said brightly, waving her hand in a circular "come on" motion. "It's 11:56, so we have a whole four minutes to think of a new idea."

"I'm trying! It's hard to come up with something that we didn't do last time." Julie's sneakered foot started shaking, her velour pant leg rippling.

"Any thoughts whatsoever?"

"Have her itemize everything and sign a copy?"

"Did that already."

"She always has a loophole!"

"Right! Anything I can actually use here?" Anna asked. The front doorbell rang, and Anna sighed. Too late. She threw back her shoulders as she swung open the door. "Bloom! Good to see you," Anna said to the small woman, midsixties in a classic Chanel suit topped with a surprising pouf of red curly hair. She smiled widely and took both of Anna's hands into her chilly grasp.

"What fun to work together again!" she said, practically licking her mauve lips.

"Yes, but this is surely a much less complicated event than the others. Shall we?" Anna said, inviting Bloom into the living room.

"So this is the party space," Anna said. They had done a few parties in the apartment, but never a sit-down luncheon before. Bloom scanned the room, calculations running through her mind. She ground her cheek, bright with coral blush, into her molars.

"I think we can seat eighty in here."

"If we want to go larger than that . . ." Anna took her through the room to the double doors into the formal dining room, where two round tables constantly waited for a dinner party of twenty.

"So one hundred then," Bloom said, turning back to the larger space. "Of course, all of this . . . every little thing"—she punctuated this with her index talon, pointing out a soft bright-white carpet under a side table, a few delicately draped furs, a particularly valuable French topiary that looked like it might topple over just because they were talking about it—"must go. Particularly these large pieces," she said, pointing at each couch. "We'll bring in wall fabrics to absorb the noise, planters for explosions of flowers, I'm thinking a strolling violinist . . . don't worry!" Bloom said, following Anna's gaze to the pillowy sectional. "You just have to get the room empty, and we'll take care of the rest!"

For a moment, it was as if dollar signs had actually replaced Bloom's eyes, her makeup momentarily macabre, clownish. Surely she had already far exceeded the relatively modest $250,000 with all these requests. Moving and replacing the couches alone would be at least ten thousand.

Instead of heading straight back to the office, Anna guided Bloom through another door into a library, where all the most serious business of the Von Bizmark family was conducted. They sat at a small table in leather chairs, a single light between them.

"Before we look at the invitations, I thought we could talk broad strokes," Anna said. Bloom raised an eyebrow. Anna wanted her to know from the start that this time was different. "Let's talk about the budget."

"Seems ample." Bloom grinned and gave Anna an infuriating half wink that said both, "Hey, it's not your money," and, more infuriatingly, "What are *you* going to do about it?"

"Our lawyer is drafting an addendum that guarantees you will not exceed two hundred and fifty thousand dollars." Whether Avi would actually do this at Anna's request was a bridge down the river. What mattered was the way the grin slackened right off Bloom's face. "Anything over that is at your expense. I'll forward that document to you for signature as soon as I have it, but in the meantime, can we agree on that point?"

"I've never signed anything like that in my entire career."

"Well, I have to tell you, Bloom, I think Mr. Von Bizmark in particular would be disappointed to hear that you balked at this request." Anna sighed heavily to underline their impasse. "Do we have a deal?"

"You'll handle preparing the space, printing and mailing the invitations, and the wine?"

"Deal."

Bloom pursed her lips but extended her hand for a shake. "I'll prepare my presentation for one week from today." The date of Anna's opening.

Anna's heart sank. "Could we do it Tuesday instead?"

"I leave for three days in Dubai tonight, and I'm in Paris after. I'm squeezing Kissy in, you know?" Bloom winked wickedly. The day her painfully brief exhibition opened was not a great day to have a huge meeting at work, but what could Anna do?

Back in the office, Julie had arranged a few proofs of the invitation. They examined various rectangles of thick cream paper and hundreds of fonts, deciding ultimately on a combination of a spring green and tangerine, which the Mrs. had been partial to lately, in a font they agreed was "kicky" to offset the most staid verbiage: *Please Join Kissy Von Bizmark and the Host Committee as They Kick Off This Year's Opera Ball at a Luncheon Honoring Felix Mercurion.* Anna's stomach lurched when she remembered this key information had yet to be communicated to Mrs. Von Bizmark, who still believed it might be possible to feature Opal at the luncheon . . . Opal, who had yet to return any of her calls.

The three grim dry cleaners arrived with their machines. These workers had been there before and had learned to fear the Von Bizmarks' taste for delicate, expensive fabrics in various shades of white, cream, off white, and light gray. As they lumbered after Cristina, quietly wheeling their large devices, bleak expressions on each face, Anna tallied up the number of workers in the apartment, which had exceeded the count technically allowed at any one time without approval from the co-op board. But what could she do? Ordinarily, she would have had all her paperwork in order weeks in advance, but this time she'd had only a few weeks total. Things were unraveling.

Like the way Anna had negotiated Bloom's contract off the cuff like that, without a prior word to Avi. But when she called him about the additional clause, he was unusually amenable—happy, even. "Good she's making plans," he said, ominously, of Mrs. Von Bizmark.

As soon as the phone was back in its cradle, Anna heard a man clear his throat behind her. Miguel, of course. Alarmingly, he held a piece of pipe in his hands. His hair was wet.

"So . . . ," he began, looking at the pipe as if he could read what to say there. "I need a few parts I don't have."

"What is that in your hand?"

"Pipe."

"From the bathroom?"

"Yes."

"So . . ." Anna stood.

"Oh, you can't use that bathroom," Miguel said, an edge of panic creeping into his voice that made Anna shudder. This was just the sort of unpleasant surprise she always sought to avoid.

"I'm getting Ariadne," Anna said.

"No! Please!" He took two quick steps into the office, one of his shoes squishing. Anna and Julie exchanged a glance; they should call in the big guns. "I'll lose my job," Miguel entreated Anna. He looked so genuinely desperate. "I'm begging you." Anna remembered he had two sons who lived with their mother in Queens. "You know the Von Bizmarks never use that toilet! Like, never!" he pleaded.

"Now that it's broken, someone will definitely try," Julie said, and both Miguel and Anna stared at her. "Murphy's law."

"Are you sure you can fix it?" Anna asked, eager to avoid having Miguel fired. He shook his head vigorously in the affirmative. "Tomorrow?" Julie pretended to fax something as a pretense to stand behind Miguel with a sign that read in large red Sharpie, *NO*. But at this crucial moment, Anna lacked the heart to swing the ax.

"One thousand percent!" he insisted. Before Anna could reverse herself, Miguel said, "Thank you. Thank you!" and backed out of the office past Julie.

"Don't push me, Miguel!" Anna shouted as the back door closed behind him.

"Are you sure that was a good idea?" Julie asked.

"Oh, for fuck's sake, Julie, of course I'm not!" Anna exploded. It was a very bad, truly terrible plan! Why, oh why, had she not insisted on calling Ariadne in the first place? Julie stood very still, her mouth agape in surprise. Anna already felt terrible for snapping at her, but she wasn't quite ready to say so and jumped on the ringing phone—a call from the Castle.

"They're gone," Phil said, exhaling the weekend's stress.

"How was it?" Anna asked.

"Pulling off a last-minute New Year's Eve weekend for the Von Bizmarks while the two of them fought like cats and dogs . . . cats and dogs *with rabies* . . . it was a trip to Hollywood." He sounded utterly drained. Almost delirious. He would have several months to recover.

"That's the job, right?" Anna said, upbeat.

He snorted. "Jesus, Anna, I don't know if they're going to make it," Phil went on. He had known them as a couple for nearly twenty years. "Maybe you can help? You know, plan a trip for them or something? To reconnect?" On its face, this was a ridiculous idea. It was hard enough choosing a shade of green for the luncheon invitation; Anna would never be able to pluck the right destination off a map of the world.

But, on the other hand, maybe Phil was on to something. There had to be a way, sitting as she was with her hands on the reins of Bambi Von Bizmark's life, for Anna to help steer it in a more positive direction. Mr. Von Bizmark's assistant would be no help, of course.

Meanwhile, Julie stabbed at her keyboard, glowering at her computer monitor, rightfully disgruntled. Anna turned to the hodgepodge of papers on her desk that served as a physical to-do list. In her hand, she found the sheet Josefina had given her that morning.

DEAR PARENT,

This is to inform you that lead has been discovered in the walls and pipes of PS 342. Unfortunately, refitting the school so that classes can continue at this location will cost $1.3 million, which is not in our budget. Starting next semester, we will begin bussing students

to PS 207. If your child is in the GIFTED program,
you MUST PROVIDE TRANSPORTATION to PS
132 in Queens, effective next semester.
> With best wishes,
> Delilah Sellers
> Principal
> PS 342

"Delilah Sellers's office," the deeply annoyed receptionist said when
Anna called the number on the letterhead.

"Is she in? I'm calling on behalf of Josefina Ruiz, who works for
Bambi Von Bizmark. Josefina's daughter, Ilana, is a student at your
school."

There was a pause. There were a lot of names in that sentence, and
Anna had spoken with authority. But surely, the principal had received
many phone calls that day.

"May I take a message?"

"Are there any fundraising efforts underway to raise money to save
the school?"

"Not that I know of."

"Please ask Principal Sellers to call me. We want to help," Anna
said, surprising herself. When she had picked up the phone, her inten-
tion was only to discover whether there might be a way for Mrs. Von
Bizmark to write a check—her favorite way to "participate" in a cause.
She would surely contribute on behalf of Josefina. But somewhere along
the way, Anna started to think that maybe, somehow, they could do
more than just send five or even ten thousand dollars. What that was,
she wasn't quite sure.

Julie quietly processed a stack of invitations Mrs. Von Bizmark had
received, her response indicated by a black Sharpie X or check mark.
She sniffed pitifully.

"Hey," Anna said. "I'm sorry I snapped at you, Jules. I just . . . this show has me all distracted. I'm making bad calls."

"No, you're not," Julie said reflexively. "OK, maybe one."

"I feel bad about Ilana's school closing."

"Do you really think we can help?" Julie asked.

Anna knew that both the school and the flexibility to bring Ilana to work had been a godsend to Josefina. Moreover, she really liked Ilana. She was extremely smart and talented. But could Anna actually extend the limited powers of her position far enough to make a real difference in Ilana's life?

Anna shrugged and sighed. "It couldn't hurt to try."

"Because, you know, we're not exactly curing cancer in this office," Julie added, a running joke between them when things got too intense. It was a way to remind themselves that even though their jobs might depend on pleasing a single impossible client, the actual work was relatively inconsequential. It did not matter whether the toilet ever got fixed, really.

"I know you're right. That Miguel is going to screw this up somehow. I just hope it's in a really small, manageable way," Anna said.

"Whatever it is, we'll handle it!" Julie said. "I mean, mostly *you'll* handle it, obviously." Which was funny because it was true.

FIVE

January 13

Anna jolted awake the day of her opening, shooting out of a nightmare where the paintings kept falling off the wall. The whole night she had to dash from piece to piece, rehanging each one just to hear another come crashing down behind her. She panted in the just-before-dawn light, Adrian snoring undisturbed beside her. Her alarm blared: 6:00 a.m.

She drank her coffee standing at her closet in the living room, trying to decide what to wear to her own exhibition. What was the image of herself as an artist that Anna wanted to transmit to the world? Von Bizmark cast-offs were too rarefied and out of character. The other candidates were almost entirely inherited from Julie, and this was where Anna found the simple Morgane Le Fay black raw linen dress that fit her like couture. She'd pair this with a statement necklace—an amber piece from Egypt—and a high bun with her thick tortoiseshell glasses. That said "Downtown Artist" as clearly as any clothing-and-accessory combination in her closet. She left these items carefully on the chair so she'd just have to throw everything on in the hour between work and the show.

As she pulled on her usual jeans and Frye boots, Adrian turned onto his back, snored once loudly, and stopped. He must have made it to bed from the couch sometime in the middle of the night. Anna had barely seen him lately—he had been working so hard—and when she did, like the night before, it wasn't so pleasant. She knew he was under pressure to churn out designs for shopping bags, fragrance logos, gift boxes. It was a "real job," he kept saying with a new ever-so-slightly superior tone, as if such a thing was removed from her realm of experience.

She turned her thoughts once more to the accolades that would soon be hers. How wonderful it would feel to finally have recognition for and income from her art. She let her fantasies run further, into the future, where she and Adrian were both flush and secure: everything would fall into place.

Anna had done everything she could think of to make the exhibit a success. She'd spent half a day interviewing and finally hiring an intern from her MFA program to help Adrian set up. She'd sent an invitation to every gallery, media outlet, artist, collector, friend, and family member she could think of and printed one on special paper for Mrs. Von Bizmark. Adrian had planned to help her prepare the space, but when he'd had to work, Julie had filled in. They'd spent several happy hours debating which piece to hang where in the one-room storefront on Greene Street. In the most prominent position, they agreed on her largest piece, a nine-foot-wide canvas of bright frolicking circles, racing and overlapping, paint dripping from one form into another, all entwined and joyful. Anna had painstakingly woven grass from an elaborate picnic with Adrian into the most prominent viridian swirl; on that breezy afternoon, they had first exchanged "I love yous."

After hanging, rearranging, and rehanging the paintings, then adjusting, tweaking, and retweaking the lighting, Julie and Anna had sat on the floor in the middle of the room, taking it in: the sum of her work since earning her MFA over five years ago. All that time and energy and inspiration. So much of herself up on the walls, each piece cradling its own cached secret. Anna imagined the way strangers would conjecture the meaning of her pieces, intuiting their autobiographical nature. The interview questions she'd have to address. Maybe more than one gallery owner would be interested in showing her work; how would she decide?

"Whatever happens after the show, you just have to keep painting," Adrian had said to her that night as she shared her anticipatory thoughts with him.

"Adrian!" Anna smacked his thigh. "That's like saying you don't think it's going to be successful."

"It just—it could take a long time to make it, whatever that means, and I don't think you should pin all your hopes on one party." Of course, he was right. But knowing this and feeling it were two different things. Anna believed in her gut it was finally her time for a big break after so much effort. "There are no guarantees. In art, anyway," he said, and she could not help but feel that he was comparing the two of them and finding her career lacking. In response, Anna had simply jabbed at her laptop keyboard in the kitchen, silently projecting her hurt feelings. But Adrian had not seemed to notice in the few minutes before he passed out, falling into a deep sleep, undisturbed even as Anna ate breakfast and got dressed the next morning.

Just before she left for her big day, Anna called from the door, "Adrian! Adrian, you never told me how many of your LVMH peeps are coming tonight." Based on his original estimate, she expected somewhere between fifteen and twenty, but Adrian only groaned in response. Anna returned to the bedroom door and asked from there, "Not that many?" already telling herself that it would be fine if only a few came.

Adrian kept his hand pressed firmly over his eyes. "I never sent the invitation." Anna's stomach lurched, and not because there would be fewer people at her opening but because Adrian had forgotten to do something important to her. Maybe for the first time. "I just . . . I'm so sorry, it's just been so crazy busy at work and . . ."

Anna walked out, thinking there really was nothing else to say.

Although Anna's main focus at her job was to prevent unpleasant surprises, each day as the elevator ding-ding-dinged on the eighth floor, she no longer knew what she was in for. She kept letting little things slip: the Mrs.'s favorite pens had run out, she patched through a phone solicitor rather than screening the call, she frequently forgot to drop the mail in the postbox. Each morning had become a possibility for a small failure. Even the foyer doors, which used to be reliably open, were now sometimes open, sometimes closed. That morning, they stood at odds—one swung open, the other shut—a metaphor for the state of the Von Bizmark marriage.

In the office, Mrs. Von Bizmark's computer beamed the family's last professional portrait all together, clustered barefoot on a borrowed yacht in New York Harbor, VBO headquarters somewhere in the cliff-like cityscape gleaming behind them. Mrs. Von Bizmark's smile in the picture said, *How could I be anything but happy?* Meanwhile, she'd come home with many bitter complaints about "being stuck on some boat."

In any case, the screen saver meant she had been there within ten minutes, an unusual early-morning visit. Or an all-nighter. The chair was angled out, as if she had risen and run. Mrs. Von Bizmark's computer suddenly went dark. Unsettled, Anna scooped up the short pile of notes on her keyboard before taking off her coat or bag.

Wake me for meeting.

Please invite Richard. Make sure Opal is coming!

Sent opera check

Tucked on the bottom of the stack of notes was one of the proofs for the luncheon invitation. Felix Mercurion's name was circled in red Sharpie, and scrawled all over it were the words,

WHAT IS THIS?

Oh no. Anna had never relayed that key piece of information. Mrs. Von Bizmark had just seemed so down, and Anna still wasn't sure if Mercurion was good or bad news. And now she had allowed a negative surprise to slip past her usually impenetrable safety net. And what was this about the check? Mrs. Von Bizmark essentially never wrote her own checks.

Anna reached into the drawer next to Mrs. Von Bizmark's chair for the oversize foundation checkbook and flipped through the stubs . . . to the last one . . . written out to the New York City Opera for $10 million. Shit. Shit shit *shit.*

While Anna dialed Marco, Julie walked in wearing a long, billowing trench coat cinched at the waist, large squarish shades, and windblown waves that either had taken her an hour to perfect or were a new wig. "She called me," Julie mouthed, "for the meeting."

"She sent a foundation check for ten million to the opera," Anna said when Marco answered so that Julie could hear also as she hung up her coat up and turned to Anna, openmouthed.

"I told you to take the checkbook away!" Marco screeched into her ear, willing for once not to go back to square one. Anna showed Julie the invitation proof with Mrs. Von Bizmark's red shrieking scrawl all over it and mouthed the word *Shit!*

"What do we do now?" Anna asked Marco placidly. She handed Julie the slip of paper that said *Please invite Richard. Make sure Opal is coming.* And mouthed "to the meeting." Julie nodded.

"Easy! All you have to do is get the check back."

"How am I going to do that?"

"I don't know. Tell them it's going to bounce. Tell them we'll wire the money from another account." Neither of those solutions would play well with the Mrs. In the meantime, she'd have to hope for an interception. Anna could not help but feel that if she had been more on her game, somehow this wouldn't have happened.

"Richard will be attending," Julie reported as Anna untangled herself from the phone cord. "Opal . . . I'm not so sure. I left voice mails everywhere."

Anna studied the calendar for the day. At one p.m., the Mrs. was supposed to have lunch at Sant Ambroeus with a few other women just like her—fighting idleness at every turn—but not true friends. This was crossed out. Dinner with another couple—business associates of Mr. Von Bizmark's—was also obliterated with a fatal Sharpie *X*. Very ominous. Anna braced herself.

Like many, rich people lashed out at those closest to them in stressful times. Unlike most, rich people sat atop many layers of staff, all of whom were prepared to take it on the chin, even when not strictly speaking deserved. She hated having to stand by while a coworker got reamed, jumping in at the earliest possible moment to defuse the situation and later counseling the employee: although staff worked in the home, the job was *not personal.*

These sorts of abuses were unusual but not unheard of in the Von Bizmark home. Generally, Mrs. Von Bizmark was simply curt when unhappy, but in the worst times she struck out at the nearest person: Phil for allowing a single piece of trash to wash up on their private beach, Julie for forgetting her Wednesday at-home nail appointment. Even the Von Bizmark family members could be on the receiving end of a loud diatribe about tardiness, rudeness, or—in one particularly disturbing interlude—weight gain. In a fit of postpartum sleep deprivation, the Mrs. had once famously screamed at Cristina for using the wrong brand of baking soda to scrub the grout in the nursery bathroom. "This stuff is poison! Poison!" she screeched. "You'll kill him! My Chester! Dead!" Once she'd recovered from what seemed retrospectively to have been a bout of postpartum psychosis, the Mrs. ate crow with

Cristina, who stood ramrod straight, hands clasped at her waist, cheeks sucked throughout the Mrs.'s brief apology.

The one person who thus far had floated above reproach in the household—safe from verbal abuse—was Anna herself. As Anna was an overeducated, reserved, highly capable professional private assistant, Mrs. Von Bizmark had thankfully placed her in an untouchable category. In a way, Anna was the only person who couldn't be replaced. There just weren't that many—if any—artistic, unflappable, worldly Yale graduates in their thirties looking for private assistant work. Mrs. Von Bizmark occasionally had to exercise extraordinary self-control over her acid tongue, a skill she hadn't needed to call upon in decades. Both of them knew that this privilege meant Anna would never look for another job.

But if things got worse in the marriage . . . irreparable. If Anna kept making mistakes . . . well, then, who could say what Mrs. Von Bizmark might do? And while money prevented the commonplace problems that troubled everyone else, even Anna's employers could suffer in ways that funds could not mend. Anna had grown so accustomed to throwing cash at problems that she had to wonder if Phil was right. Could she do something to preserve the household? Should she?

Probably not.

"Oh, shit," Julie said, having flipped ahead a few months in the calendar. "It's their twenty-fifth wedding anniversary the day before the ball."

The back doorbell rang as workers arrived to finish up their jobs. Julie routed the painter, with her assistant, to their workspace of intricate ivy detailing on the floor. The Silver Fox and his team hustled off with Cristina. Alicia and Josefina guided the dry-cleaning men with their heavy equipment. And finally, Miguel stood at the back door, thankfully no longer in a suit. He carried a slightly larger toolbox at least and a crate full of what appeared to be secondhand parts.

Anna waited for him to look her in the eye before letting him come inside. "Look, Miguel, just don't screw me on this, OK?"

"Don't worry about it!" he said, which made Anna feel not even a little bit better about the situation. But she let him inside anyway, and he lumbered upstairs to the most distant bathroom to fix the smallest of problems.

At her desk, Anna's intercom buzzed from the Von Bizmark bedroom. "Good morning," Anna said.

"Yes, what is it?" Drowsy.

"You buzzed me."

"Why did Cristina just wake me up? A little rudely, I might add."

"The luncheon-planning meeting is in about half an hour? Less even."

"That's right. Anna," she said pointedly, instantly sharper, "why didn't you tell me about Felix Mercurion?"

"I . . ." Anna usually had a litany of totally perfect defenses at her disposal: *Yes, the jet was unfortunately delayed because our rigorous safety checks turned up a loose bolt in the emergency exit. Yes, your American Express Black Card did just get rejected because I learned only thirty seconds ago your number was hacked by an Iranian arms cartel and was being used to purchase enriched uranium.*

But in this case, even her ability to spin the truth a little more favorably utterly failed Anna. "I forgot," she finally admitted. "There has been so much to take care of."

"Anna, please, it's just a lunch!" Mrs. Von Bizmark snapped. Anna remained silent, her usual gambit in times of professional anxiety. "Look, Anna, you know the drill. Get the ball rolling, and I'll be there when I can." She still had given little clue about whether the Mercurion surprise was ultimately good or bad.

"Also, I'm reminding you that your twenty-fifth anniversary is the day before the Opera Ball."

Mrs. Von Bizmark half laughed, half honked. "I can't think about that now."

Before the meeting, Anna checked in with each of the crews, assessing not only the quality of their repairs but also the carefulness with which each worker treated the space around them. She didn't need any more problems and was pleased to find everyone—even Miguel, crouching at the toilet under Josefina's watchful eye—wearing the disposable cloth booties Cristina had provided and, with stern finger, insisted that they wear at all times. Anna was less pleased to find the contractor in the same place as the day before: Mr. Von Bizmark's cognac cabinet. The Silver Fox puzzled over the door, a dash of pewter hair falling across his eyes as he leaned into the cabinet, which just refused to stay closed. Cristina had been holding it shut with putty for years.

"Your housekeeper said no noise: no drills, no hammering," said the contractor, whose business consisted of only a few very high-end clients who kept him busy in their homes all over the world.

"Right," Anna said.

"Well, I'm going to need to do some hammering here." He gestured at the door, swinging creakily on its hinges, one of which appeared to be peeling off the wood.

"How much noise?"

"Two minutes."

"OK, do it now. And please be quick." Almost immediately, he had his hammer out and banging. One minute later, Alfie the doorman called upstairs, as if on cue.

"I know, I know, Forstbacher, right?" Anna said.

"Yeah, she's threatening to call Smith and Sterling." Contacting the building's managing agent was the first escalation; they could fine the Von Bizmarks for having too many workers in the apartment without written board approval. But Mrs. Forstbacher was known to call the police, and if they didn't respond, she would report the smell of gas to the fire department until sooner or later the building was surrounded by sirens and flashing lights.

"We literally just started hammering thirty seconds ago."

"She said she set her egg timer."

"It's going to be over in about a minute," Anna assured Alfie. The hammering stopped. "See?" Anna said.

Bloom arrived a few minutes later in a maroon-and-orange suit. She stood at the head of the table fingering a sample invitation with her burgundy talons. At eleven a.m. on the dot, Richard showed up. Sullen and stout, with an unruly, curly mop of salt-and-pepper hair and a tweed sports jacket, he somehow projected self-importance from the sphere of his gut. When the bell rang a third time, Anna opened the foyer doors expecting Max, the publicist, but instead she found Renee, the dumpy, extremely persnickety building manager of Smith and Sterling, dispatched no doubt by Mrs. Forstbacher on the seventh floor.

"Oh, hello!" Anna said with dramatic positivity, as if Renee were presenting a lush bouquet rather than a bureaucratic nightmare. "I was expecting someone else."

"Yesssss . . . ," Renee said, already looking past Anna and into the living room, leaning in and peering at the strange shadows cast by the artist's floodlights.

"How can I help?" Anna chirped.

"I have had a vigorous noise complaint and allegations of unregistered workers."

"We are doing some touch-ups. No power tools and only two minutes of light hammering. I believe this falls within the co-op bylaws as acceptable routine maintenance work. Plus I am having a very important meeting in the dining room."

"May I take a look?" Renee asked, her expression pinched together around her nose. Anna took great pains to curry favor with Renee, sending her a bountiful Manhattan Fruitier basket each holiday season and always inquiring after her mother whenever they spoke by phone. None of it seemed to dent Renee's cool, arm's-length professionalism.

"Absolutely!" Anna said, wide eyed. "What great timing. I was actually going to call you to get the paperwork started for a big luncheon we're having here next month."

"Needs fourteen days' notice," Renee said drily.

"That's why we're doing some *routine maintenance* work, which should be all done by the end of the week."

In the living room, Renee cleared her throat and made a show of counting the number of workers. "Five. That's the absolute maximum allowed without written board approval."

"Mm-hmm," Anna said, willing her eyes to stay level and not drift up to indicate the presence of three additional men battling virtually undetectable stains upstairs. She locked eyes with Renee, willing her to *leave now leave now leave now.*

BANG.

Something large and heavy hit the ceiling over their heads. Renee let out a little squeak of surprise. Anna's mind ran a thousand miles an hour toward the goal of avoiding the seeming inevitability of Renee going upstairs, finding the workers, billing the Von Bizmarks . . . she couldn't remember if the fine was $10,000 or $100,000 . . .

"How's your mother?" Anna asked, grasping for a diversion. "No more diverticulitis attacks?"

"Do you mind if I look upstairs?" Renee asked.

"Oh . . . well . . ." Anna screwed up her face to mirror Renee's, as if she was full of empathy. "Mrs. Von Bizmark prefers only staff go up there unannounced, so . . . I'll call the housekeeper."

Anna hit the "All Page" button on a touch screen embedded in the wall, illuminating similar screens in every room of the house. "Cristina," she said crisply, "would you come to the living room, please?"

"I'm coming!" the housekeeper snapped back over the intercom instantly. About two hushed seconds elapsed; Anna and Renee faced off as the contractor screwed a new hinge into the cognac cabinet and the artist silently stroked a nuanced shade of green along the veins of a leaf on the floor, as quiet as a library. When Anna thought that she might hear the sound of two men lifting whatever they'd dropped, she started talking incessantly, nonsensically, and with ardor about the weather. "Here!" Cristina announced at the threshold of the foyer, wiping her hands on her white apron.

"Cristina, this is Renee from Smith and Sterling, the building's managing agent," Anna said, speaking in an unusually strained, slow tone.

"Yes, I remember," Cristina said carefully, on guard.

"What was that loud noise upstairs?" Renee asked pointedly. Anna stood just behind Renee, an odd terrified closed-mouth smile plastered to her face, eyebrows up by her hairline silently entreating Cristina to understand everything that was happening.

"Oh, you know, those guys . . . ," Cristina started. Anna drew a line across her neck with her hand—a slitting gesture. Cristina's eyes widened, and Renee shot Anna a suspicious look over her shoulder. "Alicia and Josefina," Cristina finished, eyes on Anna for a sign.

"I thought so!" Anna jumped in. "Those two! So what did they drop this time?" In fact, no Von Bizmark maid had ever, to Anna's knowledge, dropped, broken, or even scratched anything.

"Who are Alicia and Josefina?" Renee asked, not letting a possible infraction slip through her fingers so quickly.

"The maids!" Cristina said in a tone that suggested Renee must be soft in the head. "They dropped the punching bag again." When Mr. Von Bizmark had mentioned a passing interest in boxing, Mrs. Von Bizmark had had Anna transform the upstairs library into a gym that he'd subsequently used exactly twice.

"Tell them to be more careful!" Anna said sternly, out of sheer relief. Cristina scurried off, and when the doorbell rang a second later, Anna made a show of looking at her watch. "Shoot, Renee! We have a big meeting here now." She ushered her toward the door. "Thanks for stopping by." Anna could almost smell Renee's dissatisfaction.

Anna threw the front door open for Max, a small man in a pin-striped bespoke double-breasted suit, camel coat folded over his arm, light-brown hair falling in perfect, unmoving waves away from his face, which was aglow with serums and self-tanner. He extended his hand to Anna, casting Renee a sidelong glance, and drew her in.

"Anna!"—kiss one cheek—"darling!"—kiss the other. Max was a society publicist, a dealer in rarefied information and connections. A private assistant like Anna—who could let slip when might be the right time to host a certain party or what sort of causes interested the Mrs.—was a valued contact for him, and he knew enough to treat her as such. Cristina reappeared to hang Max's coat, while Anna all but shooed Renee out the door.

Max and Anna strolled to the dining room arm in arm, his hand pressed atop hers, as if they were an old couple. He leaned in his perfumed head conspiratorially and said, "What are we to do about this Felix Mercurion problem? He's such bad press."

"That's why we called you, Max!"

In the dining room, Richard and Bloom examined the invitation proofs, while Julie stood with the electric teakettle in one hand. "Chamomile, Bloom? Is chamomile good?" she asked.

"Do you have oolong?"

"Oolong, oolong . . ." Julie rifled through the tea box.

"Where's Opal?" Anna asked Richard.

"She had a prior unmovable commitment," he said with as much sincerity as he could muster. Anna tilted her head, wondering whether this explanation would suffice for Mrs. Von Bizmark. "Where's Kissy?"

"She'll be down any minute. She asked us to pick two or three," Anna said, gesturing at the proofs.

"Oh goody, the kids running the candy shop," Max said, examining the array of a half dozen various riffs on the same tangerine theme. The three of them weighed the merits of each rectangle of card stock while Anna grabbed a *pain au chocolat* and a cup of coffee. A purple file folder waited at Anna's place. Inside was a single sheet of paper titled *VON BIZMARK CONTRACT RIDER.*

By the time Mrs. Von Bizmark breezed into the room with the stressed and tired expression of a CEO who had just come from a shareholder briefing, they had agreed on two finalists. "I like this one," Mrs. Von Bizmark said, plucking the slightly oversize, most expensive one.

Cristina brought in Mrs. Von Bizmark's double espresso with lemon peel. Mrs. Von Bizmark offered everyone an espresso as well, but Cristina's glinting purple-lined eyes dared anyone to take her up on it, and no one did.

"The only thing we need to decide now is which opera," Richard said.

"And the guest list, of course," Max piped in.

"Wait," Mrs. Von Bizmark said, and everyone held their breath. "Where is Opal?" A chill settled on the room. "I thought you said she'd be involved." She leveled this at Richard. Anna winked at Julie.

A grimace passed across Richard's face a little too slowly to be completely disregarded. "She generally doesn't attend planning meetings until casting."

"Well, what opera does she want to do?"

"I'm sure she'd be open to hearing your thoughts."

"That's not helpful, Richard. I want her to be *involved*, remember?" She let this hang in the air.

"How about *Figaro*?" Julie interjected. "Remember when Opal did it in outer space, with all the servants as martians?"

"It is one of her favorites," Richard said as he contemplated Julie's suggestion. Finally he smiled, all the pieces fitting into place. "We haven't done it in at least eight years, and it's a real crowd-pleaser." He practically licked his lips.

"OK!" Mrs. Von Bizmark said agreeably. "When will we know Opal's thoughts?"

"I'll talk to her this afternoon," Richard said. Mrs. Von Bizmark only frowned.

"Can we talk about Felix Mercurion?" Max's eyes were on Richard. "What does he have to do with opera or arts education?"

"That's so funny, Max—I was wondering exactly the same thing!" Mrs. Von Bizmark agreed. Even as she smiled, her lower lip twitched in annoyance.

"I know that Mr. Mercurion is a bit of a lightning rod," Richard admitted. "But he's agreed to donate several paintings that will grace the stage for the performance and then be auctioned off for charity. Should raise somewhere between one, one and a half."

"And the charity is . . . ?" Max inquired.

"The opera education program, of course."

"It's just . . ." Max held out his manicured hands as if begging the other people at the table to help him. "He's terrible press, and the opera education program is not such a popular charity. Sorry, but true."

Richard looked as if he would like to rip Max's throat out. Everyone knew the opera was basically broke, which was why he'd had to honor the Von Bizmarks in the first place. The more money he could raise, the safer his cushy job. Instead of responding, Richard emitted a low *hmmmmmmm.*

"I know of a gifted-and-talented public school in Brooklyn that needs one point three million dollars to stay open." All eyes turned to Anna, who had not planned on speaking up like that, but the primitive part of her brain had done the math and stepped in—this was her chance. She leaned over and quietly said to Mrs. Von Bizmark, "Josefina's daughter goes there."

"Huh," Mrs. Von Bizmark said noncommittally.

"But what about our education programs?" Richard sputtered, $1.3 million slipping through his fingers.

"Yes, but if the Von Bizmarks cover almost the entire cost of the production, and the guests pay for the party through their ticket purchases, there will still be plenty of money raised and then some," Anna countered.

"I love it!" Max gushed. "With that sort of mission—to save a public school!" He pumped his fist in the air. "The sky really is the limit as far as publicity. What about our VIPs?"

"Yes, exactly," Bloom added, perking up.

"We've got the Petzers," Mrs. Von Bizmark said.

"Have you?" Richard asked.

"Anna?" Mrs. Von Bizmark said.

"Not confirmed, but I'll follow up today." Anna had in fact already emailed and called Mrs. Petzer, with no response.

"Do you know any royalty?" Max asked. "Like Prince Valdobianno? Didn't he come to your Arabian Nights party?" The prince was from an obscure European family who had somehow retained all their old-world castles and yachts without any apparent source of income other than their self-generating wealth. A young forty, he topped eligible-bachelor lists from Beijing to Beverly Hills. The only problem with people like him was that as soon as he got a better offer, he'd be making his excuses to hit up George Clooney's wrap party in Dubai. And who could blame him?

"What about art-world people?" Max asked. "Tastemakers? Artists?"

"Mercurion is inviting a few other gallerists: Charlie Humboldt and Miranda Chung."

Anna gasped, and everyone looked at her. *Oh God,* she silently prayed, *please, Miranda Chung, come to my show!* She covered by coughing lightly into her hand. "Excuse me," she rasped, reaching for her water.

Max and Bloom bantered about the critical importance of reaching outside the opera world and getting a few celebrities: this lifestyle-brand guru, that famous actress. Richard, visibly bored, excused himself from the meeting. As soon as he was gone, Mrs. Von Bizmark exclaimed, "Oh!" and withdrew an envelope from her pocket. Anna and Julie exchanged a glance—*Could this be?* The check. Anna held her breath, trying to figure out how to get it out of Mrs. Von Bizmark's hands. Bloom and Max's chatter reduced to mere nonsensical annoying sounds, and the rest of the room blurred: all Anna saw was the envelope . . . being handed to Alicia . . . to go mail. Before Anna could think of a single thing to say, it was gone. Anna considered running after Alicia, but then a loud bang from upstairs demanded everyone's attention. All heads swiveled in that direction, but there was only silence.

Eager to distract, Anna said, "So are we set on the public school thing?"

"Oh yes," Max said before another distant clank. Anna silently dispatched Julie with a nod. "With the public school angle, anything is possible!"

"You think so, Max?" Mrs. Von Bizmark asked.

"One hundred percent!"

Anna was the only one to see Josefina dashing as fast as her legs could carry all two hundred pounds of her across the dining room doorway, headed for the laundry room.

"It's not too much trouble?"

"Not at all. It's time for your PR wish list!"

Josefina ran the other way, carrying all the beach towels in the house.

"I'd like a feature in *Vogue*, then," Mrs. Von Bizmark said, her faraway gaze on the upholstered wall.

"You got it!" Max said, every professionally trained muscle in his face falling into faux positivity. No one could guarantee this sort of placement—particularly at this late date. It would be virtually impossible. Bloom smirked at him hanging himself out to dry like that. "I guess, though, I should go get to work if that's where we are setting the bar." Max needed to get out of there before Mrs. Von Bizmark came up with some other pie-in-the-sky idea.

"I'll do more thinking on the guest list too!" he tossed over his shoulder on his way out the door. "Very excited!" he called from the hallway, in rapid retreat. From upstairs, Anna heard Cristina hooting in Polish, underlined by a few Spanish curses. Bloom raised an eyebrow.

"I feel terrible, Anna," Mrs. Von Bizmark said, as if willfully ignoring the problem upstairs. "Will you please book me a day at the Peninsula and get the car?" She stood to leave, so Bloom and Anna rose to their feet. A cranking sound reverberated from upstairs. "And, Anna, great idea about the school. I'd be happy to help Josefina." The moment Mrs. Von Bizmark was out the door, Anna slid the contract rider across the table.

"Just one more thing, Bloom."

"Ordinarily I'd have my lawyers review something like this," Bloom said, "but you have my word that we will not go one cent over budget." The way she said it sounded like a threat. But how? Bloom signed in bright-blue ink just as Julie appeared over her shoulder in the doorway, her face a mask of naked panic. Anna hastily shook Bloom's hand and rushed off with Julie.

"How bad is it?" she said quietly as they climbed the stairs.

"Uh . . ." Julie hesitated. "Hard to say, but it's definitely really, extremely bad."

Anna stepped into the doorway of the bathroom to find Miguel crouched at the toilet, the whole rear machinery of it broken into three pieces—the middle section held in his hand and water pouring out of both of the other ends. Already at least two inches of water had pooled in the bathroom, and Alicia and Josefina were pressing Frette towels into the ground to stave the flow outward. In her mind, Anna calculated the damage: Carpet would need to be replaced. Possibly the tile too.

"Julie, call Ariadne and get them here ASAP," Anna directed. As she took off at a run, Miguel broke one of the parts still attached to the pipe, and water shot up and across the bathroom directly at the wall of art. With superhuman speed, Cristina grabbed a towel and held it up to block the flow, but not quickly enough. Water dripped down the wall around the picture frames. Miguel finally wrestled the part back on, and the water continued merely pouring onto the floor.

Anna removed her shoes and socks and stepped inside to examine the damage. The sketch she had noticed previously had already begun dissolving into pulp. Smudged paper goop oozed from the bottom of the frame, except for the bottom-right corner, where she could still make out the signature: Magritte. Insured but still irreplaceable. Shit. Reflexively, Anna reached out and pinched a bit of the pulp; she put it in her pocket.

Like sounds coming through in a nightmare, the phones started ringing. First one line, then three, then all five chimed insistently. Anna rushed downstairs to the living room, where the water ran across the wall-size television screen and down into the floor. Surely one of the people calling was Mrs. Forstbacher to say the police would arrive at any moment. The elevator dinged, and, slightly dazed, Anna assumed it was the men in blue already. But—even better—Mrs. Von Bizmark stood in the anteroom in her oatmeal cashmere lounge suit, spa ready. She looked confused; she knew something was amiss and hesitated in front of the open elevator.

"Mrs. Von Bizmark," Anna started, "we have a problem."

Mrs. Von Bizmark stepped back inside the apartment and followed Anna's gaze toward the living room doors. Her eyes finally found the flood, a stream flowing across the ceiling and rivuletting down the television. "What is going on here?" she rasped, her shocked lungs unable to expand to capacity.

"Remember the broken toilet upstairs?"

"I . . ."

"Well, it's still broken."

"So I surmise."

Suddenly, the parquet ceiling tiles buckled, and gallons of water and insulation poured onto the pricey, custom-made gray couch, the entire precious piece of furniture ruined in a millisecond. Mrs. Von Bizmark took a quick step backward. A wave of nausea passed over Anna.

"I should go call Mrs. Forstbacher," Anna said.

"You know," Mrs. Von Bizmark said in a daze, "I think I'll . . ." She drifted out the door like a ghost, thinking only of the healing hands of the Peninsula chief masseuse.

Anna sighed and went to her desk to commence damage control. Julie stood with her headset on, saying urgently into the phone, "OK, where are you now?" She muted it and told Anna, "I'm talking to the guy. He's coming now. Uh-huh," she said back into the phone. "No, I'd just feel much better if you just stayed on the phone with me until you get here."

Dreading it, Anna dialed Mrs. Forstbacher downstairs, but the phone just rang and rang before an ancient answering machine—one with an actual tape—clicked on. She had seen it once while on a tour of all the invisible damage the Von Bizmark renovation had done to her precious apartment, which she never left. Except for now.

She buzzed the doormen to alert them to the flood. "Miguel busted a toilet, and now we have a huge flood," Anna explained to Joe.

"I know! Mrs. Forstbacher left here in an ambulance screaming about it."

"What? What happened to her?"

"She fell running for the phone to call the police. Paramedics think she broke her hip."

Anna felt terrible that her first thought was, *Thank God!* She would not be around to complain, and even if she were around, the full-time nursing staff generally dissuaded her from calling the police more than once a day.

Anna went to answer the front door like she was walking the plank. In the vestibule, Anna found three police officers and a very pissed-looking Renee.

"Officers," Anna said calmly—after all, she had now been expecting them for at least fifteen minutes. "I thought Mrs. Forstbacher was in the hospital."

"That's where she called us from, ma'am," said the first officer, introducing himself as the chief of housing. "Do you mind if we look around?" Renee rushed upstairs while the three police drifted inside, ogling the apartment. They studied the water pouring out of the ceiling. A loud *crack* rang out as the enormous wall-size flat-screen TV split in two and a spiderweb shatter spread across the bottom half.

"Whoa," one of the men muttered.

Someone from Ariadne finally arrived at the back door, and Julie rushed the guy upstairs. The police took pictures, and the chief requested ten minutes with Anna to "ask a few questions." Which was perfect because of course she had all the time in the world to jump through hoops for Forstbacher, who was probably already unconscious and about to receive a titanium joint. They went over the timeline, starting with the faulty toilet.

"But you just have to jiggle the handle a little," one of the cops interjected.

"The Von Bizmarks don't jiggle," Anna said, and all of the police nodded in understanding.

Within ten minutes of the actual plumber arriving, the flow of water had been shut off and was replaced by myriad drip-drip-drips all over. The living room had reached the humidity level and soundtrack of a grotto. After punctuating most of Anna's story with laughter, the police took off. As she closed the door behind them, the phone began ringing. Julie was still upstairs dealing with the flood, so Anna had to run to her desk to grab it before it went to voice mail. She was surprised to hear, "Hello, this is Delilah Sellers."

"Principal Sellers!" she said, panting lightly, buying time.

"Yes, hello," said a tired voice. "How can I help you?"

"Um, well, actually . . ." *Spit it out, Anna.* "I was thinking we might be able to help you."

"Anna, is it? Look, I'm busy relocating about seven hundred kids to a dozen heated tents we had to erect in our parking lot to keep classes going. Can you make it quick?"

By the time Anna had sketched out the gist of involving the opera, the ball, and the Von Bizmarks to help raise money for the school, she had coaxed Sellers's rock-solid cynicism into healthy skepticism.

"Look, Miss, we can't just take your money for capital improvements. There's a whole DOE process that would have to be administered."

"I'm excellent at navigating byzantine regulatory bodies, actually," Anna said, since it was a part of nearly every task she undertook, from arranging Mrs. Von Bizmark's minor plastic surgeries to renting a Mediterranean superyacht.

"So let me get this straight," Sellers said. "You're going to auction off several valuable works of art . . ."

Works of art! Oh shit! Anna looked at her watch: 6:47 p.m. Her show started in thirteen minutes, and she was at least thirty minutes away by train. Certainly no way to go home and change. Or even get there on time. Or think! Or anything! She wrapped up her conversation with Principal Sellers, promising more details soon.

"I'll meet you there!" Julie shouted as Anna rushed from Park Avenue and into a cab to hasten down to Greene Street. Adrian had at least agreed to turn on the lights, so he was there with the intern, and hopefully he had the crudités out and . . . Anna dug in her bag for something, anything like makeup or an earring. She came up with ChapStick. As the driver careened around Park Avenue, she studied herself in the rearview mirror. She saw a mess of brown hair, which she quickly tied into a topknot. Her face was wan and greasy after the flood:

she looked like someone who subsisted on cigarettes and coffee. At least her long-sleeved shirt was black.

She pulled up to the curb two minutes before seven, confused to find a line of people waiting outside. Her Columbia intern was intently studying her watch just outside the locked glass doors, four large grocery bags at her feet; Adrian was supposed to have let her in an hour ago. Anna raced out of the cab to open the door, and everyone started filing in. As people crowded the drinks table, they poured themselves room-temp vinho verde because Adrian had not shown up with the ice, as planned. Before Anna started making the rounds, she took three seconds to text him:

WHERE ARE YOU????

She sloshed herself some wine and took a swig; lukewarm.

Other than the swill . . . it looked like the evening in fact was coming together! Jazz played softly in the background as people walked counterclockwise around the room as intended, taking their time as they studied the paintings. Many were also carefully reading the small plaques Julie had so painstakingly affixed beneath each canvas, listing the painting's title, medium, and date of completion. Some were reading the price lists and perusing her bio. A gray-haired couple in black wool turtlenecks gestured at the cityscape piece on the far wall; he traced the dark skyline with his outstretched hand as she nodded along. It was a small space, but it was packed by 7:15 p.m.

Adrian finally materialized at 7:23 p.m. with eight bags of ice, which matched Anna's disposition toward him. He kissed her on the cheek but seemed as distracted as she was angry. "Show looks great, babe," he said vaguely and then went to put the remaining bottles of wine on ice, though they would never cool in time.

The space stayed full for a solid two hours. Anna's MFA friends came five at a time to kiss and congratulate her. *Yale Alumni Magazine* had sent a reporter who looked like she was still in college; she snapped pictures hesitantly with her phone. Mrs. Von Bizmark showed up right at the halfway point, dressed to the nines in a velvet jade Saint Laurent gown and carrying a Leiber bag shaped like an asparagus tip. She stayed for ten minutes and left for a dinner at Eric Ripert's newest French hot spot. Anna chatted up a finance guy and his girlfriend; they seemed legitimately interested. Lindsay came late, all apologies and attaché cases and corporate speak. She gushed to Anna about how marvelous everything looked, but Anna could hardly listen because the opening was almost over, and her eyes kept darting to the door to see if Miranda Chung had arrived.

"Thanks so much for coming," Anna said to Lindsay, sparing her a quick glance.

"Wouldn't miss it. Huge congratulations," Lindsay said. Did Anna imagine her eyes doing a quick survey of the small room? *"Huge."*

SIX

B ambi woke to find a note on Peter's cards she'd had Anna get for him from his favorite stationer in Zurich. It was truly a lovely paper, made of 10 percent mulberry silk in a staid gray with the vaguest suggestion of platinum. His full name dominated the top of the card in austere charcoal serif. He'd written in blocky text with a black Sharpie:

SAW STATE OF LIVING ROOM AND WENT TO PENINSULA.

It was like a telegraph or something. Bambi felt . . . sad? Yes, sad. There it was, really, fully formed. Her husband was out. Her kids were at boarding school. She was all alone in the apartment. Well, Peony was there. With Nanny. But really, Bambi was alone.

As if searching in a dark closet, she found her outrage from the previous day at Opal's absence. Today, she'd take the bull by the horns. Bambi threw back the covers, up early (9:47 a.m.) and ready to do some business. After a shower, she buzzed Anna and asked her to tell Opal she'd be in to see her in about an hour. Anna hesitated, which was annoying. She could usually read Bambi's mind.

"Just tell her I have some important ideas that I must share with her today."

"Uh, OK," Anna said.

"Get next-door glam ASAP please."

What to wear what to wear what to wear. Well, there was always a business suit, Chanel. Or Valentino. Dolce. Pretty silk dress. Pants and a button-down. Bambi decided on a gray wool Carolina Herrera suit with a very pretty pleated skirt, a cream bow shirt, and a tidy little jacket that flattered her small waist. This would be the perfect time to throw on that lariat she'd been pining for, but she didn't own it yet. Instead she chose cabochon ruby earrings with a matching broach.

The Birkin seemed too showy, so instead she went with the Goyard portfolio, festooned on one side with painted stars. She got out her Cartier sunglasses and laid everything out in her dressing room for Cristina to meticulously steam or polish.

Her not-favorite makeup and hair duo arrived, one of them inanely snapping gum already at this early hour. "Would you mind?" Bambi said, handing her a tissue and gesturing with a pinching-at-the-mouth motion that she was to discard her gum. "Just something really simple today, guys. It's a business meeting." Ninety minutes later, Bambi looked ready for a photo shoot, her hair perfectly shiny and organized, her face pink and plump in all the right places.

Bambi marched through the empty lobby of the opera house with friendly authority and ducked through a side door into the offices. She smiled but did not slow down for the front desk receptionist, tossing at her, "I'm here to see Opal. She's expecting me."

Without hesitation, she breezed directly into Opal's office. Opal herself, in a patterned Fendi silk dress and combat boots, perched on the edge of her desk, talking to her assistant. She stopped midsentence. Her medium afro trembled with indignation. Her assistant, a former ballerina named Giselle, reclined on the velvet couch with her matching combat boot on the edge of the table in front of her, a legal pad balanced on her slender leg. They both gaped at Bambi, vaguely horrified.

Thank goodness she had come here herself to set them straight! Inflating her chest, Bambi strode forcefully to Opal and placed two kisses in the air as she pressed her cheeks to each of Opal's, who tolerated this. Then Bambi sat herself in the largest chair, clasped her hands in front of her, and announced, "Did you hear the Petzers will be joining us in our box at the gala? I know what good friends you are." Bambi smiled with all her teeth.

"Yes, well, that's great. Pippy and Charles do enjoy a good *Figaro*."

"Oh, good. That's wonderful." Bambi looked from Giselle to Opal with a broad and expectant grin. "So . . ."

"So?" Opal asked.

"Yes?" Bambi prompted.

A light went on for Giselle, who jolted as if she'd been given a shot of adrenaline. "Oh, I forgot to tell you that Anna called to see if Mrs. Von Bizmark could get on your calendar today," Giselle rushed to explain. "She said"—Giselle flipped back several pages—"Mrs. Von Bizmark wanted to share some important ideas." Giselle and Opal turned expectantly to Bambi, who let her jaw fall open.

"Oh dear," Bambi said, her head tilted to one side, brows drawn together. "No, no. no. Oh my." Maybe she was pouring it on a little thick. "I said *I* wanted to hear *your* ideas, Opal. For *your* favorite opera, *Figaro*. Oh dear, I'm afraid we've had a miscommunication. My assistant *has* been distracted lately."

Opal watched this performance with a detached, faraway expression. "I see," she intoned. "My ideas." She locked eyes with Giselle, who nervously tapped her pen on her pad. "Actually, Giselle had a thought."

"Um . . ." Poor Giselle. "What if we did it"—tap, tap, tap—"present day."

Bambi tried not to respond positively straightaway—she didn't want to let Opal off the hook instantaneously, after all. But just contemplating all the wardrobe she could provide for the production. All the guidance on hair and makeup. Set design. The lighting! The aesthetic of the evening could be entirely *VON BIZMARK*. Bambi allowed herself the slightest smile.

"What do you think, Opal?" Bambi asked.

Opal waited a beat to pretend to think about it too. "Totally. Fabulous," she intoned like a judge, and Bambi was satisfied.

SEVEN

Still January 14

"It's not just that she didn't show up . . . ," Anna tried to explain to Julie the same way she'd tried to explain to Adrian, only it was hard to hold on to her train of thought in the face of Julie's dramatic makeup: pancake-pale face with liquid-lined eyes. Her mouth was a perfectly bisected black-and-white pout. "It's just. I just . . . ," Anna stammered. "I don't think any big journalists came." Julie blinked at her, her reaction maddeningly similar to Adrian's. "And I only sold one piece!" Anna said. "It's . . ." Julie's lips were hugely distracting. Anna found herself studying the invisible line between the white and black: no gray area.

"Just the first night and you have two more days to sell?" Julie offered.

"I guess so," Anna said, the slightest bit heartened.

Why couldn't Adrian understand, though? "It's just the day-after blues, sweetheart," Adrian had said when she'd complained that morning in bed. He'd been snuggled up behind her, his words warm in her hair. "Everything went so well! A hundred people showed up."

"And where were you? Why were you late?"

He'd pulled away from her and lain flat on his back. "I do have some things going on myself, you know."

Anna's eyes had remained on the clothes she had selected for her debut, never moved from their arrangement on the chair. The black dress, the platform shoes, the oversize amber pendant carved in Arabic. Embodied in the clothes, it seemed now to Anna, there was a different kind of artist, a slightly more organized, serious, glamorous one whom she could have been. But now it was too late. Worse, it felt like Adrian would never understand.

She had sold one piece for $1,200 to that junior hedge fund–type trying to impress his girlfriend, and just like that, she'd sent her emotional portrayal of the holidays at Grandma's house (along with a secret web of thread taken from a dining room doily) to live in his glass mansion in the sky. This was good. It covered her costs. It meant something. And she did have two more days. As she sat at her desk, her sober intern could be juggling several potential buyers.

"I just need this to be *more*," Anna said.

Julie looked taken aback. Before she could gather her thoughts, they heard the telltale ding-ding-ding of the elevator door opening in the vestibule. Mrs. Von Bizmark must be home.

Anna took these forty-five seconds to review the notes that had been left on her desk and prepared to address each one in turn.

ANNA WHAT HAPPENED TO OPAL AT THE MEETING?

I hope you did not actually SEND all the invitations already?

What's the timeline on repairs?

Need New Venue Ideas!

There were so many unknowns, so many topics on which she would have to develop instant proficiency: wall repair, prewar apartment building infrastructure, navigating eight-figure insurance claims, quelling a litigious neighbor, replanning the luncheon. The phone had been ringing off the hook as word of the flood spread like the water damage in the living room. Florence called to give Anna advice on how to get Miguel fired, the sixth-floor neighbors wanted the Von Bizmarks to rent a dehumidifier for their apartment, Renee emailed an additional three-hundred-page claim form, Ariadne's billing office had some questions. Anna kept forgetting to follow up with the Petzers, and the $10 million foundation check was still at large.

Mrs. Von Bizmark was all business in her flattering gray wool suit. The bow shirt added a little whimsy. "How was Opal?" Anna asked.

"All taken care of," Mrs. Von Bizmark responded with evident satisfaction and oodles of mystery as she took a seat at her desk. Julie's lipstick immediately captured her attention, and she openly stared at it for a few seconds before speaking. "So!" She dragged her eyes off Julie's lips. "Where should we have the lunch?"

"Tavern on the Green?" Julie suggested.

"Under the whale at Natural History?" Anna offered.

"Yes, yes, but everyone's been there, done that." Mrs. Von Bizmark dismissed the ideas.

"Rent a boat?" Julie suggested. Anna gave her a very slight negative shake of the head.

"Ugh." Mrs. Von Bizmark groaned. "Definitely *no* boats." She scowled at Julie to impress upon her the absolute antipathy the entire office should feel toward watercraft. "I so wanted to do this lunch at home!"

"What about Coolwater?" Anna said, intending it as a joke, but somewhere between her brain and her mouth, the message got confused. It came out sounding all too real. To Anna's horror, Mrs. Von Bizmark jumped a little in her chair with a jolt of excitement. She was all hopped up about something, that was for sure; her eyes were practically sparkling. Anna could not stop herself from saying, "We could arrange helicopters—wouldn't take much more travel time than getting downtown. And that would be very special."

Julie's expression said it all, one eyebrow raised, black-and-white mouth halfway open: *Have you lost your mind?*

"How many helicopters?" Mrs. Von Bizmark asked.

"Well, four guests per chopper—I'd say twenty-five?"

"This would all have to be arranged with military precision," Mrs. Von Bizmark said.

"Naturally," Anna responded.

"What about . . . the Metropolitan Museum?" Julie suggested, desperate to find an easier solution. "Rockefeller Center? The Rainbow Room? Pier Sixteen? The Pierre?"

"Coolwater is perfect!" Mrs. Von Bizmark said. "Opal just decided that the opera should be present day. We can use the great room out East as inspiration for the set." She clapped her hands together in glee. "Let's call Phil."

"Hi, Phil," Anna said extra loudly into the speakerphone to alert him. "We have some really exciting news . . ."

"Oh really," he said, already annoyed. "What?"

"We're moving the opera luncheon to Coolwater!"

"Is this some kinda joke?"

"Phil, dear, it's Mrs. Von Bizmark."

"Oh, hello!" Instant sunshine. "Mrs. Von Bizmark! How exciting!"

"It's going to be about one hundred women in about . . ." She looked to Anna.

"Just under a month." Anna smiled, thinking of Phil's pained expression. He was probably biting his knuckle in rage.

"I . . ."

Phil could hardly get one syllable out before Mrs. Von Bizmark interrupted. "Now, I know what you're thinking . . . that this is going to be a lot of work for you. But Anna's on top of it. OK, Phil?" Mrs. Von Bizmark winked at Anna. "Right, Anna?"

"Right!" Anna ejected reflexively and jumped at the opportunity to answer the other line.

"Kissy Von—"

"Samuel Thomas Thorndale is going to do a feature on Kissy for their May issue," Max gushed all at once. "He loved the public school angle! Like, *obsessed*." If Mrs. Von Bizmark had not set the bar at *Vogue*, this would be quite a coup for Max. Samuel Thomas Thorndale, STT for short, ran the twenty-first-century New York City society pages, which comprised a photo-heavy website and glossy magazine titled *Park and Fifth* ("Chronicling the Upper East Side and Its Glittering Inhabitants Since 1990"). "I told him to speak to you all about scheduling a lunch so the two of them can catch up. I think he has a regular table at Sable's. Is she in?" He was like a loyal dog, happily presenting a mauled animal carcass to his owner. As if this would distract her from *Vogue*.

Mrs. Von Bizmark, always happiest when being actively fawned over, became positively ecstatic as Max repeated himself. The call obliterated everything else on the docket. "I have to see Ping and Dr. Westley before this lunch. Today. Like, now," Mrs. Von Bizmark announced. In addition to the weekly ministrations of Ping's magic hands, she paid an outrageous retainer to a SoHo dermatologist so that the doctor would recognize lunch at Sable's with STT as a medical emergency. "I need to freshen up. Do I have any gift cards left?"

"Sadly, no." Mrs. Von Bizmark spent so much on her American Express card that she accumulated rewards points to the tune of 250,000 per month, which she then redeemed for gift cards that were essentially cash. She preferred using these for anything that called for discretion: anxiety medications, yet another Birkin, her third five-digit evening dress in a single day, and, of course, any cosmetic procedures beyond mere facials. Gift cards had paid for Mrs. Von Bizmark's last trip to Switzerland, including the tummy tuck and three-week recovery at the spa, so no surprise that there were no more. The empty leather business card holder where they lived gave Anna an idea. "I'll get some more today," she said brightly.

Finished with the morning's "business," Mrs. Von Bizmark pressed her Goyard portfolio to her body with her bicep and held a slender bottle of green juice in her hands like a scepter. Before she slipped away, Anna said, "Oh, and about Opal . . . ," wanting to know what exactly Mrs. Von Bizmark had accomplished.

"I *said* I took care of it," Mrs. Von Bizmark said pointedly. That was the end of that discussion.

Thank goodness she had not had a chance to mention the invitations for the lunch, which had been drop-shipped from the printer the day before under Anna's direct and hyperspecific instructions she had written in the notes (*Make sure the flower on the crocus stamp is upright*). Nor had they gotten to the topic of repairing the apartment damage, a timeline that could not even be explored, per the Silver Fox, until the entire area had been dehumidified for at least one week's time.

So that would be next week's problem. Today she still had to deal with Bloom coming to discuss the new venue. For the first time, Anna was thrilled to have someone on board to help her dig out from the tasks she felt buried beneath. She could just imagine how this new Coolwater concept would go over with their budget-constrained party planner. Of course, this turn of events had changed everything. Anna would happily tear up the contract rider! Whatever it cost would be fine as long as this elaborate lunch went off without a hitch.

Before the meeting, Anna showed Bloom the damage. They stood side by side in the Von Bizmark living room. The wall television, shattered. Chunks of plaster hung from the ceiling; several plastic bins caught water beneath. Two enormous dehumidifiers hummed in the corner. There was no way to control this part of the process, the Silver Fox had said to Anna.

"Oh my," is all Bloom offered. "Your super did this?"

"Yup," Anna said, not mentioning that he had only been suspended for a week, not fired.

"I thought my building stunk." Bloom turned to Anna and looked up at her, even though she wore spike heels and Anna was in sneakers. "You know, Anna, it's going to be doubly hard to deliver this all within budget."

"Yes, well . . ."

Before Anna could say, *No problem! Never mind the budget,* Bloom interrupted her.

"But of course I will absolutely *not* go over!" Bloom's gleeful cackling shot a bolt of terror down Anna's spine.

"Listen, Bloom, I can talk to the Von Bizmarks about the budget—"

"Oh, no!" she cut in again, practically licking her lips. "A deal is a deal, am I right?" She paused to let this sink in. To a certain extent, Anna and Bloom were in the same boat regarding the luncheon. Bloom certainly wouldn't risk her reputation to make Anna look bad. Or would she? "Of course, the choppers are separate."

In the dining room, Anna took the head of the table to outline the logistics for the luncheon. "So . . . helicopters . . . ," Anna said. Bloom was clearly distracted by Julie's black-and-white lips facing her across the table. The three women all fingered their pens idly in silence.

"Let me think, let me think . . . ," Bloom intoned, closing her eyes. After a few minutes she said, "Let's move on to the theme. Present day, you said?"

"That's right, with Coolwater as inspiration for the set."

"OK, so that makes sense. Let's just queue everything up to highlight the Castle. We'll need a step and repeat out there. Can you resend all the invitations?"

"Already happening." She had called the fulfillment center as soon as they'd decided on Coolwater. They were out of the crocus stamps that Mrs. Von Bizmark preferred, so Anna had had to authorize them to use any other flower stamps they had, sight unseen. There was no time for her usual due diligence.

Anna was finding it increasingly impossible to do everything perfectly. Was it that there was simply more to do? Or was she getting less good at her job? Unresolved tasks crowded her desk, like the Petzers. Anna pulled their extensive database sheet out of her ever-shifting piles of papers and eyed their addresses in New York, Palm Beach, Paris, and the Hamptons. She scanned their fourteen different numbers, including one labeled *Mediterranean Yacht* and another *Vineyard Boat*. Notably no email address for Mrs. Petzer. The notes section read:

*Pippy Petzer assistant: Giosetta***

The ** was Anna and Julie's secret code to indicate contacts with big, annoying, difficult personalities: assholes, basically. Anna would try to get to Mr. Petzer's assistant first—no ominous asterisks next to her name, even though she held an intimidating "chief of staff" title.

"Oh, hi, Anna. Are you calling about a social date?" she asked. "Because all social dates go through *Mrs.* Petzer only. Do you have that number?" Efficient. Helpful. Normal.

Anna slowly dialed with dread, hoping for voice mail.

"Pippy Petzer's office, Giosetta speaking." The voice on the other end had this unnecessarily firm but rushed quality, like she was answering a red phone at the Pentagon.

"This is Anna calling from Bambi Von Bizmark's office."

"And?"

"Hello . . . I'm calling to follow up on an invitation the Petzers received from the Von Bizmarks to the Opera Ball?"

"Mrs. Petzer handles their social calendar personally."

"Is she available?"

"No."

"May I have her email address?"

"I would never share that information," Giosetta said, as if Anna had asked for a list of all her prescription medications.

"May I leave a message?"

"Is it regarding the social calendar?"

"Yes!"

"Then you'll have to call when she's in and available to speak with you." Click.

Anna put her head on the desk and groaned. She knew completing this task was not important, not in the real world. Whether Pippy Petzer attended Kissy Von Bizmark's opera luncheon was obviously no life-or-death matter. But for Anna, existentially, it did signify her effectiveness, her overall potency as a professional.

Felix Mercurion was another fish too slippery for her to grasp. Neither he nor anyone from his camp had been in touch with the opera or Mrs. Von Bizmark. His gallery and private office seemed permanently closed. No one answered or returned her voice mails or emails. Anna shot off another round of emails to him. The good news was that Mrs. Von Bizmark didn't mind his nonresponding; if he did not show up, he could neither embarrass nor outshine her.

And then there was the little matter of the foundation check. Anna dialed Richard at the opera. She just had to choose her words very, very carefully. *You can do this,* Anna reassured herself, doubt creeping all over her.

"Hello, Richard, it's Anna in Bambi Von Bizmark's office."

"Hello?" Richard said, cautious already.

Be cool, Anna told herself. "Um, OK, so listen, Mrs. Von Bizmark forgot to give you the check the other day."

"She can mail it."

"Well, the thing is, Richard, we would prefer to put this on American Express right now, and you'll have the money today." And Mrs. Von Bizmark would have a solid few years of Botox and fillers; almost nothing would make her happier. Had she stunned Richard into silence? "So I was hoping to give you the credit card number."

"For twelve point four million dollars?" Even he was impressed.

"Yup." Anna had tested this limit one other time, when a fraudulent check had frozen the Von Bizmarks' bank accounts and they'd had to put a Learjet on Mr. Von Bizmark's Amex to the tune of $13.6 million. Anna also presumed that Richard was the sort of fundraiser who knew that life was uncertain—always better to get the money now rather than later.

"OK, Anna, what's the number?"

"And we agree all profits from the sale of Mercurion's art will benefit PS 342?"

"Well, obviously, this would all need to be discussed with Mr. Mercurion."

"Have you heard from him recently?" Richard said nothing. So Mercurion was AWOL. Anna charged forward. "I think if the opera was good publicity, a school is even better. Max is already enjoying huge media response." Again, *huge* was maybe overstating it, but that was a matter of opinion.

"Perhaps . . ." Richard bristled. "But he did want the opera to benefit."

"Then isn't it fantastic that the Von Bizmarks are underwriting the production?"

"Well, I suppose." He sniffed.

"The thing is, Richard, by our calculations, you're already ahead of the game, from a financial perspective, with the money you just received. Isn't that right?"

"Well, not exactly . . . ," Richard said uncomfortably.

"As you know, the school is an area of personal interest for the Von Bizmarks." This was perhaps the best part of the job—when Anna could wield the force of her employers' name for good.

"OK, Anna."

Boom. She punched the air with her fist.

Anna rushed to find Josefina, eager to share this good news with the ones whose lives would be most impacted. She couldn't help cherishing the rare feeling that she was accomplishing something good for the world—like she was herself, in fact, a good person deserving of good things. "It's about your daughter's school." Josefina's whole face opened up with expectation, and Anna realized how awful it would be if Mercurion's pieces undersold. Or worse, failed to appear somehow. "Listen, it's not completely one hundred percent certain, OK?" Josefina, as wide as she was tall, jumped up and down, stressing the walnut beneath her sneakered feet. Tears shot from her eyes. She grabbed Anna and squeezed her, saying, "Thank you thank you thank you!" loudly and directly into her ear.

"OK, OK, look, it's not for sure. OK." Anna channeled high school Spanish whenever she really wanted to be understood. *"No está confirmado."*

"Sí, sí, entiendo," Josefina said. "Thank you." She squeezed Anna's hand, wiped her tears, and they both got back to work. For one second, Anna felt a great weight lift off her shoulders. They may not have been curing cancer in that office, but here was something important.

On her way back to the office, Cristina went *Pssst* as Anna passed the laundry room. Anna stopped—had she misheard? But Cristina waved her into the laundry room and slid the door closed behind her.

"Something wrong with Mr. Von Bizmark?" she whispered.

"What do you mean?"

"He didn't sleep here last night," Cristina said. "He took a bag too. And they came back from vacation early. There's a problem?" she said.

"Geez, Cristina, I don't really know," Anna admitted. Maybe Phil was right? Maybe they were headed for a split? Cristina's frosted blue eyes studied Anna for more information.

"I need this job," Cristina whispered. She was overpaid, with four weeks' vacation, holiday bonuses, and health insurance. It occurred to Anna that Cristina, in her midfifties, would never find a position as good as the Von Bizmarks', and her wide eyes said as much.

"Whoa, hold on," Anna said. "No one's losing their job," she whispered loudly. "Don't be so dramatic!" But when she slid the laundry room door back into its pocket, Josefina and Alicia were standing outside, wringing their hands and listening. "Oh my God, you guys, relax! Come on, she was in a great mood today!" Anna said, while internally feeling shaken by the generalized anxiety that had taken hold of the staff regarding the stability of the household.

That evening, Anna sped to the exhibition, where her intern chatted up a hipster couple in expensive sneakers. She introduced herself and happily explained her methods for incorporating the plastic sheeting into the oils, how she pressed her found materials and plastic shapes into the wet, rich oil paint. They listened attentively, but they did not even ask for a price list. She kept the gallery open until ten, though no one came after nine. The next night was a virtual repeat: many well-heeled lookers but no serious interest. With the lease up the next day, she had rented a van to cart her work back to the studio. She collapsed into bed around two a.m., Adrian snoring soundly already.

The next day, Anna told Mrs. Von Bizmark she had a migraine and raced through her tasks bleary eyed. But without the exhibition to go to, she arrived home early, only to remember Adrian would probably work late, like every other night. Unable to relax, Anna grabbed a broom to sweep their tiny apartment, already pretty dirty again after Adrian's prejob cleaning. She attacked the floor with the dollar-store broom, sending more dust into the air than into a careful pile. Anna snagged a glue trap from under the couch on the plastic bristles, and after struggling to remove such, only succeeded in separating most of the brush from the broom itself. She threw the whole mess in the garbage downstairs, poured herself a glass of wine, and sat on the couch.

Over an hour later, the wine untouched on the coffee table, Anna did not stir from the fetal position on the couch when Adrian came home. She heard him put his bag at his desk chair. He leaned over the side of the couch and kissed her cheek. She tried to smile at him, but instead a tear slipped from her eye. She wanted Adrian to make her feel better, but how?

"Aw, babe, it just kills me to see you so upset when the show went great!"

"Adrian, you really let me down!" Anna said, wanting to tell him so many things about how she was feeling. Inadequate as an artist and at work and as a partner and a human. But she couldn't put the words together for anything other than the ways he had not been there.

"I'm sorry," he said, and he sat on the couch next to Anna. "I just feel like maybe . . ." He had a strange expression. Was he being sarcastic? "You have a teensy, eensy . . ." Definitely sarcasm. "Weensy . . ." Dramatic pause. "Entitlement problem."

"I'm not sure what you mean," Anna said, the wind knocked out of her sails; she'd never expected him to turn the tables on her like this. She sat up suddenly, the blanket falling off her, ready to fight.

"I mean, careers are not made in a single two-day show, Anna! It's one thing to have high hopes, but, like, you're sulking because you didn't get picked by a gallery on your first try." It was like it didn't even matter to him that he had been late to the opening, not helped her as much as he'd said he would.

"This is not my first try," Anna insisted, indignation building. She knew he had a point, but she was having a hard time making it out through the haze of failure. And anger. "Have you forgotten about all my student showcases? My MFA thesis?"

"Well, no, it's just that . . ."

"What? They don't count? People got signed at those shows. My classmates got galleries years ago."

Adrian was silent. He only shrugged, a sardonic grin on his face, which to Anna meant, *Maybe those people were the most talented.* Maybe they deserved a gallery where she herself did not. Maybe her ship had already sailed. Was that what Adrian was thinking? Anna could feel herself losing control of her mouth as her rationales unraveled. "The point is I'm not some newbie kid. I've been at it awhile." Adrian cocked his head at her. He was definitely smirking. Like he was thinking, *See what I mean?* But Anna didn't want to see. And suddenly, she understood what was meant by the term *blind rage.*

"Sometimes I think you'll never understand me," Anna said, certain Adrian would disagree with her. Take her hand. Calm her down.

"You know, you may have a point there," Adrian conceded, and it was like the ground shifted under Anna's feet. He had always been so solid, so ready. So there. And now, out of the blue, there was this other possibility: that Adrian could go away.

Insecurity shocked Anna like a glass of water thrown in her face. "What's that supposed to mean?" she sputtered.

"It's just . . . Anna, it's hard to think about building a life with you when you get all down in the mouth about one pop-up show that failed to accomplish all of your professional goals. Like, perspective?" he said.

Oh, it was so easy for him now, in his sellout luxury-goods job with the big paycheck and the implied glamour to talk this way, like he had all the answers. Anna inhaled sharply. "I'm not sure I understand you either anymore," she tossed off, vaguely, feeling terrifically wronged. She wanted to scare him straight. Maybe she would be the one to leave! And the mere thought of this would make him embrace her and say, "Baby, let's stop all this foolishness."

But instead, he grabbed his coat off the chair, opened the front door of their apartment, and walked out.

EIGHT

"H e just walked out? Without saying a word?"

Anna nodded.

"Did he come home?"

"Really late. I don't even know when. And then . . . he's always at work! We talked on the phone yesterday, and I apologized. But . . ." Anna struggled to express her hesitation to Julie. "It just feels like Adrian doesn't take me seriously."

"Adrian? What are you talking about?" Julie's shiny side ponytail swung around as her head jerked in surprise. She wore a baggy olive jumpsuit with cuffed sleeves and a thick bright-orange belt, sedate for a change. A leather clutch made to look like an orange slice sat on her desk—definitely one of her designs. "Doesn't take you seriously how?"

"It's just, like, he . . ." Anna stopped talking as Cristina ran past the office to answer the back door. Enormous floral arrangements poured into the apartment from purveyors all over the tristate area ahead of the day's "ambience" meeting.

"It feels like Adrian has this big job now, and everything I do is silly," Anna finished. She knew this didn't quite capture how she felt, but maybe that was because she wasn't entirely sure how she felt. Instead of dwelling on this, she looked at her watch. They had only a few minutes before Bloom arrived.

"Look, Anna, if you're not sure about Adrian, that's one thing. But I think he's pretty sure about you."

"That's just it, Jules! He's not anymore. He . . ." Cristina ran past the office again toward the back door. Anna clammed up, her eyes traveling over the light-reflecting cellophane enrobing most of the floral arrangements. There were lilies five feet high and bright-purple delphinium, orange birds of paradise. Branches doused in glitter, laden with candles. Strands of crystal beads hung from birch limbs in one centerpiece so large it was like a small wintertime park.

"Never mind," Anna said of her own complicated problems. There was enough to think about, look at, and take care of at work. All the pieces were falling into place for the luncheon except the guests. Maddeningly, no one had responded! This anxiety was reflected in the notes waiting on Anna's keyboard:

Did Pippy Petzer accept for luncheon and the opera or just the opera?

Who exactly has responded for the luncheon?

Please book the big laser for TODAY.

Where are you keeping RSVPs for the luncheon?

Julie scanned Mrs. Von Bizmark's notes. "I don't think there's time for the laser." The STT lunch was just a few days away.

"Book it anyway," Anna said as she dialed Mrs. Petzer's private line, as instructed by Giosetta. This had become a ritual every morning and afternoon; each time the fear that Mrs. Petzer would answer almost equaled the fear that she would not. Only once had Mrs. Petzer actually picked up, but she said she was "running out the door" and would be in the next morning to speak. Then she simply disappeared once more into the Park Avenue ether. As the hours ticked by, Anna became increasingly panicked, so she choked on her coffee when Mrs. Petzer actually answered.

"Pippy Petzer," a tight voice answered.

Wet hacking followed by a constrained "Mrs. Petzer!" Anna cleared her throat. "It's Anna calling from Bambi Von Bizmark's office."

"Oo-oh." The way she said the single syllable was more like a whole sentence.

"I'm following up on an invitation to the Opera Ball luncheon at Coolwater . . ."

"We have received no such invitation."

"Well, you definitely should have." The fulfillment house had mailed them several days ago, but people often lied about having not received something in order to conceal their own disorganization or disinterest.

"I assure you I did not."

"The date is—"

"Please send it again!" Mrs. Petzer hung up.

Bloom arrived ten minutes after the final floral arrangement, her red hair curled and done up with a fascinator. She wore a wine-red suit with tasteful beadwork at the cuffs. Bright smudges dabbed her cheeks.

"Bloom!" Mrs. Von Bizmark said brightly from the living room. She wore a crisp white shirt over black leggings and held the arm of her readers in one hand. Her other hand extended toward the event planner with elegant warmth. Bloom's face brightened considerably.

"Kissy!" she said. They double kissed, on the best of terms.

The Mrs. had improved much since the STT news, absorbing herself completely in preparations. She worked out constantly and iced her face twice a day. She got a new couture suit in her favorite charcoal. She flipped through magazines for just the right daytime hairdo. She personally called her favorite makeup artist and begged her to cancel another appointment.

Plus, Mr. Von Bizmark had gone on his annual trip with various members of the C-suite, visiting VBO's most significant clients all over the globe in one go. This usually took him out of the country for at least a few weeks and replaced his unexplained absence with a perfectly acceptable narrative regarding why he was not sleeping at home. Without the unrest in her marriage to distract her, Mrs. Von Bizmark's interest in the opera blossomed, and she played various recordings of *Figaro* throughout the house endlessly. The stirring opening constantly rose over the house-wide sound system.

Bloom led Mrs. Von Bizmark around the flower arrangements, most of which she instantly dismissed with a simple no. They were left with a profusion of wildflowers in a substantial silver urn, which Anna was partial to, and the stiff delphinium in geometric glass, which Bloom preferred.

"Let's do the wildflowers," Mrs. Von Bizmark said. "They match the border at Coolwater."

"Of course, shipping the flowers won't come out of my budget," Bloom snapped at Anna.

"Of course not." Mrs. Von Bizmark laughed nervously. "Budget!" She tittered, completely ignorant of Avi's contract rider. Anna and Bloom locked eyes. "What else is outstanding?"

"We should start receiving responses any moment now," Bloom said.

"No one yet?" Mrs. Von Bizmark asked, anxiety creeping into her voice.

"Don't worry!" Bloom barked. "Any second the acceptances will start pouring in." Surely she had uttered these exact words to many a nervous hostess past. Bloom quickly changed the topic to a photo booth. The back doorbell rang, and Cristina appeared at the living room doors a moment later, gesturing for Anna to come with her.

Barclay stood at the back door, a luncheon invitation inexplicably in his hand. Anna blinked twice, as if to clear her sight. "I think you have a little problem," he said.

Barclay handed Anna the envelope, thick and heavy. The calligraphy looped beautifully across the front and in just the right *hopeful* spring green. Only the machine stamping of the United States Postal Service, nearly impossible to read on the dark envelope, marred the effect: *RETURN TO SENDER, INADEQUATE POSTAGE.* An actual person had circled the measly single first-class stamp—a lovely stalk of lavender, Anna noted—in ballpoint pen. Anna held her breath; could it have been a onetime mistake? She prayed that this was the one envelope that had gotten through with the wrong stamp.

"And there's this . . . ," Barclay added, and he stepped back to reveal a USPS burlap sack stuffed with invitations, none with the proper postage. The luncheon was three weeks away. She could hear Mrs. Von Bizmark laughing in the other room. To let her see this bag would be to invite all sorts of unpleasant possibilities: a meltdown, oppressive micromanagement, and eventual severance.

She had to hide the evidence.

Anna grabbed the bag, which was not that heavy but was unwieldy. Turning to hasten to the office, she almost immediately knocked a floral arrangement to the floor. It banged loudly but did not break. Cristina rushed to pick it up.

"Is everything all right?" Mrs. Von Bizmark called.

"Yes!" Anna called right back. "Just getting a large delivery." She rushed to the office and shoved the sack under her desk. Mrs. Von Bizmark, never one to leave a crashing sound uninvestigated—what painstakingly selected objet d'art had suffered?—started walking with Bloom toward the office. At the last moment Anna shoved a case of paper in front of the sack and her desk chair next to it. She crossed her arms over her chest and leaned against the desk just as Bloom and Mrs.

Von Bizmark passed by, glancing only briefly inside on their way to the laundry room to ask Cristina about the noise.

Julie watched this all with silent wide eyes. "What's wrong?" Julie whispered. "We're not curing cancer, you know." Anna held up a single envelope and enjoyed watching as Julie struggled to understand the meaning of the returned invitation the same way Anna had. To illustrate further, Anna dragged the pile of them out to show Julie, whose face looked like it might melt off her skull before she started babbling. "OK, well, we can handle this. We can . . ." Julie shut up, and Anna tossed the offending envelope behind her computer screen as Bloom and Mrs. Von Bizmark passed by again. Anna stood stiffly in front of her desk, and Julie froze, her mouth midword, a comedic tableau no one saw.

And then they were back in motion. Julie dragged the sack out, sat on the floor next to it, and started pawing through its contents in disbelief. She started to hum a single low note, a sign of extreme duress. Anna printed a map of Manhattan and divided the city into four parts, with Columbus Circle in the crosshairs. She highlighted the city's quadrants.

"OK, check this out," Anna said to Julie, ending her humming. She placed her map of a divided Manhattan on the high table. "We split the envelopes into four piles. Really, five. One for out-of-towners. Then we get four cars to deliver them today." The two of them stood at the table sorting. The process would take at least an hour. The northeast pile, home to the Upper East Side, grew quickly. Julie got five enormous shopping bags from the laundry room and labeled them: *Northeast, Southeast, Northwest, Southwest, Out of Town.* Anna sighed heavily, feeling the weight of yet another error.

"Just one question!" Julie said, steadily dropping envelopes into various shopping bags. "What will you tell Mrs. Von Bizmark?"

"What *will* you tell Mrs. Von Bizmark?" the woman herself interjected, standing in the wide office doorway in her workout gear. Anna's heart dropped, her hopes of avoiding divulging this mistake dashed.

"There was a postage error at the fulfillment house, and we have to resend all the invitations, but they will be delivered within a few hours," Anna said. "The New York ones, anyway." Mrs. Von Bizmark blinked. With all the Botox and fillers, it was hard to tell what was happening with her emotionally. Lacking any sort of response, Anna kept talking to fill the silence. "We'll have cars hand deliver them and FedEx those not in New York." Silence. Julie very, very quietly started humming again. The total lack of response from Mrs. Von Bizmark unnerved them both. Was she having a stroke? About to fire everyone? Anna could not think of anything more to say.

After an eternity, Mrs. Von Bizmark said, "You mean, *no one* has received an invitation yet?" She enunciated each word, leaving heavy pauses between each.

"That's right," said Anna.

"Oh, goody," said Mrs. Von Bizmark, pressing her palm to her chest, a wide smile spreading across her face. She looked totally thrilled. "I was panicking that no one had responded, and now we at least know why." She left for the dermatologist practically skipping.

Within three hours, they had all the invitations out except for one: Pippy Petzer. She lived in the next building. Anna grabbed a flower arrangement from the morning's display, placed the hopeful envelope carefully within it, and went to deliver the package with all her fingers metaphorically crossed.

Anna tried to hand the large ceramic urn full of forsythia to the Petzers' austere doorman in a stiff gray wool uniform full of hardware. But he held up his white-gloved hand and said, "Mrs. Petzer does not accept flowers of any kind."

"I'm sorry?" Anna said.

"Allergic," he said, this notion so ludicrous Anna's mouth fell open. Could this be a new trend in self-importance? Frequently, women of status sought ways to inconvenience those around them. First were those who resisted email and mobile phones, then came the wave of gluten intolerance, and now there were flower allergies to contend with.

"Well, what *does* she like?" Anna asked, thinking fast. But this guy was a real pro.

"Couldn't say."

She thought about throwing the pot past him into the ornate lobby, where it would smash into dirty bits on the black-and-white marble, but instead Anna thrust the invitation into his hand. "She does accept mail, right?"

"Only on Tuesdays," the doorman said with such seriousness it was impossible to know if he was joking. He took the envelope, at least.

As Anna entered the apartment, she could hear the phone ringing off the hook and Julie hectically trying to juggle all the incoming calls. *Guess the invitations landed.* Anna rushed to field responses.

"Kissy Von Bizmark's office, this is Anna."

"Why, oh why . . . wouldn't you . . ." Max could hardly catch his breath, all his words running together as he struggled to keep hold of his sentence. "Even? I mean, Anna, were you going to tell me the lunch was moved to the Castle or just wait for me to get my invitation by messenger, like everyone else? I mean, 'Helicopter transportation will be provided,'" he read off the card. "What is this, a fundraising luncheon or some sort of private-equity junket? Let me help you with your messaging, please?"

"I'm so sorry, Max, you're absolutely right!" And he was. They really could have used Max's input.

"I mean, what does helicoptering a hundred people to the Hamptons have to do with saving a public school in a poor neighborhood?" he asked, his voice rising octaves. Anna's head dropped into her palm. "I'm having a hard time coming up with, you know, a plan. You've heard of them? It's when you have a goal, and you invite all the key shareholders and influencers into a meeting, and everyone contributes, and you decide on the smartest, absolutely best course of action. Do you hear what I'm saying?"

Anna waited a few seconds to make sure he was finished. "We can fix this!" Anna said. "Right, Max? *You* can fix this!" Her mind devolved into a word jumble: *PETZER, SCHOOL, HELICOPTERS.*

"So now you want my input?"

"Oh, Max, please don't pout. We really don't have the time."

"We fly the principal of the school up for a direct appeal."

"Ouch. A solicitation at a preevent luncheon?"

"Desperate times. And she'll need coaching. She can't just ask for cash."

"Anything else?"

"Maybe a performance? Like a teaser of a scene from the show."

"We're talking about at least one additional helicopter just for the principal and a few cast members."

"So what?"

He was right again. "Sorry, I just have a lot on my plate."

"Sweetheart, I've got about ten thousand calls in to my contacts at *Vogue.*"

Avi was also no fan of Anna's grand helicopter scheme, which she was growing to regret more and more with every passing moment. It turned out that flying everyone there constituted a classic case of exposing the Von Bizmarks to unwanted and costly legal activity.

"Every guest will have to sign a waiver," Avi insisted.

"Hmmm, that doesn't sound very festive."

"How does a bankrupting lawsuit sound, Anna? *Festive?* One of those women's estates could and would sue for millions, but you'd lose four or five at a time. Way too much exposure."

"Can it be really simple? Something we can print on a postcard and have them sign as they board?"

"I'll see what I can do."

Everyone had their cross to bear, and Anna's was Pippy Petzer. Time for her afternoon attempt. Anna waited for the same old voice mail to kick in, but instead, there was nothing. Just the sound of breathing. Not even a hello.

"Mrs. Petzer?" Anna said, awash in disbelief. Two times in one day.

"Yes?"

"My goodness, I am so happy to have reached you again."

"Who is this?"

"Anna in Bambi Von Bizmark's office. I'm calling to follow up on the invitation to—"

"Yes, I have this . . . thing . . . in my hand. Listen, it's terribly inconvenient to expect people to travel all the way to the Hamptons on a Tuesday, for goodness' sake. I just don't think I can do it."

"But Mrs. Petzer . . ." Think, Anna, *think*. "Mrs. Von Bizmark was hoping you would go in her own private helicopter with Samuel Thomas Thorndale." Quiet. Blessed reconsideration. Anna held her breath. "Of course, he's eager to speak with you for the feature he's working on."

"I see."

"And you will be joining the Von Bizmarks at the ball, of course?"

"Yes, I suppose so."

"Anna?" Mr. Von Bizmark's surprising and displeased voice behind her made her jump. He must be just back from his trip. It was unusual for him to show up in the office like this. Anna felt a little quiver of panic. Was he there to fire her?

"OK thanks we'll send a confirmation bye," she said and hung up on Mrs. Petzer.

Anna spun around in time to see Mr. Von Bizmark say, "Hello, Jenna."

"It's Julie," Julie said.

"I know." He looked more tired and more annoyed than usual. "Where is she?"

"At the spa," Anna said. It was much more discreet than the dermatologist.

He snorted. "What does she want to do for our anniversary? Florence told me to talk to you about it."

"Well, I . . ." Anna went to the calendar. They had a theater series that evening, some new play about a divorce that they should surely skip. They could go to her favorite little Italian place downtown, except Mr. Von Bizmark thought it was too loud and "just too Italian, if you know what I mean." They could do something fun, like rent a boat and cruise around the island. Except she would hate that. This was a woman whose list of dislikes grew longer with every passing moment and who had everything she wanted with one exception: an outrageously expensive and completely unnecessary estate piece from Harry Winston she'd been accumulating credit toward for years. "There is that—"

"I'm not spending five million on a necklace," he interrupted.

Anna knew this was a chance for her to redeem herself; she'd been so off her game recently that this would be a big win. If she could orchestrate a glorious anniversary, not only would she improve her professional standing, but she would also enhance the job security of all those around her. And of course maybe nudge the Von Bizmark marriage to a happier place. "What if Julie and I plan something here at the house?" Anna said. Mr. Von Bizmark looked instantly skeptical about this plan. "We can get Chef to come. Make it special." Anna knew Mrs. Von Bizmark would prefer this. Well, she was pretty sure.

"Fine. Could you get me the car, please? You can tell Mrs. Von Bizmark and Cristina—"

"What, I'm right here!" Cristina announced, shooting out of the laundry room to stand in front of Mr. Von Bizmark just a smidge too closely. "What," she demanded.

"Hello, Cristina," he said. It was unclear whether he tolerated her sharp tongue or did not even notice. "I will be staying at the Peninsula until that"—he flapped his hand toward the living room with disgust—"dump is cleaned up."

"This place is not good enough for you now!" Cristina said a little hysterically. Anna forced herself to emit a staccato *ha ha* to indicate that it was a joke. Julie gamely jumped in, and as soon as the front door had closed behind him, Cristina snapped at Anna, "See?! See! There is a problem!"

"I don't know, Cristina. We're going to try and help," Anna said, but Cristina only waved a hand towel at her dismissively and disappeared. "Right, we're going to help?" Anna said to Julie brightly. The only response she got was a hangdog stare. "So that's a stupid idea, huh?"

"Like we don't have enough to worry about?" Julie said.

She was right. Planning something spectacular for Mrs. Von Bizmark would require extrasensory levels of intuition about their employer. The only predictable thing about her was the likelihood of displeasing her. Many gift givers had crashed on the shoals of Mrs. Von Bizmark's specific tastes, breadth of knowledge, and limitless budget. There was a double-door closet (right next to the stationery closet) for regifting full of unimaginative luxuries like Hermès scarves (boring), Prada bags (yawn), and a million fragrances when anyone who knew her well knew Kissy Von Bizmark wore only her own proprietary scent blended at Fragonard in Paris. Mr. Von Bizmark had planned a birthday dinner at Per Se for her once, but the next day she'd grumbled endlessly to Anna about the length of it, the volume of food, the disappointing guest list ("Who told him to invite that dressmaker from Dallas?" she'd asked of a particularly aggressive, overpriced, divorced couturier, but Anna declined to name the guilty party—Florence). Could Anna impress and delight Kissy Von Bizmark where Peter Von Bizmark had failed?

First she had to lock down Chef. The Mrs. didn't want to eat dinner every night in the city, but she didn't want to lose Chef. So she paid her a full-time salary and allowed her to live off-season at the Castle guesthouse, a sumptuous four-bedroom home tucked into the woods by the water, which was where Anna reached her.

She could hear Colombian music blaring in the background. "*Hola*, Anna!" Chef said, upbeat. "I'm making jam." She sounded so relaxed . . . just making some jam on a winter weekday. "I got these peaches straight from a friend's farm in Chile." Chef's secret weapon was a rarefied international network of food purveyors.

"Chef, Mr. Von Bizmark wants you to come to the city for their anniversary and make something spectacular for just the two of them. It's their twenty-fifth."

"All right, all right, very cool."

"I was thinking seafood—"

"Whoa, whoa. You trying to do my job? I know how to make Bambi Von Bizmark happy," Chef said. *Thank goodness someone does,* Anna thought bitterly.

"Whadoyouthink?" A cheerful mumble behind her. Anna and Julie spun around to behold a very stoned, bright-red, puffy Mrs. Von Bizmark. She looked slapped around, the skin above the collar of her Lululemon jacket furiously angry. Worst of all, her lips had tripled in size. Surely they would deflate? Anna's first thought was that she would have to push the STT lunch date as far into the future as possible. Her second was to slowly relax her upper lip and close her mouth to erase all signs of horror.

"Wow!" was all Anna could muster. Mrs. Von Bizmark's face was a hodgepodge of out-of-place textures and shapes.

"It'llbegraybytheshoot," Mrs. Von Bizmark said. Julie failed to neutralize her surprise; her lips quivered. "Cristina!" Mrs. Von Bizmark called. She appeared a moment later, openly ogling the mess the Mrs. had made of her face; her mouth fell open so quickly a little involuntary snort came out her nose. "This is photographic work, darling," Mrs. Von Bizmark explained grandly, overenunciating so as to be understood. "Ice pack, please." Mrs. Von Bizmark picked her way to the desk as if she were having trouble seeing the furniture past her enormous cheeks. Cristina presented the ice pack—teal gel encased in plastic shaped like a flattened face—on a tea towel to the Mrs. at her desk. She pressed it to her outraged skin and sighed with pleasure. Mrs. Von Bizmark's eyes covered, Cristina crossed herself and disappeared.

"Redmellhrmph," Mrs. Von Bizmark said from under the gel pack.

"I'm sorry?"

"What is going on?" she asked, which was as good an opening as any to explain how Anna had come to put a $12 million charge on her American Express card.

"Well, I was thinking," Anna started brightly. Gulp. "What if we put the opera on your Amex card?"

"I already sent the check."

"Yes, but I canceled it and got you fifteen million American Express points. You'll never run out of gift cards again!"

"*No!*" Mrs. Von Bizmark said. It was unclear whether this was good or bad news. "The card Mr. Von Bizmark pays?"

"Yes, of course," Anna said, a little confused. Mr. Von Bizmark paid all of her credit card bills.

"Oh, well," Mrs. Von Bizmark said, as if resigning herself to something.

Anna charged ahead. "And Max had this great idea!" Anna said. "Let's have Principal Sellers speak at the luncheon, and you could introduce her?"

"Fine by me," Mrs. Von Bizmark said breezily.

"Also, Mr. Von Bizmark is home," Anna said.

"What?" she squawked. "I can hardly let him see me now!"

"Well, that's good because he went to the Peninsula."

"Oh," she said, the one syllable crammed with disappointment.

The back doorbell rang, and Cristina answered it. Just outside the apartment, Alfie spoke as if he were on a Broadway stage, projecting so that Mrs. Von Bizmark could hear him from anywhere on the bottom floor.

"Hello, Miss Cristina! I brought these copies of *Park and Fifth* magazine and marked the pages with Mrs. Von Bizmark."

From her chair, face held up to the sky, mask applied, Mrs. Von Bizmark shouted, "Is that Alfie?"

"Yes, Mrs. Von Bizmark!" Anna could practically feel the breeze created by Cristina rolling her eyes at this particularly grotesque display of brownnosing. Still, this was how attentive porters like Alfie earned their tips. Which gave Anna an idea.

Cristina brought the magazines in and opened one to the page Alfie had carefully marked with a bit of newspaper. "Huh," she remarked noncommittally, unimpressed, and rushed off. The Von Bizmarks, dressed to the teeth, stood together at the top of a red-carpeted stairwell at the annual gala to benefit Calling All Chickens, a well-funded group that "rescued" farm animals from certain death. Pippy and Charlie Petzer were also on this page, her consistent updo of unmovable hair and pointed eyebrows floating near the center of her over-Botoxed forehead. The effect was vampiric, particularly so next to Mr. Petzer, who looked embalmed.

One minute later, reclining in her chair, Mrs. Von Bizmark snored lightly even as the phones rang off the hook, all of New York's most elite socialites clamoring for their seat on one of her helicopters.

NINE

B ambi wondered why people ever spoke to her as if she didn't already know something that she *did know* perfectly well. It irritated that Max insisted on lecturing her about Samuel Thomas Thorndale, whom Bambi had of course obviously so very clearly been acquainted with quite well through the years, thank you very much. Still, Max insisted on pressing one of his briefing papers into her alligator-gloved hand. On a matter of principle she refused to look at it, immediately turning it facedown on her lap.

"Yes, yes, I have known Sam forever, Max, I promise."

They crawled down Park Avenue in the Von Bizmark car, a sedate navy Mercedes with an enormous back seat that reclined slightly and allowed Mrs. Von Bizmark to avoid wrinkling any part of her bespoke Dior suit. No one, not even Pippy Petzer, had this in her closet: hot off the runway and made just for her. Bambi smiled internally with self-satisfaction and checked her glam in the rearview, tilting her chin toward the light for the most flattering angle.

Bambi noted the creaselessness of the fragile skin around her mouth and eyes—God, Westley was good! And now she had enough gift cards to last a lifetime—or at least the rest of the year. After the hot curlers, blow-drying, and multiple products, her shiny blonde long bob had the perfect amount of movement. The contouring and layers of foundation concealed any lingering redness from the laser. The downtown A-team glam squad had convinced Bambi to try something new for her nails—a khaki green she was no longer sure of.

"What do you think?" she said, holding out her hand for Max to comment on.

"Fabulous," Max said, but before she could confirm that he was complimenting her manicure and not the oversize Graff emerald bracelet, Max was charging on with his tedious STT summary. "He majored in journalism at Columbia, apprenticed with Bill Cunningham, worked for thirty years at *Vanity Fair . . .*"

"Really? I had no idea," Bambi muttered sarcastically, digging in her gray alligator envelope handbag for nothing in particular—just putting on a show of disinterest. As if she hadn't been to these sorts of lunches a hundred times! This was her job! Her profession! Bambi knew all too well the critical importance of this lunch. She would have to project charm and accessibility while simultaneously scheming and strategizing. She would have to appear real but also vaguely awe inspiring. She wanted to be taken seriously and make him laugh. Basically, she had to be perfect.

"I think he's going to want to talk a lot about Mercurion, and you should lead him back to PS 342 as much as possible. Here are some papers on the school Anna put together for STT." He slipped those onto her lap. "The talking points are talented students, motivated principal, crap building."

Bambi stopped fussing with her bag, having come up with a real question. "How much should I talk about Josefina and her daughter? I don't want to sound imperial . . ."

"Do you know the daughter?" Max asked. Bambi thought back to a few vague conversations with Anna. The day the girl had first come to the apartment and solemnly shaken Bambi's hand and thanked her. For what? Who knows. People were always thanking Bambi for something.

"Not really," Bambi admitted, realizing she couldn't even remember her name . . . Elissa?

"What about Mercurion?"

"I don't know him either."

"Just say the opera picked him."

"Right. I'm sure he'll ask about Opal, too, but we are on excellent terms," Bambi said, feeling like the truth of her statement was enhanced just in having made it aloud. They were almost at their destination . . . Sable's. She unnecessarily smoothed her hair and her cashmere silk skirt. When the car stopped, Bambi reapplied her lipstick and waited for the driver to open the door.

"One more thing!" Max whispered urgently and annoyingly. "He's known for springing things on his subjects. Like the time he brought up Charlie Petzer's first wife with Pippy."

"Well, I don't have any skeletons in my closet, and neither does Peter," Bambi said as a matter of fact. There was absolutely no way STT could know about the heated arguments Peter and she had been having about the opera payment. He railed on about whatever it was that was happening at work. Bambi could have thrown Anna under the bus, but Bambi was secretly thrilled to have all those gift cards. Botox, fillers, and lasers forever!

"Of course not!" Max instantly agreed. The driver opened the door, but Max gently held Bambi back by her elbow. "Just, you know, if he surprises you, say something like, 'I'd so much prefer to talk about Josefina, her gifted daughter, and the extraordinary school we are trying to save.'"

"Right," Bambi tossed over her shoulder as she allowed the driver to help her out of the car. Couldn't Max understand the important thing was how she looked? Even if she did everything else right, if she failed to look like the toast of the town, there was no reason to even go. Her jacket was a feat of proportioning, making her taller, thinner, younger, more chic than ever before. It had taken six fittings to achieve this effect. The wide sleeves ended at just the right point—one-third of the way from her elbows to her wrists, which were encased in long custom gloves in a matching shade of gray. The strap buckle on her glossy gray Louboutin stacked heels glimmered with a tiny green faux gem to match her bracelet. Did Max think it was easy to look so world class?

A New York institution with a landscape of niche-famous regulars, Sable's was the place to see and be seen by anyone and everyone who mattered in publishing between the hours of noon and 2:00 p.m. Bambi thought of it as a royal court of old: each person's location in the room indicated their place in the hierarchy. Dead center, that publishing tycoon who counted all the boldface names of twentieth-century literature as friends. In the light by the window, a former model who'd married a millionaire she'd met under much whispered-about circumstances and now did interior design for sultans' and sheiks' New York pieds-à-terre. There, just by the door so he could jump to his feet and greet potential customers, the duke of a defunct European province with his own overblown jewelry line. Everyone was ensconced at their usual tables.

Because one knew exactly what to anticipate, Sable's felt like a safe space. There were always friends here. And often, photographers.

Bambi appeared in the dining room's entrance and paused, her bag held at her waist, turning just a smidge this way and that as if looking for STT, when of course she knew exactly where his table was. But the top of the stairs was a stage, and it was 12:47 p.m.—prime time. She gave a quiet wave to the tycoon and the model, snubbing the duke. Bambi didn't want any more of his baubles. A few other heads swiveled: the half-in-the-bag banker in his sixties; the envious, less well-preserved socialite; the wide-eyed magazine intern on a one-time lunch with her boss. Bambi basked in the attention for a two count. No photographers. Yet.

STT's spot was a prime table just left of center in the sunken dining room, his back to the wall radiating caricatures of the dining room's most famous inhabitants, with the seat best for seeing and being seen—after all, his was a powerful pen. He regularly wrote about his lunches at Sable's, always with a picture of him and his universally female guests.

The man himself, white haired and round faced, besuited with a pocket square, raised his manicured hand. His veneered smile said, *Tell me everything*. Mrs. Von Bizmark sashayed across the dining room, willing him to include a description of her grace and style at the very top of his article. He stood; they held hands and kissed each other's cheeks before sitting again and settling into lunch, which would follow the usual agenda.

Small talk with menus open—no more than thirty seconds. Drink orders. More small talk about the kids, vacation spots, country homes. Background. They ordered food, not to eat it but because it was required. Two chicken paillards. Bambi's anticipation grew—she herself would have to be a little extra today to dazzle this man. Internally, she began marshaling her charismatic resources: the interested expression, the insignificant intimacies, the casual flattery. Her smiles, at the ready. Her eyes, clear and focused. Her mind, sharp. As soon as their glasses were full of sparkling water, the bread basket safely deposited at their table, and the servicey part of the "lunch" over, the heart of the interview would start to beat.

"*So* tell me about this school you are saving? Max said it was for gifted and talented poor kids? Is that right?" STT quietly placed a digital tape recorder on the table between them and fixed Bambi with his most encouraging, expectant face.

"I know, isn't it wonderful? It came to my attention because one of our ladies at the apartment who's been with us for nearly twenty years . . . her daughter goes to the school."

"How fabulous!" STT purred. Bolstered, Mrs. Von Bizmark continued, dutifully dropping her talking points about an inspiring principal and talented student body. Their salads arrived. STT sipped his iced tea from a straw. Bambi dared one small bite of food, and as she chewed, he said, "So, tell me a little bit about your background . . ."

"In a nutshell, I grew up in the city. Sacred Heart. Wellesley. All that. Studied art history. Worked at Sotheby's. Met Peter at an auction, and it was love at first sight."

"Yessss," STT said, stirring his drink with the straw now. The ice cubes tinkled.

"Of course, he didn't have the sort of money we do now, but he just loved nineteenth-century Russian oils. Our Russian expert was out that day, so I had to run the auction. And right out of the gate, there's a bidding war between Peter and . . . well . . ." Bambi leaned in closer to STT. "Off the record, it was Michael Bloomberg." STT's eyebrows shot up, just as Bambi had intended. "Anyway, they blew through the reserve, through anything like an appropriate price, and they're going back and forth and back and forth. I didn't know what to think—it all felt like a strange dream. And as I'm watching this man do battle with one of New York's most famous self-made billionaires, I'm thinking more and more about how attractive he is. How his hair looks so touchable and his face so kind." Bambi gave STT her gee-I-love-my-husband smile. "And he wins! Peter wins! And afterward, he comes right up to me and says, 'I need you to know I don't have money like that yet, but I had to meet you.'"

"My, my!" STT exclaimed in such a halfhearted way Bambi had to briefly wonder: Had she told him this very same story before? "That's just great background. What else are you interested in?"

"The kids took up so much of my time for so long, but now I like to focus on cultural institutions. Those things make the city what it is, don't you think?"

"Absolutely! Have you always loved opera?"

"In fact, no," Mrs. Von Bizmark admitted, allowing herself to blush just a little. "It wasn't until I saw *Madame Butterfly* at La Scala that I really started to enjoy it. Before that"—she looked around and leaned in, as if telling her deepest darkest secret—"I generally fell asleep during the first act."

STT threw his head back at this, opening his mouth wide to guffaw, revealing his incisors. "And you're Jewish?" he asked, as if these topics were related. His eyes glinted at her. Saliva pooled around his tongue.

To her credit, and Dr. Westley's, Bambi did not immediately respond to his question in any way save a quick double blink. Max's words from only fifteen minutes prior rushed through her ears again: surprise! "Yessss . . . ," she said, mindlessly picking lettuce out of her molar with her tongue and constructing rationales for why she felt so taken aback. Of course Bambi was Jewish, and of course she knew exactly this about herself. But the way STT said it, as if confronting her. His eyes glinted: gotcha! And Bambi would not allow that to happen. She was smarter than that. Of course people knew she was Jewish, Bambi told herself! Which people exactly, she couldn't quite say.

"That's so *interesting*," STT said, prompting her to say more. "So Verhuvenvel is a Jewish name?"

"I suppose so!" she said brightly, although she had no idea. Her great-grandparents had gone through the Ellis Island surname mash-up, and there were several alternate spellings from the old country. Perhaps they had even nudged the immigration official toward a more austere-sounding Austrian name. They were sophisticated people for a couple of peasants, her grandmother used to say. And of course, Bambi understood perfectly well that there was nothing to be embarrassed about, not at all. Although she could not completely prevent herself from recalling how eagerly she greeted everyone with "Merry Christmas!" instead of "Happy holidays!" and her fondness for Lilly Pulitzer shifts, pearls, bland food, stationery . . . had she intended to spell out *WASP* for everyone all along?

Just then, a photographer appeared. "Do you mind?" STT asked Bambi as he slipped his arm over her shoulder. She tensed all the muscles in her face associated with smiling.

"So you DON'T practice?" STT pressed as soon as the camera moved on.

"What?"

"You know, the Jewish faith. The traditions. Shabbat and seders and the like."

"Not since my grandmother died when I was four," Bambi said, containing a spontaneous cringe, remembering how she detested all those rituals. She had believed herself to be divorced from her past. Peter Von Bizmark was such an Anglo-Saxon; it was like she could not avoid becoming one, too, by osmosis. He would be so very bothered by this sort of attention. It would not be news to him, but still, he absolutely loathed any sort of publicity. And things were already so unsettled with him being out of the house. And everything at work, whatever that was. *Sigh.*

Bambi felt the slightest whiff of dread about the *Park and Fifth* article. Though as a twenty-first-century New Yorker, she knew there was no reason that it should come as a surprise to her circle that she was Jewish, it nevertheless would. Particularly that bitch Pippy. Bambi wasn't even certain if all her own children knew she—and therefore, *they*—were Jewish.

"That's so interesting," STT said.

"Yes, she actually grew up in a neighborhood in the Bronx not too far from PS 342." This was wholly untrue but allowed her to segue to the one-sheeter that Max had so helpfully shoved into her hand. She pulled it out of her bag and said, "Let's talk about Josefina, her gifted daughter, and the extraordinary school we are trying to save. It's really special."

TEN

G enerally, when Mrs. Von Bizmark returned from an important lunch, she flew into the office to report how *fabulous* it had been. But after STT, she wandered in without a word, quietly sat at her desk, carefully placed her bag flat on her lap, and folded her gloved hands over it. While she still looked terrific—neither hair nor thread out of place—she seemed lost in less-than-fabulous thoughts. Julie jotted down a telephone message quietly in the background.

Anna dropped her pencil and looked up from the two-inch-thick binder of materials that had arrived from the DOE that morning. Even she had rarely seen forms so extensive, confusing, and poorly worded. Once more, she wondered if it had been a mistake to step out of bounds, but it was too late to take it back now. Besides, Ilana had been going to school in a tent for weeks, and while it was perfectly warm and lead-free, it was still not the same as A fully stocked classroom. Everything would need to come together if Ilana's school building stood a chance of reopening on time in the fall.

"How was your lunch?" Anna asked, when it appeared no reportage was forthcoming.

"Fabulous!" Mrs. Von Bizmark said brightly, but her smile erased itself instantly, her eyes focused in the middle distance.

"Would you like an espresso?" Anna offered. Mrs. Von Bizmark said nothing. Anna and Julie exchanged a glance. When the phone rang, Anna rushed to answer it and escape the awkward silence.

"They've arrived. They're here!"

Anna's eardrum trembled as Richard shouted into the phone. At this point, Anna could hardly remember who was supposed to receive what, when. "Who?" Anna asked.

"The Mercurion paintings! They're in the building!" Richard must have been delirious with happiness at having actually received the art. As far as Anna knew, no one had heard from Mercurion in weeks. She breathed a sigh of relief for Ilana—maybe this would work out after all. "We'll open everything tomorrow," he panted. Max had planned the unveiling of Mercurion's donated art as the kickoff press event for the whole shebang: an official "uncrating" on the opera mainstage, with Richard, Opal, and Mrs. Von Bizmark wielding ceremonial gold crowbars.

At her desk, Mrs. Von Bizmark remained transfixed by nothing. "Who was that, dear?" she asked listlessly.

"They're here!" Anna made an effort at lightheartedness by imitating Richard. Julie laughed good-naturedly, but Mrs. Von Bizmark appeared annoyed.

"What, dear?" she said tersely.

"The Mercurion paintings! The uncrating is tomorrow." When this earned no response, Anna added, "You know, the big press event?"

"Fabulous," Mrs. Von Bizmark said vaguely. She stood and floated out of the office like a ghost.

"I guess lunch didn't go so well," Julie surmised.

"But how could that be?" Anna wondered aloud. STT was known for puff pieces at best and gossip at worst. Could he have gotten wind that the marriage was a bit touchy? From whom?

Anna dreaded having to talk about her own relationship that evening over a much-postponed dinner with Lindsay. Things had been tense since the spat, and she knew her sister would try to turn it around on her. Anna didn't want to talk about her exhibition or her "next project," whenever that might congeal. Or work, which always sounded ridiculous coming out of Anna's mouth. Lindsay was just so full of questions, like always, the words tumbling out of her mouth as she slid into a booth at Anna's favorite neighborhood Italian place.

"Hi, hi, how are you?!" Lindsay said as she looked for somewhere to put her large tote, which Anna couldn't help but notice was a Louis Vuitton as she finally settled it in the space between them. "Sorry I'm late. Traffic over the bridge was outrageous. My panel went long, and it was at the Harvard Club, so the wait for an Uber was like . . . forever." Anna was both impressed and annoyed. "Actually, the panel was on some really interesting intellectual property issues in commercial real estate." Anna realized that she was already becoming more annoyed than impressed. "But enough about me!" Lindsay said. "Your life is so much more interesting. What's happening at work?"

Whenever anyone asked Anna about her job, she sorted through a series of possible responses, looking for the one that would make her job sound the least ridiculous.

One of my big challenges will be to re-create a wall-size television screen and a huge custom Italian sectional in this very particular shade of . . . no.

This major disaster happened where the invitations to the Opera Ball luncheon were all returned for inadequate . . . nope.

Have you ever seen what $100,000 in American Express gift cards looks like . . . eh. *No.*

"We finally got all that art from Felix Mercurion I told you about for the auction to save Ilana's school. Be sure to watch the news tomorrow."

"Ooooh," Lindsay said. "I went to an opening there last year. Weird stuff and very expensive. Isn't he shady? Like financially?" But Anna only shrugged and sighed, thinking of the money Mercurion's artists made.

The residencies and guest professorships they enjoyed. The speeches and interviews they gave. "How's Adrian's app?"

Anna winced, realizing that she had been avoiding Lindsay in order to postpone this bit of news. She realized that in getting this "real job," Adrian was moving closer in the constellations of her life to Lindsay, the suit. "Actually, he got a job at LVMH."

"Wow!" Lindsay said and then grabbed Anna's arm with glee, pointing at her bag as if to signify that she was already on the team. "That is amazing. Tell me everything! I know people in the finance department. I mean, I guess that doesn't really matter. So what is he doing? Designing, right?"

"Not, like, evening gowns. More like shopping bags and websites." Lindsay's eyes were practically popping out of her head with zeal for Adrian's "real job."

Anna asked for the check as soon as their pasta plates were removed. Lindsay cleared her throat falsely and appeared suddenly . . . hesitant? Nervous?

"A, I wanted you to be the first to know. I mean, other than me. And Jack." Bringing up her husband could mean only one thing. Anna suddenly noticed a new lushness in Lindsay's face and body. How she shockingly wore a—could it be?—maternal smile as her eyes fell to her belly.

"Oh my God," Anna said. Lindsay smiled with tears in her eyes, leaned across the banquette, and grabbed Anna, forcibly embracing her, the large leather tote awkwardly squished between them. When she let go twenty seconds later, both women had wet cheeks. "Lindsay!" Anna said. It felt like she was experiencing every emotion at the same time. "I . . . you . . . congratulations!" She finally got it out.

As Lindsay told her the whole story, from conception through the first suspicions, the home pregnancy test and so on up to that day, which was somewhere in her eighth week, Anna could think only of herself. Of all the feelings seemingly crowded into her rib cage, the one she felt most clearly was a sense of mourning or loss. Like here, again, was a thing she should have had already and maybe never would. She said the words, "Lindsay, I'm so happy for you."

Anna always insisted on splitting the check with her sister, but that night, she didn't say anything when Lindsay put down her American Express Gold Card. *Let her be the grown-up,* Anna thought to herself.

Anna heard the characteristic trill of Mrs. Von Bizmark buzzing her at her desk through the closed foyer doors as she dug for her keys in the bottom of her bag. It was only 10:07 a.m., a little early for the Mrs. to be working the phones. As she slid her key into the lock, she remembered—the glam team had arrived at eight for the uncrating. She ran full sprint, getting there just the split second before it went to voice mail.

"I couldn't wait to tell you!" Mrs. Von Bizmark boomed in an over-caffeinated rush above the sound of two hair dryers. "Miguel's fired!" she said triumphantly.

"How?" Anna panted, catching her breath.

"*I* found him—" Mrs. Von Bizmark searched for the word—"*with* one of Mrs. Forstbacher's nurses in the basement late last night."

"No!" The thought of anyone having sexual intercourse with Miguel in that claustrophobic, windowless lounge was too disgusting to contemplate. But if that was what it took to get rid of the guy, so be it.

"I was thinking . . . ," Mrs. Von Bizmark continued an hour later, standing at the office door fastening a canary diamond to her ear as if the conversation had not paused at all, "the board should hire a Scandinavian superintendent."

"Huh," Anna said.

"What do you think?" Mrs. Von Bizmark said of her outfit. She wore a plain navy crepe dress that would photograph well and a pair of scene-stealing tangerine suede heels with matching nails. "It's the new Gabriela Hearst," she said of the dress. Over her arm, a mink vest.

"Fabulous!" Anna said, and she gave her a thumbs-up.

As Mrs. Von Bizmark walked down the hallway, she called back, "The Scandinavians are the best with their hands."

"I'll take your word for it," Anna said, and although they couldn't see one another, both women blushed.

As soon as Mrs. Von Bizmark was out the door, Anna buzzed the lobby. "Alfie, it's Anna on eight. So? What happened to Miguel?"

"Word travels fast." Alfie spoke quietly, muffling his voice with his hand.

"What? How?"

"Well, you know, Mrs. Forstbacher is just back from the hospital . . . hold on." Alfie put the intercom down to open the front door. "Hello, Mr. Samuelson," he said in his official doorman voice, and then he returned to covert mode. "And she has round-the-clock care. You know, twenty-four-seven nursing? And the second nurse who shows up, well, she's Dominican like Miguel, and he just starts in right away. Hold on . . ." He opened the door for the FedEx guy. "Hey, John, just right here. Thank you! Anyway, I guess he sealed the deal, because your Mrs. KGB found them in the basement on one of her late-night storage-room visits midthrust, if you know what I mean." Alfie started to laugh, which devolved into a dry smoker's cough. "Excuse me," he rasped.

"Who fired him?"

"Renee. Forstbacher got the nurse."

"Who's up for the job?"

"Some Polish guy."

"Mrs. Von Bizmark said Scandinavian."

"Maybe. What do I know?"

Anna enjoyed a nibble of her breakfast sandwich and cappuccino. She had not had a quiet moment at her desk yet that year. Her mind returned to Lindsay, her little sister. The one she used to tease and tickle and wrestle with and ditch to go out with boys. Her little sister was married and would be a mother, and Anna remained a struggling artist with a day job no one understood or respected. She texted Adrian:

Pizza and Netflix tonight?

The tranquility broke when two phone lines started to ring simultaneously.

"Kissy Von Bizmark's office, this is Anna." The third line lit up.

"Anna, it's Max, big problem. Turn on Channel Four." Anna heard a commotion or something on the television in the background at Max's office. All the lines in the Von Bizmark office and residence were suddenly alight.

"OK, my phone is on fire . . ."

"Anna, do! Not! Answer! The phone!" Max could get militaristic in a media emergency. "Just turn on Channel Four."

"You're scaring me, Max."

"Television. Now."

Anna flicked on the local news. Two uniformed cops were firmly escorting Felix Mercurion, in a sharp suit, his face a careful mask of denial, out of his own gallery in handcuffs as a few lithe employees watched, horrified. A sheet of straight brown hair quivered as a young woman wept into her friend's silky shoulder in front of the Mercurion Gallery. The anchor voiced over the footage: ". . . estimate somewhere between one hundred and two hundred million dollars and are confiscating all of Mercurion's holdings as collateral."

Cut to outside the opera house, where a large white van's rear end was opened to the stage door. Men in black windbreakers emblazoned with the white letters *IRS* were moving the large art crates into the vehicle. "We are live at the New York Opera, where the Internal Revenue Service is in the process of seizing a dozen of Mercurion's masterpieces at this very moment. Shelly, what can you tell us about what's happening over there?"

A zippy cub reporter all too happy to score a big story launched with zeal. "The IRS asserts Mercurion donated these pieces to the opera in an effort to avoid taxation and subsequently claim bankruptcy. This plan would have allowed Mercurion to maintain control of his Swiss bank accounts as well as avoid criminal prosecution. The IRS is now seizing these pieces, which they will sell to cover Mercurion's debts. And from what my sources tell me, it's going to be quite an auction."

Behind the reporter, Anna saw Mrs. Von Bizmark in her tidy fur vest and killer shoes looking on in bewilderment as the crates she had gone there to ceremoniously open filled the back of the IRS van. STT stood next to her, jaw hanging, camera up, photographing it all. At one point, he turned the lens on her, and she held up her hand. A terse exchange. Anna returned to the phone but continued to watch.

"Max? Max, are you there?"

"Can you get her out of there? There's no reason for her to be there right now," Max said, realizing. "Is that STT next to her? Oh, Jesus." The Von Bizmark phone lines rang incessantly, the little buttons all blinking like Christmas lights.

Anna thought of Ilana. How would Anna explain this to her? This devastated their chances of saving the school. Even if Anna had done her best to clarify that the auction was not completely certain, in her heart of hearts she knew that she had let Josefina think that the whole thing was basically taken care of. She had even let herself enjoy a sense of real usefulness and fulfillment. What would she tell Josefina? Or Principal Sellers, who had already had just about enough of the upper-upper crust and their problems? All they had now was Sellers's plea for donations at the lunch.

"OK, she's getting in a cab," Max said in Anna's ear, more concerned with how this would all play out in the media than for Ilana, whom he had never laid eyes on. "Just don't talk to anyone until we've decided on a plan going forward. I'll be there in an hour."

Anna watched the phones in a stupor. Everyone called: Bloom, Pippy Petzer, Julie, Florence . . . the news continued. The phone rang. All three computers dinged and buzzed and trilled, various sorts of messages piling up. The newswoman talked about how the proceeds from the art sale were supposed to go to a public school that would surely close. Anna just sat quietly, all the noise and lights swirling together into a whirlpool of dots. It almost felt good to disconnect completely like this, to give up for the moment and just exist. Why hadn't she tried this before? Dimly, Anna wondered if she was about to pass out.

"Anna?" Josefina stood in the office with Alicia. How long had they been there, witnessing both the news and Anna herself, staring into space while the office exploded around her? When she stood unsteadily and approached Josefina, it was enough to confirm the worst. "Problem?" Josefina asked, stuck on a tenacious smudge of hope, which Anna would now have to erase.

"Yes, Josefina, there's a big problem. The man with the art, he's a criminal. The government owns the art now." Josefina's eyes welled up, her big cheeks quaking. "I don't know what will happen. I'm so sorry." Josefina choked back the tears. Alicia looked on, face strained.

"I know you tried," Josefina said. Alicia put her arm over Josefina's shoulders, and they retreated to the laundry room.

Anna shook herself out of her stupor by pacing three steps back and forth. She gnawed on a cuticle until it started to bleed. What could be done? What could be done? The phone finally quieted down, ringing only every few minutes. Why had she volunteered this idea? This would never have happened if she'd just stayed in her place. Florence's favorite adage haunted her: *Never do more or less than what you're asked.* This was why.

The foyer doors opened and closed. Slow heels on the hardwood. Mrs. Von Bizmark walked past the office doors to the laundry room, and Anna followed to observe from afar.

"I'm sorry, Josefina," she said. "But we're going to do what we can."

"Oh, Mrs. Von Bizmark!" Josefina responded, her face shining with tears. Mrs. Von Bizmark squeezed her thick shoulder and returned to the office. She looked beleaguered, practically collapsing into her desk chair without taking off her vest.

"What did Max say?" Mrs. Von Bizmark asked without preamble.

"He said to not answer the phone until we have a plan. He'll be here in about forty-five minutes."

"Perfect. I called a meeting with everyone at one."

Who was "everyone"? Anna's eyes went straight to the clock: 12:13 p.m.

Max was the first to arrive, impeccably dressed but more casual than usual in a gray suit with no tie and a simple white shirt. No accessories save a small leather case that could hold a notebook or a tiny handgun. Even his generally flawless shiny waves of hair looked rumpled with anxiety.

"Max, you look . . ."

"I know. Butch. This is my emergency suit. So listen." He took Anna's elbow to keep her in the foyer for a quick confab. He lowered his voice. "Does the Mrs. really not know Mercurion, or is that bullshit?"

"She really doesn't know him."

"Terrific." He strode down the hallway, calling, "Kissy!"

"Max!" They double kissed and sat down in the dining room, which Cristina had outfitted for their midday meeting with a selection of various sandwiches—avocado, smoked salmon, turkey club—and fresh juices on ice from E.A.T. on Madison, the world's most overpriced deli. No one touched any of it.

"The key thing is that *we* say nothing about Felix Mercurion. He was a friend of the opera's," Max says. "Just say, 'I don't really know him.'"

"I don't!" Mrs. Von Bizmark parroted.

"Everyone will want to gossip with you about it, but the fact as I understand it is that you truly have no inside information."

"I just knew he was a bad idea!" Mrs. Von Bizmark said.

"Still, the less you say about it, the better. Let the opera people address it. Because you have a *Vogue* spread to think about!" Mrs. Von Bizmark's mouth fell open. "When this news broke, my people there finally called me back. They want to cover the luncheon!"

"No!" Mrs. Von Bizmark exclaimed.

"I know . . . ," Max mused. "It's almost worth it."

"The school, though," Anna chastised. "Did you talk to the principal yet?"

"They're sending Vivienne Lanuit to cover it from Paris," Max said, not done basking in his *Vogue* moment. "Apparently she knows Opal or something." Mrs. Von Bizmark actually clapped her hands like a little girl. She was smiling so hard Anna worried she would displace some of the perfectly placed filler in her cheeks.

"Max, what about Sellers. Did you talk to her about her 'ask' at the luncheon?"

Max's words slowed to a crawl. "Yes . . . well, it's a tough sell to this crowd." He was right. Children like Chester, Vera, and Peony Von Bizmark would not only never attend public school; they quite possibly would never know anyone who had. "We're working on it."

The stress had already taken a visible toll on "the opera people," as Max called them. Richard walked as if he carried a large basket of coal on his back. His darkly encircled eyes suggested he had gotten word of the IRS seizure much earlier in the day. Opal, in a green-gray Issey Miyake dress, was not downtrodden as much as deeply annoyed, a feeling she projected in her pinched expression and constant glancing at her enormous titanium watch.

Bloom and Julie arrived on the same elevator. Julie wore a vintage Italian suit made of a psychedelic paisley with three-quarter sleeves and broad bell-bottoms over beige suede platforms. She had on large square ivory shades, and her hair flowed all around her shoulders in a black wave. Bloom gave her the full once-over.

"What do you think?" Julie asked.

"Better," Bloom said.

Everyone was sitting at the table by 1:02 p.m., the food still and forever untouched. Each held various pens at the ready, save for Opal, who rested her chin on her hand and sighed every thirty seconds.

Max, asserting dominance in his emergency suit, jumped right in. "I think it's critical that we come up with a plan B before talking to the press. That way, we can say how sorry we are about Mercurion, but look over here . . . shiny object!" Having missed the last big meeting, he was not about to sit quietly through this one.

"Yes, let's just move on!" Richard nudged.

"How many pieces are we talking about?" Max asked.

"Three masterpieces and ten smaller works," Richard said.

"Only three masterpieces?" Bloom snorted sarcastically.

"Who do you know with a huge art collection?" Max, undeterred, asked Mrs. Von Bizmark.

"The Petzers, the Felidias, the Stahls, the Seamanses . . ."

"Which Seamans?"

"Isabelle and Fred."

"Would each contribute one masterpiece to save a public school?" Max prodded.

Mrs. Von Bizmark didn't have to give it too much thought. "Probably not. They think of themselves as patrons, philanthropists. Arts and diseases, you know. Not public servants."

"What about artists?" Max asked Opal.

"Yes?" she said, like a snotty teenager pretending not to understand.

Max, accustomed to divas, answered her as sweetly as possible. "Do you know any artists who produce work of value?"

"Monetary or creative value?" she said.

"Jesus Christ, Opal." Richard slammed his palm on the table, a pot boiling over. Everyone at the table jumped a little, a spotlight suddenly on the tension between them. She just stared at him while his eyes stayed carefully forward, bulging with fury. His face, fleshy and expressive to begin with, grew more and more inflamed while Opal only cooled down, relaxing into some sort of next-level uber-disinterested resting bitch face. And maybe, it occurred to Anna, it was not the easiest thing to work with the world's foremost style icon. "Do you know any artists we can sell or not?" Spittle flew from Richard's mouth.

"Well, Richard, you and I have creative differences about the importance of monetary value. Don't we? Selling and money. They aren't everything to me." She pitched her braid, thick with fresh extensions the color of peacock wings, over her shoulder defiantly.

"Yes, but we're talking about saving a school here!" Max cajoled, trying to defuse the electric air by becoming a peppy cheerleader. "I just saw a picture of you with Jonah Okanabe. At his house. In last month's *Vanity Fair*." Miranda Chung had discovered this artist's iconic metalwork in a Seattle suburb and had brought him to New York twenty years ago, jump-starting both of their careers. Anna sighed.

"Mmmm," Opal said.

"And aren't you Scarlet Koons's godmother?" Max asked. "And I know I saw you at Cindy Sherman's birthday party." These names swam around Anna's head. She'd struggled to sell one canvas from her show just to cover her costs, and these people were household names who could raise hundreds of thousands of dollars with a single piece.

"Why don't *you* ask Cindy, then, for an art donation?" Opal said to Max.

"I think it would mean so much more coming from you, Opal."

"Do you?" She was like ice.

"Opal . . . ," Richard growled. Were they really arguing about who would ask which world-famous artist to toss them some scraps? Even a Jeff Koons sketch would fetch hundreds of thousands. Like the lost Magritte. Art and money had such a strange marriage, Anna found herself musing, as disenchanted as Opal with this strategy session. A school was at stake, and all they needed to save it was one supersize metallic hot-pink balloon bunny.

"I have an idea," Julie said.

"What is it?" Richard glowered at Opal, his eyes threatening to pop out of his skull.

"How about an up-and-coming artist?" Julie suggested.

"Okaaaay, okaaay," Max said encouragingly, but Anna knew better. *Up-and-coming* was just a buzzword for "unknown but still overpriced." Definitely with a gallery or an agent. A bunch of sales under their belt but not enough to justify the five-figure price tag for some two-toned abstraction of a lower intestine. Anna saw how bitter she had become, how this half-assed attempt at "doing art" was really the worst of all worlds. Her big break might never happen, and it was time to accept that.

"Anna?" Mrs. Von Bizmark said, and she realized that everyone at the table was staring at her. Julie looked concerned. Her private self-reflection trip had taken her completely out of the meeting.

"I'm sorry?" she squeaked.

"I was just saying . . ." Julie emitted one of her odd laughs. "*You're* an artist." Anna's heart doubled its pace.

"I think it's a fabulous idea!" Bloom chimed in, her eyes narrowed. What was Bloom trying to do? Set her up for failure?

"I was at your show!" Mrs. Von Bizmark said, trying to remember the works.

Anna straightened up in her chair. *Be cool,* she told herself. "Yes, you were."

"It's not critical that we raise that much money through the auction," Richard said, but of course those were the funds designated for the school.

"Why don't you show everyone your website," Bloom urged foxily.

"Please!" Mrs. Von Bizmark said.

All eyes watched as Anna silently prayed to God: not just that everyone would like her stuff but that she could get the digital screen to work. *Be cool,* she told herself. *Deep breaths.* Almost immediately, the middle of her back erupted into sweat. She swiped a tendril of hair out of her face as she lowered the display screen by remote control. Anna poked away at her phone, searching for the right app, the Bluetooth icon, the web browser in some sort of altered state of intuitive clicking. It felt like twenty minutes passed in those thirty seconds.

And then there it was, the website Adrian had made her, her pieces filling up the screen.

"And she just had a show downtown. Greene Street," Julie added, smiling ear to ear. Richard looked completely unconvinced, while Mrs. Von Bizmark's expression stayed carefully neutral. Opal may have fallen into a coma with her eyes open. Bloom wasn't even looking at the screen; she was marking the reactions along with Anna.

Anna navigated to one of her favorites: an enormous bright canvas of spring-hued oils forming a geometric pattern around thick, opaque cellophane shapes. Various forms danced across and off the piece, large and small circles spilling over the edge of the frame; it was vibrant, fun, cheerful, strong. A few strands of Adrian's beard nestled under an overlay of blue orbs, the piece's secret. It was inspired by their first trip abroad together to Morocco. Mrs. Von Bizmark's head tilted, her lips pursing as if to say, *OK . . . I can work with this.* Richard did not appear totally repulsed.

"Plenty to choose from," Richard said. "What do you think, Kissy?" Anna held her breath. The nonsounds of the room—the hum of the electricity, the breeze at the distant window open in the office, the barely audible *shush-shush* of one of the dishwashers in the kitchen—all ascended in volume until they were screaming in Anna's ears.

"I like it," Mrs. Von Bizmark said. "Bold. Moving. Great for the stage." Julie looked like she could explode with happiness. Anna knew she should feel it, too, but instead there was already anxiety. She knew they needed three masterpieces, but besides this and one she had hung at the entry of her exhibition, the rest of Anna's stuff was smaller. She would have to create another huge piece in no time, and, crucially, all three would have to work together.

"Oh, goody," Max said. "The story writes itself. The opera stage will feature an up-and-coming artist who was the initial champion of the public school we're saving." Bloom smiled at Anna, nostrils flared, and Anna couldn't help but smile back. She tipped her head in silent gratitude. "That's the message when we leave here. I imagine you've all received a few calls?"

"A few hundred," Anna said, as the phone started ringing again.

"If anyone tries to back out of the lunch because of some, I don't know, holier-than-thou attitude, just remind them that this is about schools. Kids. Tiny creative geniuses. And now a hot young artist is stepping up to provide art for free."

"I don't know about 'hot,'" Anna said. "Or 'young.'" In her head, she knew this was a good development. On her shoulders, though, she felt the weight of an entire school. Like, the whole building. What if no one bid on any of her pieces? She put enough pressure on herself without the fates of hundreds of "tiny creative geniuses" depending on her.

"There's also an opera, you know. You can talk about the opera," Richard whined. Opal sighed dramatically and stood to go. Everyone filed out in silence, leaving Julie and Anna alone.

"Are you excited?!" Julie squealed.

"Yes, I just . . . I'm one piece short," Anna said. "And I still have to finish all that paperwork for the DOE so this will even work."

"Why do you always focus on the negative?"

"You're right. I should get to the studio tonight. I was supposed to have dinner with Adrian. We haven't had a meal together all week."

"Suck it up and do both. You're not that old. I'll make some espresso." While Julie was in the kitchen, the phone rang.

"Kissy Von Bizmark's—"

"You won't believe this."

"Phil, today, really, you can't shock me."

"I got the horses."

"What?"

"The horses Bloom wanted for the front lawn. For the lunch! I got Akha . . ." He read from a scrap of paper. "Akhal-Tekes. She thinks it might be, like, I don't know, ambience or something. And the heating is installed and almost perfect. If anything, it's too hot in there now!" That Anna was completely out of the loop on both these topics would have ordinarily alarmed her. But between the Mercurion news and the piles of helicopter contracts, flight patterns, and passenger manifests she'd had to navigate, there just wasn't time to stay on top of every last detail.

"That's great, Phil."

"Well, don't get all excited."

"You are the only person who hasn't heard the news."

"News? This is the beach, Anna. The beach, OK! I'm not like you kids, on my phone all the time. And you know I've been up to my ears with this installation . . ." Anna let Phil drone on, her mind wandering to the auction and what it might mean for her future. "A thousand degrees."

"Felix Mercurion was arrested for tax evasion today."

"Who's Felix Mercurion?"

"Aw geez, Phil. Great job on the Aka-Tatas. I gotta run."

They spent the rest of the day containing the mess, returning phone calls, talking people into attending the luncheon. Pippy Petzer in particular had to be reassured that STT was still coming, in *her* helicopter. The only person Anna could not convince was Martha Miller, who herself had been famously jailed for tax evasion. "I simply can't be affiliated in any way with that," Martha Miller had said. "I'm sure Kissy will understand." The luncheon number hovered over a hundred anyway.

The art store was right by their apartment, so Anna figured she could pick up some supplies she knew she needed at the studio, go home, change, and have a quick celebratory dinner with Adrian. They really needed one. Lately, everything seemed like such a grind. They just hadn't been in sync. But now that she had the auction to look forward to, she felt much more excited to see her man than she had in weeks. Maybe longer.

Adrian sat at the kitchen counter, working on his laptop. He barely looked up when Anna walked in. "Hey," he said. "Juuuuust finishing up one thing. And there." He closed his computer and finally rested his eyes on her. "Hi." He smiled and turned to her on the stool. He was kind of adorable, Anna reminded herself. "What's the latest?" he asked.

"My work is going up on the opera stage! For the gala!" Anna blurted.

"That's great," he said. Did she imagine his eyes darting longingly at his computer? To do more work?

"And they'll be auctioned. To help keep Ilana's school open."

"Wow, cool," he said with more oomph. But there was something decidedly lackluster in his responses.

Anna stepped into the space between his legs and put her arms on his shoulders, her wrists atop one another behind his head. He reflexively put his hands on her hips, and she said, coquettishly, she hoped, "So I was thinking . . . maybe we should start . . ." Right out of the gate, she had no idea what she was saying. She wanted him to warm to her again, to come closer and never leave. She realized with some alarm how long it had been since they had been this close. "I don't know . . . ," she stammered. "Taking the next steps."

"Wait a sec, wait a sec . . ." Adrian gently moved her away from him. He stood up and stepped as far from her as their closet-size kitchen would allow. "Let me see if I understand what's happening here. Because your art is coming together . . . because you got this break, you're now 'ready'?" He did air quotes with his fingers, even though he knew she hated it. Or maybe, it occurred to Anna, he did it *because* she hated it.

In fact, Adrian seemed a little bit . . . mad at her? "Ready!" He laughed. "To do *what*, even?"

"I . . ." He waited for her to finish the sentence, but her mouth opened and closed without issuing any further words.

"Anna, have you noticed anything about me lately? Anything different? Something new, perhaps?"

"Well, yes, I mean, your new job has occupied so much of your time. You couldn't help hang my pieces, and you were late—"

"That's right!" he snapped, interrupting. She realized suddenly how angry he was, had been for a while. Florets of rage bloomed in his cheeks, and he stood back in the kitchen with his arms held away from his body, a protective cage around himself. Anna always forgot how long it took Adrian to boil over until it was too late. "I have a new job!" He said this like it was news. "A whole new career, really! And you have asked me basically nothing about it. Except of course to get all my new friends to your exhibition."

Anna stood with her mouth slightly open, feeling as if she were at the center of the hurricane, a quiet moment before Adrian continued, when she could see clearly for one second that he was right. And for that small second she felt so, so, so bad.

Adrian continued when she failed to have a response. "The thing is, Anna, it's always about"—he dragged his hand through the air as if unfurling a banner—"'your art.' But you know, I'm here, too, and these last two weeks it's just felt like I am nothing to you, and it's all about you, you, you. I want to be with someone who isn't going to blow up our relationship over some silly party."

And into that one word—*silly*—Anna poured all her shame and guilt and disappointment in herself and forged it into rage. She breathed in all the rancor she could find in that single word. "Silly . . ." Anna said it like she was blowing on a fire. "Silly, huh?"

"Look, I didn't mean your art is silly, but I can't wait around for you to make it when it just might not happen."

Aha! Anna thought. *Here it is!* Proof that Adrian did not have faith in her. Anna's chest rose and fell in great rapid breaths. She felt a little dizzy—probably hyperventilating. Blindly, she grabbed a bag and started throwing clothes into it. Anna felt very strongly that she wanted to *flee leave get out go.*

"What are you doing?" Adrian asked.

"You're supposed to believe in me," Anna panted, knowing that soon she would disintegrate.

"But do *you* believe in *us?* I'm starting to wonder if I ever came first." The way he spoke in the past tense sent Anna further into shock. She picked up a hoodie off the floor, and a glue trap came with it. Instead of throwing it away, she folded it in half and stuffed it in her bag: a future piece where she would process and transmit the confusion encased in that moment.

But for now, all she could think about was the studio, where she could start to get her feelings out with paint on canvas. Anna knew all too well how to channel everything around her into creative output. If she could just get to her easel and have a brush in her hand, she'd be OK. She just needed to remind herself who she was again.

ELEVEN

February 10

Over the next two weeks Anna wondered if she had assassinated the best relationship she'd ever had for a nebulous and ultimately self-involved reason in the late afternoon of her reproductive life. There were even stretches where she could not remember what it was, exactly, they had fought about. Still, she remained convinced that if she was the first to cave in or call or head home with her tail between her legs, it would mean on some irrational metaphysical level that her art was no longer central but somehow had been shunted to the side.

And this was the opposite of her lived experience. Dutifully, Anna went to her studio every night for at least a few hours of solid work. She fell back in love with her shared workspace, where each artist rented a ten-foot-square plot on a giant, paint-splattered former factory floor. There was almost always another person there, scratching away at an etching or swiping bright watercolors onto thick paper. And just being around that energy made it easier to conceive of something new.

For her final large work, Anna had started on a purely geometric shapescape inspired by the glue trap, which she had carefully shredded already. But she'd trashed that a few days in. It was as incoherent as her understanding of what had happened between Adrian and her. Then she considered the Magritte pulp, taking it out of its little plastic box, a hardened dime-size mound, like papier-mâché. But it conjured nothing in particular. The sketch might have been a valuable possession, and yet no one would really care about it in the end.

Finally, she turned to a few dove-colored cashmere strands taken from a thick Hermès coat Mrs. Von Bizmark had given her offhandedly one afternoon, saying, "It's just not working for me." She had purchased the piece only three weeks prior for $27,320. The price tag still dangled from the sleeve. Anna had kept the extra threads encased in a tiny brown-and-gold Hermès envelope in the pocket and sold the thing on eBay. When she thought about the Von Bizmarks' careless generosity and her position in its direct flow, it generated a confused feeling of privilege and servitude. The piece would comprise a dysfunctional marriage of two worlds: a traditional, romantic, floral still life in oil, with a stark modernist overlay she still had not quite figured out. Once she had committed to this plan, the work poured out of her.

As the opera approached, she worked more and more intently, sometimes staying up until two or three in the morning tweaking a single detail. For that time, she was free of concern, doing exactly what she had always wanted to do, deeply in the flow of creating a piece of art with a real purpose in mind. Everything seemed manageable when she was engrossed in the canvas. She was an artist, goddamn it, and screw Adrian for suggesting it could or should ever be otherwise.

When she left the studio, the creeping anxiety icicles resumed their prodding. After the relative comfort of her workspace, the empty subway in the middle of the night headed back to Julie's miniscule apartment in Queens felt like an exercise in dissociation. Like, wait, *who* was she exactly? And *where* was she going?

Thank God Anna had Julie, but the problem with Julie was her cats, to which Anna was allergic. After that first night when she'd passed out at the studio, Anna had been staying on Julie's couch with her two felines, which meant she hadn't slept or breathed much in about twelve days. She felt less and less clearheaded outside of the studio.

At work, Anna finished up and submitted the DOE paperwork. Instead of feeling relieved to have at least accomplished this first step, she obsessed about the inevitable shortfall of cash at the opera art auction. It had been reported that Mercurion's plan had been to gift the opera his most valuable pieces, including a Cezanne and Rothko. The idea that Anna's work would somehow stand in for these treasures squeezed the air out of her lungs. The school needed $1.3 million. Any one of Mercurion's canvases would have made at least ten times that. Anna would be lucky to make ten thousand.

When Ilana stopped by after school one day, Anna tried to explain it to her. "Look, I'm doing my best, but I don't know if we can really expect —"

"Let me see," Ilana interrupted her.

"See what?"

"What you have."

Anna handed over her phone with a picture of the work in progress. The floral background was almost done, a traditional rendering of roses in musty peach and celadon that managed to read as both vintage and surreal. She had placed a few ovals made out of thin plastic sheeting over the canvas to get a feel for it.

"I'm not worried," Ilana said and winked. "We'll be out of those tents in no time."

This vote of confidence from a preteen made it possible for Anna to quiet her auction performance anxiety and endure the crescendo of various activities leading up to the luncheon.

After the Mercurion scandal, word of the Opera Ball spread far beyond the island of Manhattan. A broader swath turned their eyes toward the occasion and the Von Bizmarks, a buzz reflected in many interview requests and even an occasional paparazzo parked outside the more high-profile restaurants Mrs. Von Bizmark frequented. She had made the society pages of the *New York Times* twice in one week.

All this attention was like sunlight to Mrs. Von Bizmark, who preened at every ladies' luncheon, trunk show, and charity gala, taking calls from journalists at increasingly prestigious publications on her cell phone while en route in the car. She worked out every day and visited Dr. Westley constantly, keeping Anna in a flurry of scheduling snafus and emails.

Mr. Von Bizmark, on the other hand, felt all this attention was rather gauche and shrank from view at his VBO apartment at the Peninsula. His reticence only underlined the fact of their separate residences, a detail that was becoming harder to conceal. Peppered amid everything else, Alicia reported hearing Mrs. Von Bizmark in the upstairs office bickering endlessly with Mr. Von Bizmark whenever she had three minutes' time. He had at least agreed to dress for the evenings at home so he could, ostensibly, see Peony but, more imperatively, walk out onto Park Avenue (where a photographer could be lurking behind any number of impeccably manicured shrubs) arm in arm with his wife, smiling for all the world to see.

Anna traveled through her days like a sleepwalker, conducting business by muscle memory. Each hour blended into the next, interrupted only by creative output and the briefest islands of unconsciousness, nights punctuated by violent sneezes and eruptions of hives. Anna found herself standing on a patch of tarmac over the East River shuffling unemployed rich ladies from a heliport out to a waiting chopper. Two more zoomed East to the beach, and another trio held over the river, waiting their turn.

Dazed and depressed, Anna wondered who the architect of her life was. Instead of making choices and taking action, it was like she was watching a movie about herself; here in her hands, a short stack of waivers embossed on card stock to make them look less like the legal documents they actually were. Julie, running past her, dark hair streaming from a tense face damp with sweat, in a long tiered pink chiffon dress with two embroidered parrots on the back. Anna, standing for the moment, in her only pair of high heels and a Von Bizmark hand-me-down Etro silk cocktail dress she had never worn before, the wind blowing little artful wisps of material all around her. Both had been lent fur shrugs. Hair and nails done this morning by the "last-minute" salon team as a "treat" from Mrs. Von Bizmark, who had sensed, even from their brief phone call at dawn from the Castle, that things were still "not quite right" with Anna.

"Are you *OK*, dear?" Mrs. Von Bizmark had asked. And by *OK* she meant: Was Anna emotionally and physically well enough to carry out the tasks of the day to perfection? Was she feeling only positive things and thinking only beneficent thoughts about Mrs. Von Bizmark? And was she appropriately dressed?

"Absolutely!" Anna had said. "It's just, you know, a lot. And it's only five a.m. I'll be fine in an hour." *You are a robot. You are a machine,* she'd told herself.

Anna's most crucial remaining responsibility was to ensure Mrs. Von Bizmark would not be financially responsible for the watery deaths of any of her dear friends. Anna had handed each guest a numbered waiver to sign in the heliport while they sipped champagne. Avi, ever vigilant, had also installed a tiny hidden camera at the reception desk to record each woman as she read and signed the document. "Let's make it airtight," he'd said like a mercenary. "No deniability."

After obtaining her signature, Anna or Julie would then ferry each woman out to one of two waiting helicopters, refresh her champagne, and toss a cashmere throw over her lap, and then it was wheels up. Each helicopter took less than two minutes to fill. They would hop on the last ride out with Principal Sellers and a few cast members from the opera. Anna couldn't believe their turn was almost up; everything was moving so quickly.

Sellers, in a belted brown dress and pumps, soberly stood to the side in a knee-length down parka. She held a small bottle of water as Anna ushered out the last flute-clutching socialites making the usual high-pitched chirps. They all wore clothes and accessories in the $50,000-per-look category: the leather of the shoes, the metal of the hardware, the perfect fall of a custom-tailored couture skirt, not to mention the hides of hundreds of mink, chinchilla, and foxes.

These things did not likely impress Sellers, who silently assumed her window seat next to Anna. They lifted up, over the East River. Anna had had this pleasure several times with Mrs. Von Bizmark, but it wasn't the sort of thing she wished to grow blasé about.

"Cool, right?" Anna said, pointing with her chin at the tall buildings of Manhattan's East Side, reduced to shimmering blades of grass behind them in minutes. They were lucky to have an unseasonably warm and bright day; the sun glinted off the buildings behind them.

"This is my first helicopter ride," Sellers said. "It's not something I expected as part of being an educator." Anna knew from the programs she had prepared that Principal Sellers had come up through the public school system in the Bronx herself, attended City College, and worked her way from a grade school classroom to principal, and while she hadn't written this explicitly in the brochure, she imagined that Sellers had managed this all without having to ask a bunch of wealthy white women for money. But they both knew she needed to find $1.3 million, and Mrs. Von Bizmark's friends were a good place to start.

"Was Max helpful at least?" Anna asked, remembering with a dismal sensation that Max hadn't exactly raved about their progress with her speech.

"We'll see if he knows this audience," Sellers said noncommittally.

"If there's one thing I'd say about Max, it's that he is in touch with this crowd."

"It's just that this school isn't something 'this crowd' can use and enjoy later. You know what I mean?" She was right. People generally preferred to put their money where their interests lay: arts, diseases, and private schools.

"You have to explain what they get out of it."

"That's what Max said."

"And remember, they're just like everyone else."

Principal Sellers gestured at the mansions springing up beneath them, sprawling monstrosities with enormous amenities: the Hamptons. "Are they?" Sellers asked, pointing at a house with two pools, four tennis courts, and what appeared to be a minigolf course.

Approaching the Castle from the sky, it really did feel like somehow you were no longer on Long Island but in the Loire Valley. A lush, half-mile, tree-lined drive led up to the expansive gravel forecourt. At its center, an enormous tiered marble fountain encased in bursts of flowers bubbled to welcome those plebeians arriving by car. From the helicopter, you could make out the shape of the main house, a giant U that mimicked the cove behind it. Guesthouses dotted the peninsulas on either side. Tucked away, two tennis courts concealed a parking lot for fifty and, before that, the pool, which, even though it was the dead of winter, glimmered and gave off steam as if one of the guests might take a dip. Bloom must have insisted that the guests enjoy the mosaic at the bottom, a significant work of art in itself.

The reception was in the tent on the south lawn, by the two helicopter pads. The head gardener had carefully designed a path lined with some sort of trendy, sustainable Indonesian "sea wheat," he'd explained to Anna in order to justify some eye-popping figure that she had lacked the motivation to quibble with him about. She could see his point—it was a taller kind of grass with a lilac hue that very prettily indicated the way from the disembarkation point to the step and repeat and on to the tent.

By that point, most of the guests should have been inside already, but as they came in to land, Anna spied a bottleneck at the very start of the path. Everyone seemed focused on three gleaming blond horses on the grass. At least thirty women clustered around, watching them. And they were beautiful, but they were just sort of standing there, shaking their manes . . . or tearing and eating the Indonesian "sea wheat" as if it was the most delicious thing they had ever tasted. Many city ladies had stopped to watch this rural display. Anna could not help but wonder if this was part of Bloom's revenge plan.

Julie took Sellers past the crowd to find Mrs. Von Bizmark while Anna edged up to the step and repeat, a dramatic wall of assorted white blooms and a white carpet with diffuse lighting that would surely make for great pictures. Guests waited their turn while a cluster of three turned, laughed, and posed on the predetermined "best angle" spot, marked with a rose embossed into the white carpet beneath their pristine shoes. Pippy Petzer, one of those waiting, let out a loud cackle. They were already twelve minutes behind schedule, but no one was going to forgo being documented by the dozen or so cameras and phones snapping away from the grass.

STT grinned and snapped picture after picture, pausing to personally wave at every single guest, mouthing exaggerated greetings—"Hi, Trisha! Hi, Pam! Jane! Hi!"—like he was rushing their sorority. It was exhausting just watching him work up a sweat, pausing every few minutes to dab at his face with a handkerchief on this winter day. Anna recognized the photographer from *Women's Wear Daily*, a large blond man with a colorful slim silk scarf always looped around his neck. He never lowered his camera. The *Times* had sent their style blogger, but Anna wasn't sure if he was the willowy Asian man or the white guy in violet eyeshadow. More people crouched in the front, their phones all held aloft. Anna idly wondered if Max had paid any of them to be there or if they truly were all international style bloggers mixed in with legitimate fashion journalists, as he had promised.

A middle-aged strong-jawed waif in head-to-toe black with dark leather cuffs on both wrists lurked at the edge of the press. Tall, tan, and makeup-free, with long straight dark hair framing her face and hanging loosely down her back in a way that appeared natural and effortless and could not possibly be either: Vivienne Lanuit of *Vogue*. Anna looked around for Max, who surely should be attending to this reporter in particular. She held her large camera, which appeared to use actual film, in one tilted hand.

Anna watched Lanuit observe the women on the walkway unnoticed, far more interested in their candid moments than their posed portraits. Without sound, no sudden jerks or announcements, like a large cat stalking prey, Lanuit smoothly raised her camera and captured insincere tête-à-têtes, people feigning interest in what their friends said while covertly eyeing one another's impossible-to-get handbags and hot-off-the-runway jumpers. She spent some time capturing every angle of the golden horses eating the sea wheat. When Anna tried to cobble together a narrative or even just a headline to go with these early images, she had a hard time spinning it all that positively. Finally, Anna spotted Max, holding a glass of fresh juice, making his way across the lawn to Lanuit.

Her turn, Pippy Petzer took a few moments to compose herself to be photographed. She wore pressed camel pants and a knee-length sable vest with a feathered fedora. Locating the embossed rose, she carefully placed one toe in front of the other, tilted her head at a calculated angle, and then . . . smiled. Sort of. It was as if the expression, so painfully artificial, had affixed itself to her face like an invisible octopus. Perhaps this was the only time Pippy Petzer even attempted a positive air: in front of a camera. She squeezed the wooden handle of a tiny Gucci bag with the effort of projecting false joy.

Then, spotting Opal in the crowd, four inches taller and several shades darker than all the other luncheon attendees, Petzer shouted for her so they could be photographed together. Opal, in a crepe de chine

Prada dress covered in lips and hearts under an emerald fox jacket, was already suffering through the yapping and fawning of three opera fans. She pretended not to hear Petzer's shrill "Opal! Opal! Opal!" until the crowd parted and there was no ignoring her cries. Petzer clasped her waist and, with her other claw, grabbed Opal's hand. Opal's smile was like dishwater; she managed to break free after only a few seconds, rushing straight ahead and into the embrace of Lanuit. They double kissed and shared a whispered exchange and a quick laugh, like two old fashionista friends.

Meanwhile, Bloom, in a wide-skirted dress made of grape raw silk, looped her arm through Mrs. Petzer's, hustling her into the tent without so much as acknowledging Anna, who silently followed. Her gut churned with trepidation as she approached the reception. Shrieks—of glee? Terror?—punctuated the dull midpitched roar of an all-female gathering. The sense of foreboding she had experienced for weeks reached a peak. Was she walking into a disaster?

At first glance, it appeared not. The white silk tent stretched several stories high, a cathedral made of fabric. Ranunculus and wisteria clustered around the thick eggshell poles like fanciful moss, illuminated with lights recessed in the beams above. The sweeping curtains framed the lawn, beach, and ocean outside like a painting. Larger strategic lights bounced off the fabric above, making everyone appear more vibrant. Bow tied waiters plied the crowd with water and wine. A center table full of fresh fruit no doubt jetted in that morning from South America attracted many who loaded up their plates with nutritionist-approved melon slices, papaya chunks, and pomegranate seeds. Music from a cello and flute duo in the corner mingled with the conversations. And, most of all, everyone appeared to be having a good time, especially Mrs. Von Bizmark, who greeted each cluster of guests with verve and efficiency. Anna breathed a little easier. Fourteen minutes behind.

Against the far wall, a cornucopia of vibrant produce spilled across a table. Chef, in her toque and apron, stood at the ready with two juicers and two blenders, her burly tattooed forearms pressed against her sternum. She eyed the guests from under overgrown bangs.

"Smile, will you?" Anna said. " I think you're scaring them away."

"It's the wine." Indeed, most of the women held ice-cold straw-colored goblets, which looked extra delicious since they were off limits to Anna. Mrs. Von Bizmark toasted her wine glass with three of her club friends. Julie approached them with Principal Sellers, whom Mrs. Von Bizmark embraced and introduced all around. Anna watched Julie interject something, pointing at her watch. Mrs. Von Bizmark took Principal Sellers's arm and headed for the house, leaning in and chatting with Sellers. Good, this would get everyone moving toward lunch.

"Have you seen Phil?" Anna was supposed to check in with him before everyone sat down, but she had not laid eyes on him yet.

"No," Chef said and, marking how the guests began drifting inside, marched off to start lunch. Fifteen minutes behind schedule. Anna got out her walkie-talkie and tucked behind the side of the house.

"Phil! Phil! Come in, Phil!" Nothing. Great. "Phil?"

After thirty seconds, she got a response that was almost entirely loud static: "Problem . . . heating . . ." And then he was gone. Anna thought briefly about trying to find him in the subterranean "control room" of the house, but for what? Phil had tried to explain to her many times the complexity of the new interior climate system; she knew the installation had not been completely smooth but had long ago assumed Phil had remedied it.

In any case, it was time to sit for lunch. Instead of the usual furniture in the Castle's great room, ten round tables swathed in white linen filled every inch of floor space. Flowers dripped from the double-story window casings, and sunlight poured in through the skylights. Phil had said it would be crowded, but this was maximum capacity. A two-foot dais at the front held a microphone on its stand, waiting for Mrs. Von Bizmark and Principal Sellers. Meanwhile, most of the women clustered at the entryway, greeting Mrs. Von Bizmark like she was the president entering Congress for a State of the Union address.

Once she and Principal Sellers were seated next to one another, ninety-eight other women attempted to trickle into the seating area, wine glasses aloft, sliding their way through the tiny spaces left between the chairs. Inevitably, a glass tumbled to the floor, where it shattered. Several waiters rushed to clean it up. A guest used this distraction to switch place cards from table to table. In short, chaos was breaking out in the dining room, which meant a jam at the door. Anna took a deep breath, pulled out the seating chart, and started picking off guests to drag them, in a respectful way, to their seats.

By the time everyone had their butt in a chair, they were twenty minutes behind schedule, so Max pushed Mrs. Von Bizmark's speech to after Chef had served the main course. Despite the noise and heat level rising steadily, everyone appeared to be having an unusually good time. Anna surveyed the key media players, seated strategically around the room. There was STT in between Pippy Petzer and Opal. The *Women's Wear Daily* guy had ended up between two grandes dames. And Lanuit . . . where was she? There was the CEO of Chanel and one of those glittering ascendant socialites, and in between them sat . . . Miriam Rosenbaum, an Exeter mommy friend who was an outsider to this group. Wait a second . . .

With a shudder, Anna realized that the place card–moving culprit was none other than the dreadful Dallas dressmaker who promoted her "own line" of evening gowns at every inappropriate opportunity. Anna edged closer to the distant corner of the dining room, where Lanuit had ended up stranded. She looked on politely as Dallas scrolled through images on her phone, pointing out design details with hot-pink endless nails, forcing a response to each: "We have this lace handmade in Spain. You been to Spain?" Lanuit smiled tightly. *Nothing to be done about it now.* Anna sighed to herself. Max laid eyes on Anna and bulleted over.

"First of all, it's hot in here."

"Phil's working on it."

"Can't we just open the windows?"

"Apparently, that would trigger the heat, and it would be like an oven." She remembered only snippets of what Phil had said; something about the sensors in the wrong place, and he didn't have time to move them . . . Anna wiped the back of her neck with her sleeve.

"OK, well, I went over the speech with Kissy again. Should be super brief. Like five sentences. Wait, why's Vivienne all the way over there?"

"Place card switcher from Dallas."

"Shit," Max said. They surveyed the dining room together. The ten-vegetable salads enjoyed the usual picking over while the servers spent all their energy aggressively refilling everyone's wine. Was the room getting warmer still, were guests getting drunker, or was Anna herself just growing more and more anxious to the point of sweating? Probably all of the above. Across the room by the kitchen door, poor Julie looked like she might melt.

Another glass shattered on the ground, and this time a drunken nasal voice shouted, "It's a party!"

"Something seems a little weird, right?" Max said. "A little . . . *off.*" He went to open the front double doors to let a little air in, but the breeze only triggered the heating system to kick up. Anna could feel hot air blowing from a nearby vent. And where was the rest of the food?

Keeping a tight smile carefully plastered on her face, Anna traversed the great room and its many tables of increasingly raucous women to the kitchen, where she found a half dozen servers all waiting with two dozen plates of side dishes under warmers and no Chef in sight. She caught a glimpse of the buzzed back side of her head over the grill out the back door, which Anna quickly banged through.

"What the?"

"Phil says I can't use the oven," Chef said. "Something about the climate . . ."

"Will that feed everyone?" Anna asked, gesturing at about twenty-five large chicken breasts.

"What else can we do?"

Anna rushed back inside to tell Julie, who looked like she might actually burst into tears or throw up at any moment.

"Are you OK?" Anna whispered.

"Yes, just . . . I'll just resign, OK? You don't have to worry. I'll just quit." Oh, boy, was this heatstroke? A regular stroke? A psychotic break?

"What are you talking about?" Anna said, truly panicked.

Julie lifted a wine bottle out of the ice bucket. The label read *VIDA*. "I ordered the wrong wine," she said.

"Not the . . ."

"Grain alcohol."

"Fuuuuuuuuuuuuuck," Anna said as quietly as possible, her mind racing ahead. It was way, way, way too far along to do anything about it.

"I'm so sorry!" Julie whispered, sweaty and wild eyed.

Anna surveyed the room, the flushed faces, the women laughing so hard they couldn't breathe, others looking like they might be starting not to feel so well, and Mrs. Von Bizmark, never one to wait patiently, at that very moment rising unsteadily to her feet to make her speech. Under any set of circumstances, traversing this tight space would prove challenging. Given that she was probably very drunk along with everyone else in the room, Mrs. Von Bizmark's approach of the microphone was shaky at best. She gripped the back of friends' chairs and their shoulders, taking care to avoid legs, feet, and bags.

Halfway to the stage, Mrs. Von Bizmark fell to the floor with a thump. Lanuit and STT had their cameras out and were on their feet. Max prepared to fling his body across the dining room like a human shield. But Mrs. Von Bizmark bounced back up before anyone could capture anything incriminating and shook it off with a laugh. A pro, she smoothed her dress, and the crowd applauded a little more loudly than usual. The chairs parted ways a touch more, all eyes on Mrs. Von

Bizmark as she finally reached the microphone. She stepped carefully up onto the dais, as if realizing that she was probably very intoxicated. She grinned at the crowd, who whooped and cheered her like British football fans. The fall had endeared Mrs. Von Bizmark to her audience. A small oval of blood bloomed just below her kneecap.

Max stood in the back of the room ready with predetermined signals: slow down, speed it up, cut it short. Mrs. Von Bizmark wrestled with the stand before freeing the mic, and, collecting herself, she looked from this familiar face to that familiar face . . . the time stretched out. Max made the motion to speed it up. An uncomfortable cough at the back of the room and a few whispers.

"I want to thank you all for coming today. Many of you are dear friends, old friends. Peter's friends . . ." She drifted off, momentarily. Max mouthed the speech to her, but she was not even looking in his direction. He emphatically motioned for her to move it along and, exasperated, looked to Anna, who could only shrug: What could they do? There was no way to make the situation better, let alone perfect. Mrs. Von Bizmark continued. "But how well do we really know one another?" Max threw his hands in the air. Anna had to wonder if Mrs. Von Bizmark was so blotto she had forgotten why they were even having this luncheon. "I'd like to speak today—a little bit—about"—*public education? A great school? A bunch of gifted kids who need our help?* Anna silently completed the end of her sentence—"my heritage."

Say what?

"I am a Jewess."

More than one woman gasped. Several clutched their necklace, scarf, hair, or neighbor. Two hundred eyes rolled, evenly divided between those who were shocked to hear Kissy Von Bizmark was Jewish and those who were shocked that she should feel the need to confess it. STT shot video on his phone, documenting the various astonishments, an unguarded look of glee on his face. This display pierced Sellers's coolness; she openly gaped at Mrs. Von Bizmark. Max's expression slackened in disbelief.

Of course, this was no news to Anna. After over a decade in someone's home, knee deep in every single document, appointment, contact, and communication that pertained to their life, there was no avoiding the information. Even so, the fact had never been spoken before, and all implications ran to the contrary. The kids had attended Saint David's and Sacred Heart, for example. They may have even believed themselves to be Catholic for all anyone knew.

And even though this news was no big deal, really, to anyone, what else might Mrs. Von Bizmark say? Anna must stop her, not only from embarrassing herself further but also from tanking Sellers's fundraising chances. She grabbed a knife off a nearby drunk woman's place setting and held it up, trying to deflect a ray of sun from through the skylight directly into Mrs. Von Bizmark's eyes. She could see the slice of light bouncing around on the wall behind her.

"And do you know what is most important of all to the Jewish people? To *my* people?" She looked around at all those friends, many of them astonished, oil tankers full of Botox making it difficult to glean much more nuance than that. "Not money," Mrs. Von Bizmark said sagely, and the room positively tingled. The sliver of sun was on her chin, her hair, her earring.

The loud nasal voice asked, "What did she say?" No one bothered to answer, hanging as they were on Mrs. Von Bizmark's every word. STT held his phone up higher. Lanuit furiously took notes with a fountain pen on a spiral notebook, transcribing this weird speech in French.

Just then, eureka! Anna bounced the light right in Mrs. Von Bizmark's eyes. She startled a little, squinting for a second. Then she saw Anna, who dragged the knife in front of her neck. A moment of understanding. "Schools!" Mrs. Von Bizmark said, laughing lightly, relieved to be back on script. "Education! A ladder out of poverty! I want to introduce you to an extraordinary woman. Principal of PS 324. Delilah Sellers."

Now that she was extraordinarily intoxicated with an unusually intoxicated group of friends, Mrs. Von Bizmark's little oratorical blunders could bounce this way or that: Charming divulgence or cry for help? Whatever it was, it was certainly riveting. Lanuit jotted down page after page of notes, ignoring Dallas's attempts to reengage her. STT tapped out something furiously on his phone (a text to Page Six?). Max rushed to his side to try to spin the story in a positive way.

Whatever tomorrow's publications would say about today's events, Sellers had her work cut out for her. After Mrs. Von Bizmark's bizarre ditty, how, exactly, would Sellers capture and hold the attention of the room? Whispers broke out and quickly escalated in volume as Sellers strode to the stage, on much steadier, more sober footing than everyone else. Mrs. Von Bizmark embraced her and relinquished the microphone. Sellers looked out at the sea of women in full gossip, smiled warmly, and waited for a break in the chatter. Agnostic Anna prayed. Max rejoined her at the back of the room and whispered in her ear, "Let's see if she can save this."

"She's right," Principal Sellers said loudly into the mic, denting the din. "Kissy Von Bizmark is exactly right." She waited, gave it a second to sink in. The attention in the room resettled itself on Sellers. "PS 342 is a ladder out of poverty. And I know this because the New York public school system was the way I escaped. I know education works because it worked for me," she said. "I grew up in that neighborhood. My mom worked three jobs . . . three real hourly-wage jobs." She held up three fingers and let this data point hang out there in a room where there were probably not three real jobs among all the guests. "And today, I'm a principal. I own my Manhattan apartment." Some applause at this. Something clicking into place. Max nodded along encouragingly.

"And what do you get out of helping me and my kids and their school? What do you get out of it?" Another strategic pause. "Freedom from guilt." A few nervous laughs. "Freedom. From. Guilt." A few more titters. "Don't laugh, I'm not kidding. I get it. Your kids go to beautiful private schools, and that's fine, but they don't have all the answers! They are going to need raw talent . . . the grit . . . the real-world experience that the kids at my school bring to the table. I make sure smart, motivated, talented poor kids get an education. And if our school closes, I can promise you most of them will not go to gifted programs, and some of them will stop attending school, period." She bowed her head with the gravity of her own words, and when she lifted her face, Principal Sellers looked dead serious. "But you women here today . . . you can give them their futures." She raised her hands, theatrical but effective. "You women can keep a school open, and if we meet our goal, it will remain open for decades and touch thousands of lives."

Everyone sat very still for a beat, not knowing what exactly to do. Max mouthed the words along with her: "Please consider a generous, completely tax-deductible contribution now."

"Who do we make the check out to?" Opal shouted from across the room, her checkbook already splayed across her empty place. She walked across the dining room to personally deliver her contribution to Sellers. Along the way, Opal stared down every single woman in that room and, arriving at the dais, threw her arms around Sellers: the only two black guests embracing. Some idiot started applauding, but it didn't catch on, and thankfully she stopped. Opal and Sellers exchanged a sincere, off-mic moment, something not meant for the rest, and then Opal returned to her seat via a different route, eyeing more women with her silent instructions. Miraculously, a hundred hands reached for their checkbooks. Max was practically doing a jig in the back of the room.

"Will you take American Express?" someone shouted.

"Yes!" Julie responded. Dishes with a few pieces of grilled chicken over lentils finally streamed from the kitchen. Anna walked the room collecting checks while Julie swiped card after card through an attachment on the office iPad Anna had never seen before.

"Let's get them moving in ten," Bloom hiss-whispered into Anna's ear. "I think they're going to need a little extra time." She chuckled ominously before disappearing out a side door as quickly and inexplicably as she had materialized.

It wasn't like anyone ate anyway, and the room had become quite warm. The guests bubbled out into the tent, most clinging to at least one other person, everyone laughing as if caught up in a collective hallucination. A few nondrinkers hung at the periphery, vaguely bewildered by most of the women's behavior.

Through the magic of lighting, Bloom had transformed the tent into a springtime stage while the guests were inside. She framed the white wall of flowers in dune grass and moved it from the step and repeat to the ocean side of the tent, adding swaths of white silk over and around a small hardwood platform. Three performers took the stage, accompanied by the cello-and-flute duo. As the soprano sang her first few clarion notes, two horses wandered to the side of the stage, a beautiful tableau. Almost as if they were part of the show. One of the horses, a large stallion, came ever closer, drawn no doubt by the sea wheat there.

Then the horse, all shining muscle, stepped onto the stage and started munching on the dune grass. The violinist abruptly trailed off. Someone shouted, "Security!" The other unsaddled horse soon joined her friend. The two animals crowded the performers off the stage. Bloom seized the mic. "Thank you so much for coming, but we need to get you back to the city now. You each have a number from your place setting. Number ones, please make your way to Anna and Julie, standing right over there." And just like that, they were back on schedule.

Anna and Julie handed each woman two bottles of water from a giant cooler full of ice by the helipads, along with a paper napkin and a barf bag. By the end of the boarding procedures, it was approaching three p.m., Anna's back was killing her, and she might have had to amputate a toe. There was one chopper of guests left and one woman left to get on it. None other than Pippy fucking Petzer.

Anna's feet felt like chopped meat stuffed into her shoes as she ran around looking for Mrs. Petzer. She pulled up a society page picture and directed all the Coolwater staff to help her find the missing socialite. The chopper would soon leave, and then what would they do with her?

"Anna, come in." Finally, a maid on her walkie-talkie. "She's in the pool house."

From steps away Anna could make out the sound of violent puking. She peeked inside the cabana and through the bathroom door saw Mrs. Petzer's broad ass in her camel pants, marred by a three-inch-long brown stain: Pippy Petzer had pooped her pants!

"Get Kissy!" she shouted from the toilet. Anna was too shocked to argue and eager to pass this problem along. She walkie-talkied for someone to bring Mrs. Von Bizmark and told the helicopter to leave without Mrs. Petzer. After an interminable amount of time, Mrs. Von Bizmark finally appeared, looking herself like a zombie, her skin a strange green color over the loose neckline of her tangerine silk caftan. Her sunglasses hid most of her face, and over them she pressed a cool washcloth to her forehead.

"I think we need an ambulance," Anna said, but Mrs. Von Bizmark breezed past her. The index finger in the air said, *Wait*.

"Yes, Pippy, darling, what is it?" she called from outside the open bathroom door, pinching her nose with her free hand.

"What took you so long?"

"Well, I am hosting a luncheon today, darling. With helicopters." It sounded like Pippy Petzer might be throwing up a lung. "We'll get you an ambulance, darling," Mrs. Von Bizmark called through the open door. There were both Petzer and Von Bizmark wings at Southampton Hospital; surely they would be more than happy to save the day with some IV fluid. "We're just going to give you a little privacy, dear," Mrs. Von Bizmark said, then closed the bathroom door and sprayed half a bottle of lavender scent into the air.

Anna went outside to call the hospital, and the woman on the other end said, "Yeah, we see this all the time. We'll send the paramedics. How many IV kits do you need out there?"

"Just one." Anna peered through the french doors of the pool house at Mrs. Von Bizmark, collapsed on the wicker couch, washcloth on head, sandaled foot on the coffee table. "Actually, make it two."

Without being asked, Anna brought Mrs. Von Bizmark a cold bottle of water from the fridge, but she did not move to accept it. Anna left it on the table in front of her.

"Is there something you want to tell me about today?" Mrs. Von Bizmark rested her head on the back of the couch. Her words were barely audible. When Anna hesitated, she kept going. "How on earth did that shrew from Dallas end up next to the *Vogue* reporter?"

"I . . . ," Anna started, with nowhere to go. The question was not how it had happened, of course, but how Anna had not prevented it from happening. There was no right answer. Should she have ejected the woman from Dallas? Grabbed Lanuit by her skinny toned arm?

"Any other snafus, Anna?" Mrs. Von Bizmark said rather snittily.

Might as well face the music! "We ordered the wrong wine."

"And no one noticed?" That was an interesting point. Had Bloom, in her seventy-two hours of setup, not seen the garish hot-pink label that in no way matched the wine on the menu, a fifty-dollars-a-bottle French white chardonnay?

"Unfortunately not. Of course, I take full responsibility."

Mrs. Von Bizmark lifted her head a few inches and then set it back down. A hand fluttered to her washclothed forehead. Anna stopped breathing; she probably deserved to be fired. One of the luncheon guests required medical assistance because of an administrative error. "I really appreciate your work, Anna, but consider this an official warning," Mrs. Von Bizmark said. Though this was far better than getting fired, Anna was still crestfallen. She had never in her career been reprimanded like this before. Shame washed over her. A Yale degree and she couldn't even organize a ladies' lunch? *Do. Not. Cry,* she told herself, backing out of the room.

The last helicopter waited for Anna, but on her way there she spied none other than Bloom, overseeing the deconstruction of the tent. Without actually deciding or thinking it through, she found her feet carrying her there. For what? A confrontation? "Hey," Anna said, annoyed.

"Hey," Bloom said, matching her tone without averting her gaze from the workmen. "Careful with that! Careful!" she shouted pointlessly, an effort to blow Anna off.

"Bloom!" Anna demanded her attention. "Did you know we were serving the wrong wine?" Anna half shouted. Bloom finally looked at her.

"Were we?" she said with exaggerated surprise, a hand dramatically positioned at her breastbone. "I had *no* idea!" She took a small step closer to Anna, that hand reaching out to Anna's shoulder, pulling her closer. "And if I *did* know," Bloom rasped into Anna's ear, "I wouldn't say anything because we *must* stay under budget." It was like a tiny fist of iron punched Anna in the solar plexus with each word. Anna, run down, exhausted, traumatized, and confused, felt tears building.

Just then, Phil ran out of the house toward them, green T-shirt soaked through with sweat, which gave Anna a chance to swipe the tears away. "I fixed the heating!" he announced, triumphantly, grinning ear to ear with pride, utterly oblivious to how little it mattered anymore. The guests had barely felt the temperature in the dining room because they were all so drunk. Or maybe, Anna realized, they were all so drunk because of the heat. Phil stopped a few feet away, panting a little, hands on his hips. "I stink. So . . . how'd it go today?"

"Great!" Bloom said, and with that, she excused herself to scream at a worker attacking the silk tent with too much gusto.

"You know, I'm not sure," Anna said, looking past him at the blinking lights of the ambulance. "Can you show the paramedics to the pool house?" Before he could ask, Anna said, "I don't have time to explain."

Anna rushed onto the final waiting helicopter with the performers, Sellers, and Julie. A strange silence fell over everyone. Anna didn't know what to make of the day. Sellers, her impermeable shell pierced by Mrs. Von Bizmark's confessional, shook her head a little, trying to process it all as they lifted up over the Castle.

Julie quietly got out her iPad to total the credit card contributions. Sellers pulled up the calculator on her phone and the envelope still tucked discreetly in her purse and started tallying the checks. Periodically, she heaved quietly or said, "My goodness!" Slowly, Sellers slipped into a state of shock. Anna looked over her shoulder to make out a check written for $50,000.

"Four hundred and twenty thousand dollars in credit card payments," Julie finally said.

"Holy shit," one of the sopranos said.

"Seven hundred and thirteen thousand dollars in checks," Sellers said, disbelievingly. "That can't be right." She flipped through the checks again. "But it is. And I didn't even count this . . ." She held out a wad of hundred-dollar bills, rolled up and rubber banded. It had to be several thousand dollars in cash.

Sweet relief flooded Anna's frayed psyche. Even if everything was all messed up, even if the next day a raft of terrible publicity and embarrassing stories would cost Anna her job, she could at least feel good about this one thing. Maybe somehow, everything would work out for Ilana and all her classmates.

"I gotta be honest: I think the wine mistake paid off," Julie said.

"Big-time," Sellers said. "I don't even know what you're talking about, but whatever it was, it worked."

"See? Sometimes this crowd can be very helpful," Anna said.

"That may be true," Sellers mused. "But they are certainly not like everyone else."

That night, Julie and Anna drank beers in Julie's tiny kitchen at a table so small it was nearly child size. "I thought I'd have it all figured out by now, Jules." Anna sneezed into a tissue.

"But you do!" Julie said. "What's the problem?" Anna turned her red and weepy eyes on Julie. She sniffled a little and scratched at a fresh patch of hives on her inner arm. "OK, so there's the Adrian thing. That's an issue . . . ," Julie said, going to the fridge for another beer for Anna to press against her rash. "But is it really? Like, a real issue?" she said.

Anna sighed heavily before answering. "I can't seem to make up my mind. I don't have time to think about it now."

"Well, it seems like the sort of thing you should make time for."

"I'll deal with it after the ball."

"Yes, that's something people say. That's totally normal."

TWELVE

"So glad you came!" Bambi exclaimed to Prince Valdobianno, who inexplicably wore tails and a bright-red sash across his chest. Like a fairy tale, Bambi thought, even if it went against dress code. Never mind. He bent over at the waist to kiss her hand, and she sighed with pleasure. All around her, the candlelit faces of her friends and supporters glowed happily, warmly in her direction. It was the Opera Ball at last, and it was a tremendous, huge, massive success. Looking at the crowd, Bambi counted everyone she had ever known, it seemed, and was that . . . Meryl Streep? Sitting next to her Swiss boarding school headmistress? That Max was a magician!

As the prince receded, Pippy Petzer sprung up in his place, next in a long line waiting to greet her. Goodness, it was hard work being the honoree; she had to be gracious to each one. Especially Pippy, who wore a never-before-seen genuine smile. Won over, perhaps? Her baby-pink Chanel suit and pillbox hat underlined Bambi's impression that Pippy had come in kindness. She gushed, "Bambi, my darling, congratulations! I brought you a present." An oversize leather embossed jewelry box materialized, and Bambi just knew, instinctively, what was inside.

She opened it to find the lariat—a gorgeous piece designed by none other than Jeanne Toussaint herself and worn by . . .

"Stable now. Should be feeling much better soon." A strange voice was talking just to her right and too loudly. Bambi jerked her head to see and lurched awake in the pool house. And who was that sprawled just across from her, an IV bag jutting from her—from *both* of their arms? Oh my Lord, Pippy Petzer!

Bambi suddenly remembered everything. Oh. No. Why had she said that? About being Jewish? It had felt so critical to get those words out into the world at that moment, and yet . . . it had been the alcohol talking. Oh dear. She felt like she might vomit again—oh dear Lord, the bile rising, how awful. But it wasn't physical. Bambi was, for a searing flash, full of shame. And it was all Anna's fault.

"But can we transport her?" Phil said to whomever was outside. From the flashing lights and the IV situation, Bambi deduced paramedics.

"To where? She should rest." Where was she going? Who were they talking about?

"The city. Is it safe to send her in a car, or do we need the ambulance?" They must be talking about Pippy. No way was Bambi going to take an ambulance to her apartment building. What would people say? Someone could snap a photograph!

"Obviously an ambulance would be safer. Is there someone there to receive her?"

"I'll call Mr. Von Bizmark."

"Nooooo!" Bambi croaked. Call Peter and say what exactly? He'd be angry enough as it was, depending on whether media coverage of the lunch somehow reached him from the faraway land of fashion journalism and then how negative the articles turned out to be. He hated to be the subject of strangers' attention as much as Bambi craved it. She cleared her throat and said with more authority, "Phil, absolutely not. Come in here, please!" He appeared but stayed by the open door, lingering a good fifteen feet away. "What are you doing, standing over there? Why is everyone outside?"

"It's just . . ." Phil started to gag a little. He helplessly gestured at Pippy. As if suddenly awoken to it, Bambi could smell it too. She had become inured to the godawful stench during her long unconsciousness. Phil took a few tentative steps forward, covering his face with the crook of his elbow.

Pippy Petzer smelled like poo. And even though Pippy had never been particularly nice to Bambi outside of her dream—or to anyone, for that matter, as far as Bambi knew—her heart went out to the old battle-ax, sprawled across a lovely piece of upholstery that would now need to be replaced. Sure, what Bambi had said at the luncheon was embarrassing. She blushed even before the memory had fully formed in her mind and she could close it out. *Ugh.* But somehow Pippy, here, exposed like this, wrought compassion from Bambi. Plus, her sympathies for this society doyenne made Bambi feel much better about herself and her unconventional public address.

"Just get the car, will you?" Bambi asked Phil, who began to retch again, which Bambi thought a tad dramatic. She dispatched him to get a stretcher and the paramedics too; Pippy could not just linger forever in their pool house. Surely her people would care for her.

Bambi, feeling suddenly much, much better, came to her feet. Modern medicine was such a glorious marvel! The luncheon receded into less and less embarrassing territory; maybe it had played as a joke? Not been so bad! Bambi stood eye to IV bag and read the ingredients: saline, vitamins, a bunch of other stuff, and something called midazolam, which Bambi suspected played a large part in the incredible serenity with which she viewed everything that had happened—ever in her entire life and perhaps everything that ever would happen. Stiff, exhausted, but definitely on the mend, she minced over to Pippy, rolling her IV cart and its magical potion with her.

"Pippy," she said quietly, standing over her. "Pippy."

Her head rolled against the back of the couch, her mouth halfway open. All Pippy's makeup had shifted a half inch from its proper place, a macabre smear. Hair pieces dangled in spots. Her eyes, a mixture of grays and reds under a glassy sheen, blinked open and moved in Bambi's direction. She moaned lightly.

"Pippy, I want you to know this will stay between us." Bambi tried to impart this communiqué with all the seriousness and dignity with which it was intended. "OK, dear?" she said, patting the inside of her outthrust and exposed arm.

Pippy nodded ever so slightly, just a subtle rolling of her head along the back of the poor couch.

Getting home was a pleasant blur due to the hospital-grade anti-anxiety medication in Bambi's blood. She wasn't worried about Peter and what he might say, didn't fret over the press or the ball or the school or . . . anything. They went out for steak, which Bambi did not mind in the slightest since she was the furthest thing from hungry. She sipped her unusually tasty bordeaux—Peter really did know his way around a wine list. When the steak came, Bambi helped herself to a few slices, which were more delicious than her distant recollections of red meat. She talked a lot about the lunch, omitting her gaffe and painting the whole event a triumph. Peter remained a neutral listener, though he did yawn once. Twice. Perhaps she was a touch monologue-y. His eyebrows shot up into his hairline when Bambi ordered ice cream, which was much sweeter than she remembered but still a very nice feeling on the tongue. She scooped some into Peter's mouth, and he smiled.

Which made the next morning so, so . . . upsetting. Peter woke Bambi up early, throwing newspapers on her sleeping body. How rude! "Bambi!" he snapped. "Bambi, wake up!" She lifted her satin eye mask and blinked at him. "Bambi, it's almost ten, for God's sake." Goodness, how long had she slept? It had been the most thorough rest. She didn't remember a thing after the . . . ice cream. Dear God, had she eaten ice cream?

"Is everything all right, dear?" she asked.

"No, it's not! Look at these articles!"

She didn't have her glasses on, so they were a mass of newsprint, nothing more. "But . . . are they positive?" She picked one up and tried to find the arm's distance where she could see the print. No luck. She looked at Peter again. "Anything nice about me?"

"Bambi, you flew a hundred people to the Hamptons, and it's in every major paper somehow. How did that happen?" Bambi thought of Max and smiled to herself. It was so important to have good people. "It's not funny! Bambi! We have security and money issues. This is not helping! Do you think the mayor likes us more or less now? And the Petzers are suing us!" He let this sink in, Bambi's face falling. "I know you aren't used to hearing these exact words in this order, but how much did this whole thing cost?" Bambi winced. "I noticed you put the whole opera on a credit card, even though I told you not to."

Anna did it! Bambi wanted to say, but that would sound childish. She had already gleefully used several of the resulting gift cards.

Peter collected the papers again before she could even read any of them. "I was going to come home, but now I don't want to," he said. "I'll be at the Peninsula."

This seemed so unfair. Hadn't they had a nice time on their impromptu date night, or was that just the drugs talking? How could Bambi be sure? She chased him down the stairs, surprised to find that she was still in her cotton pants and pressed shirt from the night before. "Peter, Peter . . . wait!"

THIRTEEN

February 11

Anna and Julie were so on their game they even remembered to grab a coffee for Brian on their way to the Von Bizmarks', which he discreetly slipped under the doorman's podium. "You two look chipper today," he said. They were physically exhausted but emotionally elated.

Mere hours after the lunch, Max's handpicked bloggers with followings big and small had started posting. Opinions and stories about the luncheon ranged from mildly satirical to incandescently positive. The whole thing was just so over the top that it was hard for these professional aesthetes not to fawn. There were, of course, many pictures of the golden horses masticating thousands of dollars in heirloom sea wheat, whatever that was. Since none of these online-only publications had been allowed into the luncheon itself, zero information had yet trickled out about the shenanigans inside.

Women's Wear Daily online went with straight fashion, making only upbeat allusions to the many idiosyncrasies of the day—"an unusually good time" with "many unexpected moments"—but mostly Scarf Guy covered the various designers and styles. A picture of Julie's embroidered parrots made its way into the story.

Then, just before midnight, Max had issued the press release about the money raised for the school, and all the major papers had jumped on the story. They had a little dirt from first-person accounts, but Mrs. Von Bizmark's bizarre confessional had been eclipsed by overall intoxication and extraordinary fundraising. Anna felt an anticipatory tingling: maybe today would be the right time to ask for a raise.

The elevator door dinged and opened, depositing them in the anteroom behind the foyer doors, which remained closed all the time now. Anna pointed wordlessly at Mr. Von Bizmark's briefcase, leaning against the wall. Maybe the Von Bizmarks had had a romantic evening at home together? For a second, it was like everything was perfect.

Then they heard the shouting.

"Embarrass you?" Mrs. Von Bizmark screamed. Anna wondered if word of her speech had gotten out somehow. "Is that why you're not coming home?" she wailed at top volume. She sounded frantic.

"Drunk . . . lawsuit!" Mr. Von Bizmark shouted back. "Deal with the city . . . billions!"

Anna motioned for Julie and unlocked the door as quietly as possible. The two women attempted to pass the living room entryway without incident. The Von Bizmarks faced off, the site of the flood a backdrop to their confrontation. The television screen had finally been dismantled and all the debris cleared away, including the destroyed couch. Construction was due to start just after the ball. Mr. Von Bizmark, suited and ready for work, clutched the *New York Post* ("No Free Lunch! The Rich Shell Out"), the *Observer* ("Billionaire Luncheon Gets Boozy, Saves School"), and the *New York Times* ("How Many Inebriated Ladies Does It Take to Save PS 342?"). He glowered at Mrs. Von Bizmark. Everyone knew he despised mainstream news gossip and only coveted the attention of a very specific, very small, very wealthy circle of equally inaccessible associates.

Anna and Julie had nearly made it safely to the hallway when Mrs. Von Bizmark called for Anna, who frowned at Julie before entering the living room to stand a few feet away from the Von Bizmarks. Julie took up a protective post by the door. So much for that raise.

"What's taking so long with this wall, Anna?" Mrs. Von Bizmark asked, arms crossed over her chest. This could happen—emotional turmoil diverted onto the nearest staff member. The luncheon was thirty seconds ago, the press couldn't get enough of it, they'd nearly saved the school, the anniversary dinner approached with the Opera Ball hot on its heels, but of course, a construction update needed to happen at that very moment. Mr. Von Bizmark pointedly looked at his watch and resumed glaring at Mrs. Von Bizmark.

"First we had to wait for all the plaster, the floor, ceiling, wall, insulation, and so on to dry completely. Remember we had the dehumidifiers here? It rained a lot. Anyway, that took the longest. Now—"

"But, Anna, surely there's something you could do to speed it along. Mr. Von Bizmark has been living in a hotel for weeks now." Ah, the Mrs. wanted to blame Anna for her husband's absence. Mr. Von Bizmark was so annoyed Anna could almost hear his teeth grinding; he did not want to be pulled into this scene, but Mrs. Von Bizmark would not be deterred. Once she started in on a staff member, Mrs. Von Bizmark had to fully crush the screws in. Though Anna had seen it many times, squirming in discomfort until the earliest moment she could jump in, she'd never expected she herself would end up on the receiving end.

"I mean, after yesterday's gaffe at the lunch—*tssk, tsssk.*" Mrs. Von Bizmark could literally *tsssk*, a verbal embellishment she reserved for only the most dire circumstances. "I would just *hate*, after all these years, to have to *micromanage* you, but I don't see *any* progress here." Even Julie shrank away, both of them shamed by this unprecedented confrontation. Anna suddenly understood how difficult—how downright unbearable—her work environment could become. At any moment, Mrs. Von Bizmark could fire her for any reason and withhold references, essentially halving her earning potential in a split second. Here she was, faced with an impossible employer looking to exorcise her demons through verbal abuse. And she would have to take it.

It felt like withstanding a great storm as Mrs. Von Bizmark detailed the experience from her perspective, a narrative that Anna dizzily dipped in and out of. "Come home . . . water pouring out, Mr. Von Bizmark clutching his valise . . . endless fans . . . the smell . . ." She paused, and when Mr. Von Bizmark took a half step toward the exit, she grabbed his arm and looked expectantly at Anna. "What do you have to say?"

Both Von Bizmarks turned their eyes on her. He was impatience personified, desperate to conclude this whole nuisance as quickly as possible. But Mrs. Von Bizmark's eyes clouded over with unhappiness, her emotions so clearly *not* about the wall and much more about their marriage, and this seemed so obvious to Anna that she knew her usual catchphrases—*I'll take care of it right away, I completely understand your frustration, How about I make some calls right now*—would be useless.

Instead, Anna said, "I hadn't noticed the smell."

Mrs. Von Bizmark's left eyebrow spiked for a moment before resettling. Mr. Von Bizmark inhaled deeply through his nose, his expression blank. But the Mrs. would bring the situation to a head in one way or another; this was as cathartic for her as popping a pimple. "I have to imagine you've just been *distracted*." She employed her haughtiest tone. "But this is *our home*, Anna. You know? We *live* here? We don't get to *go home* at night."

"Neither do I!" Anna blurted, so surprised to hear these words come out of her mouth it was almost like she saw them—cartoon bubble letters flying across the room and hitting the Von Bizmarks in the face. She covered her mouth as if she could get the sentence back, and for a single surreal moment, everyone in the room gawked at one another in surprise. Even Mr. Von Bizmark forgot his desire to leave for a half second. Anna stormed out before anyone could see the tears springing from her eyes and stomped blindly down the hallway to the office.

Anna had expected for so long that her life would organize itself into neat little bins. That she would, one day, wake up and be an artist, a wife, a mother, a part-time private assistant, and a grown-up. But she could see clearly then that there were just too many bins! Everything had suffered. And now this breakthrough moment would be snatched from her. No way her art would be part of the Opera Ball if Mrs. Von Bizmark fired her.

She heaved with rage, sadness, and fear. Not knowing what else to do, she grabbed a large pair of office scissors and ever so carefully, confidently, like a surgeon, snipped three little matchsticks of cork off the board next to her desk on the wall. She wrapped them in tissue and stuffed them in her pocket, a ritual that helped to contain the overwhelming tide of feelings. Aimless, she threw herself into her Aeron chair without taking off her bag or jacket.

A hand on her shoulder. Cristina. Alicia and Josefina hovered in the background. Cristina handed Anna a tissue, which was when she realized tears were streaming down her face. They must all think she was or would be fired, and they were probably right. Here it was: the most unexpected thing. And it was happening to Anna.

"It's OK," Cristina said. "You're a good assistant." She shoved a warm croissant wrapped in linen into Anna's hand. "You eat, you feel better," she said. Anna took a bite of pastry and, indeed, instantly felt a bit more human. She sighed heavily and wiped her face with a tissue.

The ladies all watched her take another bite. Josefina's own eyes were full of tears.

Anna leaped to her feet, taking both of Josefina's hands in hers. So what if she was about to lose her job when she had helped to save a school? "Did you hear?!"

Josefina blushed and smiled, reaching into her powder-blue maid's uniform pocket to withdraw the *New York Times* clipping. "Everyone in my neighborhood knows," she said, chuckling.

"It's not done yet," Anna said.

"Ilana wants you to come for a barbecue," Josefina said. "To celebrate."

"OK, but it's not really done yet!" she said, more emphatically. "We still need over one hundred and fifty thousand dollars!"

Josefina smiled, all pink cheeks and twinkling eyes, like a coquette. She winked. "Ilana says she's not worried."

"Excuse me," Julie said to the ladies from the office door. They scattered when they saw both Von Bizmarks right behind her. Anna stood up to prepare for the firing squad. She considered taking off her bag, but why? Then she caught Julie's eye—a glint of mischievousness punctuated one of her wacky indiscernible expressions, a sort of palsied smile. Julie took her seat at her desk while the Von Bizmarks stood together at the doorway. Mrs. Von Bizmark looked rather pleased with herself, smiling beatifically at Anna while one arm warmly circled her husband's back. Mr. Von Bizmark could barely breathe through his rage.

"*Anna!*" Mrs. Von Bizmark chastised. "You didn't tell me that you and Adrian were having trouble." Anna darted her eyes at Julie, perturbed and thankful at the same time. "We're in a very stressful time here, dear. We can't have you sleeping on a mattress of cat fur, can we?"

Anna's eyes widened. Oh God, she prayed they would not try to make her move into the apartment: talk about boundaries collapsing, worlds colliding, and the general end of life as she knew it.

"Also, Julie tells me it was *her* mistake ordering the wrong wine?" Anna looked at Julie, who still had that goofy half smile on her face. "But Mr. Von Bizmark has agreed to come home so you can stay at the corporate apartment!" she said, beaming at him. Mrs. Von Bizmark gave her husband a teensy elbow to the ribs. He stepped forward, wordlessly extending an old-school hotel key, large and metal. Anna reached out to take it. Their eyes met, and he held on to the key for just a split second too long before releasing it.

"Jenny, get the car, please," he said, turning to go.

"It's Julie!" Mrs. Von Bizmark corrected, but he just glared at her as he stormed past. "See you here tonight, Peter!" she called after him, still smiling like an angel. She put one bony hand on Anna's shoulder. "Better?" she said, wanting with this generosity to erase any lingering bad feelings associated with both Anna's messy breakdown and the nasty assault that had catalyzed it. Forgetting both immediately was the cost of using the apartment. Anna had felt a twinge taking the key from Mr. Von Bizmark, the breadwinner and rightful inhabitant, but then she couldn't refuse without crossing her employer. Plus, she was dying to get away from Julie's cats.

"Thank you!" Anna said brightly.

"Because we have a lot to deal with today." Mrs. Von Bizmark took her seat at her desk. "First, we must reach Pippy Petzer. Apparently her lawyer called Avi this morning." The thought of trying to reach Pippy Petzer again by phone was enough to throw Anna back into emotional turmoil.

"About what?"

"Apparently she wants to sue us."

"For what? Getting drunk?" Julie asked.

"And in any case, she signed a waiver," Anna said, quickly scanning a copy to make sure it covered "any and every possible event, including acts of God, for the duration of the event until off heliport property in Manhattan."

"No kidding!" Mrs. Von Bizmark said, tickled to death. With the unpleasantness of the morning behind her, she could bask in the glow of (mostly) positive publicity, her husband's return to the hearth, and getting something over on Pippy Petzer. If Anna could reach her on the phone. Meanwhile, Julie dug up Mrs. Petzer's signed waiver.

From all those times dialing it, she still knew it by heart, and as Anna's fingers flew over the buttons, she said, "I should warn you, Mrs. Von Bizmark, that she never answers the phone." Sure enough, her voice mail clicked on.

"Try from my private line. And, Anna, stay on with us, please."

Anna switched over, and Mrs. Petzer picked up on the first ring. "Kissy?" she hissed.

Mrs. Von Bizmark winked at Anna and said, "Yes, darling, you rang?"

"Listen, I know that wasn't just plain old wine. My private physician tells me I may have permanent liver damage. I could have died. My neurologist is in Brazil, but when he's back . . ."

"What are you saying, darling?"

"I'm going to have to sue you. For one billion dollars. For my family."

Mrs. Von Bizmark forced herself to laugh. "You must be joking," she said.

"Not in the slightest."

"Even after the pool house?" Mrs. Von Bizmark said cryptically.

"I have no idea what you're talking about." This seemed to surprise Mrs. Von Bizmark more than anything else.

"But, Pippy, darling . . . ," Mrs. Von Bizmark said, hesitating as if she truly did not want to be the one to break the news to Mrs. Petzer. "You signed a waiver."

To her credit, Mrs. Petzer did not hesitate in her false denial. "I most *certainly* did *not*." She insisted so emphatically that Anna started to panic about the possibility of having missed her somehow. After all, there were a lot of women and helicopters and two cameras and . . .

Julie slipped a copy of Pippy Petzer's signed waiver under Mrs. Von Bizmark's nose. "Pippy, dear, I have it right in front of me."

"Then it's forged. I never signed anything."

Anna mouthed, "We have video." Julie dialed Avi.

"Listen, Pippy, I think you must still feel awful, so let's talk about this a little later when we've both had time to think about it, OK? I have to run to a meeting." As soon as she hung up, Mrs. Von Bizmark said, "Get the video," as if they were on an episode of *CSI*. But instead of running to a crime scene or a courtroom, Mrs. Von Bizmark rushed out for a different kind of full day: the gym, lunch with Sophia Bronwenmiller, and then Westley for a peel.

Julie gestured for Anna to sit. The freeze-frame was Pippy Petzer herself, midblink, yesterday, at the heliport. The video was only thirty seconds long; what could possibly happen?

Play.

Mrs. Petzer chatted with another waspy, old-money patron of the opera who drifted in and out of frame. In the video, Julie slid in between them and handed Mrs. Petzer a waiver. "I need you to sign this, please," she said, which Mrs. Petzer acknowledged with the slightest twitch. Without looking at Julie, she sidled up to the counter, seamlessly continuing her conversation.

Julie held out a pen, which Mrs. Petzer grasped while still listening to her friend, who was hard to understand since she was far from the tiny camera. Anna leaned in as Mrs. Petzer started talking. The first part was obscured, but then she turned toward the lens. "Kissy . . . just tries too hard. I mean, helicopters? Doesn't get more nouveau than that," Pippy Petzer muttered directly into the microphone as she signed the waiver and handed it back without ever looking Julie fully in the face.

Julie grabbed Anna's desk chair, and they sat right next to each other, mesmerized, watching the video again and again. Anna raged at Pippy Petzer, whom she had detested all along. How dare she come to a party, take the prime seat, and bad-mouth the hostess to another guest. Talk about tacky! Anna dreaded showing Mrs. Von Bizmark the video, which would invoke an emotion she hardly ever experienced: shame. After all, the helicopters had been Anna's idea.

The back doorbell rang, and Cristina called, "Annnnaaaa!" in a singsong voice Anna had never heard from their grumpy housekeeper. Then she called again, in a more familiar screech. Then Cristina laughed, heartily, which was also rather unusual. As Anna approached the back door, their stern housekeeper looked softer—flushed and younger. And she was smiling. Very odd. Anna turned her attention to the person at the door, a tall blond man in his late fifties. Aging but attractive, with a small gut and a contagious smile.

"This is Villson, the new super. He is Polish." She giggled like she was introducing Anna to George Clooney.

"Anna," she said, a detail Cristina had omitted. They shook hands.

"Hello!" he said gregariously. "I'm here to take a look at the toilet upstairs. Ariadne didn't fix the tile, right?"

"Can you do that?" Anna was skeptical of superintendents.

"I used to be a contractor," he said, and it looked like Cristina might swoon. She sighed quietly as she handed him little cloth booties to put on to protect the Von Bizmark floors from his workman's shoes.

"I can show you," Cristina said, but the subtext clearly read, *I will be a good wife to you.* He picked up his toolbox and followed her inside, both of them immediately speaking Polish. They meandered down the hallway like two lovebirds.

It felt like a whole day had passed, and it was only eleven a.m. Anna's uneaten breakfast sandwich sat on her desk next to the mauled croissant and her coffee, untouched and cold. Which made it easier to gulp it down. She had to do something to counter the wave of exhaustion that had suddenly washed over her. Julie would nudge the Silver Fox about the wall while Anna tried to make progress on the office's next big event: executing an anniversary celebration so memorable that it would fully restore Anna in the eyes of her employer and stall a Von Bizmark divorce for a matter of years.

"Silver Fox coming at three," Julie said.

Which gave them both a few hours to catch up on all the things that had to happen on an hourly, daily, weekly, monthly, and annual basis: Deposits for the next year's tuition; payroll for the staff; insurance premiums; appraisals for new jewelry and art purchases; ticket purchases for upcoming galas, luncheons, and symposiums; thank-you notes; birthday greetings; letters to co-op boards, social club admissions committees, and school directors; and general social correspondence via letter, email, phone, and text. Restaurant reservations, theater tickets, flight arrangements, birthday gifts.

The Silver Fox arrived two minutes early with his small technical tools, including a moisture detector and syringe. The new superintendent, Villson, should meet their contractor, and it occurred to Anna suddenly that he might still be in the apartment. Upstairs, rollicking Polish banged down the hallway. Cristina sounded like an entirely different person. The tile around the toilet looked as good as new. In the place of the Magritte sketch, the interior designer had installed a small Cezanne pencil drawing, called up from storage. The bathroom was finally back to normal—nearly a month and hundreds of thousands of dollars later—and no one would ever have to jiggle the toilet handle, thank God.

"Sorry to interrupt," Anna said, since neither one of them had noticed her standing at the door. "But the contractor is here, and I'd like him to talk to you both about the renovation."

Downstairs, the Silver Fox and Villson were hitting it off, talking about various requisite surveys, construction schedules, necessary equipment. "Of course, I'll have to call Renee. There's no way she'll agree to let us start before Labor Day," the Silver Fox advised sagely.

"Maybe if you talk to the neighbor downstairs?" Villson suggested.

"Mrs. Forstbacher?" Anna said, incredulously.

"She's friendly?" Villson asked.

Cristina laughed. "No!" she snorted.

"Maybe I can speak with her," he said, smiling slyly at Cristina. Getting Mrs. Forstbacher to agree to allow construction at all was a complex feat only achieved with the participation of a half dozen lawyers. That Villson thought he would simply ask her and she would say yes was a triumph of naivete, but Anna didn't think there was any harm in letting him learn the hard way. Cristina showed him out like she was sending him to battle.

Back in the office, Julie motioned for Anna to join her on the phone. "Max," she mouthed.

"This is one of those good news, bad news situations," Max said without preamble.

"OK. Bad news first."

"I spoke to Vivienne and STT, and they're both being very tight lipped. Frankly, I think they're not sure what to make of the whole thing, and they don't want to let me influence their view too much. But I did get Vivienne to send me some pictures. I'll forward them to you now."

Vibrant photographs filled Anna's computer screen: three socialites in pastel suits clearly gossiping about the woman behind them—one pointing at her and another actually covering her mouth to whisper; Delilah Sellers speaking to a roomful of red-faced drunk women; a horse eating the set while a soprano silently screamed. Altogether, the effect was artsy, weird, alarming, beautiful, and kind of gross.

"Huh," Anna said. "Did you tell them how much money we raised?"

"Yes, of course, Anna, but a story about more money is not exactly enough of a cover for the circus that luncheon turned into, ahem . . ." Max cleared his throat so vociferously that Anna suspected working on the Opera Ball had driven him to pick up smoking again. "So, OK, the photos are what they are, but they certainly got the attention of the higher-ups at *Vogue*. So . . . are you ready for the good news?"

"Please!" Anna said.

"I got them to agree to a photo shoot. Like, immediately."

"Wow, Max, you did it!" Anna said, glancing at the calendar and calculating the days from the peel—at that very moment searing the fine lines and sun damage off of her employer's face—until Mrs. Von Bizmark would be photo ready the day before the anniversary. Max argued with her until Anna, out of fresh ideas, admitted that she would need the time to heal.

"But she has to bring a few looks herself, OK? Black tie from her wardrobe—that's what I promised."

As if on cue, Josefina brought the garment rack from Bergdorf's into the office with a half dozen gowns to be fitted. Anna glanced at the clock: 4:55 p.m. The buzzer rang, and Julie told the doorman to send up the seamstress. "Max, I don't think that will be a problem," Anna said.

Twenty minutes later, Anna was berating herself for her optimism. Mrs. Von Bizmark stood on a podium in front of the mirrors in the dining room. The Hungarian seamstress clutched her stern chin with one hand and shook her head no. The dress, a burnished blue silk satin Tom Ford with beaded embroidery at the waist, was so oversize you could fit two Mrs. Von Bizmarks inside of it. It was a surprise the dress even came that large, let alone had somehow arrived here at Mrs. Von Bizmark's house of green juices. Over the curtain of steel-blue material, the Mrs.'s angry seared face floated like a red polka dot.

Julie, more shocked than anyone, stammered out an excuse and ran to get Mrs. Von Bizmark's personal shopper on the phone. Meanwhile, Mrs. Von Bizmark changed into the second gown behind a screen in the dining room.

"When we're done here, Julie and I have something to show you," Anna said, eager to get it over with.

"Oh," Mrs. Von Bizmark called. "Can you give me a clue?"

"It's . . ." Anna searched for the right word. "Something," she said.

"So is this," Mrs. Von Bizmark said drily, stepping out from behind the screen to reveal that the second dress, a burgundy chiffon number with beaded detailing at the neck, remained several inches apart at the back.

Julie rushed back in. "Camille says they sent us the wrong gowns. These are for some Russian oligarch's wife and her overweight daughter, apparently."

"I was just telling Mrs. Von Bizmark about the thing we have to show her," Anna said, wanting to rush through all the bad stuff. Twenty minutes passed as Mrs. Von Bizmark extracted herself from the tiny gown, got back into her Lululemons, visited the bathroom, and generally dawdled to passively express her annoyance about the dresses by making them wait. Anna felt like the day was about five years long. A huffy Mrs. Von Bizmark finally sat down at Anna's computer.

"How long will this take?" Mrs. Von Bizmark asked.

"Thirty seconds," Anna said and hit play.

Mrs. Von Bizmark grasped the edge of the desk when she saw Pippy Petzer on the screen and leaned in as the scene played out. Julie handed her the waiver. Mrs. Petzer leaned over the counter and uttered her line: "Kissy . . . just tries too hard. I mean, helicopters? Doesn't get more nouveau than that." Mrs. Von Bizmark inhaled sharply, wounded. Anna put a hand on her shoulder. Mrs. Von Bizmark replayed it a few times as if trying to work something out. Anna felt for her. It had to sting.

"Has she seen this?" Mrs. Von Bizmark asked, her eyes never leaving the screen.

"Avi sent it to her lawyer, along with a copy of the signed waiver. So I presume so."

Mrs. Von Bizmark started to pace, her cotton candy quilted Burberry sneakers squeaking away on the floor polish. Perfect tendrils of light hair fell around her cheeks, which grew redder and puffier by the minute.

"You should ice your face," Anna suggested "Shall I get Cristina?"

"In a minute. Get Pippy on the phone."

Anna dialed from Mrs. Von Bizmark's private line and flushed with fury when that bitch answered in the middle of the second ring. Anna chided herself again for not thinking of this sooner.

"Calling to gloat?" Mrs. Petzer said tightly.

"I'm calling to say that you're still very welcome in our box at the opera," Mrs. Von Bizmark said breezily.

"You can't be serious."

"No hard feelings," Mrs. Von Bizmark said, quite pleased with her own canny social maneuvering.

There was a heavy silence on the phone. "Are you blackmailing me?"

"You mean because I expect you'll make sizable contributions to the opera and the public school?"

"And sit with you." While Mrs. Petzer's fate hung in the balance, she could still be a potent ally in New York society. As long as the video never got out.

"Yes, lucky me," Mrs. Von Bizmark said, as if suddenly it dawned on her that she would have to pass an entire evening in this woman's acerbic, litigious presence.

"Well, I—"

"You know what, Pippy? Don't bother coming, then. Is that better for you? Toodle-oo." Mrs. Von Bizmark hung up and called for Cristina with the ice packs. "That takes care of that," she said to no one in particular and leafed through a file of the day's personal hard-copy correspondence while Anna and Julie waited for her to say more. Was this a rash move Mrs. Von Bizmark already regretted, or had she just delivered a strategic death blow in a battle for social dominance? It was impossible to tell from the way her eyes placidly passed over the various notes and letters, opened and sorted by priority.

"Moving on!" Anna said finally. "Any ideas about who else to invite into your box?"

"Not yet," Mrs. Von Bizmark said, closing the file folder of personal notes and handing it to Anna. "You can handle all this, can't you?" she asked. "Just, you know, do everything—"

"Perfectly," they all said at the same time.

FOURTEEN

Anna picked the following Tuesday morning to kick off Operation Anniversary, just after the building staff got out of Renee's weekly meeting with them. Villson covered the door, which was ideal since he would be of little use to her. Barclay retrieved Anna and Julie in the service elevator and took them down to the basement, a maze of storage rooms, bikes, a tiny and never-used shareholder gym, and the tainted employee lounge, which everyone crammed into. The doormen, Joe and Brian, and the porters, Alfie and Barclay, stood in a tight cluster, while the ladies occupied the sofa. Alicia blushed furiously like a teenager, and Cristina glowered at all the men aloofly.

Julie wore a vintage navy Ralph Lauren knit suit with epaulets, beige pumps, aviator glasses, and a bun, a portrait of white-collar seriousness. This was a business meeting, after all. Julie video chatted with Phil at Coolwater, along with the housekeeper, grounds crew, and Castle ladies, who all sat on the floor of his office, presumably because Phil didn't know how to adjust the webcam on his laptop. You could only see Chef's striped legs and apron, leaning in the corner, off camera. So unusual was this meeting that no one chatted as Julie and Phil adjusted the volume and tested the sound. Julie placed the phone on the shelf that held a TV so that everyone could see everyone else.

"The reason I've called an all-staff meeting is that the Von Bizmarks' twenty-fifth wedding anniversary is coming up, and I have been charged with impressing Mrs. Von Bizmark," Anna began.

Unused to the microphone on his laptop, Phil snorted directly into it, followed by a loudly whispered, "Good luck."

"Phil, we can hear you," Anna said.

"Look, Anna, it's your funeral. You'll never impress her."

"That's why I need all of your help! Over the years we have all handed Mrs. Von Bizmark gifts; overheard her discuss events, meals, parties; seen her happy and sad, and I thought the only way to solve this riddle is to pool our knowledge." A sea of stony faces. There wasn't much incentive to go out on a limb when the chances of success were so low.

"OK, you guys, let me be frank. It's my understanding that since the Von Bizmarks own two floors and six shares, they are head and shoulders the largest tippers in this building. Is that roughly accurate?"

A few heads nodded. Alicia and Josefina watched Anna wide eyed. Julie stood with a pen poised over a legal pad, ready to record anything useful.

"And what do you think is going to happen if there's a divorce? Here's a newsflash: Mrs. Von Bizmark will never leave that apartment." She'd frequently said as much. "But without his income, you can bet your tips will be halved at best." She let this sink in.

"And you, Phil. All of you out there. I have news for you. If the Von Bizmark union dissolves, Coolwater is a major asset that I can all but guarantee will be instantly liquidated." Phil cocked his head to show Anna she couldn't scare him, but they both knew he was way too much of a prima donna to work for anyone new.

"So help me help you," Anna said. "Help *me* help *you*." She looked around the room, face to face, for any hint of an idea.

"She hates ice cream?" Alfie said uncertainly. Julie wrote *Likes* and *Dislikes* at the top of her pad and put *ice cream* in the Dislike column.

"No, she *loves* ice cream," said Alicia. Julie drew an arrow into the Like column.

"But once, someone sent her all these fancy ice creams packed in dry ice, and she looked like she was gonna cry. She gave 'em right back to me."

"It's because she loves ice cream too much," Cristina said sagely. Julie crossed out *ice cream* entirely.

"She likes sorbet? Ices? Like that," Chef said, off camera. Julie wrote in *sorbet*. "But only in, like, crazy flavors. Wild honey and lavender. Basil. She hates, like, chocolate?" Julie wrote in parentheses: *herbal?*

"She hates orchids," Barclay said, jumping in. Almost all the hundreds of white orchids that had been delivered to the residence had been sent to live elsewhere. Everyone suddenly had something to contribute.

"She hates the smell of salmon."

"And citrus."

"Traffic noise."

"Slow drivers."

"Wilted flowers."

"Video games."

"White chocolate."

"White dogs."

"Annoying ringtones."

"Styrofoam."

"Loud kids."

"Ethnic food."

"Except Italian."

"That's not ethnic."

"OK, OK, what about times we've seen Mrs. Von Bizmark *happy*," Anna prodded. A few beats. It was a much harder question. She held her breath.

"She loves cherry blossoms," Barclay said. "I remember once I brought a huge bouquet of them upstairs—as big as a small child—and she actually hugged them."

"She's gettin' real esoteric about the sort of vegetables we plant in the garden. All heritage-breed this and imported-from-Italy stuff," the head groundskeeper offered.

"She studied Renaissance art," Julie added.

"She loves juice," Josefina offered, wrinkling her nose. "Like, vegetable juice."

"She likes dusk," Joe said. "Years ago she would go for walks at dusk. Said it was her favorite time of day."

"That's true," Phil confirmed.

"I heard her say once how romantic the carriages in the park are," Alfie offered.

"She loves live piano," the middle-aged housekeeper from Coolwater shouted unnecessarily. "She had a guy who would come play years ago. But always with earplugs!"

Julie wrote, *pianist + earplugs*.

"She likes tangerine," Evangeline, the newest maid, offered.

"Tangerines?" Julie asked to clarify.

"No, like the color tangerine."

"Yeah, all the roses had to be tangerine this year. Like, not orange. Tangerine," the groundskeeper confirmed.

"And you know what? I once saw her get really excited about fireworks. The polo club had this one that exploded into a big pink heart, and then it dissolved into, like, a sea of sparkles . . . ," said Phil, suddenly engaged. "If you could get some fireworks like that . . . like up and over Park Avenue . . . that would be so great, Anna. I think that would really do it."

Anna saw Julie write down *fireworks* and circle it with a big heart. She drew sparkles exploding out of the heart, and underneath she wrote, *PARK AVENUE*. Yep, that would be no problem whatsoever.

Sumptuous evenings at the Peninsula had their luxuriating effects on Anna, who felt better rested and more physically relaxed than she had in years, thanks mostly to the absence of cats but also to daily (or even twice-daily) visits to the cushy, creamy spa. There, the floor and walls glistened with pastel mosaics; rolled-up fresh Turkish towels in pyramids proffered themselves at the feet of cushiony chaise lounges. Sometimes she did twenty minutes on an elliptical in the gym before making a leisurely circuit of the whirlpool, seawater plunge, steam room, and sauna, resting in between, reclining while sipping icy lemon water.

When the weekend came around, Anna didn't want to be piggy on the Von Bizmark dime, but not ordering anything extra—food? A massage?—seemed monkish. Martyr-y. As Mrs. Von Bizmark had said: this had been a tough week. Everyone needed to be at their best. Of course, she said that every week. Anna ordered a porterhouse steak, mashed potatoes, and creamed spinach with chocolate cake for dessert. Plus a bottle of burgundy and a massage.

Saturday morning Anna went straight to the studio. The handful of other artists there didn't mind her leaning her three large canvases against the wall. She put on *The Marriage of Figaro* and stared at the paintings. The first two were done: the joyful one of the picnic with Adrian and the foreboding one about her feelings of inadequacy compared to her successful sister. These two were definitely finished.

The new piece was supposed to represent the joining of two worlds most thematically reflective of the opera itself. *The Marriage of Figaro* told the story of a count who plotted to exercise his lordly right to bed his manservant's new bride the evening of their wedding. But his servants outwitted him in the end. Not only was the valet married and his wife unmolested, but the count himself happily returned to the loving embrace of his wife.

Anna studied her piece. It still felt like an open-ended sentence. The intricate oil roses in the background stirred feelings of nostalgia. Overlaid, a crisp re-creation in plastic of Julie's black-and-white lips hovered as if from another world. The lips were superenlarged and hyperdetailed—Anna had painstakingly executed the skin's contours with teensy dots. The cashmere fibers made up the pistils of one fully open flower as well as tiny wrinkles on the skin. But what, exactly, was Anna trying to conjure about these two worlds? She felt like the piece loitered in the "interesting idea" space without having yet arrived at its stirring conclusion.

"It needs a third element," the watercolorist a few spaces away said just loudly enough to be heard. She barely raised her braided mullet. Nearby, a pale twentysomething who could have passed for fourteen looked up from her colored pencil drawing to look at Anna's unfinished piece. She nodded, agreeing with Mullet Woman's assessment. Anna had never seen either before, but the stranger was exactly right. "Not too much," Mullet Woman said. "Just a touch of something."

"Thanks," Anna said.

What exactly that third component might consist of was a detail best left for the next day, Anna decided. Now that she knew something was missing, no need to rush the full epiphany—it would come when she was ready. She spent the rest of the weekend on a circuit between the Peninsula spa, the roof-deck, and the free movies on her hotel room television.

On Monday, Anna felt downright enthusiastic about devoting herself to the Von Bizmark anniversary fantasia. The all-hands brainstorming meeting had generated a list so rarefied she knew that if she could pull it off, Anna would not only preserve her job and the relationship but quite possibly set Julie and herself up for that raise. She studied the list, each day ticking off one more item.

Sorbet (herbal?)

Cherry blossoms!

"Esoteric" heritage vegetables (?)

Dusk

Carriage ride

Pianist + earplugs

Renaissance art?

Tangerine—the color

Fireworks

(in a heart bubble with sparkles shooting out)

Nothing too challenging, really, except for that final item. Fireworks at dusk over Park Avenue in the shape of a heart. If anyone could pull it off, it was the famed Gafrucci fireworks family, whose sons had been sacrificing fingers on the job for a half dozen generations. But Anna's calls to their office had been answered by a deeply disinterested family member with a heavy Queens accent who insisted both the timing and location of her request was "totally impossible, goodbye."

Stymied, Anna focused on nailing everything else. She knew it annoyed the staff when she tried to tell them how to do their jobs, but she had to be sure Chef understood the task in front of her. "Like, dinner of a lifetime!" Anna said on the phone. "Dazzle her!"

"I have this idea, but it's a little expensive . . . ?" Chef said with a rising inflection. That she would even mention cost signaled to Anna that perhaps Chef had in fact come up with something extraordinary enough to impress the unimpressible. "See, my friend, Paolo in Puglia, he has this biodynamic heirloom farm. And I got him to send me a dozen tomatoes by plane, and, Anna, you cannot even believe how she loves these tomatoes."

"Uh-huh," Anna said, calculating the cost of a jet to Bari, Italy. What if she was on that jet? Anna imagined herself there, cushioned in the cool beige leather of the G-7, a large basket lined with one of those napkins from Provence on the seat next to her. She would gather the vegetables from Paolo, spare time for a glass and a half of verdicchio, hop back on the jet with the rest of the bottle, and zoom back to reality. Chef had been talking, but no words penetrated Anna's brief respite in the south of Italy.

"Chamomile sorbet for dessert."

"I'm sorry?" Anna said.

"Look, just get me the jet, and Paolo can take care of all our sourcing. Just there and back . . . Quick, yes?"

"Um." This was right? Right? This made sense? All Mrs. Von Bizmark ate was fresh fruit and vegetables. What did Anna expect Chef to do? Rely on Whole Foods produce? "OK?" Anna said, mimicking Chef's speech pattern. "Do you think Paolo could throw some seafood in a cooler?" Anna asked, recalling that raw fish was also on the approved list for Mrs. Von Bizmark's waistline.

"What, you don't listen?" Chef asked, and Anna decided the job was in the best hands. Chef did not need Anna's guidance any more than the reverse. She hung up and hoped for the best. The food, after all, would never be the main event for Mrs. Von Bizmark, who was focused squarely on the *Vogue* shoot. She doubled up on training sessions and water consumption. She cut the lemon peel from her espresso. She iced her face on the daily.

Which gave Anna some time to devote to each aspect of the anniversary. She created a tangerine tabletop, from the flowers in the cloth underneath to the enameled Tiffany silverware to the vintage Hermès plates. Julie wrangled her way into a wholesale channel of cherry blossoms and intercepted every branch due in New York City the week of the dinner. Anna found a Renaissance art show coming to the Cloisters and purchased a table at the preview evening as one of Mr. Von Bizmark's gifts. Julie booked a piano player happy to wear earplugs, which the entire staff knew was the Mrs.'s strange preference whenever there was only a single player performing in their home.

The one nut Anna could not crack was the Gafrucci family. She kept getting transferred to the same aloof guy, who now seemed dead set on turning her down as a matter of principle. She studied their website for clues on how to appeal to them. She had tried every number and email on their contact page and was just aimlessly clicking around their bare-bones website when she stumbled on a familiar name under *MEDIA CONTACTS*.

"Well, hello, Max, how are you today?"

"Oh boy, Anna, what is it? What's wrong?"

"We need a favor."

"You mean it's not enough that I got her the goddamn spread in *Vogue*!" It seemed these days like Max was always an inch from hysteria.

"Well, this one is a bit different. It involves arranging a small fireworks display over Park Avenue in a few weeks."

"Ah, you want the Gafruccis."

"Not just any Gafrucci. I can't get the boss on the phone, and the guy I keep talking to says it's not possible. Can you get whoever Gafrucci Senior is to come here and meet with me?"

"And you know what you are going to do for me?" Uh-oh. Anna had not anticipated a tit for tat. "Convince Kissy to pose for *Vogue* with Sellers and Josefina."

"Huh," Anna said, wondering how this would fly. Would Josefina feel used as a prop? Would Sellers find the whole thing silly and wasteful? Between this and the luncheon pictures, Lanuit was shaping up to have a real doozy of a piece.

"I think they've picked up on the *Marriage of Figaro* thing," Max said as if reading Anna's mind. "Vivienne mentioned it. You know, *Upstairs, Downstairs.*"

"Inevitable, I guess," Anna said, though even she was unclear to what extent Mrs. Von Bizmark was eager to participate or even understood that the opera could be interpreted as a statement about class in America in the twenty-first century: that despite the enormous advantages of money and social rank, cleverness would always triumph. Anna was not even sure if Mrs. Von Bizmark would agree or disagree with that statement. In any case, the only thing that really mattered was whether her overall personal social stock would rise or fall in value.

Ernesto Gafrucci arrived promptly when the Mrs. was at back-to-back SoulCycle classes. He understood that the gift was entirely to be a surprise and assured Anna that "you don't stay in this business without discretion."

On the phone, the guy she'd spoken with had been coarse, bordering on unprofessional. Ernesto Gafrucci in the flesh was anything but. In an Armani suit and an Hermès tie, hair slicked back, and with a deep tan, Gafrucci reached for Anna's hand with a pinky ring so enormous it almost completely distracted from his missing right thumb and index finger. He smelled like gardenias.

"Anna, I presume."

"Excuse the mess," she said as they stepped into the living room, still damaged: an enormous hole in the ceiling, a fractured wall, and the destroyed hardwood floor waiting for Forstbacher's unlikely consent to start work. Gafrucci graciously averted his eyes from the mess. "They'll be here." She stood at the broadest window in the center of the living room wall over Park Avenue. Gafrucci took up a post next to Anna, hands clasped behind his back. He seemed to be chewing something with his front teeth behind closed lips, mulling it over with his jaw.

"What time?"

"Just after dusk."

He raised his chin, as if doing some last calculation. "Possible," he finally said, just above a whisper.

"Really?"

"But you're going to need a 1047 form and a 21C lenience. We can start the process, but we're a little late."

"Anything we can do to expedite?"

"Do you know someone in the mayor's office?"

In her mind, she could hear Mrs. Von Bizmark's response: *We certainly* do not *know that socialist!* The mayor, famously liberal, existed at the opposite end of the city's social spectrum, far from the aerie perch of the Von Bizmarks. Nonetheless, someone at VBO must be in touch with the mayor, inasmuch as the web of VBO influence traveled to the farthest corners of the earth. Who that person was and how to find them was the trick.

Sensing her hesitation, Gafrucci rubbed his chin. "Well, hold on." Gafrucci surveyed the jobsite from eight stories up, mulling it over. "Dusk, right?" Anna nodded. "On a Wednesday?" Anna nodded again. He massaged his jaw some more. "I think we can do it on the sly—you know, no paperwork." He turned his ice-blue eyes on her. "But it won't be—in the strictest sense—legal."

"Meaning we all go to jail?"

Gafrucci guffawed a little too heartily. "No, of course not. We get fined."

"How much."

"Depends."

"Range?"

"Fifty to two hundred and fifty thousand."

"Fifty dollars?"

"Yup."

"What are the chances we get caught?"

"Low! My guys are the best."

"How low?"

"Twenty percent."

Anna tallied up the assets in her anniversary party basket: Chef cooking privately imported (technically smuggled) fresh produce and seafood from Italy, New York Philharmonic pianist (in earplugs), rafts of cherry blossoms (from Seoul!); but still . . . the real wow factor was the heart firework. Even Phil couldn't get over how much it had impressed Mrs. Von Bizmark. But the risk of having to explain a quarter-million-dollar fine to an already hostile Mr. Von Bizmark weighed heavily on Anna's shoulders.

"And you can do the pink heart thing? With the sparkles?"

"Anna, *bella*, don't worry! You're a friend of Max's."

Still, she worried! Anna had to at least try to get the permits Gafrucci had mentioned. But when Anna asked Avi who at VBO might have some pull with the mayor or someone in his office, he almost laughed her off the phone. She kept at him, insisting this was an extraordinary situation and that it would be a win-win for everyone. He finally relented. Anna studied her notes from Gafrucci as she waited on hold for the mayor's chief of staff. Asking for favors was part of her job, but this one felt odious. She had pushed Avi, her eyes never wavering from the prize, but suddenly she felt so wasteful. Reprehensible, even.

"Chief of staff speaking," said a strong woman's voice. "How can I help?" Anna introduced herself again. "Yes," the woman said, *Get on with it.*

Anna stalled, cleared her throat, looked down at her notebook. They needed a 21C lenience for a private fireworks display. That was what she had to ask for. If she wanted to stage the fireworks *perfectly* legally.

"Perhaps you read about how the Von Bizmarks raised about a million dollars to save a gifted and talented school in the Bronx?" she said, the words surprising in her own ears. Anna realized that if she was going to go out on a limb, she might as well go all the way out there. This whole business of saving Ilana's school had been her idea, and even though they had raised a substantial amount of money, the distance left to go was more than her art would likely cover. Anna had to find another source of revenue.

"I did," the mayor's chief of staff said, growing a touch impatient.

"And we're going to raise more! But we were hoping that the city would consider closing the gap?"

"Gap to what?"

"One point three million. It's only about a hundred and fifty thousand. And there will be an auction at the event that will also go toward this deficit."

"Hmmm," the chief of staff said. Anna could hear her flip open a pad and write something down.

"There will also be many publicity ops. Perhaps a ribbon cutting? Does the mayor like opera?"

"I'll see what I can do," the stern voice said, promising a callback within twenty-four hours. Anna would simply have to keep her fingers crossed about the fireworks display, she thought to herself as she answered the ringing phone.

"Is this Anna?" an angry male voice demanded.

"Yes. Who is this?"

"The concierge at the Charles Hotel. We spoke yesterday?" Anna said nothing, surprised into silence. "About Chester Von Bizmark's postoperative recovery in the presidential suite." Anna's mind reeled, trying to keep up.

"Oooookaaaay," she said.

"And I know you said not to disturb him for at least four days, but other guests are complaining about loud music, and also there's a distinct smell . . ."

"I'll take care of it right away."

As she speed-dialed the least intelligent Von Bizmark child, Anna chided herself for trusting Chester or any of her employer's children with the power of her office. She had been the one to suggest impersonating herself! Chester could have easily gotten her in trouble. Real trouble. Legal trouble. And himself.

"Mummy?" Chester said. Of course he answered a call from the Von Bizmark residence midday, an extraordinary occurrence. Anna heard about a half dozen college kids hanging out listening to music and the television at the same time. The sound of clinking glasses distinguished itself.

"Guess again," Anna said.

"What's up, Anna?" Chester said, laughing at something.

"The concierge just called me, Chester," she said, clipped. She wanted him to hear her displeasure. "About your surgery."

"Uhhhhhhhhhhh."

"Do your parents know about your recuperation? And subsequent expenses?" Of course, the worst thing that could befall a kid like Chester was the revocation of credit cards. It had happened once to Vera after a particularly energetic afternoon at Bergdorf's, and she had not stepped (that far) out of line since.

"Well, you said to call here and pretend to be you."

"To get a dinner table, Chester. Look, let's forget that. Listen to me, Chester. You have five minutes to get yourself, your friends, and everything you all brought with you out of that room. You never do this again, and I will forget it happened. Deal?"

"OK . . ."

"And apologize to the concierge! I'm going to call and make sure you do that."

"Geez, Anna, OK."

Anna grappled with approaching Josefina about *Vogue*. It seemed so
. . . frivolous. Would she care about a fashion magazine when her kid's
excellent local school was about to be shuttered for unsafe conditions?
And funding for the school still hadn't been guaranteed. But Anna had
made a deal with Max, and she would live up to it.

Anna found Josefina and Alicia ironing sheets in the laundry room,
speaking urgently and quietly in Spanish. When Anna appeared at the
door, their conversation stopped immediately. Josefina reached into
her uniform pocket. "Here," she said, handing over a letter from the
Department of Education informing her that Ilana's school was still
scheduled to close. The date, four weeks away, in bold letters.

Josefina pointed at the words. "What does it mean?"

"We have to raise more money. I told you." Josefina's eyes welled
up with tears. "OK, here's the thing. Mrs. Von Bizmark is going to be
in *Vogue*, talking about the school." Josefina waited to hear how this
news would impact her. "And they want you to be in the magazine too."

Anna had expected resistance or at the very least shyness, but upon
hearing the word *Vogue*, Josefina threw back her shoulders and straightened up, lifting her chin and sucking in her cheeks just a little as if the
camera were already there and ready to capture her image.

"Me?" Josefina said, a dimple deepening in her smiling cheek. She
smoothed her hair in its shiny ponytail, the sides held back by two silver
barrettes. "*Vogue?* Whoo!" She fanned her face. "Who's the photographer?" she asked.

"Um . . . ," Anna said, forgetting.

"Franny Rosenblatt!" Julie called from the office.

"*Ay, Dios mío!* I have to text my sister in El Salvador. She won't
believe it!"

Josefina's unexpected eagerness gave Anna an idea. It was time to
follow up with the mayor's office.

"Chief of staff."

"This is Anna in Bambi Von Bizmark's office."

"Oh, yes, I haven't had a chance—"

"Listen, Mrs. Von Bizmark is going to be featured in next month's *Vogue*, and there will be a photo shoot with Franny Rosenblatt. Perhaps you've heard of her?" Anna asked snootily. "Mrs. Von Bizmark, the school's principal, our maid—who is a school parent—and the mayor, if he wanted to participate, would all be photographed for the piece. But we need to know today since the shoot is tomorrow." Since Mrs. Von Bizmark had no idea this was happening, Anna could play hardball. If it didn't come together, no one would be the wiser. Ten seconds ticked by.

"OK," said the chief of staff.

"OK what?"

"OK, he'll do it."

"Does that mean he'll come to the opera too?" Anna suddenly saw the two empty seats next to the Von Bizmarks occupied by the mayor and his wife, president of the New York Public Library. Politics aside, this was guaranteed good press.

"Let's take one step at a time. Yes to the money and yes to *Vogue*."

"Great!"

Thirty seconds later, Anna wasn't sure. Was it *great?* Appearing in print with the mayor could surely be read as some sort of "statement." But whose statement? She stared at the phone as if she might find an unsend button on the keypad.

Julie, as excited as Mrs. Von Bizmark about the photo shoot, refused to let Anna beat herself up. "You know what, Anna? You saved a school. Who cares if everyone makes some sort of message out of it? So what if she has to take a photo with the mayor? He's *the mayor*. It's still cool." Somehow hearing Julie voice her own logic failed to soothe Anna. The Von Bizmarks very loudly hated the guy. "My only worry is, What if there isn't a gap after all?" Julie asked.

"What do you mean?"

"What if your art sells well, and there is no gap in funding? Then they'd have given him a publicity op for nothing. And in an election year."

"Julie, please, be serious," Anna said. No one would spend that much on a totally unknown artist, regardless of the quality.

"I'm just sayin'."

"What about Mrs. Von Bizmark's gowns? Are they all fit and ready to go?"

"One hundred and fifty percent."

She wasn't exaggerating, Anna thought to herself as she thumbed through the two racks of clothes Julie had secured from Bergdorf's for the shoot. Julie made sure they'd be ready for any creative Rosenblatt whim, from jeans to sequins to the in-between. Suits, frocks, summer dresses. The evening gowns were evenly divided between wearable pieces Mrs. Von Bizmark would take home and fully editorial, clearly meant for a camera's lens and not real life: a giant hot-pink pouf that came together in some mysterious multihooked invisible corset, a simple black number with cutouts that would require miles of fashion tape and no underwear. Gown after gown, look after look. It was unusual for her to wonder, *How much did this cost?* but when Max had said to bring "a few looks," Anna had had a much smaller budget in mind.

"I know what you're thinking," Julie said, smiling as Anna finished going through the second full rack of clothes. "How much, right? That's what you're thinking?"

"Sort of," Anna admitted. The tally in her mind hovered near several hundred thousand dollars.

"Nothing! The clothes are on loan. Anything she wears for the shoot is hers gratis!"

"No!" Anna said.

"And anything she wants is discounted."

"Julie, oh my God." It was better than the Amex gift cards. It was another step toward that raise. "Does she know?"

"Not yet!" Julie said brightly, rubbing her hands together in gleeful anticipation.

The morning of the shoot, Julie obsessively steamed the clothes at the *Vogue* studio. She wore her practical outfit: "sweatpants" from her last trip to Paris and a perfectly proportioned white knit crop top of Julie's own design. Her tousled top bun completed the effect. It looked like she'd fallen out of bed and yet was also ready for her close-up. This was her natural habitat. Even the *Vogue* stylist soon migrated over from her racks to inspect the Bergdorf pieces, dispatching her two assistants to grab accessories and shoes. Soon Julie and she were fast friends, steaming and draping and debating the merits of a wedge versus a stiletto for a particular plum skirt with a kicky pleated detail.

Anna, on the other hand, felt like a goblin on a rare excursion out from underneath her bridge. It wasn't her outfit—which was a perfectly fine Stella McCartney hand-me-down blouse over her favorite "fancy" jeans and her new metallic Birkenstocks. It was her attitude, which was positively not fashion. It seemed that her lack of interest, skills, and experience was obvious to the pods of busy interns who evenly divided into artsy professionals and model hopefuls darting by with coffees and clothes.

Mrs. Von Bizmark finally stepped off the elevator in owl sunglasses, a polished ponytail, and head-to-toe Lululemon. The producer rushed to direct her to makeup. Instead, Mrs. Von Bizmark's eyes landed on Julie, compulsively steaming the fluttery hem of a black Tom Ford gown. Mrs. Von Bizmark drifted over, completely taken in by the dazzling sartorial display.

"How fabulous!" Mrs. Von Bizmark gushed over the clothes. Julie and Anna stood at her elbow, holding their breath. At first, Mrs. Von

Bizmark was happy to see so many options. Somewhere in the cocktail dress section, she started to really admire and cluck. By the time she got to the evening gowns, she seemed a little perplexed. But when Julie explained the arrangement with Bergdorf's, Mrs. Von Bizmark's head swiveled around like it was on some sort of spring. "You mean we didn't pay for them yet?"

"Nope! Whatever you use in the shoot is yours to keep *at no charge*, and whatever you decide to buy is yours at forty percent off!" Julie explained again, intoxicated with this good news. In one fell swoop Julie had eliminated any lingering negative feelings from the luncheon. Mrs. Von Bizmark threw an arm over her shoulders and squeezed. "Great job!" she said, smiling from invisible face-lift scar to invisible face-lift scar.

Yet somehow, Anna had allowed them all to arrive at that moment without having told Mrs. Von Bizmark who else would be part of the photo shoot. She had to pounce before Mrs. Von Bizmark saw Josefina. "And guess who's here!" Anna interjected, one eye traveling over to where Josefina was undergoing a transformation at the hands of a dead-serious trio of hairstylists and makeup artists.

"Rosenblatt?" Mrs. Von Bizmark said breathlessly.

"Not yet! But! She wanted to do a few pics of you *with* Josefina *and* Principal Sellers." Confusion clouded Mrs. Von Bizmark's expression, and Anna decided it was best just to blurt it out. "And the mayor!"

"The mayor of what?" Mrs. Von Bizmark said.

"New York!"

"City?"

"Yes!"

"You mean, the communist?"

"Well, I mean, he's technically more of a socialist . . . ," Julie started, but she stopped when she saw Mrs. Von Bizmark's narrowing eyes.

"The city is going to cover the rest of the budget to keep the school open," Anna said, pausing in the hopes that Mrs. Von Bizmark's slight affirmative head tilt would grow into a small smile. When this failed to happen, she continued, "So *Vogue* thought it would make sense to include all the stakeholders. School mom, mayor, private philanthropist, principal . . ."

"One big, happy, family!" Julie said, smiling with both hands in the air.

Mrs. Von Bizmark sighed, slid in her earpiece, and sat in the makeup chair. Who was she calling? Anna inched up behind the *Vogue* glam team, who commenced their preliminary fussing. She could only make out every other word or so.

"Peter? So I'm at . . . *Vogue* shoot . . . OK, OK, hold on . . . . the mayor . . . New York. Mayor of New York. . . . Yes. Exactly. I don't know! Soon!" She hung up, a self-satisfied smile finally finding its way to her face.

Just by a change in the energy of the room, everyone seemed to simultaneously understand that the mayor had arrived. Interns dashed about; the producer waited by the elevator, texting Rosenblatt. A quiet descended. Then the cargo-elevator door opened, and the noisy chatter of many people talking on their phones all at once poured out. The entourage moved en masse, the mayor at its core, already photo ready with just a touch of makeup over a fresh shave.

Mrs. Von Bizmark, almost done with glam, rose to her feet: even if he was a socialist, he was a powerful and famous socialist. Although they had shaken hands only twice in receiving lines over the last five years, the mayor instantly recognized Mrs. Von Bizmark and broke free to greet her. As soon as their eyes met, their differences melted away. He strode toward her, all pinstripes and outstretched hands as if he were greeting his sister. She kissed his cheek with a light chuckle.

"It's amazing what you're doing for our public schools," he said grandly.

If this was an odd thing for Mrs. Von Bizmark to hear, she did not show it, seamlessly introducing him to Josefina. Right on cue, Franny Rosenblatt stepped off the elevator silently, camera already in hand. She walked in snapping pictures, as if this was how she introduced herself. Two lithe, ninja-esque former models in all black, each toting several additional cameras, handed them to her in rotation as the mayor and Mrs. Von Bizmark listened to Josefina talk about Ilana, all for Rosenblatt to capture.

And from there, everything flowed. Mrs. Von Bizmark donned a daytime casual look of tan slacks and a blouse with a wide leather belt. Josefina's black Brooks Brothers skirt suit fit her perfectly after the crack *Vogue* seamstress had made some adjustments. A harried Principal Sellers arrived just in time, switched into a cotton shirtdress, got a quick dusting of makeup, and took her place against the white backdrop. Rosenblatt arranged them and rearranged them, trading off cameras with her assistants every minute. The mayor was of course a total pro, turning his best side to the camera and going from serious to mid-hilarity on cue. Josefina could have exploded with pride; her grin was unwavering. Mrs. Von Bizmark looked to the elevator door each time it opened, hoping to see Mr. Von Bizmark.

But after only thirty minutes, the mayor's handlers snatched him away. Josefina took a town car home, feeling like Cinderella in her carriage. Sellers raced to the subway. And Mrs. Von Bizmark returned to the makeup chair for them to layer on darker shadow, more mascara. A deep-garnet lip. In the hands of these talented professionals, Mrs. Von Bizmark transcended mere attractiveness. The stylist picked out the slinky Tom Ford number with the cutouts and slits. The makeup artist lined her eyes in kohl. Through some combination of tape and illusion, this midfifties mom was transformed into a thirty-year-old supermodel in fifteen minutes. She changed into an even smaller dress. And then an even smaller one.

By the time Mr. Von Bizmark had stepped off the elevator just over an hour later, Mrs. Von Bizmark was in a tiny sequined slip too revealing to ever actually wear in public. His eyes scanned the edges of the loft looking for someone, not even recognizing his own wife. He drifted over to the light, his eyes on every face.

Rosenblatt, tired, directed Mrs. Von Bizmark. "Less stiff. Look more, like, loose."

Mr. Von Bizmark watched, still searching. Anna sidled up to him and said, "Good evening, Mr. Von Bizmark."

"Oh, hello . . . ," he said, reaching for her name, not knowing her out of context. "Anna!" And with this, recognition passed across Mr. Von Bizmark's face, followed by surprise to learn that the woman in front of the camera was in fact his own wife. Anna smiled to herself as he crept closer, his presence obscured by all the lights. He squinted, watching her move her hips a little. "Like, looser!" Rosenblatt barked, then gave up and lit a cigarette. "Never mind. Take a break."

Mrs. Von Bizmark looked a little dejected and walked off the set almost right into Mr. Von Bizmark. She looked up at him, and for a moment they both smiled; Anna couldn't remember the last time she'd witnessed such a calm, warm moment between them. *Cha-ching.*

"Peter!" All breathless with excitement.

"Hi there, sexy."

"Hi!"

He wrapped his arm around her and pulled her body closer. For a minute, Anna thought it would all be a home run and the perfect warm-up for tomorrow's anniversary finale. Mr. Von Bizmark leaned over and whispered something in her ear. She giggled, pressing her palm to his chest.

"Where's the mayor?" Mr. Von Bizmark asked.

"Gone almost forty-five minutes ago," Mrs. Von Bizmark said. Mr. Von Bizmark displayed his annoyance at hearing this by looking at his watch over Mrs. Von Bizmark's shoulder.

"Too bad," Mr. Von Bizmark said, taking a step back.

"Well, he's coming to the ball," Mrs. Von Bizmark said. Anna perked up, hearing this; she knew it wasn't confirmed yet. "Maybe . . . he'd be receptive . . ."

Mr. Von Bizmark nodded curtly. "All right. I've got a dinner," he said, but before he could make a clean getaway, Mrs. Von Bizmark pulled her husband in close.

As Anna watched them, cheek to cheek, she all at once knew the third element of her painting. Pencil. A sketch. Something rudimentary on vellum. What popped into Anna's mind was *The Burlington House Cartoon*: the da Vinci sketch in London's National Gallery. She wasn't one for religious art, and yet this piece was full of self-contained energy, the charcoal curves and shadows creating a movement and warmth unrivaled in most oil paintings. Mrs. Von Bizmark unclasped her husband's lapel, and he kissed her on the cheek before departing.

Anna let her imagination run, pondering the last necessary element of her final piece for the opera. She knew it had to be simple. Charcoal. She sat on the L train to the studio, her leg shaking, unfocused eyes traversing the length of the empty violet plastic seating. And then she saw it. The top of a woman's head, peeking out over the lips. She'd have to draw it, then cut it out and lay it over the oil in just the right way so that it was as if she was amid the flowers. A homage to *The Mona Lisa*'s cryptic eyes hovering over the plastic sheeting.

As predicted, it took the longest to razor out the charcoal image. Anna carefully sliced the paper so that a few of the coral and mint petals would appear to overlap the drawing. The simple black-and-white addition was the last puzzle piece. No more than a few hundred strokes of charcoal, the eyes rendered, in between lush rose petals. This, the chorus of the piece, the ones who observed. It was complete.

So high on having finished, Anna took herself to the bar at the Peninsula atop the city, ordered a forty-dollar martini on the Von Bizmark tab, and enjoyed twenty seconds of unmitigated contentment before her thoughts turned to Adrian. It was as if now that the painting was done, her mind had automatically brought its attention to the next-most pressing agenda item. She missed him.

The spa, her sanctuary, called for her. Since it was late and the middle of the week, Anna had the place entirely to herself. It was almost creepy, except for the omnipresent, professionally disinterested staff who appeared every twenty minutes to offer her ice-cold lemon water. Somewhere on her third round between steam bath and sauna, she decided she could—no, *should*—call Adrian, just to see how things would go.

She told herself she had nothing to lose and no reason to feel so nervous, but butterflies fluttered in her stomach. Anna wrapped herself in a cushy robe and tied her head up in a towel in the grotto-esque whirlpool room. As soon as it looked like she might want something, a young woman with a blonde ponytail and a Peninsula polo shirt appeared with a glass of lemon water on a silver tray.

"Actually, is it possible to have a white wine?"

"Certainly." Moments later, she reappeared with a large crystal goblet full of wine so cold the side misted with condensation the moment she set it down. Anna drank half of it before it could get another degree warmer. She took a deep breath, threw her shoulders back, and called. He answered on the second ring.

"Hey!" Adrian said, the voice so comforting, more familiar in her ear than even her own. "It's you."

"Hey," Anna said, the future before her like a blank page. In fact, her whole mind was like a blank page. The silent seconds ticked by.

"How are you?" he asked.

"OK."

"I miss you." Silence. She realized that what she really wanted from Adrian in that moment was not language. And maybe he realized it too. "You never liked having real conversations on the phone. Why don't I come to where you are?" In Anna's state, half in the bag, fully warmed up, all relaxed, the only thing this conjured was languorous makeup sex in her palatial suite upstairs, postsex room service, post–room service sex . . .

"Meet at the Peninsula bar?"

"See you in twenty."

Anna downed the rest of her wine and raced upstairs, ignoring the curious looks of other hotel guests when she stepped onto the elevator in the spa robe, toweled head and terry cloth slippers embroidered with a floral *P*, at 10:30 p.m. Way more pressing was that she had only eighteen minutes to go from wilted, damp, and basically naked to attractive enough to want to get naked with. She fumbled the key in the lock, excited as hell.

So excited that it took her a beat to figure out why something felt off in her room. A suit jacket hung from the knob of the bathroom. The lights were all on. Anna's eyes flew to the side table, where inexplicably a replica of the large key she held in her hand sat innocently enough on the table.

"Hello?" a drunken Mr. Von Bizmark called from the bedroom. "Is that the masseuse?" Anna's heart leaped into her throat, like an antelope who realized too late that she was far from the herd and the nearby bushes were rustling against the crouched back of a stalking predator. Her rational brain reminded her: *You're no antelope! Just announce yourself! Say, "Hello, Mr. Von Bizmark, it's Anna. Remember? I'm staying here?"*

But something she couldn't ignore told her to just leave and sort it all out later. These were the sorts of situations—being alone in a hotel room with your employer's drunk husband—that could easily become some sort of terrible misunderstanding or worse. Anna quickly, silently slipped out the door as quietly as possible, figuring this was the best way to neatly avoid any and all complications.

She strode through the marble lobby, past the grand staircase and the gawking Japanese tourists, and straight onto the street, all the while telling herself, *You are a rock star. This is fine. Just keep it moving.*

"Cab, please," she said to the porter, who hesitated. "I'll bring everything back!" she whispered urgently. "I promise!" And then she was safely in the back seat, the top of her head towel pressed against the ceiling of the cab, her cell phone in the pocket of her robe.

She texted Adrian: I need a raincheck.

He texted back immediately: ?

But she said nothing.

He wrote: When?

After the ball.

Ding-dong.

Anna heard the bell echo off the walls of her sister's spacious apartment. She could feel the plush carpet through the Peninsula slippers; even Lindsay's hallway boasted crown molding and inset lighting. Anna took the towel out of her hair and ran her fingers through it.

When Lindsay opened the door, Anna tried to stay sanguine. "Hi," she said, giving her sister a few seconds to take in the strange visual.

"Come in, come in," Lindsay said, eyes flying from the slippers to Anna's hand protectively clasped at the top of the robe. "What happened? Are you OK? Come sit . . ."

Anna spied Lindsay's husband, Jack, in his pajama pants, scurrying away down the hallway. Lindsay ushered her into the living room, where she invited Anna to choose from a swath of seating options: leather-padded barstools, a couch, two easy chairs pushed together by the window. Anna chose the couch. They sat knee to knee. In Lindsay's beautiful apartment. Her hand lingered protectively near her soon-to-be-round belly. "What is going on?" Lindsay said.

"I . . . am sort of taking some space from Adrian."

Lindsay tried and failed to conceal her shock. When Anna said nothing more, she asked, "And you moved to the Peninsula?"

"No, I . . . it has to do with work. Mr. Von Bizmark was staying in the corporate apartment for weeks, and I think he forgot that last week he told me I could stay there."

"And?"

"Well, he showed up, by mistake, because I think he was pretty drunk. I just left . . ." She knew how strange it sounded—how bizarre everything about her job always came off—but this time it seemed even worse. Like part of her employment involved scurrying off in the night with nothing but a bathrobe and her phone. "I know you think I'm pathetic!" Anna blurted and burst into tears.

"Oh no!" Lindsay said, instantly embracing Anna, who allowed her sister to squeeze her, jamming her shoulder into her sternum. It felt like she was pressing the tears and snot out of her. "No, no! No!" Lindsay exclaimed, not knowing what else to say. Anna reached past her for the tissues on the table and blew her nose over her shoulder. Finally, Lindsay let her go. "A, is this because of Adrian's new job?"

Anna drew back, expressions flying across her face like clouds on a windy day: rejection, consideration, acceptance. "Maybe a little," Anna admitted. "I just—I know you think I blew it. Like, blew it all. Everything. My life."

"I do?" Lindsay said. "How can you say that?"

"What am I doing? Who am I?"

"Aw, geez, A, you have to know it in your heart the way we all do." When she said *we all*, Anna felt so . . . grateful.

"I just used to think someday, I'd, like, make it and quit my job and become something else. Not just an assistant . . ."

"You're an artist too!"

"But am I?"

"Anna, you have the perfect day job. You make a great living. Great perks! And you still have time for painting," Lindsay said. Anna had thought this about herself, or tried to, but hearing it from her sister's mouth made the words more digestible. "And I get it: that it's hard. But if you doubt yourself, it's not coming from me. Or Adrian. Or Adrian's new job." Lindsay looked at her sister pointedly.

"What?" Anna said.

"It's coming from you! You always put too much pressure on yourself."

Maybe she had been wrong about Lindsay. What she said made so much sense. It was like a strange film where suddenly all the negative thoughts she had ascribed to others—Lindsay, Adrian—replayed in her mind in her own voice. Maybe if Anna believed she was an artist herself, she would not feel so under siege by other people's perceived slights. "So you don't think I'm a loser?" Anna asked.

"You'll always be my hero, A," Lindsay said.

"Hey, Linds, I'm sorry if I've been a jerk."

"What do you mean 'if'?"

"What do you mean 'what do I mean'?"

"I mean you're kind of jerky. You're rarely wrong, and when you are, it takes you forever to realize it. That's part of your charm."

"Huh," Anna said, taking this in. Made sense.

"And," Lindsay continued, seeing an opening, "I hope you won't mind me saying this, but you are just the teensiest bit self-involved." Lindsay's face scrunched up with the effort of delivering this message to her older sister. While she had never exactly said it that way before, the concept felt familiar. Anna realized with a lurch that Adrian had been right: Anna had asked about his new job approximately never. But it was too soon for her to face up to it.

FIFTEEN

Morning of March 8

"This is so much more complicated than I could have imagined," Julie said, eyeing the scattered place cards arrayed on the bistro table over Anna's and Max's shoulders. The Von Bizmarks' four boxes at the opera and sixteen tables at the ball provided a great opportunity to demonstrate the gregariousness, sophistication, beauty, and social rank of their friends and associates. A card for each sparkling guest bore their name and a tiny headshot. Max continuously distributed them, gathered them up, and arranged them again, like mah-jongg tiles.

There was an almost-lost art to seating that could elevate an evening from merely technically perfect (which was expected) to *unforgettable*. Max aimed for that alchemy where common interests, personal aesthetics, and prescription medications all vibed, and everyone left saying in unanimity about themselves and the others: "Those Von Bizmarks have the most interesting friends. I love their events!"

Max shuffled the place cards in his hand. "All the ones with the green checks are confirmed?"

"Yes, Max." Anna sighed and smiled, counting the seconds until he said . . .

"Only half?"

"So far," Anna said, and Max sighed dramatically. "The orchids go out today." These plants had begun flowing in days ago from every florist in the city, of every shade, shape, and size, ranging from jumbo to rainforest, each meant to heartily *congratulate the Von Bizmarks* on the honor about to be bestowed upon them. Cristina plucked the best buds for placement throughout the apartment, until each room, bathroom, and oversize closet housed at least one showy swoop of elephant-eared blossoms. Though the Von Bizmarks did not like orchids—"So boring," Mrs. Von Bizmark yawned whenever she passed one—there were simply too many of them to keep in the office or give away. Plus these particular flowers reminded everyone of the big event to come, lending a feeling of momentousness to the otherwise museum-like residence. Cristina would quietly discard them all the morning after the ball.

The two dozen B-list flowers unworthy of apartment placement were left in cellophane and awaited rerouting to VIP Opera Ball guests with a "handwritten" note from Mrs. Von Bizmark:

Can't wait to see you at the opera!

XO

Kissy

"Do you really think that's adequate?" Max asked, one perfectly plucked and trimmed eyebrow arched. "I can have my assistant call everyone."

Anna smiled into his negativity. "Or we could hire snipers to dart the guests and drag them to the ball by their ankles." Max ignored her.

Cristina brought yet another orchid, at least three feet high, two enormous stalks sprouting unusual neon-orange blossoms, and set it down on a distant windowsill. She hummed a nameless Polish tune and unnecessarily fussed with the ribbons. There was an aggressive quality to her happiness that grated on Anna's melancholy; for a fleeting moment, she wished Cristina would go back to being a miserable bitch.

Max pondered his newest seating arrangement. "We don't have the most important person," he said, doing jazz hands over the place cards like an incantation. The problem, front and center, was the first row of the Von Bizmark box. They needed two more people, the seats of honor. Now that the seats were no longer reserved for the Petzers, there seemed to be no one of equivalent caliber and quality. Another missing element.

"The mayor still hasn't confirmed," Anna said.

"I vote for Prince Montepulciano," Julie suggested.

"Valdobianno," Anna said. "He definitely called to accept, right?"

"Well . . . ," Julie started, her hesitation instantly calling Max's attention to her. "It sounded like he was calling from a mobile phone on a yacht in the middle of the ocean on Mars, but I'm pretty sure he said yes."

"He's too unreliable, even if he is gorgeous," Max concluded. "And besides, who will he bring? Impossible to predict."

"Martha Miller?"

"Her husband's such a bore. He'll probably sleep through half of it. No Petzers, huh?" Max asked. Anna had declined to share the incriminating video, knowing that Max could never keep it a secret for long.

"No Petzers. But Max, this is New York! Surely there's someone else?"

Max gathered up the cards and flipped through them: a lot of scions and socialites, a few luminaries, a few formerly famous faces, no real showstoppers. He muttered an ongoing commentary. "Her and her dresses. It's always big ball gowns. Too much fabric." "This one and the arm candy. Younger than his actual grandchild. Tsk." "Jail time. Tax evasion." "Too loud." "Too dowdy." "Too . . . too."

The back doorbell rang, and Cristina answered it with her usual greeting followed immediately with a hearty "So good to see you!" and then a full minute of rapid Polish in which Cristina grew louder and

louder, finally saying, "No! No! No!" several times, screeching in disbelief. The racket was unignorable. Anna, Julie, and Max paused, facing
the door in expectation, but all they heard was Polish and giggling.

"Cristina, what's going on?" Anna asked sharply.

"Come, come," she said, bringing Villson by his arm into the office,
beaming with pride. "You won't believe!" she said by way of introduction. Max took an immediate interest in their blond super of the manly
hands and easy smile. Villson wasn't used to so much attention, and
with all eyes on him after Cristina's bold introduction, he could only
rub his palms together, abashed. Finally, she clapped him on the back.
"Say!"

"Mrs. Forstbacher agrees to construction starting now," Villson said
quietly.

These words were so unexpected that it took Anna a full three
seconds to comprehend their meaning. "I don't believe it!" she finally
exclaimed. Julie's mouth hung open. Cristina broke into applause.

Max, inured by ignorance to this sledgehammer of extraordinary
news, stared at Villson in consternation. "Who," he said, "are you?"

"How?" Anna said.

"I have my ways," Villson said, and he winked. Max practically
swooned.

"He brought cookies every day!" Cristina said. "Homemade!"

"Your wife made them?" Anna asked.

"No!" Cristina snapped, instantly furious with Anna for suggesting
such a vile person existed.

"Baking relaxes me," he said, smiling at Cristina.

"This is your new super!" Max suddenly exclaimed, awestruck.

"Anyway, I heard she liked cookies. From my father. Who was her
super at her last building when I was just a boy."

"No! No! No!" Cristina said, again, totally delighted with this man.

"How's her hip?" Anna asked.

"Eh," Villson said, shrugging off his apparent irresistibility. "She's just a sweet old lady who is a little lonely."

Anna squinted at him for a moment—was this guy for real?—before moving on to the implications of Villson's accomplishment. "So we can start tomorrow. Call the Silver Fox," Anna said to Julie.

"Who's the Silver Fox?" Max demanded. "What else have you girls been hiding from me?" He batted his gelled lashes at Villson, and Cristina moved to stand between them, flashing Max her evil eye.

"Special delivery!" Barclay called from the back door. He carried an enormous explosion of pink flowers, the only nonorchid to have appeared in the deluge of floral offerings. Cristina had to move a large planter to the floor so it could find a place on the counter.

"Who are those from?" Max said.

"It's not who they're *from*. It's who they're *for*! I was told to hand you this personally," Barclay said to Anna, proffering an ivory envelope. For a few seconds, Anna hoped they were from Adrian. She had been sort of pining for him since their one brief phone call, but she didn't want to go back before her own self-imposed deadline. A small part of her still wasn't ready to admit whatever she would have to admit in order to return to her relationship.

And happily, it had turned out like a strangely ameliorative experience to stay at Lindsay's. Before washing up on her sister's doormat like that, Anna had forgotten what an extraordinary time this was, the last precious months before the baby. The sisters were hanging out like they hadn't in years. All this time, they had been separated only by a subway ride, but Anna had gotten hung up on the idea that they inhabited two entirely separate worlds. Lindsay had been gently nudging Anna to reconsider what Adrian had said from a different—more secure—point of view. He was right; it wasn't fair to expect so much from him when he himself was going through a transition that she hadn't bothered to wonder about. She hoped he had read her mind and sent these flowers to jump-start the conversation.

But no, the return address said *GAFRUCCI* with embossed silver fireworks on either side. Somehow he always knew when the Mrs. was out—today at the gym and then to the spa. Anna slipped the thick card out of the silver-lined envelope.

Dear Anna,

Fingers crossed! Just kidding. Don't worry. It's gonna be great.

Ernesto Gafrucci

PS You should probably burn this card. Just in case. Kidding!

Anna laughed. The anniversary was the very next day. Gafrucci's card made her feel better, maybe? Anna looked up and found all eyes on her, each lung in the room on pause, waiting for her to tell them who the flowers were from.

"They're from the fireworks guy. At ease," she said, confusing everyone even further. As Cristina showed Barclay and Villson out, she heard the super ask her in Polish, *"Fajerwerki?"*

Max eyed the enormous pink bouquet and asked, "How much are you paying him?"

"More exciting news, you guys," Julie interrupted. "Prince Valdobianno was photographed landing at JFK with a mystery woman last night!" She held up Page Six of the *Post.* He was smiling amiably at the camera on his way into the back of a town car. This was a relief, in that it confirmed he would bring a guest, thus answering one lingering question. But when Julie and Anna looked to Max for his response, they found him totally absorbed in his phone.

"Max?" Anna said.

"It's out," Max breathed.

"I need a little more information."

"The STT piece. It's out, up, whatever."

At a glance, Anna found nothing unusual about the length of the lede piece on the *Park and Fifth* site or the pictures, which were largely taken from the white carpet before the luncheon shenanigans. STT was a creature of society, after all. He would never embarrass the women who buttered his bread. "I don't exactly love the headline," Max said.

"I AM A JEWESS"

Fair to say most didn't know Kissy Von Bizmark was Jewish. After storming the city from the shores of the Gold Coast, she quickly rose to "It Girl" status, joined forces with none other than the ascendant Peter Von Bizmark, and promptly began checking off the usual list of socialite to-dos: Junior League, Cosmopolitan Club, the Union. She found her cause—the New York City Opera, no less—and worked tirelessly on the institution's behalf, raising tens of millions of dollars in the last decade alone to finally arrive here, the belle of none other than the Opera Ball. Bambi Von Bizmark positively defines New York Society at this particular moment. The Von Bizmarks' embracing a Bronx gifted-and-talented public school as well as Bambi's colorful ethnic past mark a break with the old . . .

"I don't think it's so bad . . . ," Anna said, intending to calm Max down. His index finger twitched over the article. The Von Bizmark phones started going; Julie hopped from one line to the next.

"Anna, it's Avi for you," Julie interrupted. "He seems . . . annoyed."

"What's this I'm reading here?" their persnickety lawyer chirped in Anna's ear.

"Yeah, I'm going to need a little more information."

"Anna, is she OK?"

"What do you mean?"

"This article . . . she sounds . . . out there." He sounded unusually flustered.

"She's fine, Avi! Come on!"

"I'm just saying, we don't need any more negative attention right now."

"OK, Avi, I'll let our publicist know."

"Know what? Know what?" Max croaked behind her.

"Please do!" Avi said into her ear.

"That was a joke," Anna said, and Avi hung up on her.

"It's not so bad," Julie said about the article before the phone could ring again. She read Anna an excerpt: "'When taken in concert with the money raised at—and the resources expended on—this particular event, well, it was just positively intoxicating. No wonder Kissy spoke from the heart! No wonder everyone drank a little too much! The mansion! The ocean! The golden horses . . . only Kissy could pull it all off with such grace.'"

"Sounds good to me," Anna said. "Right, Max?" Max said nothing, tapping out a text. "The pictures are great. He barely mentioned Felix Mercurion, saying she took it like a champion when they carted out all that art. *And* he gave her credit for saving a whole school," Anna said.

Still Max had not looked up, nor did he bid them farewell as he walked out while answering a call from his assistant. "Hold the fort— I'm coming back now," he barked into his phone.

Emails flowed in from Mrs. Von Bizmark's circle, particularly those who had attended the luncheon, avid STT readers all. Congratulations were in order! The article was a "victory," a "salute," a "toast" to KVB. These women took any opportunity, no matter how insignificant or unearned, to praise one another, and this feature in the *New York Times* of wealth was no small thing. In twenty minutes, Kissy Von Bizmark's social capital had appreciated significantly. And the *Vogue* article wasn't even out yet. The phone rang constantly.

"Hi, Anna, I know I'm not supposed to be bothering you at work," Vera said, surprising Anna out of her rhythm of taking down congratulatory phone messages, "but I could really use some help. And don't just say no right away this time, OK?"

Of course, this was the perfect time for Anna to field some outlandish request from the most manipulative Von Bizmark child. "Try me," Anna said.

"So I'm supposed to do a presentation on my hometown, and you know my favorite thing about New York, right?"

"Your family lives here?"

"Other than that."

"World-class cultural institutions."

"Bagels," Vera said. "It's bagels."

"Deep," Anna said.

"Hey!"

"Go on."

"I was thinking, you send the jet tomorrow morning, I run down to the city and pick up bagels. For my class." Anna said nothing. This teenager called upon the jet like she was asking for a lift to the mall. "As part of my presentation."

"I see. Any friends coming for the joyride?"

"Maybe. What difference does that make?"

"How about this, Vera? I overnight you a few dozen bagels plus all your favorite things from Zabar's, and you can host a New York brunch for all your friends . . . I mean, for *your presentation*." Anna emphasized the last two words.

"That's right! It's for class!"

"OK, OK."

"Thanks, Anna!" Vera gushed. Maybe this had been her goal all along; she was wily, that one.

"And remember," Anna said, already jotting off an email to their account rep at Zabar's, "don't mention the—"

"Anniversary! Yeah, yeah, I got your email, letter, text, and voice mail. I'm not as stupid as Chester, you know."

In fairness, on all the other anniversaries of the Von Bizmarks' married life, every single human Mrs. Von Bizmark encountered in their apartment building, from the maids to the doormen, and most certainly Anna and Julie, would immediately acknowledge this hallowed date, the birth of all the Von Bizmark enterprises. But to enhance an evening full of surprises, Anna had instructed no one to speak that key phrase, pretending the anniversary had been lost in all the opera planning.

Distraught, Mrs. Von Bizmark cast her eye around the office, over the sea of orchids that continued to swell. Then she loomed over the calendar, still as a statue, three fingers gracefully pressed to the day. Any other time, this alone would have prodded Anna, Julie, or even Cristina to say something, but the room was as quiet as a tomb.

Finally, Mrs. Von Bizmark went to her desk, scrutinizing its familiar clutter, undisturbed by card or gift. Eventually sitting, Mrs. Von Bizmark listlessly scrolled through the organized, sorted, and prioritized emails on her computer. Since Anna and Julie screened all correspondence, they had already siphoned away the tens of *Happy Anniversary!* greetings from every friend, staff member, former classmate, social climber, and vendor and had carefully paused her inbox so no new messages would flow in. Perhaps for the first time ever, Mrs. Von Bizmark opened each and every email, double-clicking her mouse more and more aggressively as she found nothing with those essential words. Particularly not from Mr. Von Bizmark.

Anna knew this would be a critical, difficult few minutes before Mrs. Von Bizmark was out for lunch with a friend, on to a meeting with Opal, to the gym for her final session of "boot camp" before the big day, then a facial with Ping downtown, with a little shopping in between. They had purposely stacked this day full of activities in appealing retail neighborhoods where Mrs. Von Bizmark could self-soothe. But as long as she sat there, in the office, failing to receive the attention she felt she deserved, Mrs. Von Bizmark was a grenade about to explode in someone's face.

"Should I call the car?" Anna asked.

"Fawnee is always late," Mrs. Von Bizmark said, sorting random bits of paper on her desk as if the answer to some unknown but critical question might be found amid the calling cards and thank-you notes. "Cristina!" she suddenly called sharply, which signaled Anna to hop on the intercom and summon the housekeeper in a fashion she could actually hear. The ladies disappeared into the darkest closets and bathrooms adjoining the master suite (where the majority of their employers' attention found its focus) for the bulk of the morning. As the seconds ticked by—three, four, five—Mrs. Von Bizmark grew impatient. "Did you tell her that I had the gym today?" she asked Anna crisply.

"Of course."

"Because I want to take my bag with me in the car, and I don't see it anywhere." Already huffy, she could get worked up into a lather for any reason, no matter how minor. Cristina appeared, keenly aware of the Mrs.'s fragile emotional state, with the desired monogrammed Goyard miniduffel in hand.

"Your bag is right here, Mrs. Von Bizmark. I pack two extra waters like you like and the new Lululemon that looks so good on you." Cristina deposited the hot-potato bag and, without waiting for a thank-you, scurried back to the safe, faraway upstairs. In being perfect, Cristina had deprived Mrs. Von Bizmark of the opportunity to chastise someone. Now she was doubly annoyed.

"I'll just call the car now!" Julie said brightly, picking up the phone.

Lost in a desultory haze, Mrs. Von Bizmark said nothing for a few minutes, then suddenly snapped, "Where are we on the seating?"

"I'll call Max and ask if he's ready to present."

"Why do I need to follow up with you on things like this, Anna?"

"It's certainly on my radar!"

"Anna, the ball is tomorrow. I want to see the final seating scheme when I get back." Anna did some quick math: fiveish. That would give them about six hours to confirm the most elusive guests on the list and get Max a final count.

Anna generated a quick spreadsheet of phone numbers and time zones so she and Julie could tag-team harassing Mrs. Von Bizmark's friends and associates. Their list of hardest-to-pin-down glitterati included a woman without citizenship who roamed the world in her enormous yacht with a rotating cast of attractive, jobless men and the TV personality Martha Miller, who was famous for trotting out a list of excuses (her husband's eczema, an early flight the next day, a great-godniece's favorite doll's tea party) to avoid confirming until the very last minute. The mayor's chief of staff no longer answered her phone when Anna called. Then there was the unreachable prince.

In the midst of this, Florence called to inform them she'd messengered over Mr. Von Bizmark's anniversary present for the Mrs.

"What is it?" Anna asked.

"I can't even remember. I think a bracelet this time."

"Oh, Florence, you're such a romantic." Anna sighed.

"I've done as I was asked. No more, no less. Five hundred at Harry Winston. No emeralds."

"Don't forget to get him home by seven for a briefing."

"Don't you think you might be overstepping?" Florence asked. As far as Anna was concerned, Florence was an obstructionist dinosaur whose advice always came at the worst possible time and therefore felt exactly like the jab it was.

"I guess time will tell." Anna hung up. Would this be, as Phil had predicted, Anna's funeral?

"We'll be returning that bracelet or whatever it is immediately," Julie said. In two decades, the Mrs. had kept not a single piece of jewelry Florence had purchased, an inevitability Mr. Von Bizmark had never noticed. Mrs. Von Bizmark was essentially impossible to shop for, and Mr. Von Bizmark had given up long ago. For years she had been collecting credit at Harry Winston for the mythical lariat, an office unicorn. Other than that, there was nothing she wanted. "Maybe we could do something?" Julie said. "Something thoughtful?"

To throw oneself into the certain failure of shopping for a gift for Kissy Von Bizmark seemed anathema, even to Anna. "Maybe you're in the midst of a psychotic break?"

Julie pulled out a beautiful wooden photo album from under her desk, substantial and leather bound. On the cover, hand-painted in tangerine, it read, *Twenty-Five Years*. The first picture, a retouched and blown-up print of the Polaroid taken of them the first weekend Mr. Von Bizmark had met the Verhuvenvels at their North Fork estate. The Mrs. sat on the Mr.'s lap in an adirondack chair on a lawn like the one at the Castle, sloping, flawless grass as far as the eye could see. She smiled beguilingly at the camera, but his eyes stayed on her, in adoration.

Page after page of photos of them together, through the years: vacations, pregnancies, the kids as tiny babies, all the good family fiber-of-life stuff. So many pictures of them had been taken in public, but these were all the intimate, private moments. The book itself was so beautifully assembled and well curated it brought a tear to Anna's eye. Mrs. Von Bizmark would melt.

Julie took the book to the gift-wrapping alcove by the laundry room to select the exact right paper and ribbon for Cristina, the resident wrapper, to use. When the caller ID showed a row of asterisks instead of an incoming number, Anna assumed it was some sort of solicitation.

She answered the phone curtly. "Hello?"

"Hello?" a male voice shouted over the wind in the background.

"Yes?" Anna said, struggling to hear.

"Ciao! This is Salvatore Valdobianno." It took Anna a moment to match this name with the title prince; plus, she could hardly understand him over the noise.

"Prince Valdobianno!" she finally said.

"Please! Call me Salvatore!"

"OK, Salvatore! Thank you for calling me back."

"I'm sorry, I've just been all over . . . doing so many things . . ."

"I get it," Anna said. "So the Von Bizmarks look forward to seeing you—"

He continued his train of thought. "I don't always listen to voice mail, you know? It's so boring!"

Anna laughed, forgetting for a moment why she'd called him in the first place as his image—full lips, thick hair—flitted across her mind. "But you are coming to the opera and the ball afterward as the Von Bizmarks' guest?"

"Yes, of course! I would not miss Kissy and Peter. *The Marriage of Figaro*—great choice! I have to go—my friends are arriving. Arrivederci!"

"Wait, Salvatore! Are you bringing a . . . date?" But it was too late. He was gone to fetch his guests, probably on the dock behind his Sag Harbor home as they stepped off the vintage wooden cruiser the prince was frequently photographed piloting, always in sunglasses, showing some new starlet or supermodel all the sights. Anna called him back on his mobile and tried texting him in Italian.

Per favore dimmi—farai un ospite?

She stared at her phone, willing it to buzz. Max would not be pleased.

"How am I supposed to do seating without a clue about who will actually show up?" Max asked Anna as he stood later that afternoon poring over the array of place cards.

"Max, you know as well as I do that these people can be difficult."

"That's right! And our job is to make them comply."

"Actually, that's neither of our jobs, Max." He studied the map and the cards in his hand. Moisture developed at his hairline, which he dabbed at with a lavender handkerchief. "It's going to be fine! We just have to find someone to sit in the box, right?"

"No Petzers, no prince, no Martha Miller . . . you're not giving me a lot to work with."

With only a few minutes until Mrs. Von Bizmark was due back for the meeting to review seating, Max finally came up with a scheme that hinged on everyone showing up. He put Martha Miller and the prince in the Von Bizmark box, which was dicey. Where would their date and husband sit? Anna didn't dare say anything.

Mrs. Von Bizmark breezed in from her lunch, meeting, work-out, and facial, drinking from her second 1.5-liter Fiji water bottle of the day. After the extra training, focus on green juices, relentless hydration, and trips to the aesthetician, hairstylist, and brow shaper—and all those afternoons with Dr. Westley and her fountain-of-youth supergadgets—she looked airbrushed, even in the flesh. On the other hand, she radiated displeasure. No one all day had said anything about the Von Bizmark anniversary. In Anna's belly, a little flip of anticipation for the evening ahead.

Mrs. Von Bizmark's wan hello begged someone to say, *What's wrong?* Only no one would. She looked over the seating chart, fixating immediately on the Von Bizmark box and its odd inhabitants. She pointed at the cards for the prince and Martha Miller, her index finger traveling back and forth.

"Are they together now?" she asked, perplexed.

Max forced himself to laugh, his eyes pointedly on Anna until she, too, chuckled a little. "No, of course not! But I thought they were the best people to share the spotlight with you and Mr. Von Bizmark."

Mrs. Von Bizmark looked at Max with pity, as if it was a shame he didn't have some essential piece of information. "Didn't Anna tell you?"

"Tell him what?" Anna asked, instant icicles of anxiety stabbing up and down her spine.

"That *the mayor* is coming?!" Mrs. Von Bizmark seemed on the verge of apoplexy.

"I'm so sorry, I must not . . . have . . ." Anna of course knew it was possible that the mayor might come, but she had been haranguing his office for confirmation for the previous two days. "Did you speak to him on the phone?"

"His chief of staff called first thing this morning. I'm *sure* I told you," she said to Anna, who knew that the more Mrs. Von Bizmark insisted, the more likely she was fibbing.

"Well, thank the Lord!" Max exclaimed, throwing his hands up and dispelling the tension. "We need that damn communist!" He grabbed two blank place cards and wrote *MAYOR* and *MAYOR +1* and put them next to *KVB* and *PVB* on the table. A little reshuffling and Max was clucking like the proud mother of a newborn. Max, sensing Mrs. Von Bizmark's displeasure, made a quick exit.

After a tense half hour of Mrs. Von Bizmark prowling the office; examining all the flowers, mail, and packages; and calling downstairs to ask Barclay if there was anything else waiting to come up, she announced, "I *so* do not want to go tonight."

It had been hard concocting just the right red herring for the evening: something black tie, intimate, superelite, and of Mr. Von Bizmark's world so that in the lead-up, Mrs. Von Bizmark would not discover the ruse. But it had to be enticing enough to ensure she would not put up a big fuss about going. In the end, Mrs. Von Bizmark believed the night ahead promised a private Yo-Yo Ma solo recital in the Otto Kahn mansion for Carl Icahn's eighty-fifth birthday. "It would be so nice to just stay home." She sighed. Anna said nothing. Nudging her was rarely effective. You just had to let them realize things on their own. She held her breath. "But I guess I must go. It's Carl, after all."

"Glam squad will be here in twenty," Anna said.

As soon as the Mrs. had disappeared upstairs to shower, Anna texted Chef, who was waiting in the basement lounge. She showed up at the back door in her white jacket, already annoyed and flustered, with three enormous wooden crates stamped *PUGLIA* on a dolly. "We're late," she said. Anna called for Cristina on the intercom. Alfie lifted the crates onto the kitchen floor, and Chef drove a crowbar right into the largest, cracking it open to reveal a cooler full of ice and a cornucopia of Italian seafood—enough for at least eight people. Cristina appeared, and Chef started barking at her to find a platter for the seafood. "Deep. Big, like this . . . for crushed ice!" Cristina scurried off.

Right on cue, they heard the ding-ding-ding of the elevator and Mr. Von Bizmark's heels striking the hardwood.

"Happy anniversary, Mr. Von Bizmark!" Chef said the moment he crossed the threshold into the kitchen.

Cristina, back with two enormous silver platters shaped like clamshells, ejected a terse, "Happy anniversary!"

Finally, Anna added, "Happy anniversary, Mr. Von Bizmark! Follow me."

As soon as Mr. Von Bizmark entered the office, Julie said, "Happy anniversary, Mr. Von Bizmark."

"Thank you, Jenny."

"It's Julie," Anna corrected as quietly as possible. She plucked two sheets of paper off her desk and handed one to Mr. Von Bizmark. Julie quietly watched this exchange, ready to jump in should Anna need backup. Her heart hammered in her chest as he read the minute-by-minute agenda. He chuckled at the first item, and Anna smiled cautiously.

7:00 Pianist arrives (wears earplugs for privacy)

7:15–7:30 Mrs. Von Bizmark to descend—Mr. Von Bizmark to uncork a twenty-five-year-old magnum of Pol Roger

"A magnum? Really?" he asked. "There are only two of us." *Whoa boy*, Anna thought to herself. If he balked at that, wait until he heard about the custom-imported foodstuffs.

"You know how much Mrs. Von Bizmark loves a magnum!" Anna reminded him. "Remember what she said at New Year's?"

"'They're *festive*,'" he and Julie said at exactly the same time. Who could forget Mrs. Von Bizmark remarking this very thing to justify the gobsmacking increase in expense between regular bottles and the double-size ones? But Mr. Von Bizmark breezed through the menu, already bored by it all, and entirely missed the point about the food Chef had gone to such expense and energy to procure. The most critical moment of the evening would come at:

8:15 Pianist plays "Our Love Is Here to Stay"

"Our wedding song," Mr. Von Bizmark commented, for the first time without a trace of negativity. He seemed to soften ever so slightly.

It's working, Anna thought to herself. "Yes! Exactly! When you hear that, you—"

"Ask her to dance."

"That's right!"

"It says so right here."

8:18 Ask Mrs. Von Bizmark to dance

"Are you sure I need this level of guidance?" Mr. Von Bizmark asked. "I have managed to have dinner with my wife before."

"The important thing is that you get her to the center living room window for . . ." Anna pointed to the next agenda item.

8:21 FIREWORKS

"Seriously?" Mr. Von Bizmark asked.

"They should be right outside for about sixty seconds. It's a custom display."

"She does love fireworks," he remarked. "And I'm sure that will go off without a hitch," he added unironically. Without ungluing their eyes from him, Anna and Julie reached back to knock on wood. "How much will this cost, anyway?" Mr. Von Bizmark said, perhaps for the first time ever. Before Anna could answer, he sighed, said, "Never mind," and read on:

8:30 Dessert with Peony

Additional gift

9:00 Carriage ride around the park

Harry Winston gift

"What's the additional gift?" he asked. "An Airbus?" Julie laughed too hard and stifled herself.

"A photo album. Julie put it together. She'll love it."

"But how will I keep all this straight?"

Anna produced a four-by-six-inch index card with the entire agenda simplified, reduced, and printed in two columns. "Don't forget to tell her where all the food is from!" she said, flipping it over to reveal a list of all the items and their origin. Mr. Von Bizmark tucked it in his pocket, thanked Anna, and went upstairs to get ready.

At the back door, Alfie handed Cristina a truckload of brown-paper-wrapped cherry blossom branches. When Anna tried to help place them in strategically arranged vases all over the living room, Cristina shooed her away. She returned to the kitchen to remind Chef, "Don't forget to tell Mrs. Von Bizmark about Puglia."

"Do you have any other advice?" Chef said sarcastically, backing away from the enormous ice platter half-decorated with seaweed, edible flowers, and lemon wedges. "Jump right in if you want." Her face flushed with pressure.

"Just reminding you!" Anna said and circled back to Cristina in the dining room, lining up all the necessary service items for seafood: those tiny forks, escargot holders, finger bowls . . .

"You here to tell me how to do this too?" Cristina asked.

Anna threw up her hands. *What a bunch of prima donnas,* she thought, accepting that there was nothing else she could do but let the evening unfold. When Anna and Julie passed the living room on their way out, all decked out for the big night, she found Cristina lighting the last of about fifty candles, tall and scattered in silver holders throughout the space like a fairy glen, all pink blossoms and flickering light. The flowers almost totally camouflaged the damaged wall, which the Silver Fox had draped. It was so dramatic it appeared as if the whole thing—the drop cloths, the empty space where the couch had been—had been done intentionally to prepare the room for the most dazzling anniversary imaginable.

Cristina filled the silver ice bucket and deposited the magnum with an oversize linen napkin draped over the top. "What do you think?" she asked.

"Beautiful job, Cristina."

Julie greeted the pianist at the door and handed over the earplugs and payment for the evening, plus a 25 percent gratuity. They could do no more. Let the evening begin.

SIXTEEN

Evening of March 8

As she climbed the stairs to get ready for an annoyingly unmissable evening out, Bambi wondered what the devil had gotten into everyone. She had quietly waited for someone to say *Happy anniversary!* all day. Could she have volunteered the information? Reminded everyone with a gentle, *You know what? Today is our anniversary!* Perhaps! But that sounded so thirsty. So . . . unsatisfying.

The glam squad had only eighty minutes to do the glossy waves of hair she wanted to match her new blue chiffon gown taken from the rack at the *Vogue* shoot—a preseason Naeem Khan steal for 40 percent off! The team of four worked feverishly, two drying her hair with round brushes, one applying a fan to her nail extensions, and one blending her contouring foundation. They had only until 7:20 p.m., a time Anna had printed out in hideous large font and circled in red Sharpie, including underneath, *Latecomers will not be seated*, double underlined, taping this monstrosity to one of the bulbs surrounding her makeup mirror. Occasionally her staff treated Bambi as if she had never done anything for herself, which was absolutely, 1,000 percent untrue.

She was just *busy* racing from one thing to the next, go, go, go. How many places had she been today? How many people had she smiled at and (tried to) talk to? And her lunch date with Fawnee had been such a dreadful bore. That woman's entire life was given over to pleasure. She had no hobbies, no causes, hadn't seen or done anything interesting whatsoever. But she had taken a table at the gala, so lunch must be sat through.

At least Opal was excited about the production; she'd clucked over the wardrobe of last-season pieces Bambi had provided from her own and Peter's closet for the show. The set, built to replicate Coolwater, would of course be the perfect backdrop to the drama of the opera and the garments . . . all of it fully aesthetically Von Bizmark. Just as Bambi preferred. That she had Opal's stamp of approval meant more to her, however, than she cared to admit to herself.

Bambi hurried down the steps. Peter, sipping a cognac already, sat in the foyer waiting for her and listening, oddly, to piano music on the speakers. When had they installed speakers in the foyer? He stood to greet her, reaching a hand for her grandly. It felt rather dreamy, almost too fabulous. *What is going on?*

"Let's go, sweetheart . . . we're late . . . ," she said.

"Bambi," Peter said, pointing her in the direction of the living room instead of the elevator, which was strange, all very strange, except— cherry blossoms! Everywhere! Perhaps there were even entire forests inside her living room, and candles, and it looked so beautiful inside, and Peter was holding her hand.

"Oh my! A pianist!" Bambi remarked, trying not to ask the next question, thinking she should just not even say anything, but then she couldn't help herself because she knew she would not be able to relax if she did not confirm. "Is he—"

"Wearing earplugs!" Peter said, impressing his wife immeasurably with this small gesture of thoughtfulness. He guided her to the silver ice bucket and showed her the vintage like a sommelier.

"Awww!" she said. "A magnum! Peter, my word!"

"Nothing but the best for my love," Peter said, pouring the champagne into two waiting flutes. Bambi giggled like a teenager.

Chef delivered the seafood tray to the dining room, a pizza-size platter of crushed ice covered by the fruits of the sea: a dozen different kinds of oysters, clams, mussels, crab claws, lobster, red shrimp, purple prawns . . . it went on and on, all delicious fat-free, low-calorie delights Bambi could gorge on. Chef clasped her hands. "You should know that all the food tonight was flown in from Puglia." Of course, she heard the words, but Bambi could not be certain she'd understood what Chef had said. "Just off the coast of Fasano, about"—Chef studied her watch—"ten hours ago? My friend Paolo got it for you personally."

"You're kidding!" Bambi was astonished; her hand flew to her chest. Peter reached for Bambi's elbow to steady her and prevent her from taking a step back and into the silver Jeff Koons balloon dog behind her.

"Are you OK?" he asked, pulling her closer to make sure she didn't fall.

This small gesture was perhaps the softest thing that had happened between her and her husband in about two years, and a genuine smile brightened Bambi's entire countenance. She was close enough to smell the custom fragrance she had made for him in Paris, which he never wore even after Bambi had told him she found it irresistible. Bambi did not relinquish his arm as he walked her to the table.

Chef served each of them a selection of seafood and then backed out of the room to prepare her famous homemade gnocchi that Bambi had forbidden. Chef served her only three, drizzled in truffle oil, and Bambi sighed with delight. Chef's gnocchi were the lightest, most flavorful, most velvety little potato packages the world had known. Bambi allowed herself two whole dumplings, the first carbs she'd had since that crazy ice cream. The sounds she made while eating these tender pillows were almost sexual, and soon she found Peter's hand on her knee under the table. Bambi felt like a rickety engine sputtering to life again.

Chef served a platter of wood-fired vegetables: squash, zucchini, tomato, endive, radicchio, onion, garlic, leeks, and eggplant, drizzling olive oil she poured from a repurposed wine bottle. Then she fileted a whole John Dory for them. "Taken from the Mediterranean this morning." She deboned the fish with two silver spoons in three quick strokes. The two servings barely made a dent in the large animal. She turned to the vegetables, slicing, arranging . . . making two exactly perfect plates. "The vegetables I picked myself. Olive oil from a friend in Polignano a Mare. All cooked on Sardinian wood."

"This is the same as that first night in Portofino!" Bambi gushed; they'd spent four weeks on the Italian Riviera for their honeymoon. She was brought back to their nascent marriage, how they had sunned themselves and slept outrageously and drank too much, and it all seemed so vivid. That aliveness came into their present moment in full flush, like magic, through the tastes of the food. "How did you remember?"

"I have people," he said and winked at Chef.

By the time the main course was in front of them, neither cared to eat as they both savored the unexpected beauty of a moment when neither of them harbored any ill will toward the other. The pianist played "Our Love Is Here to Stay," their wedding song. Bambi smiled at Peter, and he smiled back. They were, in fact, having the best time. The music seemed to be growing louder and louder.

"It's our song," Bambi remarked.

"I almost forgot!" Peter ejected suddenly. "Bambi . . ." He took her hand and led her to the living room. The moment felt heightened; if they were not already married, Bambi would have expected Peter to propose. The pianist extended the song a little so that they could sway together. "Bambi, I . . ."

The faint sound of multiple pops through the double-pane glass windows. Over Park Avenue, in the canyon of co-ops, just outside the Von Bizmark living room window, a sprinkling of tangerine crystals in the night sky. Bambi practically ran to see.

"You didn't!" she squealed. Ever since her father had gotten her a fireworks display for her fifth birthday, they had been her favorite sort of uncomplicated joy. There was nothing Bambi liked more, and nothing could be better than that someone knew this about her.

"Apparently, I did . . ." Peter joined her by the window. Outside, bright floral explosions. A few giant pink bursts were followed by smaller green and purple irises. *It's perfect,* Bambi thought. Exactly what she wanted. She watched, transfixed, until the very last sparkle had extinguished itself.

"But Peter, what about the . . ." Bambi didn't want to spoil the moment with something as gauche as discussing money, especially when she had known all along that things would work out, hadn't she? But Bambi also wished to demonstrate the depths of her thoughtfulness and empathy, her abiding concern for her husband's well-being. "Business 'issues'?"

"Oh yes," Peter said, smiling. "You were right. The mayor agreed to a meeting. I think we have things back on track."

Bambi took his hand and squeezed it. "I knew you would fix it."

Chef served a bowl of perfect, luscious, tiny wild strawberries, another food on Bambi's "unlimited quantities" list. Bambi popped one in her mouth, and even that was like a small sweet blast. "Oh, Peter, these berries! Are they from Puglia too?"

He pulled out an index card. They were both enjoying the evening so much more than they had expected. "Brazil!" he said as if joking, only he wasn't, and they both laughed in astonishment at their own good fortune. Peter took both her hands in his. "Bambi, I . . . I'm sorry about how things have been."

"Oh, Peter," Bambi said, her lower lip trembling.

"Never mind about the opera. I know how important it is to you." Bambi was left speechless; there could be nothing better than this. Because of course, she felt the slightest bit guilty about how it had all played out, but happily it was water under the bridge now, and she would never have to think about it again as she went through the next five years of gift cards.

"Let's forget about those silly clauses in the will. Now that the deal's almost done, we don't need them. An autopsy! What was Avi thinking?"

"Oh, my!" Bambi said. Peter wrapped his arms around her, their noses inches apart, two smiles, and then an actual lip-to-lip kiss. In Bambi's mind, the swell of an orchestra played. Nothing had ever been this romantic before in her entire life. Their lips locked for a full six seconds, an eon, leaving everyone shocked: Bambi, breathless with lust; Peter, ready to skip the carriage ride; as well as Nanny and Peony, who had quietly slipped into the room and stood slack jawed by the door.

"Oh my goodness, Peony!" Bambi said, astonished as always to see her youngest child there in her nightgown. Wasn't it . . . late? A school night? Something? She reached out to inspect Peony's hands before allowing her near her new gown.

"Hello there," Peter said, quaffing away.

"Happy anniversary, Mommy. Happy anniversary, Daddy."

"Thanks, love!" Bambi said, casting an uncertain glance at Nanny (*How long would this visit last?* she wondered) before bestowing upon Peony a loose hug. Peter pulled out the index card again and studied it.

"Would you like a strawberry?" Bambi offered. Peony's eyes popped with appreciation when she sank her teeth into the firm but tender Brazilian wild berry Chef had plucked herself about twenty-two hours prior. "Isn't that the best berry you've ever had?"

The moment Peter looked up from his agenda, Cristina came into the dining room and handed him a large heavy rectangle wrapped in turquoise with a lovely tangerine satin ribbon. Bambi allowed Peony to unwrap it, and when it fell open to the first page, she sighed. Her favorite picture of the two of them, when Peter still thought she was so . . . everything.

"Who's that?" Peony asked.

"That's Mommy and Daddy a long time ago," Bambi said, looking up, and there it was, that same expression of—dared she think it?—adoration. Her eyes blurred with tears. She flipped to an early candid shot of Peter whispering in her ear on their first date at the opera. Their cheeks pressed together, conspiratorially naughty, and they were completely engrossed with one another. "Oh!" An actual tear escaped Bambi's eye, and she pressed a napkin into her lower lid. "I just can't believe that you did this." She flipped through the pages quickly, marveling. "How did you even find all these?"

"I had some help," Peter admitted vaguely, grinning.

Incredible, she thought, that they should have a staff who could accomplish something so effective and personal on her husband's behalf. "I'll cherish this. Thank you, sweetheart." Bambi kissed Peter again, eager to keep up the physical contact. "I think it must be past your bedtime!" Bambi remarked at Peony while looking to Nanny, who quickly ushered her out of the room.

"In fact, darling, there is one more activity tonight."

"My goodness, Peter, you've already bowled me over. And I know how hard to impress I am." She tittered again when she heard these words come out of her mouth; suddenly she felt she had a great sense of humor about everything.

"You?" Peter said, pulling out her chair and offering her his arm. "No! Not you. Not my Bambi."

The wrought iron double doors of their building framed the horse-drawn carriage that awaited them on Park Avenue, and the Von Bizmarks strode out arm in arm. "Oh, Peter!" Bambi exclaimed. How incredibly long it had been since she had felt this thought of, cared for, and pampered. How marvelous to be impressed by something again. How unexpected to feel loved. She looked up at her husband, his flexed jaw, his satisfied smile. Her captain of the universe.

Waiting on the seat of the carriage, a navy leather jewelry box. As the driver flicked the whip and hooves clopped along the pavement,

Bambi gazed upon a sparkly cluster diamond bracelet, the stones like little flowers. *Not bad, Florence,* she thought to herself without a grudge. The credit from exchanging this bracelet would complete her budget for that necklace she'd been eyeing for years. And just in time for the ball . . .

How many people, she wondered, had had a hand in the evening? No matter that Peter had thought of none of the details himself and that likely no part of this had been his idea; the fact remained that he had known when to delegate and to whom, and this was the most efficient use of his time.

Bambi took Peter's hand in her own and pulled him closer as they turned west. Riding under a canopy of trees in Central Park, bathed in moonlight, Bambi made out with her husband as if it were the end of the nineteenth century and love had never died.

SEVENTEEN

Morning of March 9

For a split second when Anna arrived at her desk and saw the Harry Winston box sitting on her keyboard, she thought it was a gift for her. Then she saw Mrs. Von Bizmark's black Sharpie note:

Please return for credit toward the Lariat. Selma will know which one.

Quite possibly the entire Harry Winston staff knew exactly which piece Mrs. Von Bizmark had been lusting after for years. She had been "saving her pennies," as she put it, returning each of Florence's various Christmas, anniversary, and birthday gifts to Selma, her personal shopper there. When Anna called Harry Winston, Selma herself answered the Fifth Avenue flagship store phone on the first ring without even a hello. "I think I know why you're ca-alling," Selma cooed.

"With the bracelet, will we—"

"Have just enough with tax!" Selma cheered.

These were all excellent signs. Never had Anna known Mrs. Von Bizmark to wait for something. And now she would have that very coveted bauble for the Opera Ball that night. What luck! This singular event could be enough to jolt Mrs. Von Bizmark into a rare stellar mood.

Which meant it was time to ask for a raise. Of course, it always helped if your boss was in a good frame of mind, but in the case of household staff, where there were hardly any quantitative measures of success, this was true in the extreme.

When Mrs. Von Bizmark appeared in the office before going to Pilates and a massage, it was like her face had frozen overnight into a new position, no longer placid and unlined: she wore a permanent satisfied grin. She breezed in like a happy, fluffy cloud and thumbed through various correspondence and items left for her to see. She hummed an indiscernible tune, her demeanor the manic opposite of yesterday's moping.

Oh my God. Mrs. Von Bizmark got laid.

The time was ripe to carve out a piece for the downstairs team.

"How was last night?" Anna asked, as if the answer wasn't written on her blissed-out face.

"Extraordinary, unforgettable, total delight." She sighed lightly. "I'm the luckiest woman on earth."

"How wonderful to feel that way after twenty-five years!" Anna remarked. Surprisingly, the Von Bizmarks rarely experienced their own serendipity. The rest of the time, they were like fish: as long as it was inexhaustible, the money was only water to them.

"Isn't it, though?" Mrs. Von Bizmark leaned over the bistro table, chin in palm, and gazed wistfully out the window. Anna slipped a purple file folder in front of her marked *Anniversary Correspondence.*

"We hid these from you yesterday to heighten the surprise."

"You devil!" Mrs. Von Bizmark said playfully, chuckling to herself. She paged through cards and printed emails, but in her absolute disinterest she made it clear that nothing mattered after the glory of the previous evening.

"Mrs. Von Bizmark, before you leave for the day, I was hoping for two minutes of your time," Anna said. Mrs. Von Bizmark wasn't really listening. "In the *library*," she added. The mere mention of the library—with its built-in bookshelves, leather club chairs, and dim lamps—practically communicated the entire conversation. This was serious business.

"I see," Mrs. Von Bizmark said, looking Anna in the eye. "All right, then." She proceeded down the long hallway, humming a distinct "Love Is Here to Stay." Despite the positive vibes, despite her quick thinking, Anna's heart hammered her rib cage, and that icy sweat broke out along her spine. But this was something she had to do—as a professional. As a grown-up.

The two women ducked under a drop cloth into the library and closed the door, interrupted by only the occasional banging of the Silver Fox's crew. Mrs. Von Bizmark sat in one of the jade leather chairs, leaned back, and crossed her legs, placing each hand on the armrest, every polished finger relaxed. Even in Lululemon and sneakers, she was without question the lady of the house. Anna sat at a diagonal, which meant she had to perch on the edge of her chair to fully face Mrs. Von Bizmark.

"As you may recall, it's been over two years since the last staff salary raise," Anna began. The corners of Mrs. Von Bizmark's mouth twitched. "We have the best people in town, and we want to retain them. We've all been working very hard with the luncheon, last night's celebration . . ." Anna paused to let her reflect a bit on that one. "And of course the ball tonight. Everyone from Josefina to Julie has been going above and beyond." Here was the hardest part. *Spit it out, Anna,* she said to herself. "I propose twenty percent across the board with additional midyear cash bonuses at your discretion."

Mrs. Von Bizmark considered. "Hmmmm . . . ," she said, choreographing an index finger to her chin, a satire of someone thinking about something. Anna stopped breathing. Mrs. Von Bizmark sighed, but her eyes smiled. "I think that's a wonderful idea!" she finally agreed.

"Terrific!" Anna said, so relieved she forgot what else there was to say. Perhaps this had been the best-timed meeting. Like, ever. As they left the library, Mrs. Von Bizmark added, "And, Anna. Thanks for everything." She gripped Anna's shoulder. Did she know who'd planned the anniversary? Of course she did.

"You're quite welcome," Anna said, more warmly than usual. Mrs. Von Bizmark went back upstairs to continue various day-of-the-ball ablutions. Julie, who had slipped into the office during the two-minute library summit, finished up a call at her desk. She wore a purple kimono and sweeping updo. Enamel flower pendants swung from two large sticks in her hair. Wooden Japanese platform flip-flops and socks with a notch next to the big toe stuck out from under her hem.

"Told you so," Julie said. Anna's eyes traveled back up to her hand, brandishing Mrs. Von Bizmark's note to return the bracelet.

"I'll take care of that while I'm out. I have to go hang the art!"

"Exciting!"

"Look, I feel bad leaving now," Anna said. The phones sparkled and beeped.

"Everything's already done for tonight, right?" Julie said, waving her off. "All she has to do is get dressed!" She turned to the phone, answering three lines in a row: "Kissy Von Bizmark's office, please hold." Anna rushed out the door; the sooner she went, the sooner she could get back.

Anna had the car wait while she ran inside Harry Winston. It made her nervous to ferry such a valuable item around, and she was eager to hand the bracelet back to Selma. The personal shopper waited for Anna by the door in her sharp black suit and four-inch heels, like a sentry. This one sale would net a massive commission for Selma, a number more than double her annual salary. She brought Anna directly to the second-floor private lounge, where a bottle of champagne waited in a platinum ice bucket wreathed in gemstones and the lariat itself nestled on a black velvet pedestal under a spotlight.

"It's actually a sautoir," Selma confided as she popped the cork.

It wasn't as blingy as most of the oversize gemstones on offer at Harry Winston: coral, onyx, and a lot of diamonds. A lot. Of diamonds. Selma poured the champagne, handed Anna a flute, and, as they both gazed at the piece, whispered, "Commissioned by Coco Chanel herself."

"No!"

"Oh, yes. Also owned briefly by Princess Diana. Look." Selma gestured to the left of the pedestal, where a leather portfolio displayed two photographs of both famed beauties wearing the necklace. *This is the way to shop,* Anna thought, sipping her crisp, ice-cold champagne.

"Hey, Selma?"

"Yes, my dear?"

"Could you process the refund on the bracelet, give me a check for the full amount we have on credit, and put the lariat—I mean *sautoir*—on Mrs. Von Bizmark's Amex?" *Rewards points!* Anna thought. Selma was happy to oblige, and it was only back in the car with the necklace and the check on her way to the opera that she peered at the number: $4,703,425.63.

Oh, shit. Ten minutes before she had been nervous to courier a $500,000 bracelet. Now she had a check and a necklace valued together at nearly $10 million on her person. And every single dollar of it was uninsured. She clutched the slim rope handle of the bag with a sweaty hand and thought about taping everything to her body somehow, but she had no tape and no time because the car was already pulling up at Lincoln Center.

Anna held the bag with both hands like a lunatic all the way across the plaza and past the fountain, through the revolving doors into the lobby, down the main staircase, through the gold double doors, down the red-velvet aisles, and to the stage, where Giselle impatiently tapped her foot—somehow imbuing this ordinary gesture with grace and a whiff of sexiness—while looking at her phone. A nearby twentysome-thing guy in work boots and a tool belt silently awaited her instructions.

All Anna's pieces sat on the floor in their respective spots, awaiting her "artistic eye." It was . . . no, it should have been one of the most exciting creative professional moments of her life, but instead, all Anna could think about was what to do with the goddamn Harry Winston shopping bag crushed within her white-knuckled fingers.

She climbed up onto the stage. "Are you OK?" Giselle asked but clearly had no interest in the answer. "This is Mike. Tell him where you want everything." Anna wrapped the shopping bag handles around her wrist and worked her way across the stage with Mike, hanging first the largest, most important piece—Julie's black-and-white lips—in the center of the backdrop. Then the two other large pieces went on either side, and two smaller pieces were centered alongside the big ones toward the edge of the backdrop, and so forth. When completed, it was a visually exciting and harmonious set, if Anna did say so herself. She happily noted how at home her work looked there, in a replica of Coolwater's great room.

The one snag was that a doorway cut into where the thirteenth and final piece should have hung. It was an old one, from when Anna had first met Adrian and before they were dating heavily enough to really put a dent in her time for painting. Underneath one of the orange decal circles hid a pressed feather from Adrian's old pillow. She had finished this one quickly, wanting to complete something so she could take a bit of an absence from her work. But still, something about it captured the joy of that particular time. A breathless quality that perhaps would not have come through on stage anyway.

"I'll just put it in Opal's office for now. She likes this one," Giselle said, lifting her eyes from her phone and darting them at the piece. Then she actually looked Anna in the eye for a flash. "Really," she said with sincerity. *What an unexpected . . . ,* Anna thought, but then Giselle turned her back and strode off, as if on stilts. "*Allons-y*, Mike." He dutifully carried the small painting for her.

Anna stood on the stage, hugging the shopping bag so she could finally put it out of her mind and instead focus on the fact that her work—her real work—was up on Lincoln Center's main stage. It was something to be celebrated. *Woo-hoo,* she said to herself. She snapped a picture. Though her fingers itched to send it to Adrian, she sent it to Lindsay instead, who instantly responded with a series of *WOWs,* applause emojis, and happy tears.

Back in the car, Anna thought of the short distance between now and the end of this long hard slog. Maybe, it dimly occurred to her, all the stress had something to do with her blowup with Adrian. Soon she would return to three days at work, three days at the studio. Just a normal schedule would feel like a vacation. She suddenly missed Adrian so badly; thank God the ball was that evening. The next day, Anna would call him. She knew she owed him an apology, and she was almost ready to deliver it.

She checked the time: Mrs. Von Bizmark should be finishing up glam for the late-afternoon press junket at the opera. At least as far as work was concerned, everything seemed, for just that moment, perfectly, well, perfect: all the pieces moving in the right direction. Anna got out of the car after signing for a generous forty-dollar tip on the Von Bizmark Organization because, why not? Live a little.

As soon as Joe the doorman spotted Anna, he shooed her inside with his white-gloved hand. "Come on, come on," he said under his breath. He raced ahead of her to call the elevator, all the while wheeling one hand like he had a tic. Anna noted that today was one of the rare days when the front doors had been thrown open to the perfect weather outside. Anna tilted her head at him and hesitated at the open elevator door.

"You better get upstairs!" he said.

"What's going on?" she asked as he gently shoved her onto the elevator.

"Just go! They need you up there!" he said as the elevator door slowly closed, and she was left alone inside.

Genuine urgency occurred in the Von Bizmark world only when a complication went beyond what money could fix and into the realm of actual human problems. Someone upstairs was hurt, dead, missing, or arrested. Anna's mind started clicking through gears, downshifting, her vision narrowing onto the hand-carved etching of a maple leaf in the elevator's mahogany molding. What could have happened? Mr. Von Bizmark—heart attack. Mrs. Von Bizmark—stroke. Some sort of criminal investigation?

It felt like a three-hour journey to the eighth floor. The door finally moved at half its usual speed. Both foyer doors stood wide open like the old days. An unknown young woman in a suit and heels zipped past the vestibule on her way to the living room, holding a sheaf of papers. Inside, Anna heard the buzz of people talking, typing. A sob. Who was that? Mrs. Von Bizmark?

Coming through the doorway was like leaving her real life behind and emerging onto a movie set. Anna stepped carefully over a foot-thick bundle of black cables running through the foyer, stuck with duct tape onto the hand-painted floor, all the way into the living room. She followed them with her eyes into what could only be described as a war room. A half dozen sixtysomething dark suits commanded the crowded space. Their efficient motions, dead seriousness, and excessively tidy hairstyles gave them away as the former military officers who comprised the highest rank of the VBO personal security service.

Each of these commander types directed several staffers, who circled them like flies around a large piece of meat, this one jabbering away on the phone, that one hammering on a laptop, another menacing a document with a highlighter. Large folding tables held computers, phone-monitoring devices, printers, scanners, and other unidentifiable investigative gadgets. A few data crunchers occupied their own space by a far window at three computers, intently scrolling, occasionally scribbling notes, clearly analyzing some immense amount of information.

Seeing Anna standing there, stunned, in the doorway, Julie rushed to fill her in. Peony had had a half day at school and had been home for lunch. Around 12:30 p.m., Nanny had gone to the bathroom for three minutes—she was sick and had taken longer than usual. When she'd come out, Peony was gone. That was it. No note. Nothing on any of the seven video cameras downstairs. Nowhere in the house. Nowhere in the building. The apartment had been on lockdown all afternoon; no one could leave or communicate with anyone outside.

"And remember what the Mrs. said about the Mr.'s security concerns?" Julie asked with such emphasis she shivered. Anna recalled that first day months ago when she had found the foyer doors closed. It had seemed inconceivably ridiculous then; had there ever been a home invasion in a Park Avenue co-op? But now, Anna wished she had taken it more seriously as she watched the security personnel break up into teams to scour the entire apartment for clues, starting in the second kitchen upstairs, where Peony and Nanny ate lunch.

Another sob, from poor Nanny, sweating, crying, and hooked up to a lie detector. A wiry woman in a suit who, despite being of average size and middle age, looked like she could probably break Nanny's neck in under three seconds conducted a deadpan interview in Indonesian. After fifteen years and two other Von Bizmark children under her belt, Nanny seemed an unlikely culprit. She took a few gulps of air and returned to the beginning of her story about this terrible afternoon for the ninth time. A much calmer Silver Fox took his lie detector test in stride, answering each of the questions in the measured tones of a man with nothing to hide. Investigations like this were common in his multimillion-dollar business, where pricey items frequently went missing; he would never sell out the Von Bizmarks.

The alpha suit, a craggy, enormous, emotionless head atop a blocky body, interviewed Mrs. Von Bizmark on the couch. Tears streaked her only partially made-up face; half her hair was held up in rollers while the other half hung against her damp cheek. She clutched the top of her robe together. Mr. Von Bizmark paced along the far wall, the drop cloth a backdrop for his simultaneous passionate working of two phones, one pressed to each ear, marshaling all the political, municipal, military, and financial forces available to him.

Anna waved at Marco, spotting him perched on a windowsill behind the bank of number crunchers, appearing nervous even from across the large room. No one would mistake him, with his darting eyes, puffy hair, and pinky ring, for former military personnel. He hugged his leather briefcase like a security object. She felt for him. This investigation called for scouring all the Von Bizmarks' financial affairs, a process that featured in Marco's nightmares: *audit*.

In another distant corner of the room, Avi sat with two other lawyer types in folding chairs, his legs spread wide, forearms on thighs, leaning over fingertips pressed together. His buzz cut revealed several slim rolls of flesh on the back of his neck. Boy, did he look annoyed. He rocked on his feet with agitation. Avi eyeballed each of them for ten seconds before answering any of their questions. He kept rubbing his head and sighing. He finally rolled his eyes so dramatically that he caught sight of Anna, whose wave he met with a quick pop of an eyebrow.

One of the suits hopped off his hacker-proof satellite phone, a brick-size device that looked like it could be used as a weapon in extremis, and announced, "We have eyes on both BVBs."

"Thank God," Mrs. Von Bizmark said and reached for another tissue.

Anna looked to Julie for an explanation—*BVBs?* "Baby Von Bizmarks," Julie whispered. Apparently, they had dispatched several local teams in Boston and Concord to locate Chester and Vera, yanking them out of class (and in Chester's case, his dorm, smoking his roommate's new volcano vaporizer) and detaining them in fully secured, undisclosed locations. Anna imagined their fear being quickly outpaced by the annoyance of being disrupted in public by strangers and then held against their will. Mr. Von Bizmark talked to each of them briefly in turn on a quick rotation of mobile phones. "Peony's missing," he snapped. "Just do what security says!"

When Mrs. Von Bizmark's interview concluded, Julie and Anna took seats on either side of her. "I'm so sorry," Anna said. "I . . ." Mrs. Von Bizmark took Anna's hand but kept her eyes on nothing in the middle distance, shaking her head periodically, stunned into silence. Anna could see she was grappling with this strange reality: her child whom she frequently forgot about was now in fact missing. "What happens next?" Anna asked Julie.

"Well, I get the sense that they're trying to make a list of possible enemies." But Mr. Von Bizmark himself faced the same problem as every journalist who had ever tried to write about VBO. They all wondered what exactly VBO did to make so much money, but to know precisely was virtually impossible because corporate holdings were rigorously siloed. Mr. Von Bizmark himself preferred to remain ignorant about much of his business, but now he had no choice; he reeled off calls, explaining to each executive what had happened.

"The security service told me months ago they were tracking an active threat, but all they had was nonspecific chatter. They advised me to up the security in my home, which we did. But clearly, not enough," he spat in the general direction of one of the suits. "Come clean, because I've opened all the books," Mr. Von Bizmark nudged on the phone.

"Ask her about this one hundred and twenty-seven million dollar transfer to a DPC Unlimited in Liberia . . . ," suggested a number cruncher from behind his computer.

Mr. Von Bizmark continued haranguing the head of the weaponry group. "Did you hear that?" With each sentence he grew more incensed. "You have to look into it? One hundred and twenty-seven million, and you're not sure?"

Perched on the windowsill, Marco could not keep himself from nibbling his cuticles. He tried to make out the numbers on the auditor's screen, but it was just a few inches too far away.

"How about you call me back when you've gotten your head out of your ass." He hung up and ran his hands through his hair.

Mrs. Von Bizmark broke out of her stupor. "You don't think it could have to do with that lawn dispute? Out East?" she said.

"With the Greenbaums? No, Bambi, I don't think the new neighbors kidnapped our daughter because you told them that their landscaping is tacky." Tears leaked from her eyes again, and Julie rushed to hand her a fresh box of tissues.

A nearby suit gave Mr. Von Bizmark a phone to talk to the head of his energy group, and he launched in immediately: "That Russia deal with that really unsavory guy. What's his name? Well, please look it up now. I'll wait." His breathing was so loud and overworked that Anna started to worry about Mr. Von Bizmark having a heart attack. "Derpikoska?" he said, repeating the word for the benefit of the suits all around him. A ripple traveled among the security personnel.

"Did he say Derpikoska?" the head suit asked with quiet, crisp authority.

"Yes!" Mr. Von Bizmark said, eager and crushed at the same time. "Is that bad?"

In response, the man shouted, "All right, people, tell me everything we know about Derpikoska!" and rushed off to the nearest secure phone.

Meanwhile, Anna and Julie punctuated their stunned silence with busywork. They slipped away to make calls postponing and ultimately canceling Mrs. Von Bizmark's appearance at the press junket. Julie ordered sandwiches for everyone, which the ladies tearfully served.

The men in suits generated reports on Derpikoska and some North Korean general. Cristina updated Villson at the back door. Anna sat in silence with a devastated Mrs. Von Bizmark and felt so inadequate looking at her employer's fallen face. It was hard to just sit by, but Anna was genuinely lost for words. It was as if she was not even involved in what was happening all around her.

"What's this ten-thousand-dollar cash withdrawal in December?" a man at a computer terminal asked Mr. Von Bizmark, who had emerged from the library to resume pacing and making phone calls. "From your personal account."

"You expect me to know?" Mr. Von Bizmark said. "Marco?"

Marco broke out into an instant sweat bath. He nearly fell off the edge of the windowsill while pulling a laptop from his briefcase, which he then precariously balanced on his knees. All eyes turned to him. Here was the moment he had dreaded for at least two hours, if not his entire life. "Give me a second," he said.

Nooooooooooo, Anna thought, knowing before Marco could find it in his records that this was the money Chef had used to bribe customs officials in Colombia. While this $10,000 was unlikely to have anything to do with Peony and could therefore be overlooked, providing cash to staff for illegal payments was certainly a gray area in terms of professional behavior. Phil wasn't here to take the fall, and Anna would never throw him under the bus.

As realization dawned on Marco, he cast a glance in Anna's direction. She gave him a nod and, feeling it was the right thing to do, stood to deliver her explanation: "We unexpectedly had to fly Chef back from Colombia over the New Year's . . ." Everyone in the room paused to gape at her. Anna reached for euphemisms. "And this required greasing a few wheels at immigration. But her presence was required. Obviously, I don't have a receipt, but I'm sure Phil, the estate manager, will back me up."

"That is also my understanding," Marco added.

"Wait, what's this twelve-million-dollar American Express charge in January?" another data cruncher inquired. A moment earlier, Anna had been sorry she could not be a more active participant in the investigation; now she wished for nothing more than to just disappear back into the couch.

"It was for the opera. Tonight," Anna said.

"Oh, right," Mrs. Von Bizmark said, dazed. "For the points."

"And . . . ," the same guy said again. Young and in his twenties. His greasy complexion reflected the glow from his screen. "This one just today for four million, seven hundred and three thousand, four hundred and twenty-five dollars and sixty-three cents?" All eyes were on Anna.

"That was a necklace," she said, her voice growing weaker and almost dying in her ever-tightening throat. Mrs. Von Bizmark looked at her quizzically. "I got you the points," she whispered to her.

"That's a huge flag to men like Derpikoska," the head suit said disapprovingly. "They see this size transaction, and they know you can access that sort of money instantly." He exchanged meaningful glances with two other suits nearby, wordlessly processing the severity of this bad news. As if just remembering something, the head suit turned back to Anna. "Wait a second," he said. "Where were you from eleven a.m. on today?" Anna felt every single person in the room watching her, assessing her reaction. So self-consciousness and distressed, Anna could not for the life of her remember where she had been that morning!

Just then, the elevator dinged behind this giant, and out stepped Peony Von Bizmark herself, holding a lavender Bergdorf Goodman bag and an ice cream cone. For the first time in her life, joy overcame both her parents when they laid eyes her. They rushed to her and fell to their knees. Mrs. Von Bizmark threw her arms around her daughter, and Mr. Von Bizmark wrapped the two of them in a tight hug.

"Hey, you're smushing my ice cream," Peony said, pressing the cone into the back of Mrs. Von Bizmark's unflinching head. She kissed her daughter's face a dozen times. Mr. Von Bizmark gripped the little girl's arm as if she might suddenly evaporate. The household staff hovered, everyone smiling and shedding happy tears.

"Where were you?" Mr. Von Bizmark asked, wiping away his own tearlet before anyone could see it.

"I went to get you an anniversary present. I know how much Mommy likes the frames at Bergdorf's." Peony peered around her parents at all the people and equipment.

"Oh! That's lovely," Mrs. Von Bizmark gushed. "So that's where you've been this whole time?"

"Well, then I went to the zoo. And I got an ice cream," she admitted, licking it.

"But how did you get out without being on the security cameras?" Mr. Von Bizmark asked.

"There's a window at the bottom of the back staircase you can't see."

"How did you know that?"

"I saw Miguel do it." *That explains the cigarette smell!* Anna, Julie, Cristina, and Mrs. Von Bizmark all thought at the same time.

"Well, aren't you a quick study," Mr. Von Bizmark said. The suits started to make their quiet exits, each clapping Mr. Von Bizmark on the shoulder before leaving their personnel to pack up the room. Anna watched as some twentysomething ripped the duct tape off the hand-painted floor. Several green leaves and layers of varnish went with it.

Nanny embraced Peony. "You scared me!" she said, tears still running down her face.

And then it dawned on little Peony that she had worried quite a few people and, worse, gotten Nanny in trouble. "Oh. I'm sorry," she said to Nanny and hugged her. Over Nanny's shoulder, she saw all the activity in the living room, all those workers huffily packing up and the red faces of all the staff, tissue pressed into the corners of wet eyes and smiling at her like maniacs.

"I'm sorry, everyone," she said quietly and then started to cry herself.

"It's OK, sweetheart," Mrs. Von Bizmark said, again taking her hand. "We're just all so glad you're home right now." She cried harder. "Listen . . ." But Peony's crying only intensified. *"Listen . . . ,"* Mrs. Von

Bizmark said, with a hint of sternness. She looked into Peony's eyes until her daughter took a deep breath and met her gaze.

"I want you to come with us tonight, OK?" Mrs. Von Bizmark said for the first time ever. She pressed their foreheads together. Peony's eyebrows shot up into her blonde hairline. Definitely a first. "You too," Mrs. Von Bizmark said, twisting to look at Nanny. "And you two!" to Anna and Julie. "You've worked so hard. You can have my seat," she said to Anna, really on a euphoric roll. "I don't care! Julie, get some dresses from Bergdorf's . . . actually . . ." Mrs. Von Bizmark thought, holding her daughter's hand and looking around at the staff. She met Mr. Von Bizmark's eye. He seemed uncharacteristically tickled by her kooky behavior.

"I don't care, get a limo—everyone's going!" Mrs. Von Bizmark said. "Josefina, call Ilana. Anna, tell Richard to set out another table for some unexpected guests. Nanny, get dressed, get Peony dressed—everyone, we are all going to the ball!" As she went upstairs with Nanny and Peony, Mrs. Von Bizmark called back to Anna, "And I can't wait to wear my lariat!"

Blind panic. The Harry Winston bag! Anna rushed into the living room against the tide of hard plastic rolling trunks aggressively dragged by annoyed staffers. Any one of them could have snatched the necklace and the check. Should she sound an alarm and search everyone? Already, at least a dozen people had left. She looked around the couch where she'd spent most of the ordeal with Mrs. Von Bizmark. Nothing. She scoured her desk, in a full-body sweat. Anna was vaguely aware of Julie trailing her, offering to help; she was so frantic she could hardly hear or see beyond what was directly in front of her. Not knowing what else to do, Anna retraced her steps from the foyer to the living room to her desk and back to the foyer. Meanwhile, Julie waited by the elevator, and when the door slid open, she picked the Harry Winston shopping bag up off the little bench inside like a magician.

Anna fell upon the bag much like the Von Bizmarks had greeted their lost daughter. "You left it in the elevator. Joe found it but figured it wasn't right to bother you." Anna already had the check in her hand. She popped open the box, and there was the lariat. *Sautoir.* Everything present and accounted for. Cristina delivered the necklace while Julie hopped on the phone with their Bergdorf's shopper, who raced through the store on a cordless headset pulling dresses in sizes 6 to 16.

That done, Anna and Julie enjoyed a few minutes of downtime. The Von Bizmarks were finishing glam and getting dressed upstairs. Soon it would be Anna's and Julie's turn for hair and makeup. The day had been almost too much to contemplate.

"Hey, Jules."

"Yeah?"

"We're all getting a raise." Any other time, this would have been of significant interest, but it was as if both of them were momentarily drained, their scraps of energy reserved for an evening ahead that neither of them had planned on. They were going to the ball.

"That's great, Anna. Thanks."

"Yeah. Anytime."

EIGHTEEN

Evening of March 9

The horde of reporters and camera people crowding the plaza at Lincoln Center hungered for Kissy Von Bizmark most of all. After the scandals, preparties, press, images, allusions, and salaciousness; after that most sensational headline, "I Am a Jewess"; after Mrs. Von Bizmark herself had mysteriously blown off the entire afternoon junket, speculation ran amok as to the "true story" behind it all. Each reporter sought that golden quote to headline their own article. Each photographer wished for the front of their periodical, the home page spot, the admiration of their employer. The less flattering, more revealing, most "real" image of Kissy Von Bizmark, the much talked-about star of the evening, the better.

Max poured this information into Mrs. Von Bizmark's ear in a steady stream as the stretch limousine (an unusual conveyance but required for so many people) inched along with the preevent traffic. Mrs. Von Bizmark took it all in, serene in a simple black Armani gown that highlighted not only her perfectly prepared flesh and hair but the sautoir itself, which glimmered and blinked, flirting like a tiny celebrity nestled in her décolletage. Mrs. Von Bizmark held Peony's hand; the child, dazed and still processing how all these strokes of unexpected good fortune had fallen upon her, sat in between her parents, a rare event indeed. Mr. Von Bizmark looked out the window, studiously avoiding eye contact. He had only occasionally ridden in a car with his own daughter, let alone been in public with the entire residential staff, each and every one in an evening dress.

Josefina and Alicia had both selected gem-toned, glittering gowns. Little pearls stitched along the high neck of Alicia's dress offset the sheer bodice. Josefina had chosen a diaphanous jade chiffon with cap sleeves. Cristina had picked something in her favorite violet and had asked the makeup artist to skillfully render a matching shade of eyeliner. She kept her glasses tucked away, not wanting to obscure the effect.

Nanny appeared the least comfortable out of her nurse's uniform. She tugged repetitively at her simple black crepe rectangle of a dress. She'd declined makeup, tied her hair up in a ponytail, and, deprived of her usual seat next to the youngest Von Bizmark, looked a little lost and possibly traumatized by the day's events.

Anna straightened and resmoothed the voluminous folds of her silk gown, a flouncy, jammy, bold fuchsia, strapless with a flattering corset sewn in and two deep pockets in the skirt for her lipstick. Under Julie's direction, the makeup artist had meticulously painted on matching lips and slipped her the tube to take with her for touch-ups. Her hair was up in a perfectly frayed topknot.

Julie had, of course, gone fully, well, *Julie*, with a deep-pink floral Giambattista Valli. The dramatic puffy collar framed the low V-neck. A bright-green matching cape flowed from tiny hooks at her shoulders. The makeup artist had picked up on these hues, executing at Julie's direction green lips and pink eyes. Her hair was a tousled, tumbling, fake-flower-filled loose braid. She looked like an English garden on acid.

Max hadn't stopped talking the entire ride. When they finally pulled up at the curb, swarms of regular people—not just press—crowded the plaza. Under a tent, the corral of reporters and photographers lined the red carpet with small crowded bleachers behind them. Mrs. Von

Bizmark looked eagerly past Max. It was all so much more attention than even she had thought possible.

"So you're going to be what?" Max coached.

"Succinct, coy, and positive," Mrs. Von Bizmark murmured, rote.

Once a white-gloved attendant had opened the door, the car filled with the noise of the crowd, so loud it was a physical sensation. They rushed blindly to the press area, Nanny hustling like she was the scandal-embroiled celebrity, Mrs. Von Bizmark waving royally in tidy little wrist twists. People in the crowd yelled, "Kissy!" like she was famous. Perhaps she was? And she loved it. Even Peony was impressed and delighted that her mother held her hand the entire time.

"Everyone!" Max commanded from the step and repeat, deftly lining the staff and Von Bizmarks up for a group photo with Peony in the middle. Flashes exploded. It felt a little otherworldly to everyone except Mrs. Von Bizmark, whom Anna suspected would happily pose for the cameras every evening. She smiled naturally, arranging her face and body in the most flattering of angles. Then it was time to face the reporters waiting in a row two dozen media outlets long.

"I'll be with you the whole way," Max said soothingly to Mrs. Von Bizmark before turning and snapping, "Anna!" just as she was going to slip inside with the rest of the staff. Visions of a scotch and soda melted away. "Stay with me!" he hissed.

Mrs. Von Bizmark's conversations became monotonous droning in the background while Anna instead focused on a steady stream of VIPs, ticking them off her mental guest list. First, there was the mayor and his wife, greeted by the public in the plaza with both cheers and jeers. Lindsay arrived, radiant in a form-fitting cerulean dress. Her husband, Jack, beamed at her proudly. Principal Sellers stepped out of a taxi, ignored the step and repeat, and headed straight inside.

"Felix Mercurion was convicted today and faces twenty years in prison. What do you have to say to him?" Anna snapped to attention. The *Daily News*.

"Not much, actually. I don't really know him. What I do know is that we are here tonight for two of New York City's great institutions: the opera and an artistically focused public school. And we are introducing the work of a new artist as well . . ."

At this opportunity to change the subject, Max grabbed Anna by the arm and put her in front of the reporter. "Here she is," he added quickly before extracting Mrs. Von Bizmark.

The reporter, a brunette bob in a beat-up brown velvet jacket, took a moment to get a mint out of her pocket, eyeing Anna blandly. "So you're the artist?" she said.

"Yup," Anna offered, distracted by Martha Miller, who had, thank God, brought her husband. The crowd outside erupted, and she waved back, smiling and taking selfies with fans. She walked slowly to bathe in the attention.

"And where have you shown before?" the reporter asked.

"Yale?" Anna said. "The Yale MFA Consortium downtown." Martha Miller's husband (who could be known by no other appellation) scratched away at a red patch just above his shirt. Maybe he really did have eczema.

"And what's your inspiration?" she asked.

"You know, life," Anna said before reconsidering. *Jesus, Anna,* she scolded herself, *focus!* "We are all so lucky to live here in this city, surrounded as we are by so much of everything. My life is very . . . colorful and disparate, like so many New Yorkers'. So is my work."

"OK, well, thanks," the reporter said, indicating that Anna could move along. She chastised herself for blowing her chance to say something intelligent about her work. Then Ilana was there, pulled out of basketball practice to come to the ball. Her smile beamed across the red carpet. She wore a navy halter dress and a delicate necklace of paper flowers. Anna peeled off from Max and went to greet her.

"Hi!" Anna said, and hugged her gingerly to avoid the flowers.

"This is crazy," Ilana said, eyeing the crowds over Anna's shoulder.

"Great necklace," Anna said, eyeing the pristine edges and the careful watercolor.

"I made it."

And then Max was there too. "How about a picture?" he asked Ilana, who was all too happy to oblige. As she stepped in front of the hot, bright lights, Max started shouting, "This is a student from the school! PS 342! Ilana Ruiz!" She was a natural, her pose strong and confident, her hair a glorious espresso wave. Ilana's necklace, a skilled and inspired piece of art, spoke to the talent of the school's students.

"Oh shit." Max blurred past her toward a very annoyed-looking Mrs. Von Bizmark, who sneered at none other than Vivienne Lanuit, the terribly French *Vogue* reporter. Anna rushed over. Mrs. Von Bizmark showed signs of wear. "Well, why do *you* think we chose *Figaro*?" she sniped at Lanuit, who wore exactly the same black cuffs, long hair, and relentless cheekbones. Her silver sequined sheath would look terrible on anyone else. "I don't like the insinuation that there's something going on here tonight that escapes my understanding. I have a graduate degree in art history. That said, I shouldn't have to spell everything out. Let the *art* speak, for goodness' sake! Let events speak! Let the opera speak! It is *your* job to make meaning out of it." Max looked like he might faint. In the ten seconds Anna was distracted, somehow things had gone off the rails. Amused, Lanuit finished jotting this down and murmured, "Merci beaucoup."

Anna stuck like glue to Max for the rest of press, distracted only briefly by Miranda Chung in a black geometric Japanese frock and platform Stella McCartney sneakers. Her characteristic black bob and bold red lips matched this evening, with rimless glasses and white mascara. She looked like something out of a Missy Elliott video, despite being middle aged and of Chinese descent. She posed for only ten seconds and flew inside, jet silk floating behind her.

Julie reappeared in the press tent as Mrs. Von Bizmark began her final interview. It was almost showtime. The entire staff would be accommodated in various empty seats, which so far included two critical spots behind the Von Bizmarks and the mayor. The prince and his date, whom the seats had been reserved for, had yet to show. Worst case: they could move Martha Miller and her husband. As Julie filled her in, Anna vaguely wondered if she could somehow escape the opera. Perhaps she could get away with lingering at the bar in the lobby?

"Anna, is that"—Julie snapped her out of her reverie, drawing Anna's attention to the step and repeat—"the prince?" All by himself. He waved at the public as he strode the red carpet like he came home to one every night.

"Where's his date?" Anna asked. Only three minutes from curtain with a critical empty seat in the Von Bizmark box. Martha Miller would not be likely to abandon her itchy husband, even for a dashing Italian prince. The lights in the lobby blinked. Max interrupted the final interview to hurry Mrs. Von Bizmark inside.

Julie shrugged. "I already have a seat," she said, with her ticket and a lopsided smile. The opera would start at any moment. The prince paused on the step and repeat, a convincing grin on his tan face. He was way more handsome in person. Everyone else was inside already. As the prince sailed past, he met Anna's eye—at the very last second, he winked at her before slipping inside. "It's not like we can leave that spot empty, right?"

"I guess I'm sitting here," Anna said, sliding into the red velvet seat next to Prince Valdobianno, who exuded waves of sexual magnetism like some sort of really low, subaudible bass. His handshake felt like an embrace. "Anna," she said.

"Salvatore," he said.

"A pleasure," she said and then sat, keeping her gaze straight ahead but feeling his eyes on her like a warm light on her cheekbone. With a nervous tremor, Anna realized the prince was not one to just sit there in silence.

"I love this opera," he said congenially. "You?"

"Actually," Anna said, unexpectedly eager to announce information about herself, "I'm the artist. The pieces on stage are mine."

As if on cue, the curtain went up, and they turned their eyes forward, where a single spotlight illuminated her illustration of Julie's black-and-white lips. As the music swelled, this light brightened steadily, revealing more and more of the set, more and more of Anna's work. It was thrilling from Anna's vantage point in the box to watch hundreds of people see her art for the first time.

The prince leaned over close enough that Anna could feel his breath on the inside of her ear. "I like your work," he whispered. "A lot."

The exuberant overture swooped Anna up, and she found herself bouncing along in her seat. She had heard this so many times in the months of planning; it was like she could anticipate each note in her belly. But this gusto quickly dissipated as each song seemed to repeat itself over and over before terminating. Time slowed. Anna eyed the prince, who was wholly enraptured by the music, the stage, and the performance. He even laughed a few times.

By the time intermission blessedly arrived, Anna was desperate to move. She excused herself, leaving the prince with the Von Bizmarks and the mayor, and ran to the bathroom, where she smacked directly into petite Bloom coming out. Anna's chin crushed her cloud of red hair, which Bloom quickly repoufed.

"Anna!" Bloom greeted her with a swift double kiss.

"Bloom," Anna said with a distinct chill.

"Come on, kid. Your art looks great up there." Bloom grinned at her. "No hard feelings, right?" But she was gone before Anna could say another word, all five feet of her stomping off in stilettos.

If the first act was long, the second half of the opera felt interminable. Like purgatory. Anna made a game out of not looking at her watch until she thought ten minutes had passed, but when she finally glanced, it had been only four. Crestfallen, Anna let her mind wander ahead to the art, the sale, the future, Adrian. She hoped he would accept her apology without making her grovel too much. But she couldn't think about that yet. Anna fervently hoped that the auction would make maybe $25,000 total for the school. That would be a good chunk of the balance, and the city would make up the rest anyway. $25,000 was something after all! If it even got that high . . .

Loud noise. Anna jerked awake as the theater erupted in applause. The opera was over, and she had been fully asleep for at least, oh Jesus. Anna clapped and leaped to her feet, looking up at the prince—did he know? He looked back at her, a devilish, sexy grin on his face. Of course he knew! He was sitting right next to her.

But had the Von Bizmarks seen? They were closer to the stage, so they would have had to fully turn around. A possibility. Particularly if Mrs. Von Bizmark had tried to get Anna's attention about something. They were already filing out of the box with the mayor. Anna willed herself to wake up.

"I . . . ," she said to the prince, who looked thankfully more amused than annoyed.

"I don't think you love opera after all," he said. He offered her his arm.

"I have to ask," she said, leaning in for some discretion, "did the Von Bizmarks notice?"

"Oh no," he reassured her. "She turned around a few times, but I blocked you with my body."

I'm sure she loved that, Anna thought. "Thank you so much!"

"I think it annoyed her a lot," the prince added, and they shared a laugh. "How lucky!" he remarked when he found their place cards next to one another: Julie's doing for sure.

According to the menu card and program on her plate, the art auction was to occur between the salad and main course, which meant Anna sat and nervously picked at some lettuce leaves and carrot curlicues while waiting for the nerve-racking verdict on her work. She admittedly did not make the best tablemate, but after a lifetime of formal meals with reticent strangers, the prince was not put off.

"Where did you learn to paint?" he asked.

"Well, really I think I've been painting my whole life. Not professionally, of course, but then I studied at Yale."

"Yale! There is a great pizza place there—"

"Frank Pepe!" Anna said.

"Where they have that crazy—"

"White clam pizza!" they said together.

And then, before she could even experience another moment of anticipatory anxiety, a young fresh-faced auctioneer from Sotheby's, who plainly took the job seriously, strutted onstage in a simple black evening gown, pumps, and a headset. There, she joined an empty easel under a spotlight. Anna felt for her; it had to be daunting trying to sell an unknown's work and perhaps even insulting for her to bow to the sort of prices she might actually realize—something in the ballpark of, say, $1,200. The auctioneer called for the first piece, and a stagehand placed the lips center stage.

"I thought we'd start tonight with my personal favorite, the pièce de résistance, the cornerstone of our evening, the graphic, the stark, the intense *Julie*." From across the room, Anna made out Julie's distinctive guffaw. "Let's start the bidding at twenty-five thousand!" Anna choked on her water, spitting it out and onto the unfeeling shoulder pad of a nearby tuxedo. She coughed a few times, the prince patting her back. Once her diaphragm had finally stopped spasming, Anna heard how truly quiet it was in that enormous room. "Twenty-five thousand, ladies and gentlemen! For a school! For the children!"

Anna felt the silence in her bone marrow. No one responded or even moved. *This inexperienced nitwit is going to embarrass me and raise no money,* Anna thought. The silence extended into eternity. Anna wondered if there was a way to just restart the whole thing. Should she interrupt? Leap to her feet? Stop this car crash in progress?

"Twenty-five!" Lindsay shouted and raised her numbered sign. Anna felt tears of love spring from her eyes.

"Twenty-five, I got twenty-five!" the auctioneer shouted, trying for some momentum. "Do I have thirty?"

"Thirty!" the prince shouted, raising his number. He winked at her again, and Anna smiled broadly.

"Thirty, do I have thirty-five?"

"Fifty!" Mrs. Von Bizmark shouted from a nearby table. Anna thought she might faint.

"Come on, people, it's for education!"

Between the luncheon and the art auction, the school ended up netting almost $1.5 million. This more than addressed their structural problems, and without a single dollar from the city. The mayor applauded the loudest, jumping up from his seat when the final canvas got snatched up. Across the room, Julie mouthed to Anna, "I told you so." But surely no one would care that the mayor had scored a ton of free publicity, even if it was an election year.

Mrs. Von Bizmark herself took the podium. "Thank you, everyone. We have paid the opera's annual budget and saved a school here tonight. Enormous thanks to our artist, Anna—please stand." Anna rose to her feet, a flush of warm happiness flooding her toes and climbing all the way up to her shoulders and the tops of her ears as the room applauded. The prince grinned at Anna, proud to be seated next to her.

They talked to other people through dinner, having ignored them the entire time. So blissed out from the auction, Anna hardly remembered the name of the billionaire to her left, the male half of the international yacht duo. He wanted to do all the talking, anyway, mostly about the art collection on his boat and how hard it was to insure something like that. Anna offered a few pointers on the topic of art insurance. They traded stories of priceless pieces lost in tornadoes, fires, floods. At one point, the prince straightened the napkin in his lap; his pinky brushed Anna's thigh. By accident?

"Thanks for bidding on my piece." Anna almost had to shout as the Motown band started up.

"Don't be silly. The sheep need to know where the grass is," he said. Anna cocked an eyebrow at him. "An old Umbrian saying," he added sagely.

"That means what, exactly?" she said, smiling.

"In my town, where I grew up, there are these three old men—"

"Hey, you guys!" Lindsay interjected, popping up as if from a secret compartment behind them. Anna embraced her, squeezing her extra tight and whispering, "You! Thank you!"

"I'm so proud of you," Lindsay whispered back. "Who is this hottie?" They separated.

"Prince Valdobianno, my sister, Lindsay."

"Salvatore, please!" the prince said to Lindsay. He kissed her hand and said, "A pleasure. Would you like to dance?" Anna watched, astonished, as the prince accompanied her pregnant sister across the room. Lindsay looked back at her and jokingly fanned her face.

Dessert served, the band kicked it up a notch, and everyone hit the dance floor. Mr. Von Bizmark bopped stiffly back and forth with Peony, who giggled and bounced along. Josefina danced with Ilana while Alicia ate their cake. The head of the VBO real estate group sipped brown liquor with the mayor, softly pitching some enormous new development downtown that Anna had only heard whispers about. The mayor listened closely. The prince returned with Lindsay, all flushed.

"May I?" he asked, extending his hand to Anna. This man was every inch an international playboy, a professional charm artist, a man who would ultimately settle down with someone twenty years younger, twenty pounds lighter, twenty centimeters taller, and twenty IQ points lower than Anna. Or was she selling him short? He wiggled his hips a little and smiled. Anna struggled to maintain her cynicism in the face of such enticements.

They kept dancing into the next song and the next. Faces swirled around them. Anna spied Mrs. Von Bizmark in the arms of the tenor she'd fawned over at auditions. Julie danced with Max, who talked a mile a minute at her, probably about publicity concerns. Cristina glided by with, oh my God, Villson, in a tuxedo. How did . . . ? Whatever. Cristina looked up at him with such adoration, and he seemed to be returning this feeling, gazing into her half-blind purple-rimmed eyes.

Finally, the band broke out into a slow song: "Let's Get It On." The prince took Anna in his arms. She could not get over how unfamiliar and enticing he smelled, even as her mind drifted to Adrian. Perhaps he had a point about how easily she expected the accolades to come. She could see this now. Even though the auction had been a success, it wasn't like Anna had arrived somewhere or won something. It was just one night. There was no way for her to prove she was an artist; Anna would have to believe it for herself.

"Sorry! Sorry, sorry!" Julie interrupted, wincing. "But Mrs. Von Bizmark has been looking for you." Anna snapped to attention and apologized to the prince.

"Don't forget about me," he said.

Anna followed Julie across the dance floor to where Mrs. Von Bizmark talked with none other than Miranda Chung herself. Anna paused, not sure if she was meant to interrupt this tête-à-tête. But when Mrs. Von Bizmark spotted her waiting five feet away, she impatiently and vigorously waved her over.

"*This* is *the* artist!" Mrs. Von Bizmark said, as if she had been waiting for years to introduce them. "Anna, Miranda Chung."

"Hello," Anna said. *Be cool!* she told herself. "Hi."

"Was this your first real show?" Miranda said, all business.

"It was my first profit, if that's what you mean."

"Yes, impressive. Kissy tells me you have another piece that didn't make it onto the set. I'd love to see it." Anna listened as if Chung spoke to an invisible person standing next to her. "Now."

"We have to get our daughter home, but Anna, perhaps you could . . ." Mrs. Von Bizmark's face said it all: *Move, dummy!*

Anna traversed the packed ballroom as quickly as possible to the exit, down the back stairs, and toward Opal's office, where Giselle had said she would put the piece. It felt wrong for her to be in the opera's darkened inner sanctum by herself, but as soon as she'd popped open the back stairs door, she spied a slice of light coming out of Richard's office. The door stood a few inches open.

Focused on her goal and eager to avoid discovery, Anna rapidly tiptoed toward Opal's office. As she passed Richard's open door, she could not help but catch the slightest glimpse of the two of them, embracing, her leg up and wrapped around his waist like the dancer she used to be, his hairy hand gripping her toned, bare buttock. Richard and Opal. Opal and Richard.

"Surely you've punished me enough?" Opal said, her face coquettishly turned up at him. Anna ducked into the shadows again, momentarily stunned out of her mission.

"Yes, Opal. You'll always be the honoree." His hand slipped between her legs. Anna shuddered with revulsion. "As long as you behave." Anna silently tiptoed into Opal's office. Her piece sat like a person on the center of the couch opposite the desk. There was no one Anna wanted to love the piece more than Opal, other than Miranda. Anna crept out with it, her eyes locked on the floor in front of her.

Anna raced back to the ballroom, canvas in hand, hoping to catch the prince before he jetted off to his next destination in Tribeca or the Hamptons or Ibiza. She was not quite sure what she wanted to tell him, but she would like to at least say goodbye and thank him again. Back in the ballroom, the prince chatted with Lindsay by the door. Miranda waved Anna over and sat the piece on a chair. Anna suppressed the urge to make excuses for the work—it had been so hastily put together in a time that seemed so long ago now. A tricolor oil with plastic decals of geometric lacework in three tones of mauve, apricot, and turquoise.

"I like it," Miranda said. "I'll take it."

"You'll take it?"

"Yes, and sell it." She extended her hand. And like that, Anna had a gallery.

Across the room she could see the prince watching her, waiting. Holding his eye, she started across the dance floor. To think she was in the prince's league was already a little, well, silly, but there he was, smiling at her, and she was all made up and dressed and everything, and people did seem to think she was smart and funny even sometimes, so maybe he really . . .

"Anna!" Principal Sellers, warm, genuine, and impossible to blow off, popped up in her path. "I want to thank you." She shook Anna's hand. "You personally have made the difference for thousands of children."

"Well, I think all of us—"

"Don't do that!" Principal Sellers said sternly, every inch the professional educator. "Don't deflect praise! Feel it."

"Thank you." Anna smiled.

"That's it," Principal Sellers encouraged her. "Go on! Feel yourself!"

"Thank you very much," Anna said, surprised to find a little tear spring to her eye.

"Because of you, we'll not only have a new safe building, but we raised enough tonight to give laptops to all our eighth graders. And we have a rainy-day fund for the next disaster!"

"That's wonderful."

"Please don't forget us. We won't forget you." Sellers embraced Anna, a real warm hug, and released her to go talk to some women from the luncheon who were pulling on their jackets. When Anna looked up, the prince was gone.

In fact, the crowd had thinned considerably. Once an event started its descent, guests fled like rats from a sinking ship. Even Lindsay took off while Anna was running around. The Von Bizmark staff filed out, headed for separate cars home. Max went to meet his boyfriend at a club downtown to blow off steam. The band played its last song for a few diehard couples.

The ball behind them, Anna and Julie sat at an empty table sipping scotch in silent contemplation while waiters cleaned up around them. "Hard to see how it could have gone better," Julie said.

"I'm sure if there is a way to have made it more perfect, we'll hear about it from someone."

"To us," Julie said, lifting her glass for a toast.

"To us," Anna said. *Clink.*

They left Lincoln Center together, arm in arm. As they approached the fountain at the plaza's center, Julie shook Anna off. "Hey," Julie said. Anna looked up to see Adrian—Adrian!—in an impeccably tailored tuxedo, hands clasped in front of him, so debonair. Anna was so thrilled to see him that she gawked a little.

"Hey," Adrian said to Julie.

"See you later," Julie said and hustled off with a little wave and a goofy smile.

"You look beautiful," Adrian said to Anna.

"What are you doing here?" she asked.

"You said we could talk after the ball." Anna's heart leaped in her chest. "I came to take you home. Maybe a celebratory nightcap, if you'll let me." They turned toward the subway together. And even just this quotidian act, with Adrian, felt like home.

"I'm sorry I didn't ask about your new job!" Anna ejected. "You were right: I got all caught up in my own stuff."

"I understand," Adrian said. "And I forgive you." Their eyes locked. "I missed you. A lot." Anna could not wait to go home. She squeezed his hand, and he squeezed back. "So . . . how'd it go in there?" he asked.

"Pretty well, actually."

"Well enough to quit your day job?"

"Why would I quit my job?"

EPILOGUE

VOGUE
Bambi Von Bizmark: An American Story
By Vivienne Lanuit

Every season and city has its rituals. Spring in New York is marked by the Opera Ball, the crown jewel of that city's social season. Each year, the event salutes my dear friend, international style icon Opal. But the nature of tradition is evolution, and this year the cash-strapped New York Opera chose to honor Bambi (known to friends as "Kissy") Von Bizmark instead. In another departure from custom, Von Bizmark planned an art auction to benefit the specialized public school attended by one of her staffer's daughters. Then, the IRS swooped in at the last possible moment to seize the art intended for the auction at the literal doors of the opera house. Rushing in to fill the breach, like some sort of philanthropic superhero, Von Bizmark planned a luncheon fundraiser improbably at her estate in East Hampton. Helicopter transportation would be provided, and I was invited.

From the outside, anyone could see the intrigue and confusion swirling around one of the most staid, consistent, elitist gatherings in North America. My task would be to knit together all the various pieces—tax evasion and private-public partnerships, town and country, money and art, privilege and servitude—into a meaningful narrative.

Chopper rides to the Hamptons and a public school in the Bronx are not a natural match, and this would be no ordinary luncheon. While I doubt it was any of the guests' first time on a helicopter, the sheer outrageousness of it all was like a shot to the toned, slender arm of every hard-to-impress guest. There just is nothing else quite like quaffing champagne with a gaggle of giggling millionairesses floating over Long Island to a fairy-tale chateau. It was as if by attending this lunch, one could leave not just the grit of the city behind but the myriad constraints of our normal lives.

The ease and beauty of it all transported everyone to planet Von Bizmark. By the time all one hundred ladies had been ushered inside the great room, seated, the wine poured and poured again, it was as if a spell had fallen. Time melted. The volume and temperature in the room went up and up. The women forgot why they were there. Scarves were removed and plates nudged away, everyone eager to join the conversation that seemed to be happening like air, a modern-day, midweek, mid*day* bacchanal.

The trippy effect was complete when Von Bizmark eschewed her prepared remarks and announced, apropos of nothing, "I am a Jewess." Instantly, and weirdly, she thereby disarmed the snooty crowd, carrying us all one step further into an alternate reality of her careful design. The public school principal herself got up to make her frank case: give to avoid guilt.

The first check—written by Opal—functioned as the final ingredient in a magic potion. Every other woman mechanically followed suit, the tribal ritual of philanthropy unfolding with so many credit cards, checkbooks, and, in one case, a thick wad of bills banded together. In this way, with the help of a fleet of helicopters, a charismatic principal, and a cellar full of chardonnay, Bambi Von Bizmark managed to raise over $1 million in about twelve hectic minutes in her own living room.

On the one hand, I could argue that Von Bizmark acted in pure self-interest. Her personal connection to the school is its singular advantage over other institutions. There are surely equally good schools that will close for lack of funds and friends. On the other hand, Von Bizmark (and her staff) nearly saved an entire school—that serves 472 kids every year—which simply cannot be a bad thing.

Then there was the opera itself to consider. In *The Marriage of Figaro* a servant outwits his employer, thwarting the more powerful man's unethical efforts to exercise his antiquated right to bed the servant's fiancée (an outdated tradition if there ever was one). Many historians view the precedent play by Beaumarchais as denouncing the aristocracy and foreshadowing the French Revolution. The opera largely concerns the interactions of the residential staff among themselves and with their employers.

The first time I asked Von Bizmark about the choice of *Figaro*, she brushed it off. The second time, on the red carpet moments before curtain, she said, "I don't like the insinuation that there's something going on here tonight that escapes my understanding. Let the *art* speak, for goodness' sake!" she implored me. "Let events speak! Let the opera speak! It is *your job* to make meaning out of it."

Which is to say, I think, that we should all of us look at everything in context. Von Bizmark and the mayor of New York, a socialist, appear to be fast friends, united in the cause to save PS 342. Look how she embraced not only him (in the images that accompany this article) but her maid Josefina. Von Bizmark brought her entire household staff to the opera and ball, as if to announce to the world, "These are my people." Look at them, all on the red carpet together resplendent in brand-new evening gowns (I recognized three from this season's runway), like petals of a flower with Von Bizmark at its center.

Because one does not get to exist in the rarefied world of Bambi Von Bizmark alone. She herself must be taken in context as the head of not a household but a vast enterprise. Each and every moment of her life is a careful choreography so that Von Bizmark herself can host the party, smiling and relaxed, warm and present. Because when you see Von Bizmark at her own lunch, embracing this one and introducing that one, she is essentially at work.

What does it mean to be a philanthropist? So few understand the work of fundraising, which requires accumulating associates who can jot off checks for $10,000 without thinking. These sorts of people can be time consuming and even unpleasant, but Von Bizmark did not just wake up one day chairing the board of the New York Opera. She worked toward it for years if not decades, making "friends," cultivating relationships, writing checks, and then asking her "friends" for money. She wields not only her own funds but the power of a hundred or more purses.

So Von Bizmark simply can't worry about tens of helicopters coming and going. She doesn't wonder when the windows get cleaned or the silver polished, and she will never chase down a caterer if lunch is late. She is busy working every room she walks into. Her people will take care of the rest. Von Bizmark knows that when you want to live larger than life, you can be only as good as your staff. Bringing them into the spotlight was Kissy Von Bizmark's way of telling us that despite or perhaps because of all the help she requires to actualize her life, she is ultimately just like the rest of us.

You can doubt me, but I saw with my own eyes as Von Bizmark held the hand of her nine-year-old daughter, Peony, throughout the entire three-plus-hour opera. I watched Peter Von Bizmark, a tycoon who calls thousands of people employees, attempt to dance with his youngest child. The Von Bizmarks have been together for twenty-five years, an anniversary they celebrated privately this week, a rare evening at home for the couple.

Most other Western nations choose to leave the divvying up of financial resources in the hands of government, where rational and fair priorities can be established, simple math employed. No galas. No performances. No helicopters. This is how we do it here in Europe. In a city as rich as New York, schools for talented children should not suffer for resources.

But this is the United States we are talking about. What fun would it be, really, to sacrifice the super-rich of America in favor of, say, something as banal as health care for all? And so Americans, and increasingly the world at large, look to people like the Von Bizmarks to give them something to aspire to and live for. Von Bizmark herself embodies that unique American hope. It's a challenge she must try to live up to every day of her beautiful life.

Daily News
An Artist Is Made

At the New York Opera Ball last night, nearly $300,000 was raised from the sale of an up-and-coming artist who goes by the name "Anna." As she has no gallery or history of exhibitions, this is a record for first-time sales. Little can be ascertained about her background, but Miranda Chung snatched up this hot prospect and will be showing Anna's work this week.

Proceeds from last night's sale will benefit PS 342 in the Bronx, now due for repairs and reopening next fall. Before the ball, the artist herself appeared tense and distracted. When asked her inspiration, Anna said, "You know, life."

ACKNOWLEDGMENTS

It's quite possible this book would never have happened without my colleague Lisa Vita, whose ineffable positive qualities and loyalty kept the wind in my sails from start to finish.

To my current longtime employers, whose identity I have strived to preserve, thank you for everything. You know who you are and all you have done to support me. To employers past, thanks for the memories.

Thanks to Paul, Joanna, Andrea, Delfi, Sophie, Sandra, Flora, Aurelio, Felix, Pepe, Frank, Sal, Kenny, and Jack. You are all a pleasure to work with. Thanks, Mary Lou, for hiring me.

To my agent, Kim Witherspoon, and Maria Whelan, thanks for believing in me! Sally Willcox and Kim Yau, my fingers are crossed.

Carmen Johnson, you gently and deftly guided this manuscript to its best possible iteration. Thank you for your skill and enthusiasm.

Thanks to Alexis Averbuck, who gave the artist's life depicted in this manuscript its verisimilitude. To Liz Sarosi, thanks for being my resource on public schools and best mommy friend.

To my parents, thanks for all that education and encouragement— also, the childcare that makes writing possible.

To Matthew, there's no one else I'd rather be hustling with. And to our Anna, my heart, my light. I love you both so much.

ABOUT THE AUTHOR

Elizabeth Topp is a graduate of the Dalton School, Harvard College, and the Columbia School of the Arts. Topp coauthored her first book, *Vaginas: An Owner's Manual*, with her gynecologist mother while she worked as a private assistant, a job she still holds. Topp lives in the same Manhattan apartment from her childhood with her partner, Matthew; daughter, Anna; and their cat, Stripes. *Perfectly Impossible* is her debut novel.